New York Times Bestselling Author
HELENA HUNTING

I'm NHL defenseman Lance Romero, AKA Lance "Romance."

I'm notorious for parties and excess. I have the most penalty minutes in the league. I get into the most fights. I take the most hits. I'm a player on and off the ice. I'm the one women with no inhibitions want.

Not because I like the notoriety, but because I don't know how to be any other way.

I have secrets. Ones I shared with the wrong person, and she used them against me. Sometimes she still does. I should cut ties. But she makes it difficult, because she's the kind of bad I deserve.

At least that's what I believed until someone from my past gets caught up in my present. She's all the good things in this world. She lights up my dark.

I shouldn't want her.

But I do.

I should leave her alone.

But I won't.

ACKNOWLEDGMENTS

Without my family, I wouldn't have the time or support to do this; thank you for always being here to support me on this crazy road.

Pepper, salt is boring without you.

Kimberly, thanks for being my rope.

Nina, you're an amazing human. I'm ever grateful for your support.

Jenn—thank you for being such an amazing part of my team. You're awesome.

Shannon, you bring it every time. Thank you for making this series amazing on the outside.

Teeny, you're amazing, especially when you're haunting my messages.

Marla, you rock. Thank you for being so amazing.

Sarah, I honestly have no idea how I managed before I had you.

Hustlers, I'm so excited for this one. Thank you for being my team. For making this such an exciting journey, and for always having my back.

Beavers, you're my safe place and the best cheerleaders. Thank you for loving these characters.

Ashley—you're a special person. I would make Lance real for you if I could.

To my Backdoor Babes; Tara, Meghan, Deb and Katherine, I'm so glad I have somewhere to talk about inappropriate things.

Pams, Filets, my Nap girls; 101'ers, my Holiday's and Indies, Tijan, Susi, Deb, Erika, Katherine, Shalu, Kellie, Ruth, Melissa, Sarah, Kelly, Melanie, Jessica—thank you for being my friends, my colleagues, my supporters, my teachers, my cheerleaders and my soft places to land.

It's an honor to be part of the indie community. Thank you for embracing me, and for being so amazingly supportive, even when I take you on a different journey.

To all the amazing bloggers and readers who keep traveling this road with me; thank you for believing in happily ever afters.

For the most amazing husband in the world. Thank you for loving me.

TRAP

LANCE

I grip the steering wheel and take a few deep breaths, willing myself to put my Hummer in reverse. It's what I should do. But I don't. Instead, I shift into park and cut the engine. I don't move, though. My internal battle is fucking endless. This is the very last place I should be. But I'm here anyway. Because even though I know better, I can't help myself.

The whole breaking-the-cycle thing is hard to do. And this is part of my cycle. I come back to the people who hurt me, and I let them do it over and over again, always hoping maybe one day the end result is going to be different. Or that the process is going to cure my guilt and alleviate my need to atone.

It never does. But I'm still here.

I check my phone and scroll through the messages that began

to accumulate late last night. Tash, my ex—or whatever the fuck she is to me—is in town. I ignored her until an hour ago. There are twenty texts. One every hour. I scroll past the first nine to the ones that brought me here, to this place I shouldn't be:

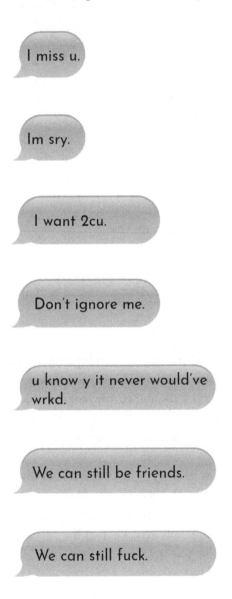

I miss u.

Im sry.

I want 2cu.

Don't ignore me.

u know y it never would've wrkd.

We can still be friends.

We can still fuck.

I still think about u.

Come to my hotel.

I leave in the a.m.

Around and around it goes. So I'm sitting here staring at the last two messages—the one containing her room number, and the one from an hour ago telling me she's getting impatient and won't wait much longer for a response.

I might've been able to ignore the last one if my teammates and closest friends, Randy Ballistic and Miller Butterson, weren't nailed down by their balls. But they are. They're both in committed relationships, so a call at nine at night for an impromptu trip to the bar isn't an option. Besides, Miller's girl-friend is expecting a baby soon, so he's not interested in being anywhere she's not.

It's understandable, but it means I don't have any wingmen to stop me from doing this. Truthfully, I could probably call Randy. But I don't really want to.

I open the door and step out into the unseasonably warm night. I let the numbness set in as I cross the parking lot and enter the hotel, heading for the elevators. I try not to think about how things went down the last time I saw Tash. I try not to feel much of anything.

When the elevator doors open at the twenty-third floor, I almost don't get off. Almost. But I'm weak for Tash. I don't know how to say no to her, even though she's bad for me. I step out into the hall. My palms are sweaty, and my stomach starts to roll the way it used to after a game when I was young. The way it used to when I didn't perform the way I should've and my mum expressed her disappointment.

But I deserved it. I took the best thing in her life away.

My feet feel like they're made of lead as I walk down the hall to Tash's room. When I get there, I shove my hands in my pockets and wait for the memories to fade. I need a drink. I need the past to stop haunting me. I need to stop doing this with Tash.

My fist doesn't feel like it's attached to my body as I lift it to knock on the door. The click of the lock turning twists the knot of my anxiety tighter. Then the door opens, and there she is.

Tash is wearing a T-shirt. My T-shirt. I don't think there's anything on underneath it. Her hair is loose around her shoulders. I know what it feels like between my fingers and on my chest. Her lips curve in a smile that looks more devious than welcoming.

"Hi."

"Hey." I jam my hands back in my pockets so I don't touch her like I want to.

"I'm so glad you decided to come." She reaches out and skims my forearm. I tense when her fingers wrap around my wrist, tugging my hand free of my pocket.

"I can't stay long."

"You always say that." She pulls me through the door, which closes behind me with a metallic slam.

Tash runs her hands up my chest, inciting the sensation of spiders crawling over my skin. She knows I hate that; I grab her wrists. "Don't."

"You're so jumpy. I'm not going to hurt you, baby. I just wanted to see you. Can I hug you?"

I want to believe her, but we've done this so many times in the past year. It's hard to know when she's being real and when she's playing games.

I release her wrists, and she wraps her arms around me, stepping closer until her hard body is pressed up against mine. I try not to tense, but the reaction is as conditioned as the sensation it inspires.

"It's okay, baby," she whispers. "Just relax."

I drop my head and turn my face into her hair. It smells like my shampoo. She does this every time. It's the little manipulations that make it so much harder to walk away and stay away. She makes me believe she actually cares, and then she finds a way to take it all back again.

"I missed you." I feel her lips on my neck, moving up my jaw.

I don't tell her I missed her, too. I wouldn't be here if I hadn't. Or maybe I'm just stupid. It doesn't matter. When she gets to my mouth, I open for her and accept her tongue. She tastes like vodka. I wonder if she's drunk. I'll fuck her either way, because that's what she called me for, and I never can say no. I ease a hand down her side until I reach the hem of her shirt and palm her bare ass. I promise myself this will be the last time.

She pulls away, that coy, devious smile turning up the corner of her mouth.

"Come. I have something to show you." She threads her fingers through mine and leads me down the short hall to the bedroom.

And the second we enter the room, I know I've been duped.

In the middle of the California king is a redhead. The color is artificial, but Tash knows what I like. She's wearing pale green satin, which, if her hair were naturally that color, would offset freckles and pale skin. But it's not real. None of this is. It's Tash's way of telling me, once again, that she's always in control. Of me. Of this thing between us. Of her emotions. Of mine.

"Lance, this is Erin. She's been dying to meet you," Tash says. Like this is normal. Like it's expected when we haven't seen each other in weeks, or sometimes even months.

My response is gritty, like the pain is coming out through my mouth. "Hi, Erin."

"Hi." She bites her lip, eyes darting from me to Tash and back again. Her excitement is as apparent as her uncertainty.

I'm a legend. I'm the one people whisper about, even though half of the rumors aren't true. I'm the man women with no inhibitions want. And I fucking hate it. But it's become an expectation.

I tighten my grip on our twined fingers and step behind Tash. Skimming her arm with my free hand, I thread my fingers through the hair at the nape of her neck, twisting it out of the way until I can lower my mouth to her ear. "You want me to fuck your friend?"

"You like her?" Tash's enthusiasm makes me want to throw up.

"She'll do."

"I picked her just for you."

This is how it is between us. Me always wanting just her, and Tash always offering something else.

I brush my lips along the column of her throat, enjoying the shiver that runs through her. "Does she know she's being used?"

"We're all being used, Lance. Some of us just choose to acknowledge it for what it is."

I bite her, my teeth sinking into skin enough to make her cry out, but not enough to cause damage that will last—the opposite of what she's done to me.

"Get her ready for me, if that's what she's here for."

I release Tash, and her expression is so familiar: confusion mixed with expectation. She doesn't know how to read my mood. Which is good. I want her on edge, because that's always how she makes me feel—on the edge. She lifts the shirt over her head, revealing tight muscles I know every inch of.

I've had my mouth on every part of her; I've been inside her, but not in the way that counts. I've never gotten inside her head the way she's gotten into mine. My biggest mistake was telling her my secrets, because she uses them against me.

She saunters over to the bed and crawls toward Erin. It's

been a long time since I've done anything like this. I don't seek it out. The last time was with Tash, too.

Four weeks ago she promised she would never do this to me again, but Tash is a liar.

I undress as they start making out. I don't join them until Tash has made Erin come. And then I do what Tash wants me to: I fuck Erin. I make her come until she cries. I refuse to kiss Tash again, but I kiss Erin until she's breathless and my name comes out on a tortured moan. And when I'm close to coming, I pull out and tell Tash to suck me off.

I cradle her face in my hands. I'm not rough with her, even though part of me wants to hurt her the way she hurts me. Instead I caress her cheek and hold her gaze as her lips move against the head of my erection.

"Who's your cock slut?" she asks.

I close my eyes, teeth gritted against what she wants me to say. Words I hate. She knows I'll never say them myself.

"Tell me, Lance."

I can't fucking stand that she wants this, that she makes me do this. Why does she want this? "You are."

Her smile is triumphant as she wraps her lips around me and waits.

"That's my girl. Suck like it's the last time you'll ever get to have my dick." I loathe the words as I say them, partially because I can't guarantee they're true. And I hate that she loves it when I talk to her like she's a whore.

I can see the moment she understands that I'm not going to fuck her too, that she's pushed me as far as she can. She's broken me in ways no one else ever has.

When I'm seconds away from coming, I lean over to kiss Erin again. She's so warm and willing. And she's just a pawn in this game Tash plays with me.

I'm so done with this. I'm so done with being used.

Tash is pissed when I meet her eyes after she takes a shot of jizz down the throat. I get dressed silently while she screams at me, calling me all kinds of names, telling me I'm useless, that I'm an asshole.

I don't disagree, so I don't know why she expects more from me. I might want more from her, but I work hard not to expect it.

She follows me to the door, getting between it and me. She's still naked. "You can't leave."

"I'm pretty sure that's what I'm doing."

She slaps me across the face.

She's said a lot of horrible things to me—things that made me wish I wasn't me. Things that make me wonder if this is the kind of hatred I'll always draw into my life. But the slap is a first.

She follows it up with a backhand to the other cheek.

For a moment I'm thirteen again, standing in the garage, apologizing for missing another shot on the goal, anticipating—with a kind of sick exhilaration—my mum's first slap to my face.

I grab Tash's wrists and pin them to the door, pressing my weight against her. Her eyes light up as if this is what she intended, as if she knew hitting me would make me give in. I hate what she does to me. I hate that she makes me weak, and I hate that she knows it.

"Don't be mad at me for giving you what you want." She arches, straining against my hold on her, rubbing her tits on my chest.

"I wanted you, Tash. That was it."

"Come on, Lance. You knew what you were getting into with me."

"I'm not a toy you get to play with anymore."

"Fine. No more games. All you have to do is fuck me; then you can go." She wraps one of her legs around my waist.

I huff out a laugh. "I think you've fucked me enough, don't you? Thanks for the present. I'm sure Erin can help you out where I can't." I release one of her hands and reach for the door-knob so I can get the fuck out of here.

"You're just a fucking whore," she tells me. "You know that, right? Your dick is the only useful thing about you." She gifts me with another slap across the face.

"Don't call me the next time you're in town. Don't text. Don't send emails. We're done, Tash. For real this time. I don't care how messed up your life is; you don't get to take it out on me."

I wrench open the door, and she follows me into the hall, still naked, still screaming. I wish I had a good reason for putting up with this. Better, I wish I could say for sure that this truly was the last time, that I won't do this to myself again.

But I can't.

I take the stairs instead of the elevator, and as soon as I'm outside, I throw up. I want to hit something. I want the feelings on the inside to be outside my body instead.

As soon as I'm able, I get in my Hummer and get the fuck out of there. Otherwise I know Tash will come looking for me, and I'll end up fucking her in the front seat. It's happened before.

Instead of heading north to where I live, I drive south out of the Loop. I keep going past everything that's familiar before I find a bar. I need to drown out all the shit in my head. I need to lobotomize myself against this night. I need the will to stop this thing with Tash.

2

FIGHT

LANCE

I find a shitty bar—somewhere I'm not likely to run into anyone I know. I parallel park the Hummer like an asshole, taking up just enough space that no one can get in behind me and fuck up my paint, which is likely based on the quality of the cars on this street.

I slip my phone into my pocket, even though leaving it in the car would be a much better idea. Potholes mark my way to the front entrance, the sign flickering, the last two letters unable to stay lit for more than a second before they go dark again.

The interior is even sadder than the exterior. Low lights can't hide the dilapidated state of this place. A group of older men in worn jeans and threadbare T-shirts sit in the corner by the dartboards. They look my way for a moment, murmur to each other, and return to their conversation with a couple of coughs.

Two other tables hold couples drinking cheap beer out of bottles. At the very back of the bar, two women dressed in tight jeans and flimsy tops play pool. No one is going to recognize me here.

It's the perfect place to get fucked up. I head for the far end of the bar, close to the pool tables and away from the group of old guys. It's dark over here, less conspicuous. I drop onto a barstool and wait for the bartender. It takes him a minute to get to me, but it's nice to be treated like a nobody once in a while. It reminds me that I'm only special in my own little bubble.

I motion to the wall of booze. "I'll take a glass and whatever's left in that bottle of Walker." It's the least offensive thing they have in the whiskey department, and it looks to be about three-quarters full.

The bartender taps the wooden bar as I flip open my wallet and pull out two bills.

He looks down as he takes the money. "You want ice?"

"No, thanks."

He slips the cash into his pocket and sets a coaster and a glass in front of me before he grabs the bottle.

"Tell me when," he says as he pours the first shot.

I tap the edge when there's about three fingers of whiskey. Then I drain the glass in one shot. We repeat the process twice more before he sets the bottle down on the bar.

"You'll be taking a cab outta here."

I salute him. "Aye, coach."

He laughs and shakes his head. "She must've screwed you over real good."

I pour myself another hefty shot and raise my glass. "That she did."

He leaves me to my wallowing. My phone keeps vibrating in my pocket. I pull it out and drop it on the bar, watching the screen light up. The contact reads DO NOT FUCKING REPLY. I wish I was smart enough to take my own advice, but apparently I'm not.

There are eleven new messages. I'm sure they're all quite lovely. As much as I know I shouldn't look at them, I don't know how long I can contain my curiosity.

Tash will be gone tomorrow, back to LA. If I can wait until she's on a plane, I won't run the risk of trying to see her again. I hate the panicky feeling that thought brings. I hate that I almost regret not fucking her. I hate that I've already forgiven her for slapping me across the face.

I flip my phone over so I can't see the alerts as the texts keep coming. There's a fight on the TV over the bar, so I focus my attention there instead. I wish I had a place to put all this anger. Since I don't, I get this feeling in my spine—it's a tingle that turns into a burn. Everything starts to feel hot, like I'm a volcano preparing to erupt.

I pour another shot, hoping it'll dull the fire. Sometimes I don't know what to do when I get like this. And Tash makes me worse. I know this. Every time I see her now it takes a few days for me to get things back under control. Last time I did five thousand dollars worth of damage to my bedroom.

One of the girls from the pool table sidles up to me. She wears her hard life in faint lines on her young face. I look over just as her friend squeezes her way between us.

She gives me a lopsided smile and scans the bar, maybe looking to score a drink while she checks me out.

"Hey." She sits on the stool beside me, knocking my elbow as I tip my glass.

The drink misses my mouth and runs down my forearm.

"Oh, God! I'm so sorry!" She reaches over me and grabs for a napkin.

I don't think she's drunk—she doesn't have the glassy eyes or loose body for that—so I have to assume she's either clumsy or did it on purpose to get my attention. Which was unnecessary. She had it the second I walked into this place, she and her friend being the only two women without a guy attached to them.

"You're fine." I take the napkin from her so she'll stop touching me.

The first girl, the one who looks like life hasn't been all that easy on her, says something to her friend and gives me an apologetic smile. It fades a bit after a moment, and her eyes narrow slightly, then flare.

"You look familiar."

"I don't think we've met before." I turn on my grin and my charm, even though I don't feel like being all that friendly or charming. "I'd remember that pretty smile."

"I've got a pretty smile," says the clumsy one. Then she points to my bottle. "Hey, you wanna buy me and my friend a drink?"

"Barbie!" the other girl chastises.

Of course her name is Barbie, although she doesn't look like one in the traditional sense, with her brown hair and brown eyes. Her friend, the one who's embarrassed now, is more Barbie-looking, with sandy blond hair and eyes that could be blue or green, depending on how the lighting in this corner of the bar messes with things.

"What? He's got a whole bottle. He can share."

"Sure. You got a glass?" These two seem like a decent enough distraction, and I need one. Besides, I probably shouldn't drink the rest of this bottle on my own unless I want practice to be hell tomorrow.

"Over there." Barbie thumbs over her shoulder. "You should come sit with us."

My phone buzzes on the bar again. I flip it over. I'm up to twenty messages from Tash. Fuck her.

"Yeah. I can do that."

Barbie helps me out by grabbing the bottle, and I follow them to their table. It's conveniently located in the darkest corner of the bar.

Barbie sits beside me on the bench seat, and her friend sits perpendicular to her. She pours them both a generous shot of whiskey and fills my glass too.

She props her cheek on her fist, mashing her face into it. "You do look really familiar."

"Oh my God! I know who you are!" The other girl slaps the table with a shriek. I cringe and survey the room. Thankfully it's loud in here. Her voice is drowned out by the blaring country music.

She leans in closer. "Don't you play hockey for Chicago?"

I put a finger to my lips and wink. "Shh. We don't want everyone to know."

"Oh my God!" She bounces in her seat and smacks Barbie's arm. "I knew it! I told you! Wow. What are the chances you'd be here, of all places?"

"Just passing by. Lucky, aye?" I'm not the nicest version of myself right now, so it comes out with a bite of sarcasm. She doesn't seem to catch it, though.

"Maybe it'll turn out to be my lucky night." Barbie gives me a coy look, like she's trying to be sweet while she propositions me. "Can we get a picture with you?"

"Sure."

The blonde comes around to my other side, and they squeeze together so we can all be in the photo. They're both touching me. I hate the way it feels, but I try to smile anyway. I want these to end up on social media so Tash can see how little I fucking care.

My phone buzzes again, and I have to fight not to look at it. Barbie with the brown hair isn't bad to look at. She's not drunk, so fucking her isn't off the table.

I'm in a bad enough headspace that if she makes another pass at me, I'll probably go ahead and make it her lucky night. And if her friend is interested, I'll fuck her too. I'll even get them to fuck each other first. Just to get back at Tash, because she's the one who calls me a whore, and she's the one who made me that way. Then I'll have a real distraction from this fucking empty feeling in my chest.

I tap the side of the bottle. If I finish what's left, I'll pass out. These girls are another way to deal with all the goddamn blackness eating at me. Neither is a smart option, but my choices feel limited.

In a way, this makes me exactly like Tash. I'll use these girls for an hour or two so I can get out of my head and hurt Tash the way she does me. Not that it will work, because I'm not sure if anything she feels is real at all.

"What're you doing when you're done with your drink?" Barbie looks around the bar, then back at me.

I finger the ends of her hair. It's dry and brittle, not like Tash's. Hers is always soft, and it smells like my shampoo because she likes to make me think she wants me like I want —wanted—her.

I smile anyway. "You, baby."

Her echoing smile is both excited and nervous, colored with a hint of fear, like maybe she thinks she's making a mistake.

She is.

"What about your friend?" I nod to the blonde, whose name I still don't know.

"What?" She looks over her shoulder, like she's forgotten her friend is even there.

"What's she gonna do while I'm doing you?"

"You mean Mindy? Um...I..." She touches her hair, flustered by the question. "I don't—"

I rest my arm across the back of her seat and adjust the strap on Mindy's top. "You two are good friends, aye?"

15

They look at each other, and Mindy answers for Barbie. "We're besties. We take care of each other."

"You do, do you?" I move Mindy's hair over her shoulder, my fingers grazing her throat, making her shiver. She doesn't pull away, though. "Do you do everything together?"

Mindy glances at Barbie. "I guess."

I lean in and run my nose along Barbie's jaw until I reach her ear. "Wanna do me together?"

She gasps a laugh and backs up a bit, maybe to see if I'm joking. Her expression is part excitement, part disbelief.

I cock a brow. I hate myself so much right now. I feel sick at the thought of having two sets of hands to deal with. But I'll do it to get back at Tash for pulling this shit on me. Again.

"Oh my God, you're serious. You want us both to come home with you?" She brings her fingers to her lips.

I know that expression. She's considering it.

"We're not that kind of besties," Mindy says, a little incredulous.

"How do you know? You ever tried?"

"Well, no, but—"

I'm still fingering the strap of Mindy's top while I close-talk Barbie, so she can't be that opposed to the idea.

"But what? You should kiss her; see if you like it."

I shouldn't be doing this. I shouldn't be fucking with them. These girls aren't bunnies. They didn't come to my party looking to ride whoever is willing so they can brag about it in their online bunny groups.

These two girls are just on the receiving end of my bad place. I'm feeling messed up, so I'm inclined to do things that aren't very nice. Sometimes I'm fascinated by the things people will do just to say they've been fucked by someone with a little fame.

Barbie turns to her friend and whispers something. I watch Mindy's eyes widen as she looks between the two of us. She hesitates for a moment before leaning in closer to Barbie, putting a hand on her shoulder. She kisses her quickly on the lips.

I laugh. "Not like that." I lean in, like I'm going for Barbie, but instead I reach past her for Mindy, the uncertain one. I caress her cheek. When she doesn't flinch away, I palm the back of her neck and pull her forward so we meet across the corner of the table with Barbie between us. "Like this."

Touching my lips to hers, I wait for hers to part. When they do, I slip my tongue inside. She tastes like whiskey and vaguely some guy's aftershave. I don't have a chance to ask about the source of that.

"What the fuck are you doing?" A loud male voice stops the party.

Mindy shoves away from me, her eyes wide with panic as we turn and come face to face with a human tank.

"Kevin? What're you doing here?"

"Looking for you," he snaps and turns his angry gaze on me.

I'm a big guy. Pushing six four, I weigh in at two twenty on a light day. This guy has got to be two fifty, and he's probably the same height as me. Based on how flat his nose is, I'm gonna go ahead and say it's been broken a few times.

"Who the fuck is this guy?" The tank grabs Mindy by the arm and yanks her out of her seat. "Fucking whore."

Now, that unkind name may very well be accurate. I have no idea, but I have never and will never tolerate that kind of shit. Not even when Tash asked to be called names could I ever give in. Also, manhandling a woman in a bar is another thing at the top of my *don't fucking do it* list.

"He was just buying us a drink. Isn't that right?" Barbie says, like that explains what her friend was doing with my tongue in her mouth.

I feel played, which is fitting since my plan was to play these girls. Mindy has a look on her face I know well. I wore it frequently as a kid. The hits I took on the ice were just a warm up for the abuse I'd sustain when I didn't live up to the expectations set for me at home.

"We have one fucking misunderstanding and you whore

yourself out to the first guy who gives you a little attention?" the tank says to Mindy.

His grip on her arm is tight, and she makes a sound that melds pain with fear.

I push up out of my seat, adrenaline rocketing through my veins, burning off enough of the alcohol to give me back my coordination. I step around Barbie, who tries to grab my arm, maybe to stop me, but it's too late. I need a way to unleash all the blackness Tash has filled me with.

I roll my shoulders. "Get your fucking hands off her."

"Fuck you and fuck her." He lets her go, though, which is what I want.

We've gained the attention of the bartender and some of the guys in the corner. The bartender calls the tank's name, but it doesn't seem to register with him.

This guy is pissed—not just angry, but drunk, drunker than me. His lazy, dark eyes tell me that. I realize now, as I take in the slope of his forehead, that there's a good chance he's a juicer and his rage and mine are not going to be quite matched. My red and his are on totally different levels. Still, the hot tingle that runs down my spine fires me right up.

I'm probably not going to come away from this unscathed, and the karma in that makes me happier than it should. I anticipate the first punch and block it with my forearm, feeling the sharp pain that travels all the way to my shoulder and up my neck.

I don't retaliate right away, aware that if I do, it's no longer self-defense. But it's more than that—I want this pain. I would've screwed these two girls and maybe gotten them to do something that, under any other circumstances, they wouldn't have considered. This is retribution for what could've happened.

When Mindy throws herself between us, I'm forced to absorb the third punch—in the jaw—so she's not on the receiving end. It feels like his fist is made of titanium. I reel and stumble back, hitting a table and knocking over chairs as I go down. The tank is on top of me before I have a chance to do anything beyond raise a defensive arm.

I'm past letting him have the advantage now, but being on the bottom makes it tough to gain leverage. He grabs me by the shirt and yanks me back up, slamming me into the table while high-pitched girl screams echo in my head. They're joined by a hollow ringing when my head hits the wooden tabletop a second time. His fist connects with my face, and I taste blood. An elbow to the ribs and subsequent searing pain tells me tomorrow is going to hurt.

I roll to the side as Mindy comes flailing at the tank, screaming for him to stop.

No matter how much Tash has fucked me around, no matter how bad it's been between us, it doesn't give me the right to headfuck someone else, I remind myself. And particularly not someone else who's already involved, even if the relationship was undisclosed and appears to be screwed.

But I'm still not willing to take any more hits now. Especially when the tank comes after me with a chair. He doesn't get very far, though, because that's when the police show up.

NO CHOICES

LANCE

I give the police my statement while a doctor fly-bandages my eyebrow. Just because I didn't start this doesn't mean I'm not going to catch heat for it. I'm notorious for starting shit on the ice. I never throw the first punch, though. I'm smarter than that. I push buttons and needle players until I piss them off enough that they lose their cool.

This isn't like a hockey fight, though. This was a brawl in a very public bar that caused more than ten thousand dollars damage. Because of Tash. Because I can't stay away from her, and I keep letting her screw with my head. I'll need to call my publicist to deal with the fallout, but right now I've got a throbbing headache, and I just want to go the fuck home.

I hate hospitals. I'll do almost anything to avoid them. I'd rather get stitched up on the bench without any kind of painkiller than be sitting here. I'm edgy because of it, and a little panicky. Hospitals bring back all sorts of shitty memories.

The last time I was in a hospital was when Waters, our team captain, took a serious hit that knocked him unconscious. The time before that was the night my brother died.

I was eleven. He was eight. It was my fault.

The doctor wants me to stay the night for observation, but I lie and tell him I've got a roommate who will wake me up. I can't stay here. I'll lose my mind if I do.

The doctor makes me call my "roommate." Ballistic is the most likely to wake up and answer, as well as give me the least grief over this.

As predicted, he doesn't ask any questions, just says he'll be there as soon as he can.

I sit in the chair rather than on the bed while I wait. I stare at the empty mattress and fall back into memories I've tried to bury for years, but can't.

WE WERE GOING to be late. It was my fault because I'd been screwing around, playing ball hockey with some of the guys after school even though my mum said to come right home. Now we'd have to run if we were going to make it.

Quinn wasn't a fast runner, though, so he kept falling behind, and he was whining about being out of breath. He had asthma, so I slowed down and found his puffer in his bag.

There was a shortcut we could take, but my mum always told us never to go that way, 'cause it was through a bad part of town. It'd cut ten minutes off our walk, though, and then we wouldn't be late and Quinn wouldn't have to run.

"Don't tell her we came this way," I ordered. "We'll get in trouble if we're late."

He hesitated for a second. Trouble in our house didn't mean losing privileges and not having time to play video games. It meant my mum losing it. Sometimes when she was mad, she hit me. It'd been happening more often.

"I don't want you to get in trouble," Quinn said.

Decision made, we slipped through the broken fence and down an alleyway. It was dank and dark and smelled like urine. We were halfway through when four guys appeared out of the shadows. They were older—I couldn't tell how old—maybe in high school still, maybe beyond that.

My heart kicked up a notch, and Quinn sucked in a breath as I moved him behind me. There were too many of them for me to protect him.

They circled us. Taunting. We had money. We wore it in expensive rucksacks and nice clothes. They wanted what we had. Quinn got mouthy, which he only ever did in my presence, and when they tried to take his rucksack his books fell out, scattering over the ground, so I pushed one of them.

And that's when everything changed. The sharp sting of something hard hit me in the back. And then again and again. I knew what it was: rocks in socks. Fill an old sock with rocks and it becomes a violent, effective weapon.

I covered my head and spun, searching for Quinn, who was screaming.

The sound cut short when one of the teenagers' makeshift weapons slammed into his temple.

Quinn's mouth was open, and his eyes were suddenly blank as his body swayed and crumpled to the ground.

Sirens wailed like crying babies in the distance. The teenagers shouted and swore and disappeared like vapor.

I shook my brother, blood dripping from his temple. I screamed his name, but his eyes were vacant.

He was gone. And it was my fault.

"LANCE? BUDDY?"

I rub my eyes to black out the memories and hiss at the pain in my right one. I look up to find Randy standing at the door of the room in pajama pants and a wrinkled T-shirt.

His eyes go wide as he takes in my face. "What the fuck happened to you?"

I push up out of the chair and bite back my groan. I'm already sore, and it's only been a few hours. "I'll explain in the car."

We don't talk in the elevator.

"Wiener's in the truck," Randy says as we cross the parking lot.

It takes me a few seconds to process that. "Miller and Sunny's dog?"

"Yeah, we're watching him for a few days 'cause he's making it difficult for Sunny to sleep. If I didn't take him, he would've whined at the door until I got back and kept Lily up. She's gotta skate first thing in the morning."

"Shit. Did I wake her?"

"Nah, she had a busy day. She was KO'd when I left." The truck beeps as he unlocks it.

I open the passenger door and Wiener barks at me, then runs to the other side like he's never seen me before. Wiener is a wiener dog, hence the name. Miller and Sunny have been fostering him for awhile, and Randy and Lily have taken him for sleepovers or whatever. It's like training wheels for kids, I guess. The thing is freaking skittish.

Climbing into the truck hurts. And it's only going to get worse, which isn't great since we have skate practice tomorrow afternoon in preparation for next week's final exhibition game before the season. I buckle up as Randy turns over the ignition and talks to his dog as if it's a person.

"So, you wanna tell me what happened that I'm picking you up at the hospital in the middle of the night all beat to shit?" Randy asks.

"Tash happened."

He pauses with his hand on the gearshift. *"Tash* did this to you?"

"No. Tash didn't do this." I motion to my face. "She's what happened tonight that resulted in this bullshit."

"You're gonna explain that so it makes sense, right?"

"Tash is in town. She wanted to see me."

"Again? Wasn't she just here a few weeks ago?"

"She came back. As she does."

Randy knows I'm not good at saying no to her. "Ah, man. You should've called. You could've come over. Or I would've gone for beers with you or something."

"You had a night planned with Lily."

"We were just watching a movie. It wasn't a big thing."

"The season's starting soon. I'm not going to interfere with your time with her." Especially not since his dad blew in and out of town not long ago and that sure as fuck didn't go well. I think he might still be repairing the damage.

"Lily would've understood."

Wiener turns around three times beside me and settles his butt against my leg. I know better than to pet him right away or we'll have to go through the whole barking-skittish thing again.

"Maybe, but I don't want to be the friend who's a problem."

"You're not a problem, Romance." Randy taps his steering wheel. "So I'm guessing things with Tash didn't go well?"

"Nope."

"What happened?"

"Just the usual bullshit. Me wanting things I shouldn't, expecting it to be different when it never is."

Randy doesn't know how things go down between me and Tash. He has a vague understanding that I wanted more out of it than she did, and that's about it. As far as most of the team is concerned, I'm the asshole because we were fucking in the gym locker room and got caught, resulting in Tash's termination from her job as team trainer. The real story behind that scenario isn't quite so straightforward.

"What happened that your face ended up being used as a punching bag?"

"I went to a bar, and some chick recognized me. She and her friend propositioned me, and one of them had a boyfriend she failed to mention. He showed up and got all aggressive, and I stepped in the middle to make sure she didn't get a fist in her face."

It's the abridged version. Randy doesn't need to know the less-than-flattering details. He's aware of what I'm like when I'm in a bad mood, especially after I've seen Tash.

"Jesus."

"Pretty sure he wasn't looking to save me based on the state of my face." I close my eyes. My head hurts. I can't tell if it's from the concussion or the whiskey, or both.

Wiener nudges my hand, which is his way of telling me he's ready for pets. I scratch his head, but keep my eyes closed. I'm so tired of everything.

Randy nudges my shoulder. "'Kay, man, we're home."

I crack a lid, disoriented until I realize I've fallen asleep and we're parked in Randy's driveway. "You brought me to your place?"

"You have a concussion. You gotta be woken up every two hours."

"It's mild. I'm fine."

Randy strokes his beard. "And if Tash calls again?"

"She's not gonna call again."

"You sure about that?

"If she does I won't answer."

That's bullshit and we both know it—especially after a night like this. My phone's full of messages from her, waiting for a reply.

"That's what you said last time, and look where that's gotten you. I don't know why she's got such a hold on you, man, but you need to get her out of your life. She's fucking toxic. You gotta cut her out like cancer."

"I know, man." I tap my temple. "She just gets in here, and I can't get her out." And sometimes I want her there, because the pain she causes is something I understand.

Wiener lets me pick him up and carry him into the house. Randy's place is nice, in a nice part of town, but it's not reflective of the money he makes. He could live in a monster house if he wanted. Instead he lives in a very reasonable house.

"The spare room's already made up." He leads me down the hall and shows me where the towels and stuff are. "I'll be back in two hours to make sure you're still alive."

"Thanks for coming to get me."

"It's no problem. Get some rest. You need to be on it for practice tomorrow."

He leaves me alone in the spare room. I go to the bathroom and check out my face. It's beat up. I took a couple solid shots to the ribs, and being slammed into the table definitely didn't feel good. I brush my teeth and spit out a lot of pink thanks to the lacerations in my mouth.

I pop a couple of aspirin and lie down. My phone still goes off every once in a while. I should turn it off and leave it until the morning—or longer. But I don't. Instead I hit the button and the screen lights up.

In addition to the thirty text messages, I have three voice-mails from Tash. All in just a few short hours. I don't have the energy to deal with them, and if I check them, I'll end up calling her back. Then she'll come here, and then I'll do something I'll regret even more than not fucking her, so I finally turn my phone off. Only about seven hours too late.

Randy's right. I need to get her out of my life, or she's going to put more than my career in jeopardy again.

"LANCE?" Fingers poke at my shoulder, followed by snapping close to my ear and a familiar female voice. "Lance, can you hear me?"

I grunt and roll over, but that hurts, a lot, so I roll back the other way.

"Sorry, buddy, I know you want to sleep. I just need confirmation that you know who I am and where you are and then you can go right back to dreamland."

Randy's girlfriend, Lily, pries my eyelid open.

I bat her hand away from my face. "Fuck! I'm awake. Jesus."

"Such a sweet mouth you have. You're welcome for making sure you're not brain dead."

An image of my brother's vacant eyes appears behind my lids. I cover my eyes with my forearm, hissing when I hit my eyebrow. The pain erases the memory.

"I have aspirin and water for you, both of which you could use, judging from the state of your face."

I peek out from under my arm. "Why're you so nice?"

Lily snorts. "Probably because Randy gives me at least one orgasm a day."

I cringe. I already know those two get it on all the time; I don't need additional confirmation. Not so long ago, Randy spent a lot of time partying with me, but not so much since he and Lily got serious.

"I think you're spending too much time with Violet."

Violet is my team captain's wife. I married them while we were in Vegas a few months back, because I happen to be ordained. I did it a few years ago, when a friend needed a favor. I did it over the internet, but it's legitimate. I never actually thought it would come in handy again.

"That's also probably true." She passes me a glass and sets the pills on the comforter. "Randy'll be your next wake-up call. I'll be back around noon."

"I'll definitely be gone by then."

"Don't worry about it if you're not."

I down the pills and the water as she closes the door behind her. I'm exhausted. I close my eyes, trying to find the will to pry them open again and get out of my friend's house before the next two-hour block passes. That's not what happens.

I must pass out hard again, because the next time I remember anything, Lily's waking me up to tell me I have practice in a couple of hours. Randy's already gone because he had a meeting with his agent.

Our last preseason game is this weekend. It doesn't matter how shitty I feel; I have to be on the ice today. I throw the covers off and hit the bathroom. I've been out for a lot of hours, but the sleep hasn't done anything to offset the myriad aches in my body. If anything, they've multiplied.

I turn on the water and strip off my shirt and pants. I must've left my boxers in Tash's hotel room. I hope she's gone already like she said she would be in her messages yesterday.

I'm quick about showering. I still have to get my car—which is at some bar on the south side from what I recall—and stop at my place before practice. It isn't until I'm drying off that I get a good look at the damage I sustained last night. It's no wonder I feel like I've taken up a second career as an MMA fighter.

Beyond the fly bandage on my left eyebrow and the corresponding black eye and split lip, I have bruises along my ribs and lower back. There are a few on my legs as well.

I put my jeans back on, but my shirt has blood on it—most likely mine. I'd prefer not to drive by that bar wearing it, so I open the door, ready to find Lily so I can ask about borrowing something of Randy's.

Wiener's sitting outside my door. He barks and scampers off in the direction of Lily and Randy's room. At my feet is a pair of dark-wash jeans, boxers, and a fresh T-shirt. She's also left me deodorant and more aspirin. I'm grateful for the thoughtfulness. I don't want to be shirtless in Randy's house, alone with his girlfriend.

My reputation is an issue. I'd never go after one of my teammate's girls, but I don't want to make Lily uncomfortable, or give Randy a reason to mistrust me around her. It's better to avoid those kinds of situations altogether.

I pick up what's been left for me, but before I can disappear back into the guest room, Lily steps into the hall from her bedroom, Wiener running around her feet. She's dragging a brush through her chin-length black hair.

"Oh. You got the—" She scans my torso, then reaches out like she's considering touching me, but thinks better of it. "Oh, God. Are you okay?"

"It looks worse than it is. It's just bruises for the most part. Thanks for these." I nod to the clothes I'm holding, step back into the room, and close the door with Lily still staring.

I change into Randy's clothes. He's a little narrower, so the jeans are snugger than I'm used to, but at least they're clean and don't smell like a bar—or have any blood on them. I probably should've pressed charges, but being drunk didn't help my cause last night. Neither did being in the hospital.

I'm careful pulling the shirt over my split eyebrow. It's tight on my arms and across my chest, but it'll do until I get home.

Once I'm dressed, I fold up my clothes and make the bed, even though I'm sure they'll be changing the sheets after I leave. I hear noise coming from the kitchen, so I follow the sound.

The smell of food cooking hits me as I round the corner. "Thanks for the hospitality. I'm gonna grab a cab and head out."

Lily looks up from the stove. "You don't need to do that. I don't have to work this afternoon. I can drive you wherever you need to go."

"You've already done more than enough."

"Well, I'm making grilled cheese, and two of these are for you, so you have to stay now, or it'd be rude."

I lean against the doorjamb. "You didn't have to do that."

She props a fist on her hip and points her spatula at me. "You're part of Randy's team, and you're his friend. That makes you like family. There's coffee on, and there's cream in the fridge if you want it. You can't go to practice without eating."

She's so matter of fact about it, like it's nothing that she's making me something to eat. I pour a coffee for myself and search the cupboards until I find plates. Then I get the ketchup from the fridge and find dill pickle spears at the back of one of the shelves.

I set everything out on the kitchen island, leaving a stool between us so we're not sitting right next to each other. Lily sets a plate in front of me. Cheese oozes out of the middle of the sandwiches she's cut in half.

"Sorry they're a little messy. Randy has a hard time keeping weight on when the season starts, and, well, that's the story of my life, so I go a little overboard with the cheese. I hope this is okay."

My throat closes like I'm being choked, like my body is preparing for a backhand to go with her kindness. But it doesn't come. All there is is a plate in front of me with two golden, gooey sandwiches and my friend's girlfriend looking apologetic for going out of her way to help me.

For a second I'm jealous of what Randy and Lily have. I try to imagine Tash doing something like this for me, but I can't. I don't think it's in her to care about people this way. It was always just about her, and what she wanted. And that was never really me.

Lily sits in the place I've set for her. She squirts an ungodly amount of ketchup on her plate, dips the corner of her sandwich, and takes a bite, chewing thoughtfully.

"When I was growing up, we only had plastic cheese slices, but I'd go to Sunny's house and her mom always made grilled cheese with Gouda or Swiss. There were always globs of melted cheese on my plate at the end. Even though it was messy, I loved it so much. I loved the ones my mom made for me too, but God, it was like cheese magic at the Waters' house."

"Sounds pretty awesome." Waters has known Lily his entire

life. His sister is her best friend. They're close like family should be. I don't have those kinds of memories from my childhood, even though it was a privileged one. After my brother died, everything good fell apart.

Before Lily takes another bite she asks, "Did your mom ever make you grilled cheese?"

I shake my head. "Nah." My mother never would've done anything like cook. "My nanny did, though. We had grilled cheese and onion sandwiches."

Lily pulls a face. "Cheese and onion?"

"It's really good."

"I'll take your word for it."

We eat in silence for a few minutes. It's been ages since someone made me something to eat who wasn't paid to do it.

Lily pauses with her sandwich. "Can I ask you a question?"

"Sure. I might not answer it, though."

"Why does that not surprise me in the least?"

I've learned how to avoid or fabricate when necessary to protect myself. My entire life has been a lie. A glossy, dressed-up lie. My mother is the kind of beautiful people carve into stone, but inside she's ugly—like most people seem to be. I don't think Lily fits into that category, though.

She gestures to my face. "Why do you let Tash do this to you?"

"Tash didn't do this; some pissed-off juicer with a God complex did."

Lily dips her sandwich in the ketchup again. For someone as small as she is, she sure can pack it away. "Before I met Randy, I dated this guy Benji for seven years."

Tash was probably my longest relationship, if I can even call it that. It was never monogamous. She made sure of that. There was a girl I dated my sophomore year of high school, but I was young, and even then I couldn't handle getting close to people, so while it went on for a couple of months, it never felt like anything real.

"That's a long time to be with one person."

Lily nods. "We started dating when I was in grade nine. He was...stable. Well, more stable than my own situation. I grew up without a dad, and my mom wasn't very good at picking decent guys. Neither was I."

"We can't make good choices all the time." Randy's mentioned Lily's douche ex a couple of times. She's a good person, so I can see how an asshole might use that quality to his advantage.

"He wasn't always a bad choice. For a lot of years he was good to me, or at least relatively speaking. Anyway, after a while it stopped being a good thing. He spent a lot of time bringing me down. He could be mean, abusive."

I think about what it would be like if Randy lost his shit on her and got physical, the kind of damage he could do. She's so small—one hit could break bones. I can't believe Randy hasn't knocked this guy's teeth out if that's what she's talking about.

"He *hit* you?"

Lily raises a hand, and I realize I'm halfway out of my seat, like I'm going to find the guy and beat him for her.

"It wasn't like that," she says. "It was emotional. He manipulated me a lot. He was subversive, antagonistic. He said things that were intentionally hurtful. It got worse over time, and I just sort of put up with it, thinking it must be normal. I stayed with him a lot longer than I should've."

"Tash is good at manipulating, but that bullshit is done." I don't buy the words as I say them, even if I want them to be true. I haven't even listened to her voicemails yet, or read her messages. But I probably will, because I torment myself this way.

Lily finishes the last bite of her first sandwich, swallowing before she responds. "Benji and I used to break up a lot. He would make threats, tell me he was going to sleep with other girls."

"That's a dickhead thing to do." And exactly what Tash has

done to me. And still does even though we're not together, except it's not isolated to one sex or the other.

"It is."

"Did he screw other girls?"

"Probably. I can't ever be sure one way or the other because he lied a lot, and sometimes it was just to make me jealous. But the not knowing was hard. His actions caused a lot of damage on the inside. The kind you can't see, but affects a lot of things. I get that now. For a long time I kept letting it happen until I realized it wasn't going to get better."

I get what she's saying. I understand it perfectly. But there's a distinct difference between me and Lily: She's actually a decent human being.

"What changed?" I ask.

"I decided I didn't want him to have any more power over me, so I took it away."

"Was it that easy?" I think about how things went down last night. How Tash duped me again. How I shouldn't have gone to see her in the first place, but I couldn't find it in me to stay away. I knew it wasn't going to go the way I wanted. I knew there had to be a ploy, but I went anyway.

"It wasn't. Randy made it easier."

"He's all about you."

"And I'm all about him."

I don't have anyone to distract me from Tash. Of course there are bunnies. Lots of them, and they're always interested in getting fucked. But that's as far as it ever goes.

"Can I ask you something else?"

"Sure."

Lily's eyes dart away. "It's personal."

"I'll continue to reserve the right not to answer if I don't feel like it."

She chews her lip, and a flush creeps up her cheeks.

"Why didn't things work out with Tash?"

"I wanted something she didn't."

"Which was what?"

For her not to fuck other people, or bring me other people to fuck. "I just wanted it to be her and me, but she didn't."

"So she wanted to see other guys?"

"Or women, whatever. She was very inclusive."

Lily looks confused. "And you told her what you wanted?"

"Yeah."

"And she didn't want to be exclusive?"

"Nope."

"But you were still with her, even though she was with other people?" The flush in her cheeks deepens to a red that touches the tip of her ears.

"I thought maybe it would change eventually." No need to tell her Tash and I have been with the same woman at the same time. She's shocked enough as it is.

"The thought of being with anyone other than Randy makes me feel sick." Lily cringes, and I drop my head.

I don't want to see how her opinion of me has changed.

"I'm sorry, Lance. I shouldn't have said that. It sounds judgmental, and I didn't mean it to."

"It's okay. I get what you mean. How you feel is the way it's supposed to be."

"Still, it's not my place to put my feelings on anyone else." She shoves the last bite of her second sandwich in her mouth and pushes away from the table.

I've made her uncomfortable. But I don't want her to look at me like there's something wrong with me, even though there is.

"I don't know. I kept hoping she'd decide I was enough. Stupid, huh?"

"It's not stupid, Lance. Sometimes it's hard to tell your heart not to want someone, even if all they do is hurt you."

Lily drives me to the south side, and I'm embarrassed to discover I can't remember exactly which bar I went to. After twenty minutes of driving around, I finally find the place, but my Hummer isn't on any of the surrounding streets.

Eventually I realize it's been towed. I'm already cutting it close. I still need to go home and grab my gear before I go to the rink.

I feel like shit having Lily drive me to get my stuff and drop me off at the arena, but she's nice about it, not making it a big deal. Still, this would've been easier with Randy. By the time I get to the rink, the aspirin I took this morning has worn off, and all the aches are back.

I'm stiff and slow during practice. Evan Smart, the team trainer who replaced Tash, pulls me aside.

"You wanna tell me about this?" He motions to my face.

If my shorts had pockets, my hands would be in them. "I ran into a problem last night."

He crosses his beefy arms over his chest and waits.

"I got into it with some asshole who thought degrading women was an awesome pastime."

"So you started a fight? Jesus, Romero, it's pre-season. You need to keep your shit together."

"I didn't start it. A guy the size of a tank came after his girl, and I stepped in the way of his fist."

Evan doesn't look like he believes me. Which isn't a surprise. He and I don't like each other all that much. I'm thinking it's 'cause he's under the impression I'm the reason Tash lost her job. I'm also aggressive and volatile on the ice. I spend the most time in the penalty box out of all the guys on the team. Actually, out of almost all the guys in the league.

Evan sighs. "Where's the damage?"

"I'm fine. Just a little sore. I'll do some stretches so I'm good to go for tomorrow's practice." I use the hem of my shirt to wipe the sweat from my face.

"Jesus Christ, man." Evan prevents me from dropping my

shirt and covering all the bruises I'd forgotten about. "You look like you got steamrolled by a truck. You're not fine. Is anything broken? Did you even go to the hospital?" When he tries to touch my ribs, I pull away.

"I saw a doctor last night. It's just bruises and some glue in my eyebrow." I smooth my shirt out.

"I want to see the X-rays and reports on that. You need to see a massage therapist at the very least, and get in a couple of physical therapy sessions if you think you're gonna play on Sunday."

"It looks worse than it is. I'll be fine."

"This is not a request. I'll set up the appointments, and you'll go or you'll be benched."

"Fine. I'll do the therapy, but I don't do massages."

"Again, not a request." He pulls out his phone and makes a call. I think I'm in the clear when the team massage therapist tells him they're all booked up, except he gets another number and makes a second call. There are a few minutes of back and forth during which he glares at me. "In an hour? Yup. Perfect. He'll be there."

"Fuck." I run a hand through my hair. I want to argue, but there isn't an option. Explaining why I hate massages will raise more questions than I want to answer.

"Get your ass in gear, Romero. I called in a favor. You need to be on the ice on Sunday for the sake of your team, and that's not going to happen if you don't take care of yourself. The clinic I'm sending you to is about twenty minutes from here. Get showered and changed and go. I'll get a call if you don't show up, and you'll be watching the game from your couch at home if you don't make it."

He messages me the directions. I hit the shower, and Randy offers to drive me since I still don't have my vehicle. He's got Miller with him. Apparently Sunny and Lily decided to do pedicures or some girly crap and won't be home for a couple more hours, so they're happy to chauffeur me around.

I'm fifteen minutes early for the appointment, so I pull my

hood up and make a half-assed attempt at filling out the paper-work. I don't want to be recognized, and I don't want to invite conversation. The receptionist is chatty, and if I make eye contact, I know she'll have all sorts of questions I'm not interested in answering.

My picture's already ended up on a few sites in the past twenty-four hours. My agent and publicist are going to be on my ass. I haven't called either of them, though I have messages from both on top of all the ones from Tash I haven't looked at yet.

I put my phone on silent, stuff it in my pocket, and close my eyes. The messages and problems aren't going anywhere. They'll all still be waiting for me after this torturous massage.

THIS IS NOT A HAPPY ENDING

POPPY

April sticks her head in the door and makes a face. "Good Lord, Poppy, how do you manage? It looks like you sheared a black lab in here."

"He's as friendly as one." Mr. Stroker has more hair on his back than a hibernating bear, but he's a nice man. He also has a herniated disc, and vertebrae three through five have been fused, so his mobility depends a lot on his weekly visits. Excessive hair aside, I like that my treatments help alleviate some of his pain.

The sheets I'm rolling into a ball are covered in his black fuzz. I wonder if his wife has ever suggested waxing and what kind of bribery would be required before he agreed. I have to use an excessive amount of oil on him to avoid ripping out too much hair. Even so, the sheets are always covered in man fur when I'm done with him.

The bodies I'm exposed to on a daily basis are as interesting as they are disgusting at times. But despite the excessive hair on my last client, I'm still starving.

"Want to run across to the bakery with me? I was thinking about walking to the park and eating there since I have lots of time before my next appointment. It's such a beautiful day." I'm irrationally excited for a ham and cheese croissant—and maybe one of those delicious tarts—and an ice-cold soda. It's a warm day, and I want to take advantage before the cooler fall weather sets in.

I toss the sheets in the laundry basket.

April makes another face, along with a weird, sucky sound.

"I don't like that face, or that noise."

"About your dinner break…" She trails off, still making the face.

I prop a hand on my hip. "Don't tell me they booked me another appointment."

Her expression holds genuine apology. "We're all back to back today, and you had the only spot left. It's a favor for some big NHL player or whatever. You know how Tim's always trying to get them in here for rehab. Well, it looks like you're the guinea pig."

Tim is the owner of the clinic. He's a nice guy, but I don't like him much right now. I'm also the one he comes to when he's in a bind because I'm the least likely to say no.

Normally I'd agree that this is a fantastic opportunity. Athletes tend to have interesting muscular issues, and helping to resolve those is something I'm usually excited about.

I loved studying human physiology in school, and while I wasn't great at sports, I was always good at figuring out how to manage the injuries that occurred, which is a big part of the reason I went into this field. Helping people makes me happy.

But not so much when it interferes with my dinner plans.

"So I get to rub oil all over an NHL player instead of eating? Awesome. I'm overwhelmed with joy."

April rolls her eyes and passes me the clipboard with his information. "If it's any consolation, he's a serious hottie. I'm sure most women would trip over themselves for the honor."

"Yeah, well, I'm not most women." My experience with NHL players, while limited, hasn't been particularly fantastic. The form is covered in masculine, barely legible scrawl. I blink a few times as I read the name, positive I can't be seeing this right.

I close my eyes and take a deep breath, then open them again. Heavy black pen still spells out *Lance Romero* across the top of the page.

Talk about ruining what started as a moderately decent day... I must groan out loud because April makes another one of her faces. It should be unattractive, but April is stunningly beautiful, so it's just animated.

"What's wrong?"

I try to pass her back the clipboard. "Why don't you treat him and I'll treat your client. Who is it?"

April's jaw drops, and she taps the paper, right beside Lance's block letters. "Are you high right now? Do you even know who this is?"

Oh, I know exactly who Lance Romero is. He's number twenty-one for Chicago. I saw him for the first time in more than a decade just over a year ago—not that he remembered me from when we were kids. If I could never see him again, that would be awesome, and extremely preferable to being locked in a room alone with him. For an hour. Where I have to touch him. With my hands.

I don't say any of that, though, because then I'd have to offer an explanation. No thanks to that.

"Can you trade?" I ask again.

"I would love to, but I have Ms. Thong next, and that won't fly. What's the deal? Why wouldn't you want to get your hands all over this guy? Maybe he'll want a glute massage."

Sometimes we nickname our clients. Ms. Thong is seventy-six years old and wears the kind of panties you'd find on a stripper. Usually I think that's funny, but right now I'm panicking.

"April."

"Seriously, Poppy, what's the deal? Why's your face red? Why don't you want to treat him? Do you have a secret crush on him? Do you *lurrrve* him?"

April and I have become good friends over the past year, since we took massage therapist positions at this clinic. We were in the same program in college, but we had opposite schedules, so we only ever saw each other in passing. We're pretty close now, though.

Sometimes we even go out on the weekends together. Most of the time we just watch movies, because I'm not much for partying, and most of the time neither is she. On rare occasions we'll go to a bar and laugh at the ridiculous guys who try to pick us up. But I have never, ever talked to her about the time I spent the night at Lance Romero's house. Not in his bed. Oh no, my no-longer-friend Kristi was the one who had the pleasure of messing up his sheets. I know all about how outstanding Lance is in bed, thanks to her detailed recount.

Not that I'd want to sleep with him—or would have had opportunity presented itself. He's an absolute dog. Who's apparently amazing in bed. And a real giver.

I offer April a version of the truth. "I went to school with him." And he's the first boy who ever kissed me with tongue.

"No way!"

"It was grade school. It's whatever. It's not like he'll remember me. We were kids. It's not important."

Mostly I'm trying to convince myself. He didn't remember me last time. I can only hope it'll be that way again. Otherwise this hour is going to be the worst. I wish my face didn't feel like it was on fire right now.

April narrows her eyes. "Why do I feel like there's way more to this story?"

The little buzzer goes off, signaling my next appointment, who happens to be the first guy I ever crushed on.

April points a finger at me. "We will talk about this later. I want to know why you look like you're about to burst into flames."

I ignore her and grab fresh sheets so I can dress my table.

April stops before she opens the door. "I can't believe you went to school with him. I want a firm ass report."

"Way to keep it professional."

She slips out of the room, leaving the door open a crack. I finish putting fresh sheets on the table and arrange the pillows before I take a few deep, cleansing breaths to prepare for what is likely going to be a painful hour.

There's so much irony in this situation. If this was a year ago, I probably would've fainted at the sight of Lance's name scrawled across a patient sheet. But no matter how I feel, I need to put aside my personal issues and focus on the purpose of him being here. People come to see me when they're in pain. If Lance is here, it's likely an issue that's impacting his ability to do his job, and my role is to help. I manipulate the human body in simple, gentle ways to help make that pain go away. I can keep this professional.

Armed with my clipboard, I walk down the hall to the waiting room. Lance is impossible to miss. Despite the fact that he's wearing a sweatshirt and the hood is covering half of his face, he's more than six feet of broad, hockey-playing man.

He's so wide his shoulders encroach on the chairs on either side, which would explain why no one is sitting next to him. He's slouched down so his head rests on the back of the chair, and his hands are clasped in his lap, a baseball cap hanging off one knee. His lips, plush and soft—I know since I've had them on mine; it might have been a decade ago, but I remember it clearly—are parted. He looks like he's asleep.

I clear my throat. "Lance Romero?"

He doesn't move.

Bernadette, the receptionist, gives me a meaningful look.

I clear my throat again and call his name a second time. He jolts awake and the hood falls back, exposing his face. It's not in good shape. He has a black eye and bruises on his left cheek. There's a fly bandage across one eyebrow.

Sadly, he's still hot.

He blinks a few times, yawns, and smacks his lips, his tongue touching the split in the bottom one. His gaze sweeps the room and finally lands on me. Heat explodes in my cheeks and courses through my limbs, warming me from the inside out as he starts at my sneaker-clad feet and roams up over my yoga pants to my company-issued T-shirt before stopping at my face. I can't look directly at him for more than a couple of seconds. I sincerely hope he doesn't remember me. I cannot go there and also be professional.

I'm sure the smile he gives me has melted many a panty off a slutty bunny. Mine stay right where they're supposed to, wedged up my ass.

I force a polite, professional veneer. "I'm ready for you now."

He pushes slowly out of the chair, a tic in his left cheek indicating some discomfort.

I extend a hand when he's close enough. "I'm Poppy. I'll be your massage therapist this afternoon."

I note the newly formed scabs on his knuckles and how warm and wide his palm is when it envelops mine. I try not to think about that night a year ago. About the way it felt when he put that hand on my back and led me through the crowd to the bar. About the feel of his lips against my ear when he asked my name. How it was too loud to hear, and I didn't correct him when he got it wrong. How Kristi got in between us and hijacked him less than a minute later. How I let that happen, even though I didn't want to.

I doubt he remembers any of it. He was drunk. Everyone was. Even I was tipsy, which isn't something I do all that often.

I'm typically not a much of a drinker at all. Still, the entire horrifying night is clearer than polished glass in my memory.

His sleepy eyes stay on my face long past what's comfortable. He wets his bottom lip and smirks. "If I sniff you, will I get high?"

I hold his gaze, not returning his flirty grin. It falters, and he blinks a few times. When I try to free my hand from his, he grips it more tightly and cocks his head to the side, as if he's trying to place me. I look away, afraid he's going to see through me.

Eventually he allows me to pull my hand free. I spin around, calling over my shoulder, "You can follow me."

Oh yes, this is going to be an unpleasant hour for sure.

My palms are sweaty as I lead him down the hall. After we left the bar that night, it was almost like I didn't exist. It had felt a lot like high school, except with more R-rated activities. God, this is humiliating. Hookerslaw. My face is hot, which means it's definitely red. Mortification is hard to hide as a freckly redhead.

I inhale deeply as I open the door to my therapy room—a bad idea because Lance smells delicious—and motion him inside. He shoves his hands in his pockets and rocks back on his heels. He glances at me, and then at the massage table.

"You can go in. I promise it's not a torture chamber."

He makes a sucking sound with his teeth and looks me up and down—not in a sexual way, but in an assessing-whether-I'm-serious way. He seems a little edgy.

Eventually he steps inside, but he doesn't go very far. I have to slip in behind him because he takes up so much space. My arm grazes his, and he jerks out of the way, muttering an apology. Jeez, he's as tense as I am.

I close the door and pat the massage table. "You can have a seat. I'd like to go through your profile and discuss the purpose of your treatment today."

"Right. Yeah. Okay." He hops up on the table with a grimace.

Based on his beat-up face, I assume the purpose is to work out whatever knots or aches the fight he was in has left behind.

Hockey season hasn't even started, so I'm curious what happened.

I review his medical history, which is vague. He gives short responses while his knee bounces.

"Are there any particular areas you'd like me to work on?" God, I'm nervous. Maybe because he seems nervous, which makes no sense. People have their hands all over him all the time. Bunnies to be exact. And my former friend Kristi.

"Um, I don't know?"

"Are there any areas that are particularly tense? Neck, back, shoulders, arms, or legs?" I prompt.

"Sure?"

"So all of them?"

"Yeah." His knee stops bouncing, and he replaces it with finger tapping while I check them all off.

"Are there any areas you'd like me to avoid?"

"Avoid?" Now he looks confused.

It's almost like he's never had a massage before. Which is unlikely. These guys must have regular massages all the time because their job is so physically intense. If anything, they need the treatment.

"Any areas that are uncomfortable as a result of your injuries?" I motion to his face. "Or areas you prefer me not to work on? Some people would rather I avoid their feet."

"Oh aye, my sneakers probably stink, so you should steer clear." A hint of Scot creeps in.

"Okay, then. No feet." I smile at his look of revulsion. "Anything else?"

He taps his lip with his fingers before dropping them to his lap. "Uh, nope."

I give it a few more seconds, because it looks like he wants to say something, but then he just stares at me, so I point to the chair beside him. "You can leave your clothes there and then lie face down on the table."

"Like, all of them?"

Please don't blush, please don't blush, please don't blush. Or imagine him naked. "You can leave your underwear on if you prefer."

"Uh, I'm not wearing any."

"That's fine." The memory of Lance stripping off his shirt on his way outside to the hot tub at his place punches me in the proverbial face.

And then he pulls his shirt over his head and the memory becomes a reality. Except this time I'm not just looking at fantastically chiseled muscles and the massive cross tattooed on his back that reads *Forgive me my sins.*

"Oh my God." I cover my mouth with my hand, because that's not an appropriate response, even as shocked as I am. "Are you okay? Have you seen a doctor?"

Lance runs a hand over his ripped stomach. "It's not that bad. Just a few bruises."

It looks like way more than a few bruises. I'm instantly angry at the person who did this to him. The purple on his ribs indicates the hits were aimed at the kidneys, with the intention of causing pain. He kicks off his shoes and hooks his fingers into the waistband of his sweats. Oh my God. Is he going to drop his pants with me in the room? They slide down over his hips, and I get a front-row view of the magic V.

Yes. Yes he is. I rush to the door. Just because I've seen him half-naked before doesn't mean I need the reminder right before I'm about to touch him for an hour.

"I'll give you some privacy. Lie on your stomach when you're ready. I'll be back in a minute." I catch a glimpse of his bare ass before I can close the door.

"Get it together, Poppy," I mumble as I hurry down the hall. I step into the bathroom and wash my hands, checking my reflection in the mirror. My face a terribly bright shade of red.

"It'll be fine. This will be fine," I tell my reflection. "He's going to be face down for the next hour. He doesn't remember you. Dammit." I splash a little cold water on my face, then heat it back up and run my hands under the hot stream.

I don't think my pep talk has done much, but honestly, it's just an hour. I should be able to handle it.

Once my hands are warm, I return to my room, knocking before I enter. "Ready?"

"Aye," comes the reply.

I open the door to find Lance lying face down on the table, as instructed. Except he's not lying under the sheet; he's lying on top of it in all his naked, hockey-playing hotness. The huge cross spanning the width of his shoulders shifts with his breathing. Instead of putting his face in the cradle, his head is turned to the side, so he's looking right at me, rather than at the floor.

I avoid making eye contact and head straight for my supply of sheets, draping one over his body—his incredibly amazing body that's covered in bruises. I might get a good look at his ass before it's covered by the sheet. It's unreal. Like beyond fantastic.

But it's just a body. I've had plenty of naked, attractive men on my table. And plenty of unattractive ones. Most of the time I can compartmentalize those thoughts. Usually I don't get to see quite so much of them all at once, though. I need to keep it professional so I can get through this. It's one hour. One favor. Then he'll go back to seeing his regular massage therapist, and I don't ever have to see him again.

"Can I get you to move up so your face is here?" I tap the cradle.

"Oh. Yeah. Sure." He mumbles something else, but I don't catch it. The tips of his ears go red, as if he's embarrassed. He shifts around, and his shoulders tense as he gets into position.

His split eyebrow and black eye might not feel too good like that. "If it's too uncomfortable—"

"It's fine. Let's just do this thing."

"Let me know if any area I'm working on is too painful, or if I'm using too much pressure, or not enough."

"Okay."

I prepare myself to put my hands on him in a way that is nothing like what Kristi did all night in the privacy of his locked bedroom a year ago. Because like the pushover I can sometimes be, I backed down the second she made it clear what she wanted. It's also not the way I put my hands on him more than ten years ago when Lance came crashing into my world and turned it upside down.

He tenses as soon as I touch him, even through the cover of the sheet. I can't decide if it's the situation that has him so on edge, or me. Or both. So far I'm managing to keep my swoon in check, but then my hands aren't on his skin, yet.

"I'm checking alignment before I get started."

"'Kay."

Telling him what I'm doing doesn't seem to have the desired effect. His muscles are all bunched up. I have a feeling his hands are balled into fists. Maybe once I start the actual massage he'll ease up.

I lift the sheet and fold it down, exposing the broad, defined expanse of his back again. Up close, I can make out the intricate details in the cross tattoo. *Quinn* is written inside it, along his spine. That must have hurt a lot. I stop when I reach the dimples that tell me if I keep going I'm going to get an eyeful of hockey butt again.

Since there's nowhere to anchor the sheet on Captain Commando, I pull it a little lower, intending to tuck it under his hands. As predicted, they're balled into fists. But when I graze his forearm, Lance's hand shoots out and grabs my wrist, fingers lapping over each other. God, his hands are big. Just like the rest of him. And he's touching me. That familiar hot feeling from forever ago rushes through me. I freeze as he turns to look at me, panic and uncertainty flashing in his eyes before a wall comes up and they go blank.

"Sorry. I didn't expect that." He releases my wrist and resumes his completely un-relaxed position on my massage table. Now that he's not touching me anymore, I can breathe again.

I give him a few seconds before I move around to the other side. "I'm going to tuck the sheet under your left hand." I say, to avoid startling him again.

Once the sheet is secure, I move to the top of the table, taking in the bruises along his lower back and the ones that span his ribs. Hovering my palms over his shoulder blades, I take a deep breath, exhaling my own anxiety as he seems to do the same. The energy in this room is thick with emotion—his and mine—and I don't know what to make of it.

"I'm going to start now," I tell him.

"'Kay," his voice holds the same tension as his muscles when I place my palms on his clammy skin. I seem to be in control of my physical response to him this time, maybe because he seems so uncomfortable.

I stay perfectly still, hoping some of it will dissipate, but it doesn't. "Lance?"

His muscles tighten even more. "Aye."

"Are you okay?"

"Aye."

"Does this hurt at all?" I don't see how it could, considering I'm using no pressure.

"No."

If his tension isn't pain-based it must be anxiety-based. I'll never work out any of his knots if he can't relax. "Can I get you to breathe with me?"

"Huh?"

"It will help you relax." At least I hope it will.

"Oh. Yeah. Sure. I guess," he says something else I don't catch.

"In and out to the count of four, okay?"

"Sure."

"Inhale, one, two, three, four…exhale, one, two, three, four," I murmur.

It seems to work, and after a moment his shoulders feel less like a wall and more like tight muscles. On the third inhale-exhale combination, I move my hands lower, and he tenses all over again.

"Just relax, Lance."

HANDS

LANCE

I hate it when people touch me. Like, I lose my shit when someone puts their hands on me, particularly if I don't expect it. A psychiatrist once told me it's a result of some kind of post-traumatic whatever from when my brother died. He didn't know my mum also used to use me as her punching bag, or that I'm edgier about it when it's women, not men.

I don't like contact even when I know it's coming. So that explains why I'm tense as shit lying on this massage table, anticipating the hour of torture that's about to occur.

What makes it worse, or what made it worse until a few seconds ago, is that this woman—this curvy slip of a woman—is likely going to become the star of every whack-off session for the rest of my life.

My massage therapist is a ginger. A strawberry blonde. A redhead. A real one. Like me. Even though I'm lying facedown on the table, I can envision all that long, pretty hair hanging down her back, her sweet body and perfect round ass hugged by black yoga pants. She's wearing running shoes—I can see them right now through the hole in the face holder—and her feet are small.

I didn't get a chance to study her face all that well, since I'm busy freaking out about this whole situation. She looks familiar, though. But that's often the way it is with redheads. We're all a little familiar-looking to each other, because we're such a rarity.

I'd been ready to tolerate the physical discomfort of having her hands on me for a prolonged period of time, but my anticipated reaction never comes. I'm tense as her palms and fingers move down my back, because that's a conditioned response when someone of the opposite sex makes skin-to-skin contact, but the sensation I usually associate with it is absent.

Instead of feeling like there are bugs crawling under and over my skin, all I feel is warm. Warm skin. Warm hands. *Warm.* And that sensation radiates through me, shooting through my veins and jump-starting my adrenaline. A wave of goose bumps flashes across my skin, and I have to work to suppress a full-body shudder. What the fuck is that about?

"Are you cold? Should I get the heating pad for you?" she asks.

Even her voice is familiar and warm. I feel like I'm being wrapped in it.

"I'm fine."

I'm actually not fine at all. I don't know how to deal with this new development, especially while all I can do is lie here and take it.

"If you get cold, let me know."

"Sure."

She smoothes her palms down my back and back up again.

And then her touch is gone. I'm about to express my displeasure at this when her hands return. This time they're slick. She starts circular motions up and down my back—a light touch that I want more of. Which freaks me the fuck out, because I never *want* hands on me.

Not even when I was with Tash. I tolerated her touch because it was expected, but I never liked it. It never felt good—not like this.

I honestly don't see how this girl can be effective, considering she has to be a foot shorter than me, but she's strong—like, crazy strong. When she hits a knot, and there are loads of them, she runs her forearm over it, repeating the motion several times. She moves on to my shoulder, and I groan. The aches there are worse; maybe because I deflected a bunch of punches.

"Is that too much?" She pauses, but she doesn't lift her palm from my skin. I'm starting to feel high from the contact.

"It's just sore," I grumble. "You can keep going."

"If the pressure is too intense, let me know and I'll ease up."

I don't say anything unless she asks me a direct question. I'm too busy focusing on the feel of her hands and how it should be unpleasant but isn't.

Eventually she moves down to my lower back, which is really sore, probably from landing on the table. I don't know how long it's going to take for those aches to go away, but I'm going to need a lot more painkillers over the next couple of days to take the edge off.

"Would you like me to massage your legs?" she asks as she pulls the sheet up over me again.

I don't want her to stop touching me, and if she's done on my back I guess it makes sense to hit the lower half of my body. "Uh, sure."

"Would you like me to include your glutes?"

It takes me a second to understand the question. "You mean massage my ass?"

I hear a puff of breath leave her; it sounds a little like a laugh. She clears her throat before she answers. "It's a fairly common area for athletes, especially hockey players because of the high level of muscle strain and use."

When she puts it that way, it sounds much less like she wants to feel my ass up, and more like she's trying to do her job.

"Right. Sure." If her hands feel good everywhere else, I'm sure they'll feel just as great on my ass.

She rearranges the sheets, exposing one of my legs, and runs her hands down the entire length. It's a strange sensation. I think the only place I've ever been touched on my leg is my thigh—when a bunny is getting ready to ask me if I want to go somewhere private so we can stop talking and start fucking.

Based on my body's reaction, it seems like my dick thinks it's the next thing Poppy's going to massage. That reaction wanes when she gets to my IT band, which kills as she uses what feels like her shoulder to dig in.

"Does your trainer encourage any of you to do yoga?" she asks.

"No, why?"

"It might help with this." She runs her forearm across the outside of my thigh, and I hiss.

"I don't think yoga's my thing."

"Maybe not, but more stretching could be helpful. I can give you some exercises to do at home, if you want." Her hands smooth down the back of my leg again.

"You could, but I probably won't do them."

She laughs. It's a pretty sound. "At least you're honest." She starts working on my ass, which isn't nearly as sexual as I expected. It actually hurts a lot.

"At the very least you should try to soak in an Epsom salts bath for a good twenty minutes after this."

"I have a hot tub; will that work?" I get this odd feeling, like this isn't the first time I've had this conversation with her. But that doesn't make sense at all.

Her arm slips, and her elbow digs hard into tight muscle. I grunt, and she gasps.

"I'm so sorry!" And then her palm is on my ass, kneading the spot, and my dick once again thinks it should be next on the massage list.

After that she doesn't give me any more advice or ask questions apart from whether the pressure is okay. By the time she's done with my legs and my ass, I have the most insane hard-on. The top of my dick feels like it's going to pop off.

She moves away from the lower half of my body after she covers it, and settles a palm in the middle of my back. "Lance?"

I grunt out a *yeah*.

"If you'd like to turn over, I can work on your quads."

"No!" I don't mean for it to come out so aggressively, but there is no way I'm turning over so she can get a load of my hard-on. "I mean, that's okay. I'm good."

"You still have another ten minutes. I could work on your neck and shoulders, if you'd like."

"Do I have to turn over?"

"It would be easier."

"But you can work on my neck like this?" Beyond not wanting her to see my problem, I don't think looking at her face is going to help my situation. I might not have been paying close attention when she brought me in here, but she's a natural redhead, and I have a serious weakness for them. They remind me of the good things about Scotland. And their personalities tend to be fiery like their hair, although I'm not so sure Poppy fits that mold. Either way, propositioning my massage therapist seems like something I'd definitely do, and certainly shouldn't. Especially when having her touch me feels so damn good.

"If that's what you'd prefer."

"Yeah."

"Okay."

Her fingertips trail a line up my spine through the sheet. At this point it feels like all contact is directly connected to my cock. It twitches between the table and my stomach. I fully expect the neck massage to help calm the issue below, because she's no longer near that part of my body, but it doesn't. Instead I get harder—if that's even possible. I try to stay focused on something other than my goddamn hard-on, but it sure isn't easy.

I'm almost glad when it's over. Almost. And then the moment she finishes, I realize that unless I schedule another massage with her, she's never going to put her hands on me again. Weird panic accompanies that thought.

"Take your time getting up. I'll be waiting for you in reception." The door clicks quietly behind her.

I flip over and throw off the sheet. My erection stands straight up. I wait a full two minutes after she leaves the room for my hard-on to deflate. While I'm waiting, I send a message to Balls to let him know I'm done.

Our next stop will be the impound lot where my Hummer is waiting to be picked up, and once I get home, I'm thinking I need a nap. For two days. But first I'll have to rub one out or the ache in my balls is going to be unbearable.

My hard-on shows no signs of giving up, like it thinks Poppy's coming back for a happy ending.

I'm almost positive I could make it happen in less than a minute, but that's sketchy, even for me. Instead I get dressed. I'm fumbly and uncoordinated. I end up having to sit on the chair to get my sweats back on.

As I'm tucking the head into my waistband so it's not too obvious that I'm sporting wood, I notice the wet spot on the sheets where my cock has been weeping tears of sadness over not being touched. For fuck's sake. It's like I'm a damn teenager.

I bunch the top sheet over to hide it.

I feel groggy and out of it as I adjust my baseball cap and prepare to leave, and I don't think it's just because most of my blood flow has been redirected to my cock. I move toward the reception area, rolling my head on my shoulders. I'm a lot less tense than I was when I walked in an hour ago—except for my dick.

Poppy's standing at the desk, talking to the chick behind it. I take the opportunity to check her out, and my hard-on starts crying again. She's short. Maybe five three or five four, tops. She's soft around the edges, nice and curvy. Her black yoga pants hug her ass. I can see her panty line. She's rocking those boy short things.

Her strawberry blond hair is pulled up in a wavy ponytail, the end of which kisses the space between her shoulder blades. For some reason I have the urge to tug on the end as I approach her. I shove my hands in my pockets so I don't. I also readjust my hard-on. I wish I had my Hummer, because I need to get my ass home so I can resolve my problem.

Poppy and the receptionist are whispering away when I reach the desk.

"Hey."

She jumps and spins around, fumbling her clipboard. I catch it before it can hit the ground.

"Wow. You have amazing reflexes," the receptionist says.

"That's why they have me on defense." I wink reflexively and turn to Poppy. The tips of her ears have gone pink, along with her cheeks. "Thanks for fixing me."

She smiles, but avoids making eye contact. "It would probably be a good idea for you to schedule a follow-up appointment with your regular massage therapist for later in the week."

"I don't have a regular massage therapist."

This time when she looks up she meets my gaze briefly. "But your team must have someone."

We do, but now that I've had Poppy's hands all over me, I kind of want them again.

"Maybe I could come back and see you?"

The receptionist coughs a little, and Poppy fidgets with her clipboard. She looks tense. Kinda like I was when I first came in here.

57

"Can you check the schedule for later this week, say Thursday or Friday?" Poppy asks.

I lean on the counter and observe her profile. The bridge of her nose and her cheeks are dotted with pale freckles. A faint sunglasses tan circles her eyes. She's been enjoying the unseasonable weather and sunshine over the past few days. I wonder what she looks like in a bikini. I bet her ass is amazing.

The receptionist clicks away on the computer for a minute before giving Poppy an apologetic look. "You're fully booked both days."

She taps her pen against her lips. "What about Marcie, or April? Do they have any openings?"

"No," I bark.

Poppy jolts, looking up. "I'm sorry?"

"I want you." I honestly don't mean for it to come out sounding like a line, but based on the shade of red she's turning, it does. "I mean, you've already worked on me, so it'd make more sense for me to come to you, right?"

She clears her throat. "If that's what you prefer."

"It is. I do." I lick my lips. "I prefer you." I don't know why her touching me feels different, but it does, and I want that feeling again.

"What's Saturday look like?" she asks the receptionist who's now gawking between us.

"You have one opening left, but it's only half an hour at four in the afternoon."

"We fly out for our last exhibition game on Saturday."

Poppy taps her pen against her lips. She's not wearing lipstick. They're dark pink, full. I bet they look good wrapped around a cock. I bet they'd look amazing wrapped around mine. Fuck. I need to stop this shit. I can't be imagining a blow job from my massage therapist. Even if she is hot.

"What if I put you on a waiting list? If there's a cancellation, I can call you. Then if it works, you can come in before you leave for your game."

The receptionist's eyes widen, which tells me this isn't something Poppy usually does.

"You'd do that for me?"

She looks away for a moment. "I'd do that for any of my clients. You need another session before your game and you're right, I already know the issues. Bernadette, can you make sure Lance's number is in the system so I can call if something comes available?"

"Other than workouts and practice, I'm open to come in almost any time."

The bell over the door to the clinic chimes, drawing Poppy's attention away. Her eyes go wide, and once again her cheeks flush.

"Hey, Romance, you all loose and limber now?" I hear Miller ask.

Randy snorts. "He's always loose."

I turn away from Poppy, annoyed by the interruption.

Miller looks at her and his face changes. "Hey! Poppy from the garden?"

Poppy's expression is somewhere between embarrassment and mortification. "Heeeeyyy," she says.

"How crazy is this? How you doin'?"

"I'm fine. Good. And you?" She's focused on his forehead.

I look back and forth between them. He better not have fucked her. "You two know each other?"

Miller frowns. "Uh, yeah." He's not looking at me; he's looking at Poppy.

When I turn back to her, she's making hand gestures that she quickly turns into a ponytail adjustment.

"It's nice to see you again. I have another client." She gestures over her shoulder and looks at me briefly. "If something comes available before Saturday, I'll be sure to have Bernadette call you." She spins around and rushes off down the hall.

Bernadette confirms my number, and I take one of Poppy's cards, slipping it into my pocket as we leave.

I wait until we're outside before I start with the questions. "How do you know Poppy? Did one of you fuck her?"

Miller stops walking to stare at me. "What?"

"Poppy. You know her. How?" Jesus. Why the hell do I sound so pissed off?

"You seriously have no idea?" Miller seems surprised.

"No idea about what?" I glance between him and Randy, trying to figure out what the hell is going on.

Miller runs a hand through his hair. "She's been to your house before, dude."

I guess that explains why she looked familiar. "So she's a bunny?" I don't like that possibility. She doesn't seem like that type, or maybe I just don't want her to be that type. I try to place her in my memory, but come up with nothing.

"No, man, she's no bunny," Miller replies.

The only girls who come to my place are the ones looking to get fucked by a hockey player. "Why was she at my house then?"

"Because you invited her."

"That doesn't make any sense."

"Oh, fuck." Randy smacks Miller's arm. "Isn't she the chick who rubbed the dick off your forehead last season?"

Miller grimaces. "That's the one."

I vaguely remember pictures of a dick drawn on Miller's forehead going viral on the internet last year. But I don't remember Poppy at all, let alone her being the remover of the dick. However, that night is pretty fucking vague, as are many nights over the past couple of years.

"Does someone wanna fill me in here? Did one of us fuck her?"

"No, jackass, she came to your house with her friends, one of which you ended up fucking," Miller snaps.

Well, that explains why she won't make eye contact. "At least I didn't fuck *her*; that woulda been hella awkward."

Miller gives me a look and shakes his head.

"Is there more to the story?" I ask.

"Nope. You fucked her friend; she wiped a dick off my fore-head. That's about it." Miller's SUV beeps as he unlocks the door.

I'm not so sure I believe him. Something about this still isn't quite falling into place.

TOUCH ME,
TOUCH ME NOT

POPPY

I head straight for my therapy room to change the sheets. I don't have another massage for a little bit, but I need to get away from Lance and his hockey friends before one of them says something and outs me. That's a level of embarrassment I can't deal with right now, if ever.

My room smells like massage oil and Lance. I close the door, and try not to get all swoony over his cologne, or deodorant, or whatever that awesome scent is. I can't decide if I'm relieved or sad that he didn't show any signs of recognizing me—not from last year, or when we were kids.

This day was so normal prior to an hour ago. Everything in my life was normal. Maybe even a little boring and predictable, but I don't necessarily think there's anything wrong with consistency. Now that normalcy has been turned inside out by the reappearance of Lance, I can't decide whether it's good or bad or somewhere in between. Although, I managed to put my hands on him for an hour without inadvertently groping, which is definitely a good thing.

My plan is to prepare quickly for my next appointment and run out to grab a bite to eat, because I have back-to-back sessions for the rest of the evening. I toss the balled-up top sheet in the laundry hamper. It takes a lot of effort for me not to sniff it first, like some creepy obsessed fan.

"Stupid." I pull the rest of the sheets off the table, tossing them into the laundry as well. I miss, and they land in a heap on the floor. When I crouch down to pick them up, I notice a cell phone lying under the chair in the corner—the one where clients leave their clothes.

It vibrates across the floor toward me, a contact lighting up the screen. I blink a couple of times, sure I can't be seeing it right, but I am. The caller has been named DO NOT FUCKING REPLY in all caps. Maybe it's a joke. It stops ringing, and the screensaver pops up. It's definitely Lance's phone, because the image is the Chicago team logo. A few seconds later, it starts ringing again.

Maybe it's Lance calling his own phone. I debate whether I want to answer. It could also be someone he doesn't want to talk to, and if that's the case, I probably don't want to talk to that person either.

A knock on the door startles me, and I fumble the phone, nearly dropping it.

"Poppy?" It's April.

"Come in!" My voice is high and pitchy.

She peeks in, taking stock of the stripped table, the pile of sheets on the floor, and the phone buzzing in my hand. She slides in through the crack and closes the door behind her.

"So? How'd it go?" She looks again at the phone. "Did you get a picture of his ass?"

"No. I didn't do something that could potentially cost me my license, April."

"Wow. You're testy. I'm guessing it didn't go so well."

"It was fine. He left his phone here, though."

"Oh my God! Lemme see!" She grabs for it, but I hide it behind my back.

"You can't get into it. There's obviously a passcode." I haven't checked to verify this, but who doesn't have a passcode on their phone?

"I know that. I just want to see it."

I roll my eyes and hand it over because there really is nothing she can do besides check out his screensaver.

April rubs it on her shirt before she examines it. "Dammit, it's thumbprint activated."

"Seriously, April."

"Don't tell me you didn't try it." A sudden flash nearly blinds me.

I raise a hand. "What're you doing?"

"Sorry! That was an accident."

"Did you take a picture of me?"

"I didn't mean to!"

I grab the phone, but without a password, I can't delete the photo. "Thanks a lot. How am I going to explain that when he comes back to get it?"

She makes her sorry face. "Tell him the truth. It was an accident."

"Should I include the part where you tried to get into his phone because you can't contain your curiosity, or maybe the part where you rubbed it on your boobs?"

"I was cleaning the screen!"

"On your boobs."

"I bet you stuck it down your pants!"

"That's just too far." We both snort laugh.

"Do you think he left it here on purpose?"

"I doubt it. He was looped by the time I was done with him."

April wags her brows. "Oh, I bet he was. Bernadette said he was all kinds of flirty with you."

"Bernadette's full of crap."

She gestures to the phone. "So what're you going to do?"

"I guess I'll try to call him to let him know it's here so he can come pick it up."

We check the system for his contact information and discover he's only left one number. Instead of letting Bernadette do the calling, I use my personal cell, and the phone in my hand rings. I assume he'll come to the conclusion that it's here and return for it—but who knows how long that could take.

I only have twenty minutes left for dinner now, so I run across the street, grab a sandwich and a Sprite and scarf it down as quickly as I can before my next appointment.

I follow my rushed meal by working on a man with the worst bacne ever. It's a stark contrast to Lance's flawless, freckled, tattooed skin. I try to stay out of my head and remain focused on what I'm doing with my hands, but back acne isn't all that pleasant, and mostly I'm just trying not to gag.

My final client of the evening, Debbie, is fifteen minutes late for her appointment. She relies on an independent transportation company to get her here because she can't drive, so I always try to build in extra time in case they're late, as they sometimes are.

This means I'll be the last one out of the clinic. April wants to go to a pub for snacks and details about Lance's massage, but I tell her not to wait. I'll catch up with her.

It's after nine by the time I finish my last client, and I know I'll be responsible for cashing her out because Bernadette always leaves at eight thirty. I wash my hands and wait for Debbie to appear.

"Any plans for tonight?" she asks as we walk down the hall.

"I think I'll curl up with a bowl of popcorn and watch *Vikings*."

"Great idea! I have the best dreams after I watch that show. Ragnar is sex—" She comes to an abrupt halt.

I'm confused until I see what she sees. Lance is sitting in the exact same place he was earlier today. He's wearing a pair of jeans now instead of sweats, and a T-shirt with his team logo instead of a hoodie. His hair looks like his hand has been in it. He proves my theory correct when he looks up from his lap and runs his fingers through it again. No man should have the right to look this good, especially as beat up as he is.

"Hi." Wow, my brain is on point right now.

"Hey." His knee bobs a couple of times.

"Holy Jesus," says Debbie. She grabs my arm and does this swoony thing, falling into me for a second before she pushes away and flaps her hands in front of her face. "Oh my God! You're Lance Romero! You play for Chicago!"

I suddenly feel far less ridiculous about my reaction to this man.

She takes three steps toward him and then two steps back. "I'm so sorry. I just—can I please have your autograph? I know I shouldn't, but I can't be this close to you and not ask." The whole time she talks, her hands are flapping. She looks to me. "That's Lance Romero. I'm in love with him." I think she means to whisper the last part, but she doesn't.

The side of his mouth quirks up. "I'd be happy to sign anything ya want." That hint of Scot drops.

More hand flapping follows, and she turns to me imploringly. "Can I get a piece of paper and a pen?"

"Of course." I move around the empty receptionist desk, trying not to be smug about the fact that this woman is losing it over Lance and I've had my hands on his ass today.

"Why don't I sign this for ya?" He spins the ball cap in his lap around his finger—he can't have been wearing it, based on his lack of hat head.

"Really?"

"Sure."

"You have no idea how much I appreciate this! Seriously, isn't he the best?"

"That's the rumor," I mutter.

"Pardon?" Debbie asks.

"He sure is."

I pass him a Sharpie from Bernadette's desk. Lance signs the cap and hands it to Debbie. She squeals and hugs it, then puts it on so she can get a selfie with him. Apparently Lance isn't great at taking selfies, and her arms are too short to be able to get his whole head in there, so I'm commissioned to take the picture. Lance flinches as she wraps her arm around his waist and hugs his side—I remember the bruises on his ribs, the ones I avoided as I massaged his back. She promptly posts the picture to all of her social media sites.

Once she's done fawning over him, and talking to him about how much of a team player he is, and blah, blah, blah, she thanks him half a dozen more times for being so nice.

As soon as she's gone, Lance exhales a deep breath and taps on the counter. And I'm alone with him, again. For the second time today.

"I'm so sorry, and thank you. You really didn't need to do that, but I'm pretty sure you made her entire year."

"It's cool. I'm used to it." More desk tapping.

I try not to fidget or touch too many of Bernadette's things. "I'm sure you are."

"I didn't mean for that to sound cocky."

"It doesn't. I assume you're here about your phone?"

"Aye. The receptionist lady said you had it."

"Yes, I meant to leave it with her, but I forgot." The lie feels thick on my tongue. Despite the awkwardness of this entire situation, I still wanted to be the one to give it back. "I hope you weren't waiting too long."

"I would've waited to see you either way, so it doesn't really matter." The last part comes out heavily accented, sounding more like *It does nae reee-lly mah-ter*.

"Oh." I don't know what else to say to that. I don't understand why he'd wait to see me, unless he wanted to make sure I didn't jailbreak his phone.

He looks down and smoothes his hand across the counter. His knuckles look sore, and his nails are bitten to the quick, a bad habit I used to share, but have worked hard to curb. There's nothing quite like wearing your worry on your hands for everyone to see. He makes a fist when he notices me looking and drops his hands to his sides.

When he doesn't say anything else, I shut down the computer and push up from the chair. "Well, I'll just go get your phone for you."

I beeline for my massage room and try not to freak out on the way there. His phone sits where I left it: on top of my pile of towels, where I could see every message come in while I massaged my other clients.

Lance is standing in the same place when I return with his phone. He has thirty-seven new messages, six missed calls, and two voicemails from DO NOT FUCKING REPLY. I only know because the tally appears every time the phone lights up again.

I pass it over to him. "You missed a lot of calls."

At the quirk of his brow, I rush to explain. "I wasn't snooping. It just went off a lot."

The phone buzzes again. His grin drops and his eyes go wide as he scans the screen and does some scrolling.

"Fuckin'ell." He jams the device in his pocket and shakes his head. "I, uh—thanks for holding on to my phone for me."

"Of course." I'm anxious now. His proximity does things to me that I don't know how to handle. And he's staring. "Did you forget anything else?"

"You."

I blink a couple of times, certain I'm misunderstanding. My heart does this stupid fluttery thing. "I'm sorry. Pardon?"

Lance shakes his head. "My teammate Miller says I know you, but I don't remember, and I should."

"I don't—"

"I should remember someone as beautiful as you." It sounds very much like a line, but he taps the desk again. He's agitated, his frustration obvious. "I want to remember you."

I look away, because I don't want him to see my hurt. I should be relieved, but I'm really not. "It's not a big deal. You meet a lot of peop—"

Lance interrupts me. "I hope I wasn't an asshole. I get that way sometimes; when I've been drinking I'm not always nice. I wouldn't have wanted to be a dick to you."

"You were perfectly fine." It's only sort of a lie. He was nice to me until Kristi got in the way and made it clear she was interested in a lot more than conversation.

He watches me for a few long seconds, and I know he's assessing whether I'm telling the truth. "I probably wasn't if I don't remember you. I must've been fucking wasted, so however I acted, with you and your friends, I'm sorry."

"It wasn't a big deal." I adjust a few of the papers on the desk to have something to do with my hands. I could say something. Maybe I even should, but I clam right up instead, too caught up in my own embarrassing memories.

He pulls his phone out of his pocket again and hits a few buttons on the screen, mumbling something I don't catch. "Can I get your number?"

When I just stare at him, likely with that blank look store mannequins can pull off effortlessly, he's quick to correct my stupid assumption that he's asking me out. Because that would just be crazy.

"So I can call you for massages. Do you do home visits?"

"Pardon?"

"Like, have table, will travel? You do that, right?"

I don't even know what to do with that question. "You want me to come to your house?" I can't tell if this is some sort of weird proposition, and whether I want to be flattered or affronted.

Lance runs his jagged nails through his hair and drops his

head, his jaw working. When he raises his head, there's a hint of panic behind his pale green eyes. "I'll come see you again here if that's the only way I can do this, but it'd be good if you could come to me…if there's, like, an emergency situation or something."

"Emergency massage?" This is the worst pick up in the history of the world. Except, as I observe his mannerisms and expression, I don't think he's trying to pick me up at all.

"Sometimes I get into fights on the ice."

"So you want me to be your on-call massage therapist? What about the team therapist?" I can't treat him on a regular basis. Well, I can, but I'm not sure I should. I might have successfully managed myself around him so far, but I'm not sure if that's going to last. Not with the way I feel right now, and how upside down this all seems.

"I—I don't really like it when people touch me. It makes me…uncomfortable. But it wasn't like that with you today. So it'd be good if you were the person I saw when things like this happen." He gestures to his face. "If that's okay with you." He bites his split lip, staring intently at me while he waits for a response.

What does he mean he doesn't like to be touched?

While rumors are typically embellished, based on the many accounts of Lance's exploits *and* what happened with Kristi that night at his house, I find that hard to believe—at least when it comes to sex. But I keep this to myself. Beyond it not being an appropriate observation to voice, it's really none of my business.

"It's more expensive for me to do home visits," I tell him. "I have to factor in things like transportation time."

His panic flares. "Is it about the inconvenience? What if I can come to you?"

"I don't know—"

"Please, Poppy? Whether you come to me or I come to you is irrelevant. I just want to know that it's going to be your hands on me."

Based on his expression and his pleading tone, I don't think he's playing games. Or maybe I just don't want him to be.

"My trainer's gonna make me do this again, and if it's you I'll feel a lot better about it. Please?"

Eventually I give in. I'd like to say it's because he needs the treatment, which he does, but I'd also like to see him again.

"Okay, fine. But this needs to be cleared with your trainer. I took you as a favor today, but only certain therapists are covered for team treatment, so it's up to you to make sure this arrangement is okay."

"That's cool. Even if it's not covered, I want you." He passes me his phone. "Maybe you can give me your cell, so if I need you, I can text or whatever works best."

Giving Lance my cell number isn't a smart move. I know this. But I type it in anyway, clearing him to contact me outside of work hours, which is probably the worst idea I've ever had.

I tell myself this doesn't mean I'm actually going to hear from him. Or answer his calls. But I can't imagine ignoring Lance if he messages me.

Which is exactly what he does as soon as I pass him back his phone. I hear mine chime in my purse.

I go to the message and add him as a contact while he fiddles around with his phone some more.

"We're all set?" he asks.

"All set," I echo.

"You didn't reply."

I pull up the message from him, add a smiley face and a thumbs up emoji, and hit send. His phone vibrates, and the smile he gives me reminds me of the boy I met when we were just kids. I wish he'd been like this at the bar last year.

"Better?" I ask, maybe a little snidely.

"Much. I'm gonna let you go home now. Maybe I can walk you to your car?" He shoves his hands in his pockets and rocks back on his heels.

If I didn't know better, I'd almost think he was nervous.

Except this is Lance "Romance" Romero, and I can't imagine he gets nervous about much—except massages apparently.

"Umm, I guess that's okay."

"I promise I'm not going to kidnap you or anything." He makes a face and crinkles his nose. "That wasn't very reassuring, was it?"

"Not really. As soon as you say you're not going to do it, that kind of makes me think it's part of your plan."

He takes a step back from the desk. "I can just go, if that's better."

"Yeah, but then I'll find you hiding between cars in the dark with a rag soaked in chloroform. Better to keep an eye on you until I'm safely locked away inside my vehicle." I lower my voice to a whisper. "Besides, there are video cameras in the parking lot. If you steal me, people will know."

Lance arches his split brow. "Wow, this got macabre pretty damn fast."

"Sorry, my sense of humor is a little off sometimes. I think it's from all the crime drama marathons." I cringe at how stupid that sounds, but he doesn't look at me like I'm an idiot, so I feel a little less ridiculous.

I shove all my things in my purse, make sure the computer is shut down, and gather the keys to the clinic and my car.

My stomach does all sorts of spins and twists and turns as Lance opens the door for me and waits while I lock up. He's hulking behind me. I can see him in the reflection in the glass. He absolutely dwarfs me. It makes my skin hot.

When I turn around, he's right there. I take a step back so I don't accidentally slam into him. He puts his hand on my elbow, as if to steady me. He's wearing the oddest expression, as if he's expecting me to burst into flames, which is entirely possible with how hot my face feels.

He drops his hand and stuffs it back in his pocket. "Sorry."

"Trying to get close enough to get high from sniffing me?" I ask.

His white teeth flash. "That was fucking awful, wasn't it?"

"It's not the first time I've heard it." He said exactly the same thing once before, all those years ago.

"I swear I'm not always an asshole."

"I know," I whisper, and when he looks confused, I realize my mistake and shake my head. "I mean, I believe you. My car's just there." I point across the lot, where a bright light shines. I know better than to park at the back. This might be a decent part of town, but it's late, and I'm not very imposing, so I try not to take risks. Usually when I do, it backfires. The case in point is walking beside me.

I also drive a car that matches my size. Beside my Mini is a massive, ostentatious Hummer in lime green. I snort. "I bet some five-foot-nothing bald guy drives that thing."

"Why do you think that?" Lance checks out the beast of a vehicle.

"Oh, come on, you know what they say about guys who drive big trucks." When all I get is a look of confusion I continue. "That they must be compensating for something?"

"What if it's a girl who drives it?" he asks.

"No girl would drive something that big. It's not practical." I hit the unlock button and shimmy between the Hummer and my car. Of course I have to become the least graceful person on the face of the Earth and bang my head on the Hummer's side mirror, dropping my keys in the process.

"I got them." Lance swoops into the confined space and bends to retrieve them. I just need to get out of here so I can stop acting like an idiot in front of him. I rub my head, checking for a bump.

"Are you okay?" Instead of handing me my keys, he shoves them in his pocket.

"I'm fine."

"Let me have a look."

"Seriously. I'm just clumsy."

He ignores me and turns me around. "Whereabouts you hit your head?"

I rub the small lump forming at the back. Lance shifts my ponytail out of the way and slides his fingers under my hair, beside mine. I'm glad I washed it this morning, otherwise it would be a greasy mess.

"There's a bump. I think you should probably sue whoever owns this asshole ride." Lance knocks on the passenger side door. "Should we leave a note?"

"Stop making fun of me."

"I'm totally serious. What if you have a concussion?"

"Can I have my keys now?"

"Concussions are dangerous business."

I hold my hand out.

He shrugs. "Suit yourself, but if you end up with memory loss, you can't say I didn't warn you."

"Well, I won't remember anyway if that happens, will I?"

"I guess not." Instead of dangling the keys from his finger, Lance's places them in my palm.

I'm positive I stop breathing. I look down to where his hand molds to mine, and then up to his face. God. His expression is intense. He drops the keys into my palm and closes my fingers around them, covering them with his other hand.

"I should know you." He looks so forlorn.

It reminds me of when I was just a girl with a silly crush.

I'd wanted him to remember me when I saw him in that bar last year, to be the same honest, kind boy I'd met all those years ago. When we'd been invited back to his house that night, part of me had still hoped he'd remember me. But he didn't.

I feel like I'm melting inside, and a rush of emotions makes me want to tell him he does know me, but I tamp that down, biting back words that will probably cause me more trouble than good.

My phone buzzes in my purse, and he expels a sharp breath,

retracting his hands. He reaches for the handle and stands there a moment before he says, "Thanks for taking care of me today." As he opens the door for me I mumble, "You're welcome." I don't know how else to respond. I feel like his words are loaded, and I'm suddenly terrified of the mistake I've made in giving him my number.

Because now I'm not sure what's going to be worse: him finally remembering who I am and how we know each other, or me realizing I never left enough of an impact to warrant being remembered at all.

COMPENSATING

POPPY

L ance closes the door and taps the roof of my car. The Hummer beside my Mini beeps. I look around excitedly, expecting a paunchy bald guy to appear out of nowhere. That's not what happens.

Lance rounds the front of the vehicle, waving and grinning sheepishly. I drop my head and give it a shake. Of course I insulted his choice of vehicle—well, him, actually.

I start my car, but the sound of my engine is drowned out by the Hummer revving to life. The thing is a beast. Lance's passenger window rolls down, and his face appears in the dark space.

He waits until I do the same before yelling over the rumble of his engine. "I swear I'm not compensating."

"Suuure," I reply. "I'd tell you to drive safe, but since you have a tank..." I shift into gear and pull out, waving again as I pass him.

I think he waves back, but his windows are tinted, and all I can see is light reflected off the windshield. Lance follows behind me and turns in the same direction I do. He leaves lots of space between us, maybe respecting the fact that he could drive over my car if he were impatient enough. My little Mini looks like something his vehicle expelled from the exhaust pipe.

My phone keeps buzzing in my purse. It's likely April, since we're supposed to meet up and I'm way later than I thought I'd be. Part of me wants to talk to her about Lance, and the other part—the part that remembers exactly what it was like to get burned by him last year—doesn't want to rehash that experience any more. I've already done it once today. For an hour. While I massaged his glutes.

I rummage through my purse when I come to a stoplight, digging out my phone. Before I can check my messages, a honk comes from my right. It startles me, and my phone lands on the floor of the passenger side, bouncing out of reach. I look over to find Lance's Hummer beside me, his window down again.

Mine descends with a whir.

He revs his engine. "Wanna race?"

I laugh. "Pretty sure your car can eat my car for breakfast."

"Maybe more of a light snack." He winks and throws a handful of what appears to be candy in his mouth, then tosses the package on the dash. It looks like gummy bears. The light turns. Lance lifts his hand in a wave and puts his foot on the gas, proving me right as he speeds away while I obey the posted speed limit. I drive home and park in front of my row house. The pub is only a ten-minute walk, and it's a nice evening. Besides, I need the time to clear my head.

April's in a booth close to the pool tables. I feel bad about being so late, especially since she's alone. She looks up as I slide onto the bench across from her.

"What took you so long?"

"Lance stopped by to pick up his phone." I try to sound nonchalant, but I'm sure I fail based on how high my voice goes at the end.

"Oh my God! What happened? What did he say? Did you explain the picture?" April looks like she's going to pass out. "Did he ask you out? Was I right about him leaving it there on purpose?"

I raise a hand to stop her. "You need to stop chugging Red Bull."

"I still need that firm ass report."

"It's solid as a rock." I look around, seeking out the server so I can place an order. I'm starving, and I'll do just about anything to get out of answering questions about Lance's assets.

A waitress stops at the table, so I order a Shirley Temple and some sweet potato fries. Fiber makes them healthier than the regular ones.

"You're not even going to have a real drink?"

"I have to be back at the clinic at eight tomorrow morning." I'm also concerned that if I order something with alcohol, I might not stop at one. This whole thing has me discombobulated enough that getting tipsy doesn't seem like such a bad idea. Which is exactly why I won't do it. Alcohol isn't a coping mechanism I like to use. Sweet potato fries, on the other hand...

"What about a white Russian? It's like drinking chocolate milk."

"Really, I'm good."

"Suit yourself. Go wild and drink from the kids menu. Anyway, back to Lance. What happened when he came back? What did he say? What's he like? Do you think all the rumors are true?"

"Seriously, April, how much Red Bull did you drink today?"

"None. Just a lot of coffee. Come on, Poppy, you had your hands all over one of the hottest, most notorious hockey players in the league. You need to share that experience with me."

"It was just a massage." I wish I had my Shirley Temple already so I could do something with my hands.

"If it was just a massage, why is your face the color of your name?" April asks. "Oh! Did he remember you from when you went to school together? Did you get his autograph?"

"I didn't get his autograph."

The waitress drops off my drink.

"Did he remember you?"

I stir my drink with the straw, swirling the grenadine around, and shake my head. "I was a kid, and he only went to my school for, like, maybe a month or two. He didn't even know I existed."

That's not quite true, but it doesn't matter because it was so long ago, and those sweet childhood memories had already been replaced by something much less pleasant.

I'm responsible for allowing that to happen, I suppose both when I was young, and again last year. It's funny how the few times I've made the decision not to play it safe all seem to involve this man. Even today I could've told my boss I knew Lance. I could've intimated that I didn't feel comfortable treating him, but I guess the truth is I wanted to. Just like the last time I ran into him, I wanted to see if he would be the same as I remembered. He was, and he wasn't.

Today he was awkward, and intense, and maybe even a little sweet—exactly like he was the first time our worlds collided, and nothing like the way he was last year. I wonder if I'm inviting discord into my life, or if it's just my insecurities that make me feel this way. A kiss is just a kiss. Especially one that happened more than a decade ago. Maybe it should be nothing, but there's so much spark caught up in that one memory.

When I saw him last year, I wanted to find that feeling again. But that's not what happened at all. I hope this time his appearance doesn't lead to second-guessing and the consumption of a lot of comfort food like it did before.

It took me three months to lose the five pounds Ben and Jerry's added to my waistline last time. Which is ridiculous,

79

because it was one stupid night where nothing happened, so it shouldn't have meant anything. But it did. Because it destroyed a perfectly preserved moment in time. A highly romanticized one, obviously, but I was twelve, so that's totally acceptable. Not so much at twenty-three.

"Poppy? Are you okay?"

"Huh?" I look up from the drink I'm still stirring.

"You gapped right out there."

"I'm fine. Just tired. It was a long day. How was Ms. Thong?"

"Oh God! I wish you could've seen her today. She was rocking the craziest hot pink butt floss. I thought it was going to snap it was so tiny!"

April doesn't ask me any more questions. Instead we move on to other topics. When the fries come, I scarf down the entire plate. April and I live in the same neighborhood, so once she finishes her drink and I polish off my snack, we walk home together. I'm quiet, trying my best not to think about Lance and all the feelings he's stirred up.

I don't have a lot of girlfriends living around here. I'm kind of a homebody by nature, and my high school friends are back in Galesburg. Most of my college friends have moved to other places, and my sister never stays in one place very long. Right now she's living in Boston, but I assume that will change in the next few months, as it often does. I love my sister, but we're exact opposites. She lives on the edge, and I'm usually safe inside the lines.

"Are you sure you're okay?" April asks.

I can't decide if I want to tell her what happened last year or not. We hadn't been close enough for me to divulge it back then. But now things are different. "Do you remember Kristi?"

"Who?"

"That girl in our program who used to party all the time?"

"You mean the one with the Kardashian butt?"

I snort. "Yeah."

April makes a face. "Sure. You hung out with her a bit, right?"

I nod. "Last year I went out with her and another one of her friends downtown." She'd had a lot of connections because her family had money. I'd made a decision I normally wouldn't. Later, when I had perspective, I realized Kristi was only nice to me because I aced all the tests. The invitation was a trade of sorts; she allowed me into her circle for a night, and I'd taken on the bulk of a group project. I definitely lost out on the deal.

"I bet that was a trip."

"She had VIP connections or whatever. Anyway, she got us into this exclusive club where all these rich people hang out. Lance was there with some of his teammates."

"What? When did this happen? Why is this the first I'm hearing about it?"

"Because it wasn't exactly an awesome night, and I didn't think I'd ever run into him again, so what was the point of talking about it? Besides, it's more embarrassing than anything."

"Embarrassing? Why? Oh my God. Did you sleep with him? Why didn't he recognize you? I'm so confused."

That makes two of us. "I didn't sleep with him, but Kristi did."

"Ew. She's so dirty. I hope he used a condom."

I don't comment, or tell her about how I told Kristi I'd been following his career since he'd been drafted and then she used that line to get his attention when he started talking to me.

"I don't get why that's embarrassing for you."

I debate how much I'm willing to share. Talking about it makes it all fresh again. "He started talking to me first when we were at the bar, but after that Miller guy wasn't interested in anyone, I guess because he had a girlfriend, Kristi decided she wanted Lance's attention, so..."

"She jumped on him before you could."

"Pretty much."

I leave it at that. Not that I would've jumped on him anyway, or at least that's what I tell myself now. I honestly don't know what would've unfolded had I been his sole focus of interest that night.

"Did he recognize you then?"

I shake my head. "He was drunk—everyone was except for me. I was…tipsy, not drunk, though. And like I said, I was a kid when we went to school together, and it wasn't for long, so it's not a surprise he doesn't remember me."

I don't share anything about the party my sister took me to when she was a freshman and I was still in seventh grade. Lance hadn't recognized me then either—but what happened cemented him in my memories forever.

I also don't tell her we exchanged phone numbers.

April and I walk together until we reach her apartment, and then I keep going to my row house a couple of blocks away. My neighbor, Mr. Goldberg, is sitting on his front porch as I climb the stairs, phone in hand texting April to let her know I'm safe.

"Out late tonight?" Mr. Goldberg asks.

"I stopped to have a bite to eat with a friend," I reply.

"Got yourself a new boyfriend?"

I laugh. "Nope. Just April."

"Well, that's a relief. I'm not looking forward to the day you cancel our Wednesday tea dates."

Mr. Goldberg lost his wife of fifty-three years almost ten months ago. When that happened, I'd started bringing over care packages once a week, which turned into Wednesday evening tea and cookies. He was a sweet man, and his loneliness made me sad sometimes. I didn't have a boyfriend right now, but my life was still pretty full with good people and a job I loved.

"No boyfriend could get in the way of tea and cookies."

"Ah, one day you'll find someone better looking than me to spend time with, Miss Poppy."

"Impossible, Mr. Goldberg."

He smiles. "You're good for an old ego." He pushes out of his chair. "Well, now that you're home safe, I can go inside and watch the news. You have a nice night, dear."

"You too, Mr. Goldberg."

I check my mailbox and bring in all the flyers and bills, sorting through them as I kick off my shoes. I live in the house I grew up in. When we moved out of Chicago, my parents decided to keep this place as a rental property, and when I came back years later, they gave me the keys with the understanding that I would pay the balance of the mortgage. It's worked out well so far.

I drop most of the flyers in the recycle bin and toss the rest on the kitchen table. I'll go through it tomorrow, when I'm not so tired and in need of my bed.

I change into my sleep shirt and brush my teeth. As I lie down, I try to think about anything but Lance. It's impossible. He's dominated everything every single time he's come in to my life, even if he doesn't know it.

I try to go all the way back to the beginning, when he was a boy in grade school and there was still some innocence clinging to all of us, but I can't get past the night at the bar.

I'd been on the dance floor, which wasn't really my thing at all, but Kristi had assured me it would be fun. I could already tell she was getting tired of trying to persuade me, so I didn't argue. It was better than standing by the bar getting elbowed constantly, or hit on. I'd been about to call it a night when I'd spotted Lance making his way across the club with his friends. He was impossible to miss, his huge frame parting the crowd, the blacklights making his freckles glow and his hair look like flames.

Kristi had followed my gaze.

"Oh my God. Who are those guys?" she'd asked.

"They're NHL players." I'd rhymed off their names and Lance's stats, because I knew them.

Kristi started screaming in my ear about how hot they were. I

83

hadn't paid much attention because I could only focus on my childhood crush less than fifty feet away from me.

And then I'd realized they were headed our way. I turned around, thinking it would be a great time to make an emergency trip to the bathroom, except there was no clear path off the dance floor.

"What are you doing?" Kristi grabbed my arm and looked over my shoulder. "They're headed over here right now."

I didn't have a chance to answer because the next second I felt a tug on my ponytail. "I like yer hair," a deep voice with only a hint of Scottish accent said in my ear.

I turned around to find Lance Romero standing right behind me, smiling.

In that instant I was eleven again, shoving books in my backpack after school. That lovely memory faded an instant later when I realized all of them were totally wasted, especially when Lance linked his pinkie with mine and said something about doing shots.

He shouldered his way through the crowd and pushed his way to the bar, maneuvering me into a gap that had opened up, and flagged down the bartender.

He ordered a bunch of shooters and passed them out, handing two to everyone. Knocking his glass against mine, he shot the first and then the second. I sniffed mine.

He smirked, his eyes heavy with alcohol. "You don't think you're gonna like it?"

"I don't really do shots. What's in it?" Shooters didn't seem like the best idea when I was already tipsy.

"A bunch of stuff. You wanna know what it tastes like before you try it?" he asked.

I tilted my head to the side, unsure what he meant. But before I had a chance to answer, Kristi was yelling in my ear about how she was going to get him to take her home that night and stealing my shot.

"I'll do hers. She doesn't drink." She gave Lance a simpering smile.

They did another round, and I took a tiny sip of the one Lance had handed me. I must have made a face at how strong it was, because he laughed and took it from me. He put his mouth to my ear. "You're not a big partier, are you?"

"Not really."

"That's good. You look like a good girl. You can take care of me, tonight, 'kay? Make sure I don't do anything I might regret." He ran his fingers through my ponytail, and I felt the end of his nose touch my cheek. "What's yer name?"

I yelled my name over the music, but it was hard to hear and he got it wrong.

"What're you two talking about?" Kristi yelled in his ear before I had a chance to correct him.

"Hey, Romance, you gonna take a little break from your friends and order more shots, or you need me to do it for you?" Randy asked, his arm slung around Kristi's friend Felicity's shoulder.

Lance sucked in a breath, but lifted his head. I watched shadows pass behind his eyes as he turned to his teammate.

"Wanna get off my dick, Balls?" A sloppy grin broke across his face, and he ordered yet another round of shots, doing mine for me once again.

Kristi slid in beside him, taking my place, and I did nothing to stop her.

When he invited us back to his place, I considered going home, but Kristi had my phone and wallet in her purse, and she told me I should live a little. I could've insisted on getting my things from her, but my curiosity and fascination won out, and I went along for the ride.

When we got in the limo, Randy and Felicity got friendly, Kristi dropped down beside Lance, and I found out all the rumors I'd tried so hard to ignore about him were true.

BLANK SPACES

LANCE

U sually I don't have a problem coming home to emptiness, but tonight I don't like it. Panic makes me jittery every time my phone pings with another message. Being alone means free time, and I could use a distraction from the forty-three text messages—it dings again; make that forty-four—currently unread on my phone.

They're all from Tash.

Not having my phone today was a blessing because it meant I couldn't read or respond to anything. But now that I have it back, it's hard not to check them, though I know it won't do me any good to read them.

I take a minute to call my agent and my publicist. Turns out the guy I got into a fight with has a record a mile long, including several charges for domestic violence, so my stepping in actually makes me look good—not bad like I expected. It makes the aches and stitches almost worth it.

I toss my phone on the kitchen counter and open the fridge. Vodka seems like a good choice. My mum used to drink a lot of vodka. She always said it was water, but then her breath smelled like rubbing alcohol. I find a glass and fill it halfway, not bothering with ice or a mix. I grab the bottle and the glass and pass through my living room to the sliding glass doors.

Poppy said I should spend some time in the hot tub. That seems like a better idea than getting dragged into more Tash-style crap tonight.

I step out onto the back patio. The pool is covered to keep it warm, as I haven't emptied it yet. The weather has stayed nice longer than it usually does. I set the bottle and the glass on the bar out back and flip the lid off the hot tub. Steam billows out, fogging the air briefly. I haven't had a party in a while, so I know it's clean. I strip down to nothing—there's no one here, and my neighbors can't see me—grab my drink and the bottle, and climb into the tub. Sinking down, I close my eyes. The heat feels good, but the silence is hard to take. It makes it difficult to drown out all the shit in my head.

I keep thinking this thing with Tash is going to end—that she'll get tired of screwing me around. But every time she's in town, she sends me messages, and every time I give in and the same stupid shit happens.

It's a lot like how my mum used to be with me. There were good moments, times when I thought she gave a shit about more than the bottom line, more than status and prestige. But after Quinn died, everything changed.

She'd always been a live wire of a woman. She had cycles. I didn't understand them as a kid, but as I got older I learned they were medication based. When my mum was on her meds, she was almost sweet. She didn't yell as much, didn't get angry, didn't start fights with my dad. But when she was off them, she was out of control. Any little thing could send her reeling.

Quinn had been the easy kid. He listened, did what he was asked, didn't push buttons. I wasn't the same. And then she blamed me for his death, understandably. If I hadn't taken the shortcut, he'd still be alive.

Once he was gone, my dad worked longer and longer hours, and my mum couldn't cope. Most of her family had moved to the States, and so we did too. It was supposed to be a fresh start. My dad stayed four weeks and went home—not to Scotland, but to Italy. He filed for divorce as soon as he was gone. So he became another thing I'd taken away from her.

After that I focused on hockey, and my mum focused on my failures.

After practice, in front of all the coaches and other parents, she'd tell me I'd tried hard and done a good job, and I could do better next time. But the second we got to the car, the real her would come out. She was all fangs and rage. And even that was nothing compared to what I'd endure once we were home and there weren't any witnesses. My failures gave her license to use me as an outlet for her anger.

Tash knew all of that. For some ridiculous reason I believed I could share it with her. I told her all about how messed up my childhood was, about my brother, about the abuse, and about how I deserved all of it. She'd listened quietly, and then used it against me.

She keeps doing it even now, probably because her childhood was equally messed up, maybe even more. But I'll never know, because Tash is good at telling me what I want to hear, or what she thinks I want to hear—or maybe what she wants me to hear. She never said the most important thing: that I was enough for her. Just me. Because I wasn't.

Maybe that's why I keep showing up when she calls. She affirms what I already know: that I'm not worth giving a shit about. What they say about victims is true when it comes to me.

I don't know how to exist without the chaos, and I seek it because it confirms the message beaten into me as a kid: I deserve to be a victim, because my little brother was mine.

I down the glass of vodka in three long swallows and pour a refill. I polish off the second glass, hoping it will stop the turmoil that swirls around and around in my head.

I close my eyes, wishing for a way to shut down my mind for a while. Flashes of Tash with Erin make my stomach roll. I can't keep those images from pushing their way to the front—the look on Tash's face when I denied her, my satisfaction at making her mad, my anger over falling for her bullshit again.

I try to think about Poppy instead, about her softness, about how her touching me wasn't something I immediately hated, and had eventually liked. I want that feeling again.

But I can't hold on to any good thought, because Tash overrides everything.

I try a different tactic and consider what Miller said about Poppy having been at my house before. As hard as I try, I can't find any memories of her, even though she feels familiar.

I shouldn't have asked for her number tonight. I should focus on keeping things as professional and straightforward as possible, if I want her to have me as a client again. It's obvious she recognized me. Something must've gone down—probably something I should feel bad about. But I don't feel capable of letting it go. I want to know what I did, or said. And if it was bad, I want to fix it.

I sift through all the parties I've thrown since I moved into this house a year and a half ago. There've been so many, and I'm not great at moderation when it comes to drinking. It's either one beer or a lot of hard liquor. And when I throw a party, it's all about the booze and the bunnies and the fucking. Or at least it has been. But I was never as bad as the rumors made me out to be. Until Tash made them a constant reality.

Ever since things fell apart with Tash, I've been looking at my choices and where they've gotten me. It's not anywhere good.

I have to stop fighting to remember Poppy because it's giving me a headache. All I keep getting are flashes of parties from high school, which isn't even remotely helpful.

I can hear my phone buzzing on the counter. There's a good chance it's Tash. Maybe I should answer and get it over with. But I'm tired, physically and mentally. I need some space from her before I can deal. I still hope I've pissed her off enough that she's going to stop messing with me. But she's calling after I told her not to, so that doesn't seem to be her plan. She always does the opposite of what I want.

I down a third glass of vodka and pour a fourth. Numbness is starting to kick in, working its way through my limbs and into my brain. I close my eyes and focus on the aches and pains in my body, rather than the one in my head.

Fifteen minutes later, my phone goes off again, ruining my calm. I attempt to pour another glass of vodka, only to realize I'm out.

I hoist myself out of the hot tub and weave unsteadily toward the sliding glass door. My brain is foggy, and the emotions I've been contending with all day are blissfully dampened.

I grab my towel, wrapping it around my waist, then trek through the living room, leaving wet footprints on the hardwood and the rug. My phone vibrates on the granite counter, the screen lighting up. It's a phone call, not a text.

My stomach flips and rolls. A cold sweat breaks out across my skin.

I'm almost looking forward to hearing her voice. I'm almost excited for the fight we're about to have and all the shitty, nasty things she's going to say to me, because I deserve them. I fucked Erin, and I left her hanging. I came down her throat and refused to give her more—I wonder if that makes me just as bad as her. I let her do this to me. I let her make me into this person I hate.

I check the phone and realize it's not Tash but Rookie, as I've named him, mostly because I was too drunk to remember his name when I took down his number. Rook Bowman is the newest addition to our team and the replacement for Kirk, whose only choices were retirement or being sent back to the farm team. Rookie's a good trade and an excellent player.

I answer the call. "Hey, Rookie."

"He picks up! How's it going, Romance?"

"All right. Wassup?" I'm slurring already. It's not a good sign for positive decision making.

"Me and a few of the guys are heading to Rush Street and figured you might be interested in coming out."

I check the time. It's not even eleven yet. We don't have practice until later in the afternoon tomorrow. That's plenty of time to sleep off a hangover. And then I won't be as inclined to cave where Tash is concerned.

"You guys wanna come here first? I can make a few calls, see if there are girls looking to party."

"For real?"

"Yeah, man, why the fuck not, right? We're gonna be on the road soon enough. Might as well take advantage while we can."

"Awesome. We'll be over in half an hour, sound good? You know any bunnies who might be interested in hanging out?"

"I'll make some calls." I don't really want them here, but they're a distraction, and that's what I need the most right now.

I end the call and pull up my contact list, dialing the sure things and dirty girls who're always looking for another player to bang.

Less than an hour later, more than twenty people are hanging out on my back deck or swimming—I turned up the thermostat and put on the deck heater. It's not pool weather anymore, but skimpy bikinis are always in season.

More people show up as the night wears on. The chaos around me isn't making anything better in my head. I'm wasted and maybe a little numb to the feelings, but I don't know half of the people at my house, and I'm tired of them already.

I didn't bother calling Randy because he won't come over

anymore when I've got a party going. He doesn't ever want to risk the good thing he's got with Lily, and since his dad couldn't keep his dick in his pants, Randy's always been worried about repeating history. Miller can't and won't stop by on nights like this either. He's not interested in getting his party on, thanks to Sunny and the baby she's about to have. He just wants to be home with his girl. I can't blame either of them for staying away, but I wish they were here to ground me.

If Tash hadn't been the team trainer, and if she hadn't wanted to invite all the extras along, maybe I'd be like them right now. Maybe I'd be hanging out watching TV in my bedroom with her curled up beside me.

But even as I consider it, I know that's not how things would've turned out. Tash isn't that kind of person. She screwed with my head and made me think maybe we could be more, but we couldn't. And then she pulls things like she did last night and ruins it all over again.

The two girls to the right of me in the hot tub have started to make out. They're doing it because they think it's going to get my attention. Which it does. They're both hot, both brunettes. I've fucked them before. Together. They're the reason the rumors about me started in the first place. Until Tash, it had been a one-time thing.

The curvier of the two keeps bumping my arm as she runs her hands over her friend. Normally I wouldn't allow this, but the booze makes me numb to sensations I don't like.

I just want to feel the way I did earlier today, when Poppy's hands were on me. But these girls aren't her, and I don't have the energy or desire to entertain them tonight.

Rookie's sitting on the other side of the hot tub, watching them make out.

Curvy turns to me. "Should I take her top off?"

I've had some shots since I started the night with half a bottle of vodka, and when I open my mouth, I realize my filter is completely gone. I look to Rookie. "You think she should lose her bikini top?"

Rookie lifts a shoulder, like this is no big deal, but I know better. He's small town, and I don't think this excess is something he's used to yet, having come from the minors. I'd feel bad about corrupting him, but I'm an asshole, and I don't feel much of anything tonight. Except all the fucking emptiness.

"Are you going to take us upstairs again?" Curvy runs her hands down her friend's sides and grabs her hips. They grind against each other, moving to the shitty music someone's put on.

I remember how things went down when they came up to my room before. They'd been the ones to suggest it, and I'd been drunk enough to entertain the idea, but it wasn't something I particularly enjoyed—too much managing too many sets of hands.

While they kiss, I wonder if it would be different with Poppy. Maybe if she touched me the way those girls are touching each other, I wouldn't mind it. And then I realize how fucked up that is, since she's not supposed to put her hands on me like that. And I shouldn't want her to.

"Come on, Lance, let's go upstairs and get naked," Curvy says, trying to drop into my lap.

I stop her by the hips before she can sit down. "You should take Rookie upstairs."

She gives me a pouty face. "Let Tina have Rookie, and I'll take you."

"Not tonight, gorgeous. Go show my friend all the amazing things you can do with that pretty mouth of yours."

And they do. No more questions asked, because it doesn't matter who they're fucking—me, Rookie, or one of the other players—just as long as they're screwing someone they can brag about on social media.

I get out of the hot tub and go inside, stumbling a little on the stairs on the way up to my room. My door is locked, so I fumble for the key I keep in the secret pocket of my bathing suit and let myself in. Then I lock it behind me so I don't get any surprise visitors.

My phone is charging on the nightstand. I drop down on my bed and pick it up. My vision is blurry, but I can see there are more messages from Tash.

I give in and bring them up, clicking on her contact. The most recent was sent fifteen minutes ago.

It includes a picture of those two girls from the hot tub making out, with me sitting behind them looking bored.

The message below reads:

> I bet I hate you more than you hate me

I hate that her words hurt. I hate that they make me feel anything at all.

JONESING

LANCE

Although I read her messages, I don't respond to Tash over the next few days. There's a certain gratification in the torture of her silence and mine—although it's unlikely she feels the same way I do about it. If I'm lucky, I won't hear from her for a couple of weeks. If I'm extra lucky, she'll stay quiet for a month. It's happened before.

I don't have a game in LA until the official season is underway, so she doesn't have a reason to contact me, other than to send more pissy messages about how I'm an asshole, which basically sums up the content of her entire message feed. A bunch more pictures from the party I had showed up on social media, and Tash was pissed about that. My satisfaction over that is a problem I'm aware of. It makes me complicit in this game we play.

I also don't hear from Poppy, which isn't unexpected considering the only reason she would contact me is to report a cancellation.

My lower back still aches, and yesterday's practice didn't help at all. Still, I'm about to head out for a training session at the gym. The last thing I want is to be benched for the game. I don't want to go into the season as a target.

Tomorrow morning we fly out to Philly. We're only ever gone for a couple of days at a time, but soon there will be longer stretches. If I'm going to get relief for the aches, I need a massage or something today. I send Poppy a message asking about cancellations, then pack my gym bag and drive over to Randy's.

A few minutes after I text him that I've arrived, he comes out of his house, tosses his stuff in the back, and climbs into the passenger seat.

"How's it going?" he asks.

"Not bad. You?"

Before I can shift the Hummer into gear, Lily bursts out the front door. She's holding something as she runs toward my Hummer. Randy rolls down his window, and she steps up on the running board.

"You forgot your phone."

"Thanks, luscious."

"No problem." She kisses his cheek, then turns to me. "You're looking better."

I raise a hand in a wave. "Thanks."

"I'll see you around seven, okay?" she says to Randy.

She goes to step down, but his arm shoots out and keeps her where she is. He leans in and whispers something in her ear.

She lets out a breathy laugh. "Go burn off some energy so I can deal with you tonight."

He pulls her in for a kiss, and I keep my eyes on the steering wheel, because it sure isn't a PG one. After a moment Lily disengages, despite Randy's protest. She apologizes to me, slips out of his grasp, and runs back to the house.

Randy runs his hands down his thighs as we pull away.

"You all right?" I ask.

"Mostly." He strokes his beard. "I kinda wish we were playing this game at home, you know?"

He's not talking about home ice advantage. "Can she fly out?"

"I already tried that. She's gotta work this weekend, and we're only gone a couple of days. Besides, even if she could rearrange her schedule, she wants to be here with Sunny while Miller's away."

"Yeah, right. That's gotta be hard on him, aye?"

"He's pretty fucking freaked out that Sunny's gonna go into labor while we're away."

"It kinda still blows my mind that he's having a kid."

"If there's anyone who can handle it, it's Miller, you know? Sunny's chill, and he doesn't get all worked up about much, so they'll be okay no matter how it rolls out. And it's good that Lily's gonna be here, even if it means she can't come to the away games."

"Are you worried about her not being there?"

"I'm used to seeing her every day, so it's gonna be an adjustment."

I nod like I understand, even though I don't. Not really. When Tash and I were doing what we were doing, it was always secretive and on the down low. I saw her almost every day for training sessions, but we never actually talked to each other while other people were around.

The time we got caught in the locker room was an isolated incident she manipulated me into.

"You hear anything else from Tash this week?"

"Other than text messages and voicemails telling me I'm an asshole and she hates me, nope."

"Man, you must've really pissed her off."

97

"Yup."

"You wanna talk about it at all?"

"Nope."

"Okay. Just know if you run into problems with her, or she shows up looking to cause trouble, you can always call me and Lily."

"Thanks, but I've got it handled." That's untrue. I don't have it handled at all, but I'm not about to drag Randy and Lily into my messed up BS.

I've never told Randy, and probably never will, about the why behind the actions. Explaining the whole mess with Tash would require far more than I'm interested in divulging to him, or anyone else, about my messy, fucked-up past and the shit I had to deal with as a kid. I tried telling Tash, and I know where it got me.

We arrive at the gym with lots of time to change and warm up before the workout starts. I check my phone in case I missed a message from Poppy, but there's nothing, so I toss it in my bag and stuff that in my locker, hoping I'll hear from her by the time I'm done at the gym.

I'm slow and uncoordinated during the training session, and the ache in my lower back gets progressively worse, as does the twinge in my neck.

Smart finds me in the locker room before I have a chance to get changed and pulls me aside, looking less than pleased. "Did you make another appointment with the massage therapist like I told you to?"

"I tried, but she was all booked up this week. I'm on a list for a cancellation."

"You need to see someone today, or you're not getting on the plane tomorrow morning."

"What?"

"You were sloppy and all over the place today. You can't get on the ice the way you are, and there's no point in having you come to a game you're not even going to be able to play."

"You think Coach will go for that?"

"He's the one who told me to give you the options. You'll be stiff as hell tomorrow if you don't get this taken care of, and I don't need you out before the season's even started."

"Well, what the hell can I do if she doesn't have an opening?"

"I can get you in with someone else this afternoon."

I run a hand through my sweat-soaked hair. Panic forces a shiver down my spine. "I don't want someone else. Can't you call that clinic and get them to rearrange her schedule so she can fit me in?"

Smart snorts. "The world doesn't revolve around your wants and needs, Romero. I can get you on a table before the end of the day, but it's gonna be here, not at the clinic. That was me calling in a favor so we don't lose a good player with the beginning of the season right around the corner. I'm trying to ease Waters back in to it, and we need strong defense. Butterson can't do it on his own."

"What if I can get the clinic to take me?"

Smart raises an eyebrow. "You wanna risk not coming to the game by banking on a cancellation?"

"No." I rummage around in my locker for my phone. Poppy's gotten back to me, but it's not with good news. She doesn't have any openings—not at the clinic, anyway. I cross my fingers that she's not in the middle of a massage as I pull up her contact and hit call.

Smart crosses his arms over his chest while I hold up a finger and wait for an answer. She picks up on the fourth ring.

"Hello?" Her voice is soft and warm, the way her hands felt on me.

"Hey, hi. Are you busy? Did I call at a bad time?"

"What the hell are you doing? Planning a date?" Smart asks, incredulous.

"Hold on." I cover the receiver. "I'm seeing if I can get in with the massage therapist."

He shakes his head and rolls his eyes.

"Poppy? You there?"

"I'm here. What's up? There haven't been any cancellations since I messaged you half an hour ago."

"Yeah. I figured. Look, do you think you could fit in a home appointment like we talked about?"

There's silence on the other end of the line for a few long seconds.

"I might be able to schedule something tomorrow night."

"That's too late. It has to be tonight."

"I'm here until eight thirty."

"I could come to you. I mean, if that would work. Unless you have plans." *Fuck.* I forgot it's Friday night. Some people have lives. The possibility that she might be going out—on a date even—makes the volcano inside me bubble. What the fuck?

More silence follows.

"Please, Poppy? The team trainer says if I don't get another massage before tomorrow morning I'm not gonna be able to play on Sunday. It's an exhibition game against the team who put us out of the playoffs. I don't wanna miss it."

"I don't have plans." She sighs. "Okay, fine. You can come to me, but make sure you're there at nine."

"Okay. Nine o'clock. At your house, right?"

"At my house."

"You'll send me directions?"

"I will."

"Great. Thanks, Poppy. I really owe you."

"You're welcome. I have to go. I have a client in a few minutes."

"Right, of course. See you tonight."

"Bye."

She hangs up, and I flash a grin at Smart as I pocket my phone. "Guess I get to play on Sunday after all, aye?"

He doesn't return it. "A home appointment?"

"Lots of massage therapists do home appointments." At least I think they do.

"Don't make me regret cashing in that favor."

"It's not like that, Smart. I'm not gonna hit on her." I don't want to have to deal with someone else. I already know things with Poppy work.

He gives me a look before he turns to walk away. "Make sure you stretch and use the sauna before you take off."

The sauna part I'll do here; the stretching I can do at home. Rookie's in there hanging out with Miller and Randy when I open the door.

"Romero!" He holds his fist out for props, so I hit him up.

"Man, that was a killer party the other night."

"Glad you had a good time." I drop down on a free bench and try to get comfortable, which isn't possible with the way my back feels. Smart has a point about me not being able to play like this.

"Good time? Man, those chicks were up for anything."

Ballistic's eyebrow lifts. "Sharing your contact list with the newbie?"

"He can consider it my welcome gift."

"Best gift I ever got in my life. They gave me their numbers, said anytime I wanted to hang out just to call one of them."

I snort, but inside I feel hollow. Here's this kid from buttfuck nowhere, and I've managed to taint him before the official start of the season.

Miller blows out a breath. He's been different with me lately, not hanging around as much. I have to wonder if it's about more than his becoming a dad.

"Me and a couple of the guys are thinking about hitting Paris Club tonight. You guys wanna come?" Rookie asks, looking around the room.

"Nah, man, I'm staying in with my girl tonight," Miller says.

"Same," adds Randy.

"I've got an appointment for a massage, so I guess it depends how late that goes."

Miller's brow furrows. "You mean Poppy? From the clinic?"

I nod. "Yeah. She's doing me a favor and treating me at home 'cause she didn't have any openings and Smart and Coach won't let me play if I don't get one."

"You're shitting me, right?" Miller looks from me to Randy, his expression incredulous.

Randy shrugs, because this is the first he's heard about it.

"Dude, you fucked her friend," Miller snaps.

Rookie barks out a laugh.

I don't know what Miller's problem is. I can't get a gauge on him. "I apologized, and she was cool about it."

"You *apologized*?"

"Well, yeah."

"For fucking her friend?" Miller looks like he's about to have a brain aneurism.

"Not exactly, but I told her a censored version of what you said, about knowing her, and then I apologized in case I was an asshole. She said it wasn't a big deal, so—"

His mouth drops open. "Jesus, Romero, you're fucking clueless." He shakes his head and turns to Randy. "I gotta go. Sunny's having some kind of craving. I'm gonna cook burgers so she can huff the barbeque smell out of my shirt."

"I should probably go, too. I'm taking Lily out for dinner when she's done at the rink." Randy looks to me. "You good if I catch a ride with Miller?"

Miller's already halfway across the room. "I'll meet you in the locker room," he calls over his shoulder to Randy. The door slams into the wall as he opens it with extra force.

"What's his problem?" I ask.

"He's got a pregnant girlfriend, and we have to go away. He's stressed."

"Well, yeah, but why's he so pissy with me?"

Randy runs his fingers through his beard. "Do you remember that night you screwed Poppy's friend?"

"Nope. I got nothing on that except what he's told me."

"Yeah. Other than the shots, it's vague for me too. Maybe you should talk to Miller more about it, 'cause he's the only one who seems to remember much of anything."

I look to the door. "You think I should do that now?"

"Probably not. Maybe tomorrow."

"Sure. Right."

Randy leaves, and it's just me and Rookie. Rook then goes into great detail about the events that took place in one of my spare bedrooms the other night. It really just makes me feel worse.

ONCE I GET HOME, I spend an hour stretching and another hour in the hot tub trying to relax the muscles in my back, but they've gone into spasm, and no amount of ibuprofen seems to be helping. I could go for something stronger, but then getting to Poppy later could be a problem. There's no fucking way I'm going to miss having her hands on me for another hour.

At seven I take another shower, shave, and get dressed. At seven twenty, I whack off. At, seven fifty-five I whack off again. It only takes ten minutes, which is twice as long as the first time. At least I'm killing time, and it would be really nice to avoid the hard-on part of the program this evening. I'll be at her house, for God's sake. Stressing out about that, I wander around my house until eight twenty.

At that point I'm too antsy to wait any longer, so I get in my car and follow the directions to Poppy's place. She lives in Bucktown in one of the little row houses. It's a familiar area, not too far from where my aunt's house was when I lived with her. It's a cute little neighborhood. Poppy must make a solid living as a massage therapist, or maybe she has a boyfriend she lives with. I don't particularly like that idea.

I park a couple of houses down and look for her Mini, but I don't see it anywhere, which makes sense since it's only 8:41.

I'm already semi-hard again, which is crazy since I've whacked it twice in the past hour and a half. I drum on my dash while I wait. At eight fifty, she finally shows up. I cut the engine, check my reflection in the rearview mirror, and get out of the car.

"I'm a little early," I call out as I walk up the sidewalk toward her.

She startles and drops her keys. Her fingers flutter to her throat.

The same fingers that are going to be touching me soon.

"Sorry, I didn't mean to sneak up on you. I figured you would've seen my car." I thumb over my shoulder.

Poppy follows my gaze. "I must not have been paying very close attention."

"I guess not." I bend over to pick up her keys. Instead of dangling the chain, I hold them out in my hand.

Her fingertips graze my skin as she takes them. It's too quick to really register. I'm nervous now that this massage won't be the same as last time—actually enjoyable. What if that was a fluke?

I follow her up the stairs to her house. Her hair is in a ponytail again.

"Evening, Poppy."

"Oh! Hi, Mr. Goldberg. How are you?"

A little old man dressed in track pants and a loose fitting T-shirt with a Nike symbol on it sits on the porch next door.

"I'm good. You?" He looks me over, like he's assessing whether I should be allowed in her house.

Poppy smiles. "I'm good, too."

"Who's your friend?"

"Oh. This is Lance. He's a client. I'm treating him here as a favor."

"Ah." He gives me another speculative look. "Not your Friday night date, then?"

"No, Mr. Goldberg. Not my date."

"That's good. Means I don't need to worry about this one."

Poppy laughs. It's high and a little embarrassed. Her cheeks flush pink.

"I'll be on my very best behavior, sir," I say.

He raises a brow. "That's what they all say right before they're on their worst behavior, son."

NOT SO HIDDEN EMOTIONS

POPPY

L ance laughs while my face sets itself on fire. Of course my neighbor has to be out tonight. Well, he's out almost every night, but his timing and pith are unfortunate on this particular occasion.

Usually Friday night is April and me hanging out, and Mr. Goldberg knows that. I've probably had a handful of Friday night dates in the past year, and of course, my neighbor is usually around to witness me being picked up. Then on our Wednesday cookie-and-tea dates, he'll give me his thoughts on whether said gentleman deserves to go out with me again. It's rather sweet.

"I'll see you later, Mr. Goldberg." I manage to open the door, slap the light on, and usher Lance inside before he can say anything else.

Before I close the door, I poke my head back out and give him a look that tells him I'm not impressed. He just winks.

"Be safe, Miss Poppy. You know what they say about those redheads."

I roll my eyes and shut the door. "Sorry about that. He's a little..." I struggle to find the right word.

Lance rocks back on his heels. "Feisty? Protective?"

"Both. Definitely. He lost his wife last winter, and his kids live on the other side of the country. He's pseudo-adopted me."

"Can't say I blame him. Pretty single woman living alone... makes sense he'd want to watch out for you." Lance looks around. "You live alone, right?"

I cough as I drop my purse and keys on the little table by the front door. "I live alone."

"No roommates?"

"That's usually what alone means."

"No boyfriend?"

I raise an eyebrow.

"What? It's a legit question. I don't want some dude walking in while you're digging your elbow into my ass and I'm crying in pain."

I laugh, because I can't imagine Lance ever crying. He doesn't seem the type. "I don't have a boyfriend right now."

My internet dating experiences have been lackluster at best, so meeting prospective dates can be a challenge.

"Good to know."

I'd like to say I ignore the way his eyes move over me, but that would be a lie.

"Follow me." I lead him down the hall to the living room. It's the only space in my house open enough for a home massage. "I just need a few minutes to set up. Can I get you something to drink? Water? Juice? I don't usually have pop in the house, but I can check."

"I'm all right. Can I help with anything?" He shoves his hands in his pockets and looks around the room.

I'm suddenly self-conscious about him being in my personal space. I've been inside his massive home. It's beautiful and polished, despite the things that happen there. He has expensive taste, and my place is middle-class normal. Most of my decorative touches are knickknacks from my parents' trips around the US and pictures my sister painted when she went to college for art. She never managed to finish the degree, despite her talent. Since I'm not a developer, I haven't upgraded to the latest and most fabulous furnishings, like most of the other houses on my block.

"Why don't you have a seat while I set up?"

"Sure." He crosses over and drops down on the couch, stretching his arm across the back.

"I'll be right back." I run upstairs to the hall closet and pull out my travel massage table, two sets of sheets, and some pillows, lugging it all back down the stairs.

It's a little weird having Lance sit in my living room while I set up the table and cover it with sheets and pillows.

"Sorry I was early."

"It's fine. This won't take long." I tuck the sheets in and fold them back enough to make it easy for him to get under. "I'll be right back again, and then we can get started."

I make a stop in my upstairs bathroom to grab a lavender candle and my portable speaker. The music they pipe into the rooms at the clinic isn't my favorite. I can do better here. I bring everything back down and set it up on the coffee table in front of Lance.

He takes up half the couch with his broad shoulders and wide stance. He's wearing a collared button down and a pair of jeans. He smells amazing, even from across the room. I wish I could stop noticing these things about him.

"Would you prefer music or no music?" I ask as I set up the speaker.

"I'm good with music, as long as I don't have to dance."

I pause to check if he's kidding, but he looks serious. "No dancing."

He smiles a little. "Then we're good."

I look around the room to make sure all the blinds are closed. "Okay. If you'd like to undress in the bathroom, I can bring you a robe or a towel."

"I'm cool to do that here." He starts unbuttoning his shirt.

"I'll just give you some privacy." I pass the table and run my hand over the sheets, smoothing out a wrinkle. "Once you're undressed lie facedown under the top sheet."

Lance pauses in his unbuttoning. I can see the definition in his pecs, and I try to keep my eyes above his neck. "I didn't do that last time."

"It's fine. I wasn't clear. I'll be back in a couple of minutes." I rush out of the living room and cross over to the kitchen. I turn on the water and wait until it's hot before I put my hands under it. It also helps drown out the sound of Lance unbuckling his belt.

I imagine what it would be like to undress him. To unveil that incredibly strong, athletic body inch by toned, sculpted inch.

"Stop it," I mutter and shake my head. When my hands are warm enough, I turn off the tap and call out, "All set?"

"Good to go," Lance says.

I return to the living room and find him lying on the table, his feet hanging off the end because he's so tall. The sheet is pulled up high enough to cover his butt, the dimples above it dragging my eyes down.

Why the hell does he have to be so damn hot? This would be so much easier if he could just be unattractive and a total asshole, but so far he's been sweet, apologetic, and funny. I don't know what to think.

He lifts his head when the floor creaks under my foot. "Did I get it right this time?"

"You did great."

I turn on the lamp on the side table and turn off the overhead light, choose some music, and pull the sheet up to cover his back and the massive tattoo. The setup isn't the best because my oil is on the coffee table, which is out of arms reach.

I skim across his back, over the sheet, from one shoulder to the other, as I walk around to the coffee table. "I'm going to start now," I say quietly.

"Sounds good."

I begin the way I always do, gauging the tension in his muscles as I press my palms along either side of his spine. He tenses a little when I reach his lower back. "It's tight here?" I add a little pressure.

"Yeah. It's sore."

"Anywhere else?"

"I'm sore in general."

"Okay." I peel away the sheet, revealing his back. After pouring oil in my palm, I rub my hands together and smooth them across his shoulders.

A deep sound rumbles through Lance.

I lift my palms right away. "I'm sorry. Do you need me to stop?"

"No. Don't." He lifts his head and grabs my wrist, awkwardly trying to put my hand back where it was.

"Okay. I remember you said you don't like being touched last time, so I wanted to make sure."

He settles his face back in the cradle. "It's okay when you touch me."

I go back to rubbing slow circles on his back, warming up his muscles. His shoulders are tight, especially the right one. Every once in a while I get a low groan out of him that almost sounds like a purr and a growl intertwined. But when I reach his lower back, the contented groans turn into the kind I associate with discomfort.

"How can someone as small as you be so strong?" he asks.

"It's just using different parts of my body to achieve the right amount of pressure. I couldn't do this with just my hands."

He hums and stays silent for a minute before he asks, "Have you always lived in Chicago?"

"Mm-hmm. This is actually the house I grew up in. My parents live outside of Chicago now."

"Wow. I can't even imagine that."

"I guess being a professional hockey player means you move around a lot."

"Yeah. My contract with Chicago has another two years on it, but you never know if they're gonna trade you early or keep you on, ya know?"

"That can't be easy."

"It's part of the job. Mostly I don't mind the travel."

"So if there was a place you'd call home, where would it be?"

He's silent for a few seconds. "Here, I guess."

"In Chicago? Why here?" I shouldn't ask leading questions. It's going to get me into trouble.

"I moved from Scotland to Chicago when I was thirteen. I lived with my aunt until I was drafted, and then I started moving around a lot, depending on what team wanted me. So other than Scotland, this place has the most roots for me."

"Scotland is beautiful. Do you miss it?"

"You've been there?"

"I have a lot of family there."

"I guess with a last name like O'Connor that makes sense."

"We went on a family vacation there when I was young. I'd really love to go back one day. So how does a Romero end up as a ginger in Scotland?"

"My dad's family was from Northern Italy. My grandfather married a Scottish woman, and they had my dad. My mum went to Italy for an exchange program in college and met my dad. He followed her back to Scotland. My mum's not a redhead, but there must've been some ginger on her side, too, because this is what I got." He gestures to his hair.

"So what brought you to the US?"

He's silent for a few seconds. When he speaks again he has to clear the rasp from his throat. "My mum has sisters who moved here when she was young, so she has a lot of family in the States. She, uh, wanted to be here. My dad came with us at first, but after a while they split."

"I'm sorry. That must've been hard."

My parents have always been a strong, stable unit. Even when my sister was causing trouble and making life generally difficult when we were teens, they were a united force. I can't imagine them not together. Their relationship has always been the bar for mine. After thirty years, they're still madly in love. I want that kind of forever for myself.

"My dad worked a lot, and that included traveling. My parents weren't very happy for a long time, so it wasn't as much of a surprise as it should've been, I guess. We stayed in Chicago for the hockey opportunities."

"So you could play professional hockey?"

"Crazy, right? My cousins came to visit one summer while we were still in Scotland, and all we did was play road hockey. It was all I wanted to do after they left. That winter I came to visit them here and learned how to skate. I was a natural, I guess, and the coaches at the rink said there was potential. Back in Scotland, I took skating lessons where I could, but hockey's not a big thing in the UK like it is here."

"Does your mom still live in the city?"

"She moved to Connecticut when I was fifteen." There's a bite in his tone.

"Oh."

I don't press, because my questions seem to make him tense. What kind of mother moves her child across the ocean and then leaves him with his aunt? There has to be more to that story.

I work in silence for a while until I've done all I can for his back. It's much better than it was when I started. I still have twenty minutes left, so there are several other areas I can work on. I glance down at his sheet-covered butt. As nice as it is to look at, it's a lot different putting my hands on it in the privacy of my own home than in the clinic where everything is sterile and professional. Still, I have to ask. "Would you like me to work on your glutes again?"

"Uh, no. I think we're good there."

I'm almost relieved. "If you turn over, I could work on your neck and shoulders. There seems to be a lot of tension through there."

"Uh, yeah, okay. I think that'd be okay."

"If anything is uncomfortable, you can just tell me."

"It should be fine."

I pull the sheet up over him and get him to lift his hips to remove the pillow situated there. Then I lift the sheet. "If you can shimmy down and turn over, I'll be able to work on your neck."

He follows the directions, army-crawling down the table. His feet hang way off the end now. I rearrange the sheet once he's lying on his back and work on tucking it in around his legs. "Let me know if your feet get cold, and I can put a heating pad on your legs."

"I'm good right now, but thanks."

I fold down the sheet so I have access to his shoulders. They're massive, like every other part of him—well, the parts I've seen so far. Then I pull up my rolling chair so I can get comfortable while I work.

Lance's eyes are on me as I squirt more oil into my palm and rub my hands together. "Ready?" I ask.

"Yeah." He gives a curt nod, and I use my thumbs to adjust the angle of his head, making sure it's lined up straight with his spine before I assess the worst areas of tension, which seem to be everywhere based on the way his muscles lock up.

His eyebrow looks a lot better today than it did the last time I worked on him, and the bruises around his eye have faded a little, yellow and green replacing the edges of black and blue.

The matching split in his lip has scabbed over. His lips part as he exhales slowly.

I put pressure on his shoulders, kneading a little before I start in on the muscles that need the most work. Everything is knotted and tight in there. It's amazing he can even turn his head.

When his shoulders don't feel like they're full of stones any more—just rubber balls—I move on to his neck.

Turning Lance's head to the side, I glide my thumb along the side of his neck. The muscles there are tight, as expected, and the ones I've just loosened in his shoulders bunch at the contact. I settle a gentle palm on the side of his neck. I can feel his pulse, strong and rapid beneath my hand.

"Just relax for me, okay."

"Sorry." The tightness in his shoulders eases a little.

"That's better." I follow the muscle with my thumb again, find the knot, and start working it out. "Do you grind your teeth in your sleep?"

"I don't know." His teeth click together, and his tongue darts out to wet his bottom lip. "Probably."

"I can massage your face, if you'd like."

His eyes flip open, and he tilts his head up until I'm met with pale green. "My face?"

"Have you had a lot of headaches recently?"

He frowns. "I guess."

"You're carrying a lot of tension in your neck and shoulders. That can cause headaches. There are some small muscles in your face that might contribute to that. If you don't like the way it feels, you can tell me, and I'll stop."

"Yeah. Okay. That sounds good."

He closes his eyes, and I shift his head so it's straight again, then start by smoothing my thumbs across his forehead, erasing the lines of tension with gentle but firm pressure. I work my way down his face, over the bridge of his nose. He has so many freckles. They're everywhere.

With his eyes closed like this, he looks almost sweet. Like the boy who pulled my ponytail in the hallway in grade school. Like the one who kissed me in a closet more than a decade ago.

I wonder if that boy is still in there, hiding. I don't want to believe the man I met a year ago is who Lance really is—the man who was too wasted to remember having met me, more than once.

The rumors seem to conflict with the person on my table, I'm beginning to wonder if the hard exterior is Lance's wall, and beneath it is a man with secrets and insecurities, like his admitted aversion to touch.

I try to focus on the names of the muscles as I move my fingertips over them, but I can't stay in the present. I'm pulled into the past, back to a time when innocence disappeared one new experience at a time, and the night I fell in love with a moment I can't ever get back, even though the person responsible for creating it is right here with me.

MY SISTER HAD DISAPPEARED fifteen minutes ago, and I couldn't find her anywhere. She'd given me two options tonight: stay home by myself or come with her to the party. My thirteenth birthday was the next week, and she'd said this would be like an early birthday party, but better. Sometimes I wanted to be exciting like her, so I'd said I'd come.

I held a red cup of purple Kool-Aid that burned my throat every time I took a sip. I walked into a low-lit room where a group of teenagers were playing a game. The lights were off; there was just the glow of the TV in the corner. Music videos flickered on the screen. Women with hardly any clothes on were dancing to a song I didn't like all that much. My mom never allowed me to watch that, but sometimes my older sister, Cinny, would let me when she had to babysit me.

No one was paying attention to the TV, though. The teenagers sat in a circle, an empty beer bottle in the middle. I scanned their faces, most of them unrecognizable, although the blue glow didn't help.

I knew one girl. She had been talking to my sister earlier, so I moved into the empty space beside her, just as a boy with strawberry blond hair leaned forward and gave the bottle a spin. He was beautiful. I thought I knew him. I looked back at the bottle when he caught me staring. I watched it twirl—quickly at first, then slower until it stopped. It was pointed at me.

"Oh my God," the girl beside me said. "You lucky bitch."

The boy across the circle lifted an eyebrow, a slow smile spreading across his face as screams and hollers of excitement followed. He downed whatever he was drinking and passed the cup to the boy beside him as he stood.

The girl beside me took my cup. "Get up! Go!"

I obeyed, because I didn't know what was going on. I'd naïvely thought this was a game of Truth or Dare—that someone would ask me a question, and I would get to choose—but apparently I was wrong.

A chant began, and a flush crept up my neck as I realized I was very, *very* wrong about what was going to happen.

The girl I'd sat beside sniffed my drink. "Your sister's going to kill you." She was laughing, though.

I was ushered across the room, and the screaming got louder. Seven Minutes in Heaven. That's the game we were playing, not Truth or Dare. I'd never kissed anyone.

People patted the boy on the back and made lewd, suggestive comments. I suddenly felt panicked as he stepped into a closet and someone shoved me in there with him.

There was no way to avoid touching him as the door slammed closed and darkness swallowed us. I felt around, trying to make space among the winter coats. My hand connected with soft cotton and hard muscle. I was exhilarated and terrified at the same time.

"Hey, hey, relax." He covered my hand with his. It was warm. Clammy. "Are you afraid of the dark?" he whispered. He smelled like the same drink I'd had, but sharper, and I could taste cologne on my tongue. It was familiar.

The small space was suddenly illuminated by the glow of his phone as he flipped it open.

"No," I croaked.

"Me neither. But I don't like small spaces." He rested his shoulder against the door.

I reached for the knob, but he stopped me. "Don't bother. They locked it from the outside. We're trapped in here together."

The word *trapped* sent a shiver down my spine. His gaze was lazy and a little unfocused as it traveled over my face.

He pressed a bunch of buttons on his phone. I did know him, I realized. Last year he'd gone to my school for a little more than a month at the end of the school year. He used to flick my ponytail when he passed me in the hall. Not in a mean way, more in a gingers-stick-together kind of way. He'd winked at me once. I didn't know if he remembered. Even though he'd showed up late in the year, he'd been popular—with the teachers and all the students. Maybe because of his thick Scottish accent.

He'd gone on to high school this year, like Cinny, and I was still in seventh grade.

"What are you doing," I whispered.

"Setting an alarm for six minutes from now."

"Why?"

"'Cause I don't think you really want to make out with me for the next seven, based on how freaked out you look, and I can't lose face."

"What?"

"Don't worry. When my alarm goes off, all I'm gonna do is make it look like we've been making out the entire time, 'kay?" He shoved his phone in his pocket, blanketing us in darkness once again.

I felt the warmth of his fingertips down my arm, and goose bumps broke out across my skin. He spoke in a whisper I could barely hear because of the noise beyond the door. "I feel like I know you. What's your name?"

"I'm Poppy."

"Like the flower?"

"Yeah. Like the flower."

"You think I'll get high if I sniff you?"

"What? I don't—"

He huffed a little laugh. "Never mind. That was dumb. I'm Lance, like what you'd do to a wound."

I giggled and clapped a hand over my mouth.

"You think I'm funny?" His accent was heavy, thick. So were his words. He'd probably been drinking. I think most of the people at the party had been. I think maybe my drink had alcohol in it too, and that's why my whole body felt suddenly fuzzy and hyper-alert at the same time.

I nodded, but realized he couldn't see me so I responded with a quiet *yes*.

"How old are you, Poppy like the flower?"

"Fourteen," I lied. "How old are you?"

"I turn fifteen tomorrow."

"Happy almost birthday."

"Thanks. Where do you go to school?"

I gave him the name of the local Catholic high school. I liked that he sounded disappointed we didn't go to the same one.

He took my hand and played with my fingers. It was a heady feeling that made the hair rise on my neck and my skin prickle. "Has anyone ever kissed you before, Poppy?"

That time I didn't lie. "No."

"I should be sorry I'm gonna be yer first, then." He lifted my hand, and I felt his hot breath on my fingertips, then softness as they brushed against something. It was his lips, I realized.

"Why?" My voice didn't sound like it belonged to me.

"Because I'm going to take something you can't ever get back." His words were old. Sad.

"What if I tell you it's okay to take it? Would that make you feel better?"

"Not really." He dropped my hand, and I felt his fingers in my hair, tugging gently on the end of my ponytail, then moving down to my shoulder. I was wearing my sister's top. It had thin straps, ones my mom wouldn't approve of. It was too big on me, and it came down too low.

"Why not?" I asked.

"Because I'm not sorry the way I should be." His fingers followed the strap all the way down to where my heart was, then moved back up, traveling along my neck to my jaw until his thumb skimmed my bottom lip. I shivered.

"Oh."

His chuckle was dark like a night with no stars. "One day, when I'm a famous hockey player, you can tell your friends I kissed you in a closet." His phone beeped. He pulled it out of his pocket and silenced it. "Time's almost up, pretty Poppy."

He skimmed my arms, and when he reached my hands, he drew them up, clasping them behind his neck. "Keep them right there, okay? Don't move them, please."

"Why not?"

"Because that feels nice, and I want this to be perfect."

"Okay." I didn't really understand what that meant, but I followed his directions, my tummy flipping over and over as I pushed up on my toes in order to link my fingers.

He was so much taller than me, it brought me right up against his body. Fear and excitement merged. He released a shaky breath that smelled like sweet alcohol and ground out a curse that made me blush.

Once again I felt his fingertips on my cheek. The pads were rough, but the touch was gentle.

"Tilt your chin up for me," he whispered, guiding me with his thumb along my jaw.

I did as he asked, shaking. My mouth was dry. I wet my lips with my tongue. My head felt light.

"You okay?" I felt his warm, humid breath against my neck.

"Uh-huh." I gave a tiny nod.

"Don't be scared." His lips touched my cheek. "I won't hurt

you."

The next brush of his lips found the corner of my mouth. I sucked in a breath as weird tingles shot through me. He pressed his lips against mine, and the tingles became tiny explosions.

After a few seconds, he pulled back. "That wasn't too bad, was it?"

"No." It came out a whisper. I wanted him to do it again.

"This time when I kiss you, will you open your mouth a little?"

"Okay."

"And when that door opens, remember who I was in here, 'kay? That's the real me."

He didn't give me a chance to respond. Instead he pressed his lips to mine again. This time he pulled my bottom lip between his. I did what he asked and parted mine. His tongue touched my top lip, and I gasped. Then I felt the gentle, hot sweep of his tongue in my mouth. I gripped the back of his neck, and his arm came around me, hugging me close. His other hand came up to cradle the back of my head. He made a sound like he was in pain and angled my head to the side, his tongue sweeping my mouth again and again.

On the next slow stroke, I pressed my tongue forward, mimicking his movements, and his arm tightened around me further. There was no space between our bodies, and heat seemed to be building inside me, along with an ache low in my stomach and a wildness I hadn't known existed until then.

His phone beeped again, and he made another sound, this time almost despondent, and a trickle of regret made me hold on to him tighter.

I didn't know what to call the emotion that swelled inside me then, but years later I can identify it as lust. In that moment, I thought I was falling in love.

The door was wrenched open, darkness giving way to light that blinded me. Lance tried to grab for the handle to shut us back in, but my sister was right there, pushing her way between us. She yanked me away by the arm, and I stumbled back, off kilter.

"Poppy! What the hell is wrong with you?" she yelled.

She flattened her palm against Lance's chest and shoved him away when he reached for me again. "Don't touch my sister."

I got one last glimpse of him as she dragged me away through the crowd of screaming teenagers. He swiped his mouth with the back of his hand, his pale green eyes locked on mine. The emotions I saw there were staggering, everything from hunger to anger filtering through. I swear he mouthed *I'm still not sorry* before the crowd swallowed me.

LANCE'S HANDS COVER MINE, and his voice is a gravelly rasp, snapping me out of my inappropriate memories. "Poppy."

"Is it too much pressure?"

"I think you need to stop."

"I'm so sorry." I attempt to drop my hands, but he's holding them in place. His breathing is heavy, as if he's anxious. My thumb is below his bottom lip. That full bottom lip I was just thinking about. "I didn't mean to make you uncomfortable."

He clears his throat. "Yeah. That's not the problem."

"I don't underst—" The words get caught in my throat as I lift my gaze. The white sheet covering his body has a lump below his waist. A very obvious, ample lump.

He releases my hands, and they slide down either side of his neck. The action makes his erection twitch.

"Oh." It comes out a squeak. I place my palms on the table on either side of his head.

"Oh is right." He sort of cough-laughs.

"You really aren't compensating at all." I slap a hand over my mouth, because it's probably the most inappropriate thing I've ever said to a client. "I'm so sorry," I say from behind my hand.

This time Lance snorts.

I try to reclaim professionalism. "That's a totally normal reaction."

"Oh yeah?" Lance is looking at me with an expression that borders on amused, except there's an accompanying hunger that

I recognize. That look was only trained on me for a few seconds last year, but I'd felt it, and I feel it now—in all the wrong places. Or the right ones, depending.

"I'm going to give you a few minutes. Just, uh, tell me when you're dressed." I roll back my stool and tear my eyes away from his massive erection. I've been staring this entire time.

I go directly to the kitchen and turn on the tap. I pump soap on my hands, scrubbing away the oil and what I imagine is the scent of Lance's cologne. At least I have the restraint not to be a total loser by sniffing them first.

I try not to envision him getting dressed, tucking that hard-on away. I wonder if he's in my bathroom relieving himself. I wonder if he's still hard.

"Stop it." That I'm talking to myself again is a real issue.

I'm worried that I'm crossing lines I shouldn't by treating him, especially here. It's too personal, intimate in a way it shouldn't be. Or maybe that part is all in my head because I have these memories he's unaware of.

Either way, I don't think I'm doing a good job of compartmentalizing him as a client. Here I am, treating him in my living room, and now he's got a raging hard-on because of a face massage. My face massage.

I grip the edge of the counter, weighing my options. I should pass him over to someone else as a client. Marcie could work. Plus she's older, and not really attractive, so maybe he'd be less likely to get hard for her.

Not that it's me he got hard for. It's just the physical contact. It has to be; the other possibilities are too out-there to entertain. And even if I am the reason for his hardness, it's not like he'd want anything from me other than physical release. I've seen enough online to understand Lance isn't a guy who dates. Wishing that wasn't the case is another reason I should probably let someone else treat him.

"Hey."

I look up to find him standing in the doorway of the kitchen with his hands in his pockets. I keep my eyes at chest level. "Oh! Hey." I turn off the water and force what I hope is a natural smile.

"Got my situation all sorted out."

"What?" I cough, and this time I look directly at him.

"Oh, fuck." He raises his hands in the air. "I didn't mean it like that. I didn't whack it in your bathroom or anything."

"Right. Okay." I try not to let that image become more than vapor in my head.

He continues to explain. "I thought about dead kittens and old, wrinkly boobs, and the situation resolved itself."

"Gotcha."

"Sorry. That was probably a lot more information than you needed. I've been hanging out with Violet too much lately."

The twinge of jealousy over another girl's name is as much a problem as my fixating on Lance's hard-on.

"Is that your girlfriend?" I want to crawl into the sink and stay there for the rest of my life.

Lance laughs. "No. Violet's my team captain's wife. She's nuts, and she has zero filter. She's fun to be around, but a little crazy."

"Oh." I'm annoyed by my relief. "Can I get you something to drink? A glass of water?"

"Uh, yeah, sure. That'd be good." He looks around my kitchen. "This is a nice place."

"It's old school, but I like it."

"It's comfortable. It must've been a nice place to grow up." He leans on the counter and rearranges the apples in my fruit bowl. "My house is huge. Sometimes I don't like it. Like, there's too much space just for me. I try to fill it up with people, but that makes it worse a lot of the time."

"What do you mean?" I pass him a glass.

His fingers graze mine when he takes it. I can't tell if it's intentional or I just want it to be.

"There isn't balance, I guess. Like, it feels empty when it's

123

just me, but then when all the people are there, things get out of hand and I make bad decisions." He straightens and chugs the contents of the glass before setting it down on the counter. "It's like how I know I should know you, and I keep trying to find you in here." He taps his temple. "But I was probably wasted as shit, and everything's a big black hole."

"There isn't really anything to remember." The lie tastes bitter.

His expression is intense as he regards me. "You don't seem like the kind of girl who'd end up at my place. There's gotta be a story behind how you got there."

"Randy and Miller were there. Why don't you ask them about it?"

"They don't have the clearest memories, either."

I give him a small smile and lie again. "Neither do I."

He purses his lips and shakes his head. "Sorry. I should probably go. It's late, and I'm making you uncomfortable."

When I don't say anything, he pushes away from the counter. "Thanks for taking care of me."

"You're welcome." I walk him to the door.

Halfway down the hall he turns around. "When I get back from my away series, can I see you again? Like, can I come here instead of the clinic?"

"I don't know if that's such a good idea."

That stops him short. "What? Why not?"

Oh, God. He's just so much...everything. I can't be around him without thinking things I shouldn't. "It's just... I just... It's unprofessional."

"Is it because I got hard?"

My thighs clench, along with every single muscle from the waist down. *It's because I liked that you got hard.* My clasped hands are suddenly very interesting.

"Sorry. That was crass. I like it better here than at the clinic."

"I don't think it's a good idea."

"So it is because I got hard? I thought you said that happens all the time."

I stumble over my words, unable to find anything that isn't inappropriate. "It does. Sometimes. And that's not the reason…" I make a hand gesture.

"Is it because of what happened last year? With your friend? At my house? I told you I was sorry about that, too."

I can tell he doesn't remember anything about that night, which is almost gratifying, because it means Kristi wasn't a memorable lay.

"It's really not about that. Kristi and I were never good friends anyway."

"Then I don't understand why you can't treat me here again."

"I just don't think it's a good idea."

"You've already said that." He's agitated now, chewing on his bottom lip as he shifts from foot to foot.

"I shouldn't have done the home treatment. It blurs lines."

"Okay. You can treat me at the clinic if it makes you feel more comfortable. I like you touching me."

Those words and his tone are going to haunt me tonight. I know it already.

I can't tell if he means it the way I've taken it: suggestively. "What about the team therapist? Shouldn't you use him?"

His expression is as pleading and panicked as his tone. "I don't want to go to someone else. Please, Poppy."

He's so hard to say no to, especially with how worried he seems. I don't know why he's so intent on it being me, but I want to erase his anxiety.

"No more home visits."

"Okay. No more home visits." He blows out a quick, relieved breath and flashes me a grin. "I'm gonna go now, before you change yer mind."

That Scottish accent kills me.

He shoves his feet into his shoes and opens the door. "Bye, Poppy. Thanks again for taking care of me."

I can't make eye contact, so I look at his forehead. "Bye, Lance. You're welcome."

When the door closes, I sag against the wall.

I don't know how I'm going to manage this. Part of me wants him to know the truth: that he was my first kiss. That I never forgot it. With a decade of life and experiences, of boyfriends and plenty of new first kisses, I should be long past romanticizing Lance in my head. But I've been searching for the spark I felt when he kissed me since then, and I've never been able to find it.

Maybe it was just because it was my very first kiss. A part of me has always wanted to test that theory, and last year I almost had the chance, until I let Kristi get in the way.

When Lance made the NHL, I watched every game, because even after all that time, seeing him brought back that memory and the fleeting feelings that came with it.

But if I told him the truth, I'd also want him to know how my perfect memory was tainted when the gossip mill started churning out pictures of him with all these women. And how that night at the bar, when I saw him for the first time in over a decade, he shattered the beautiful glass jar I'd kept that first-kiss moment safe in for all these years.

PUSH

LANCE

I'm sitting in the airport, and I'm bored. I've done the Sudoku in the paper. It took me all of fifteen minutes, and it was supposed to be one of the hard ones.

If I hadn't come across hockey, I probably would've gone into some kind of career where I could work with numbers all day. I love numbers. They make sense. They're constant, and they don't change. A formula is a formula.

People don't work the same way. Emotions make them unpredictable. Like right now Miller is in a shit mood. He's been texting Sunny every three minutes and researching signs of labor and statistics on first-time pregnancies. Baby Butterson should be hanging tight for a few more weeks, but apparently he's getting antsy.

Miller puts his phone to his ear. "Hey, Sunny Sunshine, we're gonna board the plane soon. I wanted to check on you one last time—yeah...yeah. I know. I get that. I don't like that I'm not there right now."

He drops his voice to a whisper, gets out of his seat, and wanders toward the windows, watching the planes as he runs his hand through his hair, making the short blond strands stand on end.

I don't know whether to feel sorry for him or envious. I have no idea what it's like to need someone like that. Well, I guess maybe I do. Although, with Tash it wasn't about need; at least not in the same way I think it is with Miller and Sunny. It was more about want.

Sometimes I wonder if I only wanted her to myself because she'd never give me that. Which is fucked up. There are things about me that aren't right, and I know it's because of how things went down in my house as a kid.

My dad comes from money. Lots of money. So does my mum. It's the reason I have the house I do. My hockey salary is great, but I already had lots of cash flow before I started earning my own. The weird thing about money is that people equate it with stability, but there was nothing stable about my childhood.

I remember the way my mum used to go after my dad. Sometimes I wonder if my propensity for aggression is hereditary, or maybe she conditioned it into me. She was a small woman, always watching what she ate, always taking some kind of class or drinking something that was supposed to help keep her thin or whatever. I'm pretty sure it was just booze, now that I think about it.

On the days she was really fired up, she'd go at my dad, who I'm built like. He'd laugh and let her have at him—slapping him, punching, kicking—and the more he laughed, the angrier she'd get until he'd pick her up and take her, screaming and flailing, out of the room.

If my brother and I were there, a nanny would take us away,

so we wouldn't witness it. The next morning my dad would be at the breakfast table with a smile on his face, usually accompanied by faint bruises and the occasional scratch. He never talked about it, just went on and pretended like it hadn't happened.

I usually wouldn't see my mother for a good twenty-four hours after that. And when I did, she'd be back to a version of normal, but far more subdued, almost vacant. She'd be physically present, but she wasn't really in there, just a body going through the motions. Flowers would arrive. My dad would take her away for a little trip, and then things would calm down for a while.

But as I got older, the pattern started to change. The violence became more frequent. My dad traveled more. And when my brother died, everything fell apart. Eventually, when Mum's mourning turned to anger, it found a new target. An easier target. Me.

I thought maybe it would stop when we moved to Chicago. It didn't. It went on long enough that it changed the way I'm wired.

"Romance?" Fingers snap close to my face, and I jolt. "Your phone's ringing." Ballistic points to my hand.

I look down. Usually by this point Tash would've given up, but she's still calling, still leaving messages for me. I'm actually impressed that I haven't responded to her, even though I've read the messages.

"She's kind of a stalker, yeah?" Randy asks.

I shrug.

"Why don't you block her?"

"What's the point? I've tried before. She always finds another way."

Randy shakes his head. "Man, I don't know how you deal with that all the time."

"I'm used to it, I guess." I pull up my contact list to see if there are more new texts to go with the voicemail she's left. Of course there are. All I can see in the preview is a bunch of profanity. Three messages down are the texts from Poppy.

I looked her up on the internet after I left her place last night. I kinda fucked that whole thing up. Or my dick did. Everything was fine until she started touching my face. I don't think anyone has put their hand on my face without the intention of causing me pain since I was ten.

I'm damn lucky she's willing to massage me at all after that bullshit, even if I lost the home-care privileges. I should make a bunch of appointments at the clinic so I don't have to worry about being on another waiting list, and it'll probably win points with Smart.

I dial the clinic and talk to the receptionist. Unfortunately Poppy's all booked up for two damn weeks, so I can't get in right away when I'm back. Obviously Poppy's in high demand, so I just book as many appointments as I can before we get called to board the plane. I don't have my game schedule in front of me, so I take whatever she offers, hoping it won't conflict with an away game.

I catch a nap on the flight to Philadelphia, and I get paired up with Rookie to share a hotel room since Miller and Randy always stay together when we're at away games. Waters and Westinghouse do the same.

Once we're settled in our room, we head down for food, and then we get some ice time. My back is definitely feeling better, thanks to Poppy. And the nagging headache I've had for the past few days seems to be gone, which leads me to believe she was right about the teeth grinding.

Later on, Rookie asks if I want to go to the bar, but I don't know if I can go and not drink right now. I don't want to screw myself for the game tomorrow, so instead of joining him, I turn on hockey highlights and fuck around on my phone.

I find a picture of Poppy on my camera roll. It doesn't look like a selfie, not with the way she appears to be yelling at the photographer. I use it as the picture for her contact.

I kill time by screwing around on social media. Tash has tagged me in a bunch of posts, as she does. Mostly it's just stupid ranty stuff and a few old pictures. I untag myself and look up Poppy. She has the usual accounts. Facebook, Twitter—she doesn't post there much, Instagram, and Snapchat. I scroll through the pictures she's posted on Insta, hitting the follow button, even though I probably shouldn't.

There's one of her at the beach with her friends. Poppy's wearing a bikini, but it's mostly hidden under one of those cover-up things. She's wearing a wide-brim hat and big sunglasses. Her freckled cheeks are pink, and so are her shoulders. I bet she burns like crazy. I bet her skin is creamy white under that fabric.

Thanks to the European genes involved in my creation, I've at least got the ability to tan a little and not burn to a crisp. It's mostly a freckle tan, but it's something.

I pause and recognize that I'm internet-stalking my massage therapist. And I'm considering how I'd like her to be more than that, except I'm not sure that's even possible since I screwed her friend last year. But that was a long time ago. Maybe it's fine now. She keeps saying it's fine, though it doesn't seem that way. I don't know the statute of limitations on screwing one chick before you can get down with one of her friends.

Well, if they're bunnies it doesn't matter, but Poppy isn't a bunny.

I could ask Miller and Randy about it, but I get the feeling Miller would be pissed, so I decide to leave it alone for now.

THE NEXT MORNING we have a pre-game skate, followed by a team meal and a meeting. Once it's over, we've got several hours before we have to suit up for the game. I want some down time with Miller and Randy before I get out there so I can mentally prepare. But Smart pulls me aside on the way out.

"I lined up a massage for you," he says.

"What?" For a second I imagine that he flew Poppy out to treat me. Then I realize how fucking stupid that is. But it would be awesome if she could come work her magic on me before I hit the ice.

"I need you on point tonight, Romero. Butterson's off his game."

"He's got a baby dropping soon; he's distracted."

"You don't need to tell me. I know what the issue is. But I need you to be focused on the game, so I set up an appointment with one of the therapists here at the arena. It's not negotiable."

I can't argue. He has a point. As much as Miller would like to be able to focus on the game, it's got to be tough. Beyond that, maybe it's not a bad idea to see whether my reaction to Poppy is isolated. Maybe it's massages in general that actually work for me, not Poppy.

"Fine. When and where?"

"Now. Follow me."

The massage therapist Smart hooks me up with is a woman in her thirties whose shoulders are nearly as broad as mine.

Okay, that's an exaggeration, but she's substantial.

It takes all of thirty seconds for me to come to the conclusion that my reaction to Poppy is completely unique. I try to relax; I really do. But these hands are so different. Having this woman touch me for an hour is a horrible kind of torture.

After the torture-massage, I head back to my room. I'm in a shitty mood, and I'm not excited to hang out with Rookie—not because I don't like him, but because now that I've partied with him, he has the same expectations of me that everyone else does. And that's my fault.

When I get there, I find him hanging out with a chick. She looks like she's about ready to take her clothes off, and I'm not interested in dealing with that kind of bullshit. Especially in the middle of the afternoon.

"I just need to grab a couple of things, and I'll leave you two to it." I point across the room to my bag.

I don't like that there's some bunny I can't keep an eye on in my room with my stuff, but I grab the most important things: identification, wallet, phone, and iPad. I stuff them in my duffle, which still has my workout gear in it, and throw it over my shoulder.

"Text me when you're good," I call as I close the door and walk down the hall, heading for one place I know no bunnies will be.

I send Randy a text to make sure he's in his room. I get a reply as I knock on his door. It swings open a few seconds later.

He eyes the duffle as I drop it on the chair. "You get kicked out of your own room?"

"Rookie found himself a bunny."

"The game isn't even until tonight. Where the hell'd he find her?"

"Who knows? Maybe she's a friend and not just a bunny. I didn't stop to ask. I figured I'd let him expend some energy. He's still got some time before we have to suit up for the game."

"That's a bad idea before a game."

"He'll have to figure that out on his own, 'cause I'm not having that conversation."

"And if she's there when you go back?"

"She'll have to bail, or I'll help her find the door."

Randy cocks a brow. "You all right, man?"

"Yeah. Why?" I drop down on the couch and look around the room. "Where's Miller?"

"On the balcony. He's talking to Sunny."

"Is everything okay there?"

"I don't know. She's having some cramps. She thinks it's some kind of hiccups or something, and Miller wants her to call the midwife."

I shake my head. "You know, a year ago if you'd told me he'd be talking babies, I woulda laughed."

"A lot can change in a short span of time."

"Isn't that the truth?" I think about how things went down with Tash. How at the end of last summer it went from nothing to sex to me wanting just her to her not wanting the same. One minute we were whatever we were, and then we weren't anything. "When you and Lily started hooking up, it was just for the fucking, right?"

Randy sits at the other end of the couch and runs his palm over his beard. "We were just—"

"—having fun. You used to say that a lot."

Randy nods. "Yeah. I was a fucking idiot."

"So it wasn't just about the fun?"

"I mean, yeah, at first that was the whole point, but then things started to change."

"Change how?"

"I wanted more."

"I'm glad that worked out for you." I mean it, though it might sound like I don't.

Randy regards me for a few seconds, maybe judging my sincerity. "Can I ask you something?"

"Sure."

"Why do you keep letting Tash screw you over?"

I tap on the arm of the chair. "I'm not gonna let her do that anymore."

"What happened this last time?"

"I had enough. Like, every fucking time she makes me believe it's just gonna be me and her, and that we're gonna work things out or whatever. But then there's always someone else involved, and it's never what I think it's going to be."

"That's kinda your thing, though, right?"

It sucks that even one of my closest friends believes this about me. Although, I've never given him a reason to think otherwise, because then I'd have to explain more than I want to.

134

"Not like you think. And when Tash and I started hanging out, it wasn't like that. Not at first. And it wasn't supposed to be anything, but then suddenly it was."

"When did it change?"

"I don't know. I think maybe it was when you and Miller went to that camp up in Canada last summer that it started to be…something real, I guess. Or I thought it was real. Nothing really happened between us until just before Waters' engagement party, though. Tash likes to play games."

"Miller thought something was going on between you two before that."

"Before the camp thing?"

"Yeah." Randy tips back his water and takes a long drink. "Think back to the night you and that chick drew a dick on Miller's forehead. You were weird about Tash even then."

I give him a look. I know now that was also the night Poppy came to my house. Mostly I remember seeing the dick pictures on my social media feed the next day. They'd gone viral, and gotten Miller in a world of shit with Sunny.

"That chick you were with? She's the friend of Poppy's you fucked."

I try again to piece together the events of that night, but last season I spent about as much time drunk as sober, and it only got worse as I got into things with Tash. "You're sure about that?"

"Yeah. Poppy was the one who removed the dick from his forehead. You don't remember that at all?"

I'd probably been focused on the fact that Tash was coming over and there were still bunnies in the house.

I pull up my Instagram, but then I remember I deleted all the pictures because of the shitstorm the dick on Miller's forehead caused. Well, it wasn't the dick so much as the presence of the girl in the bed with him. I get now why it wasn't the best move on my part, but at the time I hadn't thought past how funny it would be.

I flip to my photo stream and scroll back through the pictures until I get to the ones from last summer. It takes me a while to find the dick forehead pics, but when I finally do, I have a hazy recollection of the girl in them.

"I don't think I screwed that chick."

"Dude, you don't even remember meeting Poppy that night. How can you be sure about anything?"

The not remembering Poppy bugs me a lot. I keep trying to find her in my memories, but she's not there—not the way I want her to be. All I get is the swish of a long, strawberry blond ponytail and the urge to pull the end of it.

I close my eyes, trying to pull up other memories from the night, anything to make a connection between that girl in the picture and Poppy.

As I start talking about the little I recall, more memories trickle in until it becomes a flood. "I remember going upstairs and stopping in my room to grab that girl a shirt. I wanted to check on Miller since he hadn't come outside." It had been my excuse to go upstairs since it was late and we had the training session in the morning. I didn't want bunnies in the house when Tash got there. She was pissy with us when she knew we'd been out partying. Me especially.

"That's when you drew the dick on his face, right?"

"Yeah. Exactly. But I didn't sleep with her after that. She had a freak out."

"What do you mean?"

I remember tears. I have a weakness for girl tears. I don't like it when women cry. My mum used to do it all the time. After she'd have one of her epic raging sessions on me, she'd feel bad. That didn't stop it from happening again, though.

I sift back through my memory. The girl had been wrapped in a towel. I took her to my room. My phone had been sitting on my nightstand, lighting up with messages. It was Tash, reminding me she'd be there in the morning. I'd given the bunny a T-shirt while I messaged Tash back a thumbs up, because typing anything more required too much coordination. Then I realized it was after two in the morning, so she'd likely know we'd been out, anyway.

The girl had come up behind me and put her hands on me. It felt like spiders crawling on my skin, which wasn't unusual. I'd grown accustomed to that sensation when any woman touched me, so I managed it for a few seconds before I grabbed her hand and tugged her toward the door instead of the bed.

I took her with me down the hall to Miller's room, not because I was pawning her off on him, but because he'd been super drunk thanks to all the shots I'd fed him. I wanted to make sure he wasn't face down in a pile of vomit.

"When I found Miller passed out, butt-ass naked and not responding other than grunts, the girl made a joke about drawing something on his face. She was wasted, falling all over the place, which should've been a solid tipoff that it wasn't a great idea, but you know how it is."

Randy gives me a short, curt nod. We've been drunk plenty of times together, and I'm sure he's made some questionable choices in those uninhibited states. Nothing like the ones I make, but then he and I are a lot different.

"So I snapped a bunch of pictures of her posing with him, and I asked if it was okay if I posted a few of them, because they were funny. When my social media feeds started lighting up, she realized how bad it looked and how many people would see them." She'd been wearing a shirt with nothing underneath— not that anyone could see that, but she was braless, and that much was clear.

"Ah, man."

"Yeah. I mean, I should've known, especially with how much shit it created for Miller, but at first I couldn't understand why she was so worked up. Anyway, it turns out she still lived with her parents, and the last thing I wanted was some father showing up at my front door with a shotgun, so I deleted them, but you know how things go viral."

"Yup. I sure do." Randy rolls his eyes.

"Anyway, this girl was all worried she'd be kicked out if her parents ever saw them. Then she really started to lose it and locked herself in my bathroom."

"Oh, shit."

"Yeah. I spent an hour trying to coax her out. She apologized and then wanted to fuck still, but I was tapping out, right? I felt bad though, so I wasn't gonna kick her out. Besides, she was still drunk, so I let her get in my bed. I ended up sleeping on the floor because she kept trying to get on me. She knew a lot of my stats, where I grew up, when I moved to what team. It was a little creepy."

"So she was, like, a super fan?"

"I guess? If I'd slept with her, it would've been a bad deal. She didn't want me to tell anyone what did or didn't happen."

"You could've had a serious clinger if you'd jumped on that."

"Right? So I guess that's why Poppy thinks I fucked her friend."

"Yep." Randy seems mildly impressed with my recall.

"Do you think I should tell her it didn't go down that way?"

"Why bother? I mean, it's not like you're going to see her again, right?"

"I have massages scheduled for when I get back."

He looks stunned. "Do you think that's a good idea?"

"Well, I can't go to the team massage therapist."

"Why not?"

"I don't like how it feels."

Randy stares at me. "I don't get it. You mean she uses too much pressure? Just tell her to ease up, or take off your pussy panties."

"It's not that."

"Then what's so special about Poppy, other than she's hot?"

The sliding door opens, and I'm glad for the interruption. I don't want to explain why I hate being touched. I've never really shared any of that with these guys. They know I had a brother and he died. That's it. It's not that I don't trust them; it's the possibility that they'll look at me differently. Getting the beats I did from my mum was a special kind of humiliation, one I don't like reliving if I can avoid it.

Miller comes inside and shakes off the cold, pausing when he sees me. "What's up, Romance? You get sick of Rookie telling you how awesome you are already?"

"Rookie's found himself an afternoon bunny."

"You share your entire contact list with him or something?"

I laugh it off, but the comment stings. "He found her on his own. No help from me. How's Sunny?"

"She's calling the midwife, and she'll get back to me. Hopefully soon." He turns to Randy. "Lily's at our place, and if things change at all, Sunny's gonna call her mom." He closes his eyes for a moment. "I just want her to hold on until I get home."

"She'll have lots of support even if that's not how it goes," Randy assures him. "Why don't we play some Xbox, or watch highlights?"

"Yeah. Good call." Miller goes over to his bag and rummages around until he finds his gaming console, which always comes with us. We play for a while until I think it's safe to go back to my room.

The bunny's gone when I get there, which is good, because I didn't want to deal with having to kick her out so I can get ready for the game. Before we head to the rink, I make the mistake of checking my phone. Tash has left more messages, which I stupidly check, so when I take the ice for my first shift I'm already amped up.

In the first period I get a penalty for checking. In the second period I get one for sticking, and in the third period McHugh, the forward for Philly, gets all up in my space and keeps pushing at me from behind. We're up by two, and they're getting desperate. My ribs are still sore from the fight last weekend, and that's exactly where he keeps elbowing me.

After the sixth time, I lose my cool and say a bunch of shit to rile him up. It works. He shoves me from behind, so I turn around and get up in his face, looking for him to throw the first punch. He swings a right hook, which I deflect. Then I let him get in a few solid hits. I rip my helmet off and shove him back, so he goes for my face, his gloved fist slamming into my cheek.

The pain is almost a relief. I need it. I want it. I don't know how to exist without it. I don't brace for the next punch, letting it take me to the ice. I'm careful to keep my head up, though, which means I take the hit with my back. I don't even have a chance to fight back before Miller and a couple of refs are between us.

Randy's right there with him. "Romance, you gotta take it down. Come on, buddy."

I swipe across my cheek and realize I'm bleeding again. I'm sent to the penalty box where I reflexively look around the stadium. I don't find what I'm looking for—which is my mother, wearing her disapproval in apathy. All I see are Philly fans cheering in the stands.

Both teams are down a player now, Philly having started the fight even though I was the one to throw the words. McHugh is pissed about it, and the chippy play keeps up. Fortunately we end up winning the game, despite the penalties, so I don't get the same level of flak that I might've had we lost.

I get held up on the way out of the locker room because Smart wants the team doctor to check me out, so everyone's settled in at the bar by the time I arrive. The bunnies are every-where, trying to get in my lap, touching me, looking for a hook up I'm not interested in. My split eyebrow reopened during the fight, and my head is throbbing. I practically have to shove my way into a seat at the team table. I end up next to Waters.

"You all right, man? You took a solid hit." He glances point-edly at my eyebrow.

"I'm good. Nothing I can't handle. That guy wouldn't let up," I reply.

"I get that. But beyond this—" He taps his own eyebrow. "—are you good? Things settled down for you?"

Sometimes, after I see Tash or she calls or whatever, I talk to Violet, Waters' wife. She's good at listening, even if I only tell her the surface stuff. Last summer I went to Waters' cottage after an altercation with Tash, and like usual, Violet was good about talking me down.

Later Randy asked about my relationship with her, and told me to watch myself.

I might look at Violet like family, but she's not, and I don't want to mess things up—for myself or anyone else—so I've given myself space from them. I never want to get between the people who are there for me. It's kinda like how I'm leaving things alone with Miller right now. I get that sometimes the things I do rub him the wrong way, and now isn't the time to hash it out.

"Yeah, man. Like I said, I got it handled. I'm gonna get a beer."

"Okay. You did good out there, Romero. I know you're keeping an eye out for Miller, and the team appreciates it."

The compliment means a lot and makes me uncomfortable at the same time. I stand as Alex gets pulled into a conversation with Westinghouse, and I flag down a passing waitress to order a pint of Guinness.

Rookie's got girls looking for action again, and he's a lot more interested than I am, so when he asks, I tell him it's fine to take them up to the room. A little while later I see Randy and Miller heading up, so I ask if I can come with them.

Miller gives Randy a look. "You're not taking a bunny off Rookie's hands?"

"I'm tired. I just wanna sleep."

"That's a first," Miller scoffs.

"Look, man, I know you're stressed about Sunny and the baby and shit, but you think you can cut me a little slack here?"

Miller blinks a few times, jaw working as the hardness in his expression eases a little. He nods. "Yeah, man. Sorry. There's a lot going on."

"You wanna crash in our room?" Randy asks, breaking the tension.

"You cool with that?" I pull my phone out of my pocket and check my messages. There aren't any new ones since Tash messaged me earlier, and I haven't read them. Yet.

"Yeah, man. Of course. You sure you're all right?" Randy asks.

"Yeah. Just one of those days."

The whole scene is losing its appeal. It brings me more trouble than it's worth these days, especially since the guys I'm tight with on the team are all committed to someone. I don't know if it's that or the crap with Tash, but if I'm going to feel alone—which I know I will—I'd rather actually be alone as well.

TOO MANY
FAVORS

POPPY

Instead of going out for a bite to eat with April on Sunday evening, I tell her I need a night in with a book because I'm tired. Which is sort of true. I also promised Mr. Goldberg a game of cribbage on his front porch, which I've already taken care of and of course I let him beat me twice. Plus, I have early appointments tomorrow. I also want to watch the game. Because maybe I'm a little obsessed with Lance Romero. Still. Again. I don't know.

I should definitely not want him to call me and beg for another home massage session. I should also not be fantasizing about him. Because he's a client. Because he's a dog. All the bunny sites tell me that.

But I am fantasizing. Because he's gorgeous and because he's been so sweet with me, and maybe a little awkward. Nothing like the guy I met last year at the bar who was drunk and cocky. Okay, so maybe he's still a little cocky, but that's not a bad thing.

My focus during the game is one hundred percent singular. I watch Lance, number twenty-one, every time he's on the ice. When I'm not watching the game, I'm checking my social media feeds. Lance is following me on Instagram and has liked a bunch of my posts. I shouldn't be all that excited, since everyone follows everyone else here, but I am.

Close to the end of the third period, a fight breaks out between Lance and number forty-four from the other team. If one could even call it a fight. It doesn't look two-sided from my perspective. The guy from Philly lays right into him. Lance even takes off his helmet, but he never hits the guy. Not once. He does go down hard, though. Hard enough to make me cringe. He'll be sore tomorrow. I wonder if that means he'll try to get another appointment with me.

By the time the refs intervene, Lance is bleeding from a gash above his eyebrow. I think it might be the one that had the fly bandage on it the other day. That'll suck if he reopened the wound.

He still gets a penalty, though. Both teams do. But Chicago manages to win the game being down a player, and it's late by the time I go to bed.

I have an early morning with an eight o'clock start, and I'm dragging a little as I get myself out the door. I arrive about ten minutes before my first client, but without caffeine in my system, because I slept through my alarm. It's Lance's fault. He not only infiltrates all my waking thoughts, but sleeping ones too. It made for a restless, thigh-clenching night.

Bernadette doesn't arrive until nine, so I don't get stuck at her desk to chat. I rush to my room, grateful I set up on Saturday night so all I have to do is throw the heating pad on the table to warm it, cue the music, and put the oil in the warmer.

My first client of the day is always pushing the late side, so I have a few extra minutes, but not enough time to run across the street to grab a coffee. I send April a text requesting one if she has time to stop on the way in.

My client arrives at 8:03, and a long, painful hour ensues. She's an incredibly chipper person. Normally I appreciate her positivity, but underslept and caffeine deprived, it's a bit much to handle on a Monday morning.

April arrives at my door as I'm stripping the sheets, coffee in hand. I toss them to the floor and practically tackle her for it. "Oh my God, I'm dying right now."

April's eyes go wide and she holds out the cup, cringing away from me. "Wow. Do I need to stage an intervention?"

"I slept horribly last night."

"Yeah. You look like you're packing for a vacation under your eyes."

"It's not that bad." I check my reflection in the mirror across the room.

April changes the subject. "Have you talked to Bernadette yet this morning?"

I shake my head. "My first appointment was early, so she wasn't here when I came in. Why?"

She gives me an eyebrow waggle. "You need to come check out who's booked into your schedule and on a wait list for you."

"What are you talking about?"

"I think you mean *who* am I talking about. Bernadette's been telling everyone who comes through the door. I think you might have a fan."

"Is it that guy who smells like cheese? Please tell me it isn't. I don't think I can handle repeated hours of that." Every time that guy comes in I'm off cheese for a good week, and normally I love cheese.

April makes one of her signature faces. "Oh, God. No. This is way, way better."

"So who is it?" My stomach does a little flip, but I quash that quickly. It has to be someone else. It can't be who I want it to be.

"Guess."

"I have another appointment in a few minutes. I don't have time to play guessing games." I don't have anyone for another twenty, but I'm not in the mood for this.

"Oh, come on! Why are you so grumpy? You're ruining all my fun."

"Fine. Is it that guy who won't takes his socks off?" I know it's not him. He only sees Marcie.

April throws her hands in the air. "It's Lance! You know, the professional hockey player whose ass you had your hands all over last week? The one who asked for your number so you could be his emergency massage therapist?"

"April!" I throw a pillow at her. "Keep your voice down!" While it's not against policy, I don't want the whole clinic to know about that.

"That's the reaction I get? Lance Romero, this famous, incredibly hot hockey player keeps calling to check for cancellations, and you're worried about my volume? Where are your priorities? Are you sure he doesn't remember you?"

"As far as I know. Wait. What do you mean he *keeps* calling?"

"He called yesterday and left messages, and he's already called twice this morning."

"It's only nine."

"Yeah. He left a message at, like, seven thirty."

"You're kidding." I squeeze past April and root through my purse until I find my phone. I have missed texts and a voicemail from Lance.

Now it feels like Leprechauns are dancing in my stomach.

"Oh my God. He's texting you? And he left a voicemail? You have to check them! You need to listen to it!"

I hold my phone close to my chest. "You need to calm down."

"You need to be more excited!"

I roll my eyes but check my messages. I missed quite a lot sleeping through my alarm and being without coffee this morning.

146

Hey. I have an emergency.

The appt warden says u have nothing avail 4 2 wks.

Poppy? u there? I called but no answr.

Getting on a plane soon.

I need you.

"Oh my God!" April rips the phone from my hand. "Did you read this? He *needs* you. Can't you hear him saying that in his sexy Irish accent?"

"He's Scottish."

"Scottish, Irish, whatever—it's sexy as hell. You need to find a way to fit him in."

I'd like to fit him in all right.

She pushes me toward the door.

"What're you doing?"

"You need to talk to Bernadette before your next appointment so you can call him back and tell him he can come in."

"He's getting on a plane; it can wait."

"Are you crazy? You don't make guys like Lance Romero wait."

"I'm sure it's a skill he could probably use a little help with," I gripe. "And can we stop calling him by his first and last name? It's a little weird." But I stop fighting and let her push me. I'm curious to see what exactly Bernadette has to say about this and whether April is blowing it out of proportion.

As soon as Bernadette sees me, her eyes light up. "You'll never believe who's trying to get an appointment with you this week, and who's booked appointments for the next two months."

"Lance?"

Her face falls, and she shoots April a dirty look.

April lifts a shoulder. "I got excited."

"How many appointments has he booked?" I ask.

"Twelve."

"Pardon?"

"He's booked twelve appointments. And he took a cancellation for next week, but he says he really needs to see you this week. I tried to explain that you don't have any openings, but he didn't sound very happy about it. That accent is so sexy. Where's he from again? Australia?" Bernadette sighs.

"Scotland," I reply. "Can I see the appointments?"

She turns her computer monitor toward me and flips through them. He has two appointments a week for seven weeks, starting the week after next since I'm already booked up until then.

I pull up my appointments for tomorrow on my phone. All I have are two half-hour breaks, one at eleven and one at three thirty. The clinic closes at eight on Tuesdays, but since I already have six appointments, Bernadette won't schedule me another one, no matter how much time I have at the end of my day. As I'm contemplating whether it's a good idea to give in to Lance, my phone rings.

"It's him!" April shrieks.

I glare at her.

Bernadette's hands flutter. "Oh! You should answer! He's been very persistent. He only wants you."

I wish people would stop saying things like that. "You both need to stop fangirling." I wait until they stop twittering like birds before I answer. "Hello?"

"Poppy?"

"You're speaking to her."

"Thank fuck." He mumbles something, maybe to someone on the other end of the line. "Sorry about that—the swearing, I mean. I'm boarding the plane back to Chicago. Listen, I know you said no more home treatments, but I really need to see you, and your appointment warden won't book me in for anything in the next day or two. Can you help me out? Please."

Why do I have no resolve? "What time does your flight get in?"

"Uh, like, before noon, I think? Maybe a little later? And we have a team meeting as soon as we get back, but I'm totally free after that. I'll take anything right about now. I got into a scuffle on the ice last night, and it undid all the good you did last time."

Oh my God. The word *scuffle* coming out of his mouth does funny things to me. "I saw that."

"You did?"

I cringe at his surprise, and the fact that I've outed myself as a hockey watcher. Like this man needs his ego fed any more. "Mmm. Let me check my schedule this afternoon."

Bernadette shakes her head and motions to the screen. I came in early today so I could get out early. My last appointment is at six thirty and it's only forty-five minutes. Technically I can fit Lance in, although that's going to put me up to seven sessions today. And I'll miss yoga. Although our new instructor isn't nearly as good as the girl who'd been teaching the class since early spring, so I'm really not missing all that much, apart from exercise.

I point to the computer screen and give Bernadette a questioning look. She shrugs, and April makes flailing hand gestures. "I can take you at seven fifteen."

"Tonight?"

"Yes."

"At your house, or the clinic?"

"At the clinic. We close at eight, though, so it can only be forty-five minutes." I want Bernadette to be here when he leaves, just to be safe. Lord knows I'm stupid around this man.

"Okay. That works. Yer a precious angel. I really owe ya, Poppy." His voice becomes muffled. "Yeah, yeah, I know. I'm hanging up. No, ya does nae hafta do that." His voice becomes clear again, the Scot thicker with his agitation. "I gotta go or they're gonna kick me off the plane. I'll see you tonight, Poppy. Thanks again."

I listen to dead air, still processing the *precious angel* comment, before I finally hang up.

Bernadette and April are squeal-flapping.

"You're worse than teenage girls at a boy band concert. You can't act like that when he's here."

April huffs. "This one starts treating famous hockey players, and she's suddenly Ms. Serious."

"It's one hockey player, and he's asking me to treat him, not marry him."

"Yet," April says.

"I have another client, so I need to get ready." I leave the two of them to go set up, trying not to squeal-flap myself.

The rest of the day moves in an anxious blur. I don't want to fixate on Lance, but really, I have a lot of time to think about him and the fact that he's scheduled all these appointments and insisted on seeing me today. I also try not to think about what it means that I've given up my evening plans so I can treat him. I'd like to say it's because I'm nice, but I'm not so nice that I'd give up my evening for just any client.

I'm antsy by the time seven rolls around. Typically I'll work a little longer on my clients, particularly if they're regulars, but knowing that Lance is likely waiting out there makes me feel rushed. Still, I don't want to short-change anyone, so it's seven twenty by the time I finish up.

I slip out of my room and down the hall to wash my hands before I check reception for Lance. He's sitting in the same chair as the last time, wearing a pair of jeans and a long-sleeved henley pushed up to his elbows. Its dark green hue makes his eyes and hair pop more than usual. He has bruises along his jaw, and his eye has a dark shadow under it. There's a new, bigger fly bandage across his split eyebrow. He's still gorgeous.

But that's not the most shocking thing. Clutched in one hand is a bouquet of red flowers. Poppies, to be exact.

His eyes move over me. "Hey. Hi. I brought these as a thank you." He stands and thrusts them at me.

God, there's far too much fluttering in my stomach. Lance Romero brought me flowers. Because I managed to get him an appointment with me. It's a little weird.

I take them, aware that everyone is staring at us. Someone snaps a picture to my right. "Um. Thanks?"

"They're poppies."

"I see that. They're beautiful, although unnecessary." I bring them to my nose.

"They have that water stuff in the bottom, so they won't die before you get home."

"That's very thoughtful. They're lovely." Geez. My face must be the same color as the flowers.

He stuffs his hands in his pockets and gives me a cheeky grin. "I didn't get high when I sniffed them."

I laugh. "I'm sure you tried really hard, though."

"I did." Silence follows while we look at each other, and no one says a thing.

"Sooo...you ready for me?"

It takes a second for me to realize he means the massage, not that he's picking me up for some date.

"Al-almost," I stutter. "I'm a few minutes behind. I'm just finishing up with my last client."

"Oh. Okay." He drops back into the chair. His knees start bouncing.

My client comes out and settles up with Bernadette. We rebook for three weeks from now, and I excuse myself to change the sheets, taking my flowers with me.

Of course, April catches me in the hall and follows me into my room, closing the door. "Where'd you get those?"

"Lance."

"He brought you flowers?"

I'm assuming she doesn't need an actual answer to that.

"Oh my God. He's so into you. You know what this means, don't you?"

"The marriage proposal is next?"

"I wonder if he'll wear a kilt."

I set the flowers on the chair in the corner, careful not to crush them. I know exactly what this means. I shouldn't be treating him anymore. But I don't say that. "He's being nice. He's not into me."

"Bullshit."

"Will you just help me? I don't want to be here until midnight."

She takes the corner of the sheet and pulls it over the opposite end, helping me dress the table.

"Seriously, Poppy. He's into you."

"Yeah, well, he's already slept with someone I know. I don't want to be an addition to his list of conquests. Plus he's a client, so I can't accept his marriage proposal." I put the heating pad on the table, adjust the cradle, and force April out so I can get Lance.

As soon as I round the corner he's out of his chair. "We're good? You're ready now?" he asks.

"I am. You can come with me."

He's right on my heels, practically mowing me over to get to the room. As I close the door, he's already got the hem of his shirt in his hands. He pulls it up, over his hard, incredibly toned abs.

I drop my eyes to the floor. "I'll give you a minute."

"I'll be naked in thirty seconds."

I have to bite my lips together to stop from laughing. "Okay. I'll be right back, then."

I still knock a minute later, just in case.

"I'm ready," he calls.

And ready he is. That mountain of muscle is stretched out across my table. The sheet is pushed down to his waist.

I need to keep the ogling in check. I feel like I should go to confession or something, and I haven't been to church since my cousin's wedding last year.

"Would you like me to work on the same areas as last time?"

"Yeah. That'd be good." He shifts a little, and the muscles in his shoulders jump. His fists clench and release a few times as I cross over and pull the sheet to cover his back.

He lifts his head. "Why're you doing that?"

"It's how I start. Would you prefer me to leave it the way it is?"

"Yeah. Please."

"Okay." I fold the sheet back down. Once again I have no underwear to tuck the sheet into, so I push the edges in around his hips. He jolts a little, then settles again. "I'm going to get started, okay?"

"Yup." More fist clenching follows.

Usually when I drag my fingers along his spine, moving up to the top of the table, the sheet acts as a barrier. But this time I watch the shiver run through his body and goose bumps break along his arms, the same reaction echoed in my body. When I settle a palm on either side of his broad back, he groans.

I freeze and try to keep my tone professional, rather than breathy. "Are you okay?"

He clears his throat. Twice. "Yeah." It still sounds like he swallowed the contents of a gravel truck.

"Do you want the heating pad?"

"No. I'm good." More gravel.

"Take a couple of deep breaths for me, okay?"

He does as I ask, his back expanding with each full inhalation. I do nothing but keep my palm on the center of his back, right in the middle of his cross. When he's a little more relaxed, I grab the oil and make a few easy passes, moving down his back, gauging where he's the tightest. When I reach his lower back, he jolts. It's red, but not bruised. "Is this where you landed when you went down?"

"Yeah. It's a little sensitive."

"I'll be careful around there, then."

"'Kay."

"Are there any other tender areas?"

"Other than my back and face, nope."

"Okay."

Lance doesn't say much during the massage. Apart from the occasional grunt when I hit what I assume are sensitive spots, and the fist clenching, he doesn't complain at all about the pressure.

I don't even ask about his glutes this time, because it's already after eight, and Bernadette will be gone from her desk, even if a sexy hockey player is here. Lance was right, though, he's all knotted up again, and there's no way I'm going to be able to sort it all out with one treatment. He needs at least one more this week, and I'm fully booked.

"I still have some time left. Would you like me to work on your neck and shoulders again?" I've done what I can for his back.

"Uh...yeah, I think that'd be okay."

I'm relieved he doesn't have the same problem as last time. Mostly.

I get him to lift his hips so I can take the pillow out from under him. Lance makes a sound of discomfort as he rolls over.

"Everything okay?" I ask.

"Oh yeah, just managing the aches. Good to go."

"Great."

I won't be touching his face this time because of the bruising and the fresh fly bandage, but he keeps his eyes closed while I work on his neck and shoulders, so I can study his gorgeous, pummeled features.

No matter how hard I try not to, I can still recall—rather vividly—how prominent Lance's *issue* was last time. I must make a sound because his eyes open and flip up to mine. I decide it's a good time to end the massage.

It's eight thirty, and I'm alone in the clinic with Lance. I give him some privacy and wash my hands in the bathroom before going to the reception area so I can prepare his invoice, which I find already waiting for me. Sometimes Bernadette can be so sweet.

It takes a few minutes for him to come out—longer than it did the last time he was here. I consider what might be happening in that room. When Lance appears, he looks groggy and disheveled.

I put on what I hope is a natural-looking smile. "Feeling a little less tense?"

His eyes go wide before his expression flattens. "Uh, yeah. A lot less tense."

He pulls his wallet out of his back pocket and drops it on the counter. Flipping it open, he pulls out his card. "I need to get you for last time, too."

"Huh?"

"At your house. I didn't pay you. I need to do that."

I'd totally forgotten to even prepare an invoice for that massage. "You could email-transfer the funds for that one if you want."

"Why don't you add your email to your contact?" Lance passes me his phone.

My name comes up as Pretty Poppy, and it's accompanied by the picture April accidentally snapped of me. I look like I'm yelling at her. Probably because I was. "April took that picture by accident when you left your phone here."

"So it's not a selfie?"

"If I was going to take a selfie, I'd make sure I didn't look like a troll."

"I think you look cute."

"That's even worse." I type in my email address and am about to delete the picture when Lance snatches the phone back.

"That's my phone. You can't delete my pictures."

"But it's a picture of me!"

"Which I like, so I get to keep it. It's not my fault your friend has a slippery finger. What was she even doing with my phone in the first place?"

"Trying to jailbreak it so she could get all your personal information," I say.

"Seriously?" Lance looks legitimately worried.

"No. Not seriously. Although she did check to see if it was locked, which was when she took the picture. I forced her to give it back to me."

"So you were trying to protect my privacy."

"Mmm. That I was." I swipe his credit card.

"So you think maybe you can fit me in again this week?"

"I'm fully booked, but I can see if someone else is available."

"No," he snaps, then amends, "I mean, no thanks. Like I said before, I only want it to be you."

"I could try to fit you in at the end of a day again, if that works?" That's the opposite of what I should do right now, but I've decided I'm not going to keep questioning myself. I want this time with him. What I'm doing is helping him, and beyond how much he seems to appreciate it, I like who he is when it's him and me and I'm treating him, even if this relationship is supposed to be strictly professional.

"Yeah, sure, whenever you can. I have practice a lot this week, cause the official season starts this weekend, but I can usually do these later ones. Unless you want to treat me at my place or yours."

"It's better if we do it here."

He chews on his bottom lip. "All right. If that's how it's gotta be."

Like last time, he walks me to my car. This time I have the flowers with me, which makes getting in my vehicle even more awkward. Lance takes them for me so I can unlock my door and toss my purse on the passenger seat. When I turn back to him, he has this strange look on his face.

He takes a step toward me, and for a second I think he's going to kiss me. In that instant I'm transported back to that closet at the party. But he doesn't kiss me; instead he leans past me and drops the flowers on the dash. Then he straightens and wraps his arms around me. The hug ends as quickly as it began. He steps back, shoves his hands in his pockets, and looks at the ground, as if he's embarrassed.

"Thanks for taking care of me again."

"You're welcome."

He holds my door open and waits until I'm in the driver's seat before he gestures to the flowers. "Is it weird that I gave you those?"

"Not weird. Unexpected and unprecedented, maybe."

"Okay. I can deal with unprecedented. Night, Poppy."

"Night, Lance."

I wait until he's in his Hummer before I move the poppies to the passenger seat and start my car. I'm not sure what just happened, but this feels different than any of my other client-therapist relationships.

UNPLEASANT CONCESSIONS

POPPY

I t's been a week since I've treated Lance. I haven't been able to fit him in at all, though against my better judgment I did try. The nights where I could've tacked him on to the end of my day, he had practice, and then he had back-to-back games to open the official hockey season.

I watched those in the privacy of my living room, alone, almost like it was porn.

And he texts me daily. Sometimes multiple times. He always starts off by asking if there have been any cancellations. When I tell him no, he resorts to begging. Occasionally he sends me pouty-faced selfies, which I secretly love.

Today we're finally making our schedules work, which is good, at least for him, because he told me if I don't treat him, he won't be able to play the next game. I squeezed him in as my last appointment of the day, working against the tingles in my tummy to convince myself this will be the very last time.

As I work out the horrible knots and kinks in his back, neck, and shoulders, I promise myself that after this massage I'm going to tell him someone else has to treat him. I don't think I can keep up the professional front much longer, and I'm getting attached to these appointments. I don't want it to become an issue, or another source of humiliation.

He's talkative tonight, so I'm learning new things about him. His teammate, Miller, the one who had the penis drawing on his forehead, just had a baby, and Lance has plans to visit him tomorrow. I imagine him holding a newborn, and it makes my insides feel all warm and melty. Lance only goes back to Scotland once every two years. His favorite color is green, followed by orange, and his favorite foods are anything traditionally Scottish. He loves chocolate but breaks out in a rash when he eats it. Gummies are a special weakness for him. His favorite music is mellow, but he listens to heavy stuff when he works out.

I steer clear of discussing my childhood or my going-out habits. Mostly the conversation is easy and limited to safe subjects. Except there are a couple of times when he seems to want to say something, but can't quite get it out. He starts and stops and then goes quiet.

When I'm finished, I leave him to change while I wash my hands. It's another late session, so the reception area is empty when I go out there to manage Lance's invoice.

It takes a few minutes for him to change, whether because he's slow to get off the table, or because he has an issue to manage in there, I don't really want to know. Well, I sort of do want to know, which is the main reason I can't keep treating him.

When he comes out, he's got his hat in his hand, and he's twirling it around his finger, chewing on his bottom lip. His nervousness ramps up my own. I have no idea how I'm going to broach this subject, because knowing I have to and actually following through on it is not at all the same.

He drops his hat on the counter and taps anxiously. "I want to tell you something."

Please don't mention your hard-on again. "Is everything okay?"

"Yeah. No. I don't know. It depends on how you react."

I sit up straight in Bernadette's chair; all the hairs on the back of my neck stand up.

"So...uh, I remember the night I met you."

I drop my eyes. "Oh."

"Well, not you exactly. Well, kinda. But it's all real vague until I went upstairs to check on Miller."

And now my stomach is churning in a not-so-good way. My voice is a whisper. I fiddle with Bernadette's sparkle pens. "With Kristi."

"Yeah. Anyway, I didn't sleep with her. Well, like, I fell asleep, but I didn't sleep *with* her. As in fuck her. I didn't, I mean. Do that. I thought it would be good to tell you."

I blink a few times, shocked. "But she said—"

"—a lot of bullshit, I'm betting." Lance looks annoyed.

I don't know why he would bother to lie to me about something like this, and Kristi liked to brag about all the guys she'd slept with, so it's entirely possible nothing did happen.

"Oh. Okay. Well, thanks? We don't hang out anymore, sooo..."

"Right. Yeah, okay. Good." He taps the counter some more. "I still wish I could remember meeting you that night. I guess it explains why you're so familiar, aye?"

"I guess." I can't look him in the eye. "They kind of dragged me along."

"So—" He slaps a hand on the counter, startling me. "Uh, I don't know how much free time you have, but maybe you wanna go out for dinner with me sometime?"

Well, that's quite the segue. Now I have no choice but to look at him. "Like on a date?"

Lance's eyes dart around. "Aye. Like a date."

"I can't go out to dinner with you." *Oh my God. What the hell am I doing?*

His brows pull down. "Why not?"

"It's against the clinic policy to date clients, not to mention the association that provides me with a license to practice." This is it. This is the best way to pass him off to another therapist. He's given me the perfect excuse, and I don't have to own up to anything. *And* he wants to take me on a date. I think I'm in shock.

"You can't even go out to dinner with me once? Just to see if, you know, you'd wanna hang out again?" He's doing that thing where he chews on the inside of his lip.

"Not if you want me to treat you."

"So it's not about the Kristi thing? 'Cause I'm serious when I say I didn't sleep with her."

"It's really not about Kristi. If I agree to go out with you, I can't treat you at the clinic anymore." The Kristi revelation does mean I might agree to the date, though.

His expression turns hopeful. "Just at the clinic?"

I dash it with my next response. "Or at my home. But that was already off the table."

Lance taps his lip while he thinks about that. I don't know whether to feel good about his hesitation or not. I guess it means I'm a decent massage therapist.

"What about the ones I've already scheduled?" he asks.

"You'll have to see someone other than me. Devon is great, and so is Marcie."

"What about the other girl who works here? Your friend with the blond hair?"

"April can't work on you."

"She's not any good?"

"We'll go with that."

The corner of his mouth pulls up in a slow smirk. "You don't want her to touch me?"

Now he's poking fun. "Never mind. This isn't a good idea."

"Whoa, whoa. Okay, no April. We'll go with Marcie then, or I can see the team therapist if I have to." He huffs out a breath. "So how long will I have to wait for you to be able to work on me again?"

"I won't ever be able to treat you again." I don't mention that if one date turns into many, and I end up being more than just someone he sleeps with and tosses aside, I'll be more than happy to provide all services free of charge. He doesn't need to know that.

He runs a rough hand through his hair. "Never?"

"You can't be my client anymore. Not ever."

"Fuck. It's really that final."

I nod solemnly. "I could lose my job otherwise."

"For going on a date? Shit. Well, I don't want that to happen." He dips his head resolutely. "Okay. So two dates, one coffee and one dinner, in whatever order you'd prefer them."

I have to force my face to stay neutral. "One date. Dinner or coffee."

"I think we need to do some negotiating. If I have to give up massages from you forever, it's only fair that I get more than one kick at the can here."

I raise a brow at his choice of words. I also have to bite my tongue to keep from telling him that technically this would be his *third* kick at the can.

"In case I screw something up," he continues, "which is entirely possible since this whole dating thing is off the grid for me. So one dinner date and one coffee date?"

It doesn't surprise me that he hasn't had much dating experience. Girls have probably thrown themselves at him his entire life. Still, it's obvious he's trying.

"Fine. One dinner and one coffee. Any more stipulations you'd like to add to the bargaining table?"

Lance tips his chin in the air and regards the dusty lights above. "The dates have to occur within a week of each other."

He's rather charming. "Very practical. We wouldn't want to drag it out unnecessarily."

"You're sassy. I like it a lot. What're you doing Friday night?"

"I work until six."

"I'll pick you up for dinner at seven thirty? Is there any type of food you're particularly averse to?"

"Food aversions?"

"Things you don't like to eat."

"Oh. I won't eat things with tentacles, or meat babies." I shiver at the thought.

"Meat babies?"

"Like lamb or veal."

"Oh, got it. No lamb or veal. Anything you love?"

You wearing nothing, lying on my table. "I like comfort food. Pasta, things like that."

He smiles. "Great." He taps his forehead. "I'm locking all that information away in here."

"Okay. Well, I guess I should get my things and go home."

"Right. Yeah. Sure. I can walk you to your car?"

I find it interesting that he makes it more of a statement than a question. "Sure, I'll grab my purse and coat."

"'Kay. I'll wait here." He pushes up on his toes a couple of times.

I can feel his eyes on me as I head back to my room to get my things. I've agreed to go out with Lance. On a date. Two actually. I don't even know what to think. I grab my purse and slip into my jacket. As fall settles in and the temperature drops, layers are becoming necessary.

When I return, Lance is standing at the desk, checking his phone. He's smiling.

"Ready to go," I say.

He hits a couple of buttons, pockets his phone, and turns that grin on me. "Cool."

I lock up the clinic, and Lance walks me across the lot. This time he doesn't leave the usual space between us, and the back of his hand grazes my hip.

I'm nervous when we reach my car. His Hummer is parked right behind my Mini this time. I adjust the strap of my purse and look up at him. Strangely, he looks as nervous as me.

He scans my face and takes a small step closer. I can see his hand lifting in my peripheral vision. My hair is in a ponytail, which is sitting on my shoulder. He fingers the end of it.

"Why do I always want to pull this?"

It's on the tip of my tongue to tell him he used to do it when we were kids. But I don't have the opportunity, because he drops his head and his lips skim my cheek.

"I want to kiss you, pretty Poppy."

"You just did," I whisper.

"I want do it again, but here." His thumb touches my bottom lip.

"Oh."

He's so close. His lips almost touching mine as he asks, "Can I do that?"

"Yes, please."

His lids grow heavy, and he kisses the corner of my mouth. I'm transported back in time, to a dark closet at a party I never should've been at. Lance strokes my cheek and rests his palm on the side of my neck. The other hand skims the length of my arm until he reaches my fingertips.

He leans back a little, and for a second I think it's over before it's even begun, but he takes my hand in his. Uncurling my fingers, he lifts it and presses my palm against his cheek. A full-body tremor runs through him, and his eyes drift closed. He turns his head toward my palm, and I smooth my thumb along the contour of his bottom lip. A deep sound comes from the back of his throat, making my skin prickle and heat blossom in my belly.

When he opens his eyes again, the fire in them matches the

heat flooding my entire body. "Can you keep yer hand right here?"

"If you want me to, yes."

"I definitely do."

He leans in and brushes his lips over mine again. It's soft and warm. The next time he takes my bottom lip between his, he releases it slowly, and then does the same with the top one. When his tongue flicks out, I might whimper. Light fingers cup my head, and I tilt it back farther.

I part my lips, and his tongue sweeps my mouth. His groan is low, sending a shiver down my spine. He drops the hand that's keeping mine pressed against his cheek. His arm winds around my waist, and he pulls me in tight against him.

I expect the kiss to grow in intensity. It doesn't, though I can feel the heat building inside me. That feeling I've been searching for all these years is finally back.

My other hand abandons the strap of my purse, because there are far better places for it to go. I follow the contour of muscle in his arm to his shoulder. As soon as my cold fingertips connect with the warm skin on his neck, Lance makes another needy sound and tightens his hold around my waist.

The flash of headlights reminds us we're in the middle of a parking lot. Lance disconnects his mouth from mine, and we turn to see a police cruiser moving through the lot.

"Fucking cops, ruining my goddamn moment."

I laugh. It's all breathy and shaky, like the rest of me.

The cruiser stops in front of my car, and the window whirs down. "Everything all right here?"

"Just saying good night, sir." Lance has his arm thrown casually over my shoulder, but his fingertips are pressing in.

"He was making sure I got to my car safely." I gesture to the mostly empty lot and state the obvious. "Because it's dark."

The policeman regards us for a few long seconds, as if discerning whether we're likely to be thieves. He must decide we're harmless. "Careful out here at night. There've been some car break-ins lately."

"Thanks for the warning, officer." Lance raises a hand.

The police officer taps the side of his car and rolls away, the window whirring up.

Once he's moved on, Lance returns his focus to me. "Maybe you want to go out for drinks now or something?"

"I'm not much of a drinker."

"Right. Okay. What about tea? Or maybe a bite to eat?"

"You want to have dinner tonight instead of Friday?"

"It won't count as dinner. It's too late."

"So this is our coffee date, then?" I'm egging him on.

"Well, no. Not unless we have coffee, which probably isn't the best idea since it's late. Unless you want to pull an all-nighter with me." His expression is impish.

"I have to be up early tomorrow."

His eyes dip back to my mouth. "I bet you could do it."

"Just because I can doesn't mean I should." I imagine an all-nighter with Lance would be exhausting for reasons other than lack of sleep.

"What about going for ice cream then?"

"It's October."

"Or some other dessert? Please, Poppy." He tugs on the end of my ponytail. "I want a reason to say good night again."

If he means kissing me, he hardly needs an excuse. "I guess dessert wouldn't hurt."

"And that way this doesn't count as part of the dinner and a coffee date thing."

"You're quite the negotiator, aren't you?"

"I always won in debate class. So should I follow you home and we can hit a place near there?"

"Sure. That would work."

Lance holds my door open. Before I get in he puts a finger under my chin and tilts my head up. I expect some tongue or something, but all I get is a quick brush of lips. "Drive safe."

"You, too."

I drop into the driver's seat, my legs feeling like they're made of rubber. Lance's Hummer revs to life, the loud rumble drowning out the sound of my engine turning over and the music filtering through my speaker system. His lights practically blind me. I turn my head away, letting my eyes adjust to the dark for a moment, before I pull out of the lot, and he follows me to my neighborhood.

The butterflies in my stomach won't stop, and my palms are sweaty. I park in front of my house, but Lance has to drive a little farther down to find a spot for his giant vehicle.

While he's parking, I run into my house, change into a pair of jeans and a mostly wrinkle-free sweater, and return to meet him on my front porch.

"There's a little dessert place a couple of blocks away. Does that sound okay?"

"Yeah. Dessert's my favorite."

"Great." We start down the sidewalk. I have to take two steps for every one of his long strides. "They have all kinds of home-made pies and cakes and scones and things, and this amazing lavender tea."

"Nice. I'm actually kinda hungry now, so that's perfect."

"I imagine that's fairly constant for you."

"Pretty much." Lance shoves his hands in his pockets as we walk, so I do, too. "You said you grew up in your house, right? So you've lived here all your life?"

"Until high school. We moved to Galesburg for a few years right before I started, but my parents didn't sell the house. I guess they always thought we'd be back. Or maybe it was a good investment property. The neighborhood's improved a lot over the years."

Lance takes in the houses lining the street. They're pretty, and many of them have been face-lifted, if not totally remodeled, since my childhood.

"I lived around here for a few years," he says.

"Oh? Whereabouts?"

"Not too far away, I don't think. Lister Street? All of this looked familiar the last time I came here. My aunt's moved since I lived with her, so I haven't been back in this neighborhood for a long time."

"Oh? Where'd she move to?" I want to distract him from questions about me. Now that he's taking me out, I can and probably should tell him the entire truth, but I'm not sure how to divulge that information yet.

"Up to Wisconsin, out of the city. Her kids are grown and out of the house. My one cousin's married with kids in Milwaukee, and I think she wants to be close to them and all."

"How old were you when you moved to Chicago, anyway?" I think my school must've been the first place he came, based on the rumors back then, but asking keeps the focus away from me.

"Thirteen. It was late spring. I didn't expect it to be so freaking hot since it had been winter the last time I visited, and that was when I was ten. Scotland doesn't get snow that much, not where I'm from, and the temperature changes aren't as extreme as they are here."

"You must've been so sunburned that first summer."

"Oh, fuck! I had the worst sun poisoning. I was barfing for, like, three days, and I was covered in blisters. My mum was *pissed*. I had to miss two hockey practices, I was so sick." His jaw tics. "I never went outside without a ball cap or sunscreen after that."

"Was it hard to get used to winter?"

"Not too bad, since it meant playing lots of ice hockey."

"Did you start playing Rep hockey as soon as you moved? That must've been a huge change."

"I did. I was old to be starting. Most of these kids had been on skates since they could walk, but I loved playing, and it was a good outlet for me."

"Your parents must be so proud of you." Mine are happy that I have a full-time job in the field they spent all sorts of money educating me for, and that I found a job that suits me. Obviously they're proud, too, but becoming a massage therapist is a lot different than a professional hockey player.

"I don't talk to them all that much. I mean, I guess my dad is proud, but he isn't all that connected to the family, and he wasn't here when it mattered."

"I'm so sorry. I didn't mean to pry."

"It's okay. It's not your fault. My mum isn't really a good person, so I don't much blame my dad for leaving."

I don't ask any more questions about his family, because it seems to put him in a dark mood, and I'd much rather have the flirty, sweet, funny Lance. My family has always been pretty close. Even my sister, who has a hard time settling down anywhere, always shows up for the important events, though most of the time she asks for money before she leaves. Fortunately, we've arrived at the little café. It's busy, maybe because it's a Monday night and lots of places aren't open.

Lance holds the door open for me and groans when the smell of sugar, coffee, and baked goods hits him. "Now I'm really starving."

"We'll feed your beast." I pat his flat stomach, then realize the unrequested contact might not be all that welcome.

But he grabs my hand before I can pull it away. He threads his fingers through mine and squeezes before guiding me through the tables to the counter. A glass case features muffins, scones and ornately decorated cakes. On the chalkboard menu above the cashier is a list of sundaes and ice cream options.

"There's a gummy bear sundae?" Lance asks, awestruck. He looks at the girl standing behind the counter. "Is that any good? Do they really use gummy bears?"

"Um. Yes. And everything here is good."

He looks down at me. "Have you ever had one?"

"No. I usually get their lava cake, but you're allergic to chocolate, right?"

"You can still get it."

"Well, how allergic are you?"

Lance frowns, and then his eyebrows pop up, his eyes moving to my mouth. "Uh, on second thought, I guess it might be better to avoid it if you want me to say a proper good night later."

"I'd like a proper good night."

His smile is devilish. "I'd like several proper good nights."

Lance orders the gummy bear sundae and a strawberry tea—this place doesn't have a liquor license—and I get the carrot cake and lavender tea. We look around for a table, but the options are limited. Lance spots a tiny two-top in the corner, grabs my hand again, and leads me over. He pulls out my chair, tucking me in. Then he moves his chair so he's not across from me, but perpendicular, his knee touching mine as it bounces under the table.

"I like this place."

I shrug out of my jacket. "Me, too. April and I come here sometimes."

"The girl at the clinic, right? The one you don't want to touch me."

"That would be her."

Lance tugs the end of my ponytail, running his fingers through it. His smile falters, and he sifts through the strands again. "I have this memory from when I first moved here—"

The server brings our drinks and desserts over, interrupting him. My heart stays firmly lodged in my throat, though.

Lance's sundae is ridiculously huge, and as advertised, it's covered in gummy bears and some sort of white topping.

"What's on that?"

"Marshmallow fluff." Lance digs in, twirling his spoon as it gathers ice cream, fluff, and gummy bears. He shoves the massive spoonful in and makes a contented food-love sound.

"Is it good, then?" I ask.

He makes hand gestures, but he can't actually respond for the moment. It takes a long time before he's finished chewing enough to use words.

"The gummy bears are so cold and hard. It's magically deli-cious." He puts on an overdone, fake Irish accent for the last part. "You need to try this."

He shoves the spoon in and drags it through the ice cream, holding it out to me. It's heaping. I don't even think I can open my mouth that wide.

"That's too much."

He frowns and looks at the spoon, then sticks it in his mouth, removing about half the contents before he holds it back out to me. "How's this?"

I make a face. "It's got your spit all over it now."

"So? You've already had my spit in your mouth. What's the big deal?"

"Lance!" I look around to see if anyone has overheard, but no one's paying attention to us.

"It's true. But fine, I'll try again." He flips the spoon over and keeps his eyes on mine while he licks off the contents. When he's done, he flips it back over, licking the other side clean. He's incredibly thorough. I have lots of thoughts about how talented he must be with that tongue. And now that he's not my client, I allow my imagination to run.

Holding the spoon up, he asks, "Is this okay? Or do you need me to get a clean spoon that hasn't been in my mouth at all?"

I roll my eyes. "It's fine."

This time he dips the spoon in, carefully gathering a small amount of ice cream, marshmallow fluff, and a single gummy bear coated in strawberry sauce. He holds out the spoon. "How's this, precious? Can you handle it?"

I give him a look, but open my mouth. His lips part right along with mine, his tongue peeking out as he watches the spoon disappear between mine.

This feels very much like foreplay.

It also tastes like a sugar bomb has gone off in my mouth. It's so sweet it's almost pucker worthy. Lance withdraws the spoon slowly, his eyes on my mouth the entire time, his bottom lip caught between his teeth. When he notices the spoon is by no means clean, he offers it to me again.

I still have a gummy bear in here, so I shake my head.

"You don't like it?"

I chew a few times before I swallow. He wasn't kidding about them being hard. They're practically frozen. I put my hand in front of my mouth. "It's a little sweet."

He sticks the spoon back in his mouth and licks it clean. "See? I don't have a problem with your spit."

I can feel the heat in my cheeks, and I duck my head. Lance leans in close, forcing me to look up at him. "I want to kiss you again."

I survey the crowded café.

He must see my panic, because he tugs my ponytail and sits back in his chair. "But I can wait if I have to."

We eat our desserts in silence for a while. I'm too nervous to enjoy this the way I'd like to. I can feel Lance staring at me.

"Where'd you go to high school?" he asks.

"In Galesburg."

"Right, because you moved."

"Mm-hmm. My sister went to Wells for a year, though."

"Really? Do you look alike?"

"Not much. She has brown hair and brown eyes, and she's tall and thin."

"Huh." He takes a few more bites of his sundae. "Wait. What school did you go to before you moved, then?"

I knew this was going to happen eventually.

"I went to Pulaski."

"I went there for, like, a month right at the end of the school year when I first moved here." He sets his spoon down and leans forward. "Shit. I knew I knew you. I used to pull your ponytail in the hall. You were the only other ginger in the school. I noticed you right away. Do you remember that?"

I look down at my carrot cake, which sits mostly uneaten on my plate.

"Poppy?"

"I remember."

"Was I mean to you? I wasn't trying to be mean."

"You weren't mean."

"Okay. Good." His knee is going again. Rubbing against mine. "If you remembered, why didn't you say anything before now?"

"It didn't seem important." *Because I didn't think you remembered me at all.*

"That we went to school together? You came to my house. Did you know you knew me then?"

Oh, God. This is happening now? My whole body feels numb and like it's on fire at the same time. "Maybe we should go."

"Poppy?" He puts his hand over mine to stop me from grabbing my purse.

"You didn't even really notice I was there."

"So you did know?"

"Of course I did. Everyone knows who you are," I say quietly.

"No one here has recognized me."

"You're wearing a baseball cap. It's not like we were friends or anything. We went to school together for a few weeks, and you were two grades higher than me. I was nobody."

"What aren't you telling me?"

"I think we should go."

"Not until you tell me whatever it is that's making you all sketchy."

"Can we not do this right here, please?" I whisper.

I don't actually think there's an ideal location for this anywhere, ever, but a crowded café is definitely low on the list.

"Sure, okay." Lance pushes away from the table and comes around to help me into my jacket.

My stomach is twisting. I feel stupid already. I'm going to come across as some pining, idiot girl who's idolized him for years—which is and isn't the case. I mean, for a long time I

173

romanticized that kiss, and of course, like the hopeless romantic I am, I had those silly girl fantasies about meeting him again and picking up where we'd left off.

But it isn't like I never dated or had boyfriends. I've done both. I've had several long-term boyfriends, nice ones who treated me well. But the fire just never seemed to burn bright or long enough to sustain the initial attraction, and eventually those relationships turned into friendships.

What if he thinks I'm a stalker? No matter how sweet he is with me, there's plenty of evidence floating around out there to prove he's a partier with lots of willing partners. That coupled with the strangely labeled contact on his phone is enough to remind me how sideways this whole thing could go.

Lance follows me out of the café, the mood having changed from light and flirty to heavy once again.

He grabs my hand when we're on the sidewalk. "Can you tell me what's going on? I really fucking hate being manipulated, and that's exactly what this feels like."

"I'm not manipulating you." I pause while people pass us on the sidewalk. "Can we walk and I promise I'll talk?"

Lance sighs, but falls into step beside me. I wait until we're back on a quieter street before I say anything.

"My sister's freshman year, she took me to a house party. Some kids from her school threw it."

"Okayyy."

"I was in seventh grade."

"Fuck. That wasn't a good place for you to be, but what does this have to do with anything?"

"I'm getting to that."

"Was I there?"

I nod, but don't look at him.

He grabs my arm, gently but firmly, and pulls me to a stop. Stepping in front of me, his eyes are wide and haunted. "Please tell me we didn't hook up at that party when you were thirteen."

"God. No. Not in the way you mean."

He drops his hands, closes his eyes, and releases a relieved breath. "Thank fucking Christ."

"And I was twelve."

"Twelve? At a high school party?"

"My thirteenth birthday was, like, a week away. My sister didn't always make the best choices."

"Clearly."

"It was a big part of the reason we ended up moving away from Chicago for a few years. She couldn't stay out of trouble." I was always the easy child growing up. Cinny was the one who got into all the trouble. Apart from that one party.

We start walking again.

"So I didn't commit a felony, which is good. Did I talk to you?"

It hurts that he doesn't remember at all. "In a manner of speaking."

"That doesn't sound good."

"One of my sister's friends was playing a game. I didn't realize what it was until it was too late." I have to look anywhere but him in order to get out the rest. "They were playing Seven Minutes in Heaven."

Lance comes to a dead stop again. I don't want to look up, but I have to because he's not moving. "You got locked in a closet with some high school douche when you were twelve?"

"Almost thirteen." As if that makes it better. "I didn't get locked in there with a douche; I got locked in there with you."

"For seven minutes?"

"Yes."

"Did we make out? Wait. Don't answer that. We're close to your house, right?"

"It's down the street."

He laces his fingers through mine and tugs. "Come on."

"What are you doing?"

"Hoping to jog my memory."

When we reach my door, it takes me a minute to find my

keys since they're stuck at the bottom of my purse. Then I fumble and drop them on the mat.

Lance bends down to grab them. "Here. Let me get it."

When the door swings open, he pushes past me into my foyer. He goes straight for the hall closet, opening the door and parting the hangers.

"What're you doing?"

He laces my fingers with his. "I want you to show me."

"Show you wh—"

He steps into the closet and pulls me inside with him, closing the door behind us.

A hat falls from the hook inside the door, and I bat it away in the dark. "This is a really weird way to end a first date." I'm so nervous right now.

"Just go with it." He brings my fingers to his lips.

"What am I supposed to be showing you, apart from the inside of my closet?" My heart is beating so hard.

"What our first kiss was like. I want to remember it the way you do," he pleads.

"You were probably drunk."

"There's a good chance. But I'm not now. Please."

I can tell him no. He won't push me for something I'm not willing to give freely. But I recognize the vulnerability in this. In him. It makes me want to see if I can resurrect the sweet boy inside this closed man who stole my heart so many years ago.

My biggest fear is falling for real this time. I don't really know him or understand the crazy life he seems to lead. I never have, and I'm not a kid anymore, but actually spending time with him has pulled me way beyond any romantic fantasies.

I pull out my phone and key in the code.

"What are you doing?"

"Setting a timer."

"What for?"

"Because I'm re-creating the moment, and this is what you did."

"I set a timer?"

"You honestly don't remember at all?"

He cups my face in his hands. "I'm sorry. I didn't make a lot of nice memories before I got drafted, especially not when I first moved to Chicago. I had to shut a lot of things out. Please give me this one good thing back?"

He's so sincere. What's more, he's so very sad. It makes me want to know what could've been so bad that he'd choose to forget everything he could.

"Okay." I cut the light on my phone, submerging us in darkness again. It's easier to do this if I can't see his face.

I can feel him playing with the ends of my hair. "Why did I set a timer?"

"You were being sweet. I was freaked out. You set an alarm so you wouldn't lose face—those were your words. I didn't understand what you meant at the time, but then you started asking me questions. I told you my name."

"Poppy like the flower," he whispers.

My stomach does a little flip at the thought that maybe he does remember. "That's what you said to me."

"I did?"

I swallow the lump in my throat. "And you asked me how old I was. I lied and said I was fourteen. You were turning fifteen the next day."

"Why would you lie, pretty Poppy?" His fingers are light, following the contour of my lips.

Is he playing with me? It's like he's giving me back the words he used all those years ago. I don't want this to be a game for him. It's not for me.

"I knew you wouldn't kiss me if you knew I was only twelve."

"Fuck. No, I wouldn't have. I guess I'm glad you lied then."

"I'm not twelve anymore, so it's fine. And even then, I made the choice to be in there with you. I remembered you from the year before, when you went to my school. I thought you were cute. Anyway—" I swallow thickly at the feel of his fingers trailing along my neckline. His light touch sends my mind spinning into the past, and heat rushes through me. "You asked me if I'd ever been kissed before."

"And what did you say?"

"No."

"And what did I say?"

"That you should be sorry, because you were going to take something from me that I couldn't get back."

"But I kissed you anyway."

"You did."

"That was selfish of me. That kiss belonged to someone special."

"It felt special at the time."

"I'm glad. And I'm still not sorry the way I should've been."

"What?"

"For taking something that didn't belong to me. I wasn't sorry then. I'm still not sorry now."

He remembers.

14

SLAPPED IN THE FACE WITH MEMORIES

LANCE

W hen a person chooses to bury memories, there's usually a reason. The span of time between my brother dying and my aunt realizing my mom was beating the shit out of me—verbally and physically—was the worst of my life. When we moved to Chicago, her beatings got worse instead of better, so I shut down. I locked everything away—all the good and the bad and everything else in between—and kept it stored in the dark place in my head.

It was almost like the mental place I go to when I get into a fight on the ice. Keeping the memories on lockdown is a lot easier than contending with them. Or at least I thought it was. But everything just changed.

I've been slapped in the face—not literally, I don't think

Poppy has a violent bone in her body—with a deluge of memories.

Now I understand why Poppy's always felt so familiar. She is. Flickers of things long buried start to surface: my first week of school in Chicago, the still-healing bruises on my back and legs and knees, wearing pants when it was hot, all the attention from the teachers and other students.

A lot of the memories aren't very pleasant, but the good ones that contain Poppy come hurtling to the surface now, obliterating everything else. She's the strawberry blond girl with the long ponytail who looked like home.

Not home in the sense of parents and family, but familiar and comfortable, warm and welcoming.

For a while I'd tried to ignore her, but she was always in the same hall as me during third period, so eventually I caved. I pulled her ponytail because I wanted to touch her hair and see what kind of reaction I'd get. Her smile, so curious and innocent, was something I'd forgotten existed.

I'd never bothered to find out her name. Comfortable things were alluring but untenable for me back then. Hell, mostly they still are. Stability was frightening. After we moved to Chicago, everything—my mum's happiness, my well-being and safety— was contingent on my success. And failure, perceived or real, required punishment. I accepted this because I knew I had failed my mum in the worst way possible.

Even after my aunt realized what was going on and my mum moved to Connecticut, I still didn't trust the peace. I would push my aunt's buttons, waiting for her to lash out, to the fill the void my mother's absence had created. It wasn't an absence in the sense that I missed her, but without the constant verbal and physical violence that had become normal, expected, anticipated even, I didn't know what to do. I waited for the slaps—the physical attacks, the breaking me down emotionally. But they never came. And I didn't understand it.

So I picked fights on the ice, needled players until they

cracked. And I let them get in solid hits before I shut them down. If that didn't satisfy the need for violence that had been conditioned into me, I would destroy my own property and myself.

I wasn't prepared to interact with anyone appropriately, so it was better for me not to know her name. Yet here she is, more than a decade later, and she still feels more like home than anyone I've ever known. I get it now. All my reactions to her make sense. Finally.

She skims my knuckles with her fingertips. "Before they opened the door, you told me to remember who you were in that closet, because that was the real you."

That was probably the last time I was real with anyone. I remember what the rest of that night looked like. I remember the aftermath of it, too, and I know why I buried this memory. Because it was pure, and I didn't think I deserved to have something so good. So I forced myself to forget it.

"You were so sweet." The alarm on her phone goes off. She silences it.

"It's time, pretty Poppy," I whisper, and I'm right back in that closet with her, all those years ago.

I bring her hands up, and she clasps them around my neck. Her palm curves against the back of my head. She's still so small compared to me. Her body is flush with mine.

My lips touch the corner of her mouth before I press them gently against hers. She doesn't open for me, so I just appreciate the softness for a few seconds before I pull away.

"Was it like that?" I ask.

"Exactly like that. I wanted you to kiss me again, and I was angry at myself for wasting those six minutes."

"I did kiss you again." I'd tried not to be pushy, but she'd tasted so sweet, like she does now. Once I started kissing her, I hadn't wanted to stop.

"But it could have lasted a lot longer."

"I'm glad I talked to you instead. This time will you open your mouth a little?"

"Yes."

When I press my lips to hers, I feel the velvet stroke of her tongue across my bottom lip. I don't grab her ass, even though I wanted to then, and I want to now. I wrap my arms around her, pulling her in close. I skim her hip and explore her mouth with my tongue, and like that first time, she lets me lead.

She kisses me back, tentative, and then she grows bold, our tongues dancing. She's not innocent anymore, not like when we were kids. She's given someone else her other firsts, but that kiss —that still belongs to me.

She presses her curves against me and makes a small, plaintive sound. I could kiss her forever. I could live in this memory— past fused with the present. This kiss would be my heaven.

I realize, though, that I can't keep Poppy in this closet for the rest of our lives, and that if we keep going, I'm definitely going to want to get her naked—okay, I already do—and make her come. I want to know what my name sounds like as a moan on her lips. I want to see her cheeks flush when I whisper how sexy she is, because I know under these clothes is a gorgeous body begging to be worshiped.

But I've already made enough mistakes when it comes to Poppy, so instead I slow the kiss, scale back on the tongue, loosen my hold on her, and open the closet door.

I take her face in my hands and press a few semi-chaste kisses to her lips. Then I go back for one more with tongue because I don't have as much self-control as I'd like.

When I try to leave the closet, Poppy wraps her arms more tightly around me and tries to pull the door closed again.

"What're you doing?" I ask around her tongue.

"Adding another seven minutes."

I laugh, but then it's not me leading anymore, it's her. I don't try to slow her down again, but instead of staying where we are, I take a step back, then another and another until I hit the opposite wall.

If it's her against it, not me, I'm liable to find a nice warm home for my thigh between her legs, or worse, I'll use the convenience of the wall as a great way to keep her pinned as I lift her up and wrap her legs around my waist.

And she'd let me. The tension between us has been building for a while now, and all this truth is unraveling the tenuous control I've been holding on to when it comes to her.

But if I fuck this up, I stand to lose a lot. Poppy's touch is the first to be enjoyable in my entire adult life, and I want to find out exactly how good it is when we're naked. And that's not happening tonight.

She moves her palm from the back of my neck to my cheek. I have a brief moment of panic in which flashes of Tash touching me like this threaten to ruin the moment. Every hint of gentleness with Tash was balanced with aggression. But this is different. Poppy is almost careful, and as much as I like the way that feels, it makes me nervous. She has a new, different kind of power over me, and I'm not sure how to deal with that.

When her hand moves to my chest, I cover it with mine.

She pulls back; worry making her sparkling eyes wide. "Sorry."

I lift her palm back to my cheek and drag her fingers along my jaw, then I kiss the tip of each one, resisting—just barely—the urge to bite or suck on them. My dick is achingly hard.

"I'm going to go home now." Jesus. It sounds like I gargled with razor blades.

"You don't have to leave yet." Her eyes drop, her teeth pressing into her lip.

"Poppy, look at me."

Her gaze lifts. She's hurt. I can read it in her expression.

"I'm not leaving because I don't want you. I'm leaving because I do."

"But I—"

"If I'm going to have to see a different massage therapist for the rest of my life, I'm sure as hell not going to screw up my chances of getting more kisses like that from you by jumping the gun tonight. Your body is a gift I want to earn the right to enjoy. Okay?"

That changes the hurt to a tender smile. "Okay."

"Can I steal one more kiss, though?"

"Please."

I savor her—taste her mouth, sample the sweetness of her tongue and the press of her body against mine. I've never wanted anyone the way I want her. I don't want to claim, fuck, devour. I want to be worthy, and I'm afraid I never will be.

This is exactly what makes me a bad person, because that won't stop me. I'll get inside her. I'll find out how good it feels to be with her, even if I never deserve her.

15

FIRST DATE ADVICE

LANCE

I t's Friday, and that means tonight I'm taking Poppy out on a date. A real date. One that includes dinner, and whatever the fuck else I can think of to make her more likely to go out with me again, beyond the second date I've managed to pre-negotiate.

Canceling all my massage appointments made me aware of how on point I need to be tonight, which is why I'm currently sitting in Waters' kitchen, getting advice from Violet. She and I got tight when Waters had an accident last season and I beat the fuck out of the guy who took him off the ice.

I haven't been hanging around with them as much lately. However, right now I need dating advice, so here I am.

I could talk to Lily, but I haven't said anything to Randy

about this date. I figure it's better to keep it on the down low for now.

Violet's standing on the other side of her kitchen island, going through a bag of baby clothes and toys.

"Seriously. How much stuff does a baby need? Don't they just eat, sleep, crap, and cry? Why do they need so many outfits? Ohhh! This is awesome!" She holds up a onesie with an inappropriate logo on it.

Miller and Sunny's baby is only a week or so old, but apparently he's huge for a newborn. His name is Logan. I've only been over to visit once. I'm not sure I'm all that great with babies since he puked on me and crapped himself during the two minutes I held him.

"That's a lot of baby stuff. Don't tell me you and Waters are jumping on that train now, too. "

She gives me a look. "I'm not jumping on that train. Alex is another story. He keeps buying things; it's a compulsion. On the upside, he's taken a break from buying me new bras." Violet abandons the clothes-sorting project and shoves everything back in the bag. "Okay, so one more time with this. You're going out on a date with a girl you banged when you were a teenager?"

"No. I never banged her. I kissed her."

"I don't get why this is a big deal."

I've been trying to give Violet the abridged version of events. She probably knows the most of anyone about my history, and that's still not very much.

"It was in a closet. I was her first kiss."

Violet frowns. "Why a closet?"

"We were at a party, playing Seven Minutes in Heaven."

"Wow. Huh. How old were you?"

"I was almost fifteen."

"How old was Poppy?"

"She said she was fourteen."

Violet arches one of her brows and taps her manicured nail

on the counter. There are jewel things on the end. They're a little distracting. "Was she actually fourteen?"

"No. But that doesn't matter now, does it?"

"I guess not, if you didn't bone her. Okay. So let me put this all together. You were her first kiss at a party in a closet—which sounds like some weird horror movie business—and then you met her again last year at a bar, but you don't actually remember meeting her because you were drunk off your ass. Do I have it so far?"

"Yup."

"And she came back to your house, which you also don't remember, and you almost slept with one of her friends, but instead you drew a dick on Miller's forehead and posted it online, which caused the friend to have a meltdown because she was dressed like a slut and everyone on social media saw it."

"She was wearing my T-shirt."

"She was acting slutty. It's okay. I mean, I had crazy sex with Alex the first night I met him, and that's a pretty slutty thing to do, even though in general I'm not a slutty person. I had a slutty moment. He's so hot. He was hard to resist. I'd also had a lot of beer." She waves her hand in the air, like maybe she realizes she's pulling one of her overshares. "I'm just saying I can't judge her for being in a T-shirt and looking like a slut; although I can say that stupid dickface drawing caused a lot of tension between Alex and me for a while. So thanks a lot."

"That was a year ago."

"And I still remember not getting any for several days."

"Sorry." I'm not sure what else to say. I didn't know Violet all that well at the time.

"It's fine. I'm over it now that you've apologized, even if it's insincere."

"I'm not being insincere."

"Whatever. Okay. So back to this girl's slutty friend who you didn't sleep with." She motions for me to continue.

I try to explain again, as best I can without providing too

many details, but it's not easy. And when I recount the events out loud, to another female, it makes it sound a lot worse.

"Wait a second, you don't even remember seeing her the next morning?"

"I was preoccupied. Tash was there, and she was pissed off."

Violet slaps the counter. "Hold the fucking salami. Tash came over? While you had hockey hookers in the house?"

"It was before anything happened between us."

Violet assesses me, maybe trying to decide if she believes me or not.

I raise my hands in the air. "Seriously. I'm telling you the truth. It was after that when things started to get...whatever they got. But that's irrelevant anyway, 'cause this has nothing to do with Tash."

Violet rubs her temples. "You need to take it from the top again. This is like a hockey-style soap opera."

When I'm finished explaining the whole thing from beginning to end, with a couple extra rewinds thrown in for clarification, Violet closes her eyes for a moment.

"So tell me if I've got this. You were this girl's first kiss back when she was fourteen, or however old she was, and then you didn't see her until a decade later. But you don't remember meeting her again, because you were wasted and you almost hooked up with her friend, but you didn't. Then fast forward another year later and she ends up being your massage therapist, and you *still* had no idea who she was until recently, *and* she's agreed to go out with you?"

"Yeah. Pretty much."

"Wow. So that's either the most romantic thing ever, or the most twisted. Are you sure she's not some kind of weird stalker?"

"She didn't come looking for me; I just happened to find her."

"Then it's totally romantic; it's like fate keeps throwing you together! Except the part where you don't remember her being at your house and almost sleeping with her friend. That's not romantic at all."

"No. Not really."

"Can I ask you something?"

Based on the look on her face, I'm probably not going to want to answer.

"Does she know about your..." She makes a bunch of random gestures.

"My what?"

She flails some more. "About your sexual...habits?"

"Habits?"

"Jesus, Lance, I'm trying to diplomatic, and you know how hard that is for me. You were a Mathlete. You're not an idiot. Use your brain! Does she know about your reputation with the hockey hookers?"

"Doesn't everyone?"

"But does she believe them?"

"I don't know. You believed the rumors about Waters when you first started dating him."

"Yeah, but he perpetuated them all the time, so of course I believed them. It was only when they became an actual issue that he started defending himself. I know people blow things out of proportion, Lance, but in your case—"

She has a point, even though I don't want her to. "Not all of it is true, but that's not something I'm going to have to talk about."

"Not on the first date, no."

I run my hands over my thighs. "But you think I will eventually?"

She blows out a breath. "Forget I mentioned it for now. Let's focus on getting you through the first date and then we can go from there. Where are you taking her for dinner?"

"I was thinking about Spiaggia, downtown. I made reservations and asked for a private table."

"Ohhh, that's nice. You must really like her." She does that tappy thing with her fingernails. "Ever take Tash there?"

"No. We didn't go out on dates. We just fucked." I look down at the counter, unwilling to see her pity.

"Are you over her?"

"What?"

"Tash? Are you over her?"

I line up the oranges in the fruit basket so I don't have to look at Violet. "I'd be fine if she stopped calling."

She touches the back of my hand, and I pull it away, hiding it under the counter.

"Why do you want to go out with this Poppy girl if you're still hung up on Tash? Is that really fair to her?"

I run an anxious hand through my hair. "I like her, and she's different. Even when things were okay with Tash, I never felt settled, but Poppy—she's like…all this goodness wrapped up in one person. I want to have that." I look down at the counter. "I want to deserve to have that."

"Well, you deserve it. You just have to work for it since this girl isn't a hockey hooker and won't throw herself on your dick. My advice is to bring her flowers at the very least. And don't pick her up in your Hummer. That thing is big enough to have an orgy in."

"Good point." I can definitely do flowers again. "Should I take her out after dinner?"

"Take her out where?"

"I don't know. To a club?"

"No. Definitely not. You want to avoid reminders of how you completely forgot who she was and don't remember her ever being at your house. Stay as far away from that scenario as possible."

"What if she invites me to come inside after the date?"

"What about it?"

"Should I go in?"

"If she invites you, yes. If she doesn't, I don't suggest trying to invite yourself. That makes you look desperate. Unless you want to look desperate. Then go for it."

"Do I want to look desperate?" I don't think I do, but then I've done a lot of screwing up where Poppy is concerned, so it's possible I do want to. More than that, it's possible I look that way already whether I want to or not.

"Probably not? But you may want to keep in mind this advice is coming from me, so a second opinion might be helpful."

"Why would I need a second opinion?"

"Well…Alex kind of stalked me after the first time we slept together, and I didn't actually mind his stalkery-ness."

We both turn at the sound of a throat clearing. Alex is standing at the threshold of the room with questions all over his face. Waters and I are close to the same size, but he's a little broader.

He looks his wife over. "What kind of lies are you telling about me?"

"They're not lies. You wouldn't stop calling, and then you started sending my boobs gift certificates and presents. Then you showed up at my house uninvited, and my work, and you pestered me until I cracked."

Waters smirks. "That's just tenacity."

"It's also called stalking."

"Well, it worked, didn't it?" He moves her ponytail out of the way and kisses her shoulder.

"Yes. Yes it did." She looks to me. "But maybe you should talk to Lily about this, too, to be safe."

"Yeah. I don't know about that. You're the only person who knows about this for now."

"Knows about what?" Waters asks.

"Lance has a date."

Waters' eyes go wide. "Like a *date*, date? Or with someone you met off Tinder?"

"A real date, not a hook up. I mean, I'm not opposed to the hook-up part, but that's not the reason I'm going out with her."

"Wow. Uh…that's great?" He still hasn't lost that shocked look.

"Let's see if I can manage not to fuck it up."

Violet gives me a warm smile. "You'll do fine. Just remember the flowers and not to be stalkery."

"Got it all locked up here." I tap my temple as I push the stool away and stand. "I'm ready whenever you are," I tell Waters. "We're picking up Westinghouse on the way, aye?"

"Yup. I'll be back in a few hours. You still gonna be here, or do you need to go to the office?" Waters asks Violet.

"I'll be here."

He whispers something in her ear, and her cheeks turn pink. She murmurs something and pushes on his chest. "Good luck tonight, Lance."

"Thanks for the advice."

"Anytime. And if you want to know more about the ins and outs of stalking, ask this guy right here." She pats Alex's cheek.

I wonder what it's like to have that kind of connection with someone. I bet it's terrifying. But if it wasn't worth it, people wouldn't let it happen.

AFTER OUR WORKOUT and ice time, I drop Waters and Westinghouse off. I don't have to see the team massage therapist for a couple more days, thank fuck. Every single hour of torture makes me highly aware of what I've forfeited to get this date with Poppy. I hit the flower shop and follow that with a candy store. I stock up on all my favorite treats from the UK, searching for the things Poppy's said she likes.

Then I go home and whack off, followed by a shower and more whacking off. I adhere to all the first-date guidelines as set out by Waters, who gave me some of his own advice on the way to get Westinghouse. We didn't discuss it in front of Darren, and I was relieved since his relationship with Charlene is a little fucking weird from what I've witnessed. And that's saying something, coming from me.

I shave because I don't want any parts of Poppy to chafe as a result of too much stubble.

Once I'm dressed and ready to go, I pace around my house. I consider whacking off one more time, but twice should be enough, so I hit my garage to pick a car. I decide on the Audi; it's not too flashy, but it's nice. I'm going to arrive early, but I don't think I can wait any longer. It's been four days since I've seen Poppy, and I'm antsy.

Once I'm parked in front of her house, I take a few deep breaths before I get out of my car and walk up the front steps. The door is painted deep green. The mat on the front step says WELCOME. It's homey—not like my place.

I ring the doorbell and wait, listening to the sound of pattering feet coming down the hall. The only time I've been more nervous was my first official NHL game.

The last time I tried to do this kind of thing I was fifteen years old. I went out with this girl in high school before I really understood my extreme aversion to physical contact from the opposite sex—before I got how badly my mother had fucked me up, how she'd made it impossible for me to have anything resembling a normal relationship. There I was, trying to be normal when I wasn't.

The door swings open, and my dick starts crying. Maybe a third whacking session would've been a good idea based on where all the blood has redirected itself in my body. I don't plan to let the head below my belt govern my actions tonight, but Poppy is my goddamn wet dream.

She's wearing a silky emerald green dress. It's the perfect color for her hair and her peachy, pale skin. The straps are two inches wide, showing off a light dusting of freckles on her shoulders—the only sign she's been out in the sun recently. Her dress cinches at the waist and flares at the hip, stopping above her knee. It's classy, pretty, and sexy all at the same time.

Poppy is perfectly feminine, curvy and lush. She's exactly the opposite of Tash, who's all hard muscle. That could be a factor in why I'm so into Poppy too.

I want to get my hands on all of those curves. I want to get inside her and feel that softness against my body. I want her to look at me the way she did when her sister dragged her out of the closet all those years ago: like leaving me was the last thing she wanted to do.

She took more of me with her than she'll ever really understand. Maybe more than I'll ever understand. And even after all the shit I've pulled, all the ways I've fucked up, she's still willing to give me a shot. So handing control over to my dick isn't an option. But man, the last thing I want in this moment is to get back in my car and go sit in a restaurant to be civilized and have conversations that might mean talking about myself.

Poppy runs her palms over her hips self-consciously. "Lance?"

"Huh?"

She clasps her hands in front of her. Her grip is tight, like maybe she's trying not to fidget. "Do you want to come in?"

Yes. And then I want to get you naked and screw you on the closest surface. I stuff my hands in my pockets so I don't do something I shouldn't with them. "I can wait here if you want to grab your purse."

Her pretty pink tongue touches her plush, glossed lips. I wonder if they taste like strawberries, or maybe something sweeter, like vanilla.

A small furrow appears between her brows. "I thought dinner reservations weren't until seven thirty."

"They're not."

"It's not even seven. You could come in for a drink before we go."

"I thought you didn't drink."

"Not usually, but I have a bottle of wine someone gave me as a gift."

It will only take twenty minutes to get to the restaurant. There are a lot of things I could do between stepping through her doorway and the time we have to leave, a lot of ways I could fuck this up. "Sometimes it takes a while to get parking. We can have a drink at the bar if we're too early."

She drops her eyes, and her cheeks flush pink. "Oh. Okay, just give me a minute."

She leaves the door open, allowing me to watch her legs as she disappears up the stairs. Her bedroom is probably up there. I wonder if I'll ever get to see it. I fucking hope so.

I glance to the right, at the closet where I kissed her the last time I was here. I try not to think about how good she felt pressed up against me. How much I liked her hands on me. How much I want them on me again.

I back up and turn away, looking at the street instead. It seems to take forever before Poppy comes back down the stairs. She's wearing a thin, pale sweater thing that doesn't button, but covers her shoulders and arms. Her purse is a muted gold, as are her shoes. She locks her door and turns to me, her smile strained. I worry something I've done is the reason for that.

I slip my arm through hers and walk her down the stairs. Shit. The flowers and candy I bought for her are on the counter in my kitchen. I suck at this. I can drop them off at her work tomorrow and do better next time—if there is a next time.

"Wow. This is nice," Poppy says as I open the car door for her and help her in.

"Thanks. I figured it's a little classier than the Hummer, and maybe easier for you to get into." I wink.

If I'd driven the Hummer I would've had to pick her up to put her in it.

I close the door and round the hood, sliding into the driver's seat. I'm right about the trip not taking long. Poppy asks me questions, but I'm distracted, trying not to focus on how good she smells, or how much I want to put my hand on her bare thigh.

There's a line at the valet, so we have to wait while the cars filter through. I tap on the steering wheel, impatient.

"We don't have to do this," Poppy says quietly.

I stop staring at the taillights of the Porsche in front of me to look at her. "What?"

"I don't want you to feel obligated to take me out for dinner."

"Obligated?"

She looks down at her lap. "If you've changed your mind, or you're not interested anymore."

The car in front of me moves up. "Whoa. Hold up. Why would you think this is a pity date? Or that I'm not interested anymore."

She fidgets with the strap of her purse. Her hair is in her face, so I can't see her expression.

"Poppy?" I tuck her hair back, and she shies away. I drop my hand. I won't touch her if she doesn't want me to. "Why would you think this is a pity date?"

She lifts one shoulder. "Because of what I told you. You didn't want to come in for a drink, and now it seems like you can't wait to get out of this car. You've hardly said a thing since you picked me up. I'm not stupid, Lance. I don't want to sit through two hours of strained conversation because you feel some sense of duty to follow through."

Here I thought I was doing everything in my power to not fuck this up, and in doing so, I've managed to screw myself anyway.

A knock on my window prevents me from answering right away.

I roll down the window a few inches. "Hold on."

"If you exit the vehicle, sir—"

"Hold the fuck on." I grab the valet ticket from him and close the window, slamming my finger on the lock button, despite his protest. "Let's get something straight." I shift the car into park and unbuckle my seatbelt. "This isn't a pity date. The only reason I didn't want to come in for a drink is because I'm pretty low on restraint, and *this* is the only thing I can think about right the fuck now."

I slide my hand into her hair and angle her head to the side. I don't do what I want to—which is fuck her mouth with my tongue. Instead I stop half an inch away. "Tell me no if you don't want me to kiss you."

"I want you to kiss me."

I brush my lips over hers, soft, sweet, and then I suck her bottom lip between mine. She tastes like vanilla and perfection.

She grabs the sleeve of my jacket, so I figure I'm good to keep going for now. I slip my tongue into her mouth, all slow and easy. At least at first, but the second she starts responding and that hot, satin stroke meets mine, I kind of lose control. I lean in closer and rest my palm above her knee, squeezing so I keep it where it is and don't go on a search-and-rescue mission to discover what kind of panties she's wearing.

Aware my semi-good behavior isn't going to last very long, I start to move my hand away, but Poppy grabs it and squeezes. I want her to drag it higher, up under that pretty, silky dress, but we're sitting in front of the valet, so taking this further isn't an option. Instead, I flip her hand over and bring it up to rest against the side of my neck, groaning when her warmth meets my skin. She makes a matching, but much more delicate sound.

I ignore the honk behind us and the knocking on the window until Poppy pulls away.

Then I drop my hand and sit back in my seat. "Did that feel like pity to you?"

She brings her fingers to her lips. "No."

Valet guy knocks on my window again. Which is a good thing, because I'm about to reconsider this entire part of the night in favor of ordering in.

"Good. Let's go have dinner with my really blue fucking balls. "

DESSERT

POPPY

Lance has his arm threaded through mine as we navigate the uneven walkway to the restaurant. I'm not used to heels, so he's supporting me a lot more than he might realize.

The host shows us to our table. It's in a private, secluded area of the restaurant, right beside a fireplace, so I shed my shrug. Like last time, Lance pulls his chair closer so he's perpendicular to me rather than across the table.

When the waiter comes to take our drink order, I flounder, looking to him for guidance. I don't know why. I've never needed help ordering a drink before. Especially not on a date.

"Can I have sparkling water for now?" I ask Lance, not the waiter.

He picks up my hand and kisses my knuckles. "You can have whatever you want, precious."

"Would you like to look at the wine list?" the waiter asks.

"Um—" The question seems to be directed at me.

"Sure, you can just leave it with us." Lance takes it from him without even glancing in his direction. "You want anything other than water to start?"

I bite my lip and decide to order what I want without worrying about looking silly. "May I have a Shirley Temple, please?"

The smile that spreads across Lance's perfectly kissable lips is as breathtaking as it is sweet. "Make that two."

The waiter nods and disappears.

"Living on the edge, aye?" Lance bites my knuckle through a grin.

"Watch out. I'm a real wild one."

"Not even a little, eh?"

My answering smile is all mischief. "I've always been a good girl."

"Then what're ya doin' here with me?" The accent that's barely noticeable most of the time gets heavier, along with his gaze.

"I don't think you're nearly as bad as you make yourself out to be."

"I'm probably worse." He's still smiling, but for a second it goes dark. Then his expression grows serious. "You look so beautiful."

I tip my chin down. "Thank you."

He fingers the strap at my shoulder. "I love this dress."

Green is his favorite color. I already knew that when I pulled it out of the closet the night he asked me out. I smooth out the skirt, feeling self-conscious and overheated. The kiss he laid on me in his car lingers on my lips. I want him to do it again. Over and over.

There's something about him that draws me in. It's the same something that pulled me in when I was a girl.

I want to understand how he can be so sweet with me and so hard on the ice. And why his reputation is so incredibly deplorable. I want the rumors not to be true, even though I know they must be. At least some of them. But it doesn't make sense with how averse he is to touch.

I don't ask any of those questions, though, because I don't want to ruin the perfect bubble we're in right now.

"Would you like me to order wine?"

He keeps brushing his lips across my knuckles. My stomach is fluttering so much it's hard to focus on anything but the feeling. "I'd have a glass."

"To go with your Shirley Temple?"

"Are you making fun of me?"

He uncurls my fingers and drags the index one across his bottom lip. "I think it's precious, just like you."

That name sends a sweet shiver down my spine and raises goose bumps along my arms. "You're full of lines tonight."

"You think I'm feeding you lines?" I see his hurt even though he's still smiling.

I hate that I don't know whether to trust my gut with him. I want to. But I'm not sure what he wants out of this. "I don't know. Are you?"

He releases my hand, setting it on the table and propping his fist under his chin, as though he's contemplating my comment. "Why would you think I need to feed you lines?"

"I don't think you *need* to do anything. I think you're used to getting whatever, or maybe whoever, you want."

"But you're not whatever or whoever, Poppy. You get that, right?"

"I'm not?" I'm pushing now, but I want something from him. Some kind of reassurance that he's not going to play me like he does other women.

He takes my hand again and presses my palm against the

side of his neck. I feel the heavy thud of his pulse beneath my palm. "I want this. You."

"Why?" I still don't understand why me. What makes me so different from everyone else? What makes me special?

"This." His fingers caress the back of mine, still pressed against his cheek. "Feels nice." He opens his eyes slowly. The weight of them on me is almost suffocating. "It's never felt nice before."

"Why not?"

"Because it's never been you before."

"But it has been me before."

"You mean in the closet?"

"Mmm. Was it nice then?" I remember the sound he made when he kissed me, the way his arm tightened around me, the hard lines of his body as he pulled me closer and his tongue swept my mouth.

"It was. So I had to work really hard to forget it for a long time." Lance flips the wine list open.

I want to ask why he wanted to forget something I spent most of my teen years replaying over and over like some kind of dirty Disney love story, but he seems to be done talking about that.

"Do you like red or white?" he asks.

"I prefer white." Of all of the alcohol options out there, white wine is the one that doesn't give me an immediate hangover.

"And you're sure you'll have a glass if I order a bottle?"

"Yes."

"Because you want to or because you'll feel obligated?" He's reclaimed my hand and is kissing the tips of all my fingers now. The hairs on the back of my neck stand on end as his tongue touches the pad of my thumb.

"Both."

He smiles. "I like how honest you are. Why would you feel obligated?"

"Because this is a date, and that's what people usually do on dates."

"So you want to drink wine because it's conventional?"

"No."

"Then why?"

"Because I'm nervous."

Lance frowns. "Why?"

"Why?" I echo.

"Why are you nervous?"

"Because you're you."

Lance blinks a few times, releases my hand again, and leans back in his chair. The floor vibrates with the bounce of his knee. "And what exactly does that mean?"

"I didn't mean to offend you."

"I'm not offended. I'm curious."

The waiter chooses that moment to return with our Shirley Temples. He gestures to the open wine list. "Have you made a selection?"

Lance gives me a tight smile. "I think we're okay for right now."

At my murmur of agreement the waiter turns back to Lance.

"Would you like to start with appetizers?"

"We'll need a few more minutes, please." Lance's voice is as tight as his expression.

The waiter leaves us alone again. I don't like the sudden change of mood. Lance has gone dark.

"You're a professional hockey player; I'm just a massage therapist."

"You're not *just* anything," Lance replies.

"You know what I mean. People know who you are, even if they don't actually *know* you. No one knows who I am."

"I do."

"To a certain degree, yes, but we only give the part of ourselves we're comfortable with, right?" I motion between us.

"Being here means we must be willing to give a bit more, doesn't it?"

"And that makes you nervous?"

"Of course. You have an idea of who I am, an ideal even. I'm the girl who gave you her first kiss in a closet." I look down at my napkin. "I won't lie and say I haven't romanticized that memory, even if it's a silly, naïve thing to do."

Lance adjusts his silverware, his knee still going under the table. "So what's the part that makes you nervous? That I'm not gonna be the romanticized version you've built me up to be?"

I don't tell him I already know that part of him has been buried for a long time. Based on what happened in the closet after we went out for dessert earlier this week, I'm aware that the boy I knew is definitely still in there, even if he's been hiding. But there are years of time and experiences creating a barrier between us now.

"And that I'm not the same version of the girl you remember."

He nods, like maybe this makes sense.

"Sorry. This got heavy fast."

He runs his finger around the rim of his glass. "I don't mind. No girl ever gets real with me. It's kinda nice for a change."

I laugh. "I can't imagine how much lip service you get on a regular basis."

"A lot more than I want, actually. I don't like being played with by people."

It's a loaded statement. I can almost taste its bitterness.

The waiter returns to ask after our order. I decide on a glass of sauvignon blanc, and Lance requests a bottle instead, checking with me for the brand. I point to one in the middle of the row, but I won't know the difference between a high-end bottle and the cheap stuff from the local liquor store.

He also orders appetizers since we haven't even opened the menu. When the waiter leaves, I look it over. They have all of my favorite things with a classy twist. Everything sounds amazing, and I decide to go for the spaghetti Bolognese.

Once the waiter returns with the wine and takes our dinner order, Lance settles back in his chair, his knees brushing mine under the table.

"So, I gotta ask how a good girl ends up at a high school party at the age of twelve. I can't imagine your parents actually let you go."

"Absolutely not. My parents went out, and my sister was babysitting me. She didn't want to miss the party, so she took me with her."

"That wasn't very responsible."

"I could've stayed home by myself, but my sister isn't known for her responsible tendencies."

"Sounds like there's a story there."

"She was always a little wild. Fun, but she pushed the boundaries a lot. Sometimes I wanted to be more like her. The night we went to that party, I felt so cool." I shake my head at the memory. "She never really grew out of that rebellious phase. She's better than she used to be, but she still struggles with things like keeping a job for more than six months."

"Does she have a name?"

"Oh! Cinny."

"Like Cinnamon?"

"No, like Hyacinth. My parents were big into botany when we were born, so we're both named after flowers. Anyway, what about you? Why were you there that night?"

"Some girl in my class invited me, said it was gonna be a good time and there'd be booze, so I went."

"Ahh. Very responsible of you."

Lance laughs. "Not even a little."

"Cinny got in so much trouble." I take a sip of my wine. Lance has already half finished his glass.

"Your parents found out?"

"They did. She took the car without permission, and she

didn't even have a learners permit. She hit the side of the garage and dented the bumper when we came home. She accused me of ratting her out, but all the evidence was there. I don't know why we didn't take the train. Or walk! Plus our clothes smelled like cigarette smoke."

"Shit. I bet it was way worse because you're girls."

"Oh definitely. She was so mad at me, thinking I'd been the one to tell, so she told my parents I'd been making out with some high school boy in a closet."

Lance's mouth drops, but it's not shock; it's a devious look of satisfaction. "She told them about me?"

"Oh, yeah. She was actually pretty jealous that I ended up in a closet with you. It was kind of funny. Not at the time, obviously, but later, when we weren't in trouble anymore. Her telling on me backfired, though, because they blamed her for that too. I don't think she talked to me for at least a month."

"If anyone should've been giving the silent treatment, it's you. She let me steal your first kiss."

"And I'm still okay with that."

Lance grins. It's warm. "Me too, even if I shouldn't be."

"You were so sweet about it, even if you were drunk," I tease.

I slide my hand across the table. Lance watches the movement and flips his over, palm facing up. I stroke the length of his fingers.

"So what happened after that?" he asks. "Were you grounded?"

"We both were. I wasn't much for going out, so it wasn't a huge punishment for me. Mostly it meant my parents didn't go anywhere and nagged my sister all the time."

"So you really were a good girl?"

The way he says it sends a shiver down my spine. "I guess. I mean, I didn't go looking for trouble. I had a small group of close friends, and I wasn't really into parties."

"Did you like living away from Chicago after you moved?"

"It was hard to start over, but my dad had gotten a job offer in Galesburg. It was this small town, quaint and community oriented. They thought it might help tone my sister down."

"I'm guessing it didn't."

"Not really. She always seems to find trouble, no matter where she goes."

"What kind of trouble?"

It's my turn to shrug. Cinny has never had it easy. She's a restless soul. "She's reactive, and she doesn't consider the ramifications of her actions."

"Sounds a lot like me."

"I don't know if I'd agree with that. I mean, sure, you're reactive, but that's kind of your job, isn't it? I think you know what the ramifications are going to be before you take the action."

"So I premeditate my bad decisions?"

I raise an eyebrow. "Now you're putting words in my mouth. I wasn't just referring to the bad decisions; I was referring to all decisions."

"Ahh. I see."

I decide to switch gears since we seem to be getting serious again. "How hard was it to move from Scotland as a teenager? Leaving all your friends couldn't have been easy."

Lance spins his glass, watching the wine swish. "It wasn't that bad. Getting out of Scotland was…necessary. I had my cousins. I knew I'd get to play hockey, and there was a lot of talk about how I was destined to play professionally."

"Clearly they were right."

"That part wasn't so easy. I spent all my free time on the ice, trying to catch up to the kids who'd been skating since they were born. I had to work ten times as hard. A few times I got passed over for the minors. That sucked."

"But eventually you made it."

"I did. I spent three years on the farm team. A couple times they almost let me go, but then someone saw some potential, and I got picked up."

"I remember when you were drafted to Nashville."

"Yeah?" The corner of his mouth lifts.

"I remembered what you said about how I could tell people you'd been my first kiss."

"And did you?"

"No. It wasn't something I wanted to share."

Lance focuses on the table. "I guess not, after all the shit you've seen and heard about me, aye?"

"That's not why. It was *my* memory. I wanted to keep it to myself. And it's not like I believe everything I hear or see on social media, anyway."

Lance looks down at his empty glass of wine. "Some of it is true."

At my silence he glances up. He looks guarded.

"Is that a warning?"

"I don't want you coming into this thinking I'm some white knight with pure intentions."

My stomach twists. "What are your intentions?"

It's a long time before he finally whispers, "I don't know."

A lump forms in my throat and drops to my gut. I start to retract my hand, but Lance curls his fingers, catching mine. At my hard stare he sighs.

"There's a lot of stuff I'm probably going to have to explain along the way that isn't going to be easy to hear."

"I'm not a delicate flower," I snap.

"Sure you are, pretty Poppy." His face falls completely when I try to pull my hand away again. "I'm sorry. I'm overthinking everything, and I'm being a dick." He brings my hand up to his face and uncurls my rigid fingers, pressing them against his cheek again. His eyes flutter shut, and he follows with a shaky breath. When his eyes open, they're hot with want. "This feeling —what you do to me—I've never had it before, and I don't want to lose it. But I probably don't deserve it."

He's telling the truth. I can see it in his face.

"Why wouldn't you deserve it?"

"A lot of reasons. I was involved with a woman last year. She played a lot of head games. It didn't end well, and she still makes it difficult sometimes."

"To get into a relationship?"

"Yeah. Something like that. Shit. Why is this all heavy again? Look, I really like being around you, and I want to see where this goes between you and me. Just us."

"Okay. I'd like that, too."

Lance seems relieved. "Great. Good."

Appetizers arrive, so we dig in. In the time it's taken me to get through half a glass of wine, Lance has had two.

Part of the reason I'm not much of a drinker is because it hits me hard. The other part is because of the problems it's caused Cinny over the years. I have to assume Lance has a much better tolerance than I do since he outweighs me by about a hundred pounds.

Tonight I'm having a glass to help calm the butterflies in my stomach, but every time Lance reaches for my hand, fingers the strap of my dress, presses his knee up against mine, or pays me an idle compliment, they start fluttering around in there, making it hard to breathe.

Dinner is a long, slow event, and thankfully our conversation moves away from serious subjects and turns lighter. Lance gets a message from his friend Miller—the guy whose forehead I rubbed the penis drawing off of—and shows me a picture of his newborn baby.

"I got him that outfit," Lance says proudly.

The tiny baby's fist is wrapped around a massive finger, and he's trying to eat it. The onesie he's wearing says LADIES MAN. He's blond and blue eyed, just like his dad.

Lance flips to the next picture, which includes a blond woman I recognize.

"Hey! That's my yoga instructor!"

"Huh?"

I tap the screen over her face. "Sunshine teaches me yoga. Or she did until she stopped to have the baby."

"Oh, yeah. I guess Sunny's gonna have to take a break for a while, right?"

"I hope not too long. I miss her."

A text message alert pops up, and the contact I saw when Lance left his phone at the clinic appears: DO NOT FUCKING REPLY. Lance expels a curse and powers down his phone, shoving it in his pocket.

"Sorry about that. No more interruptions for the rest of the night."

I give him a small smile, but it's hard not to wonder who that person is. I'm pushing myself to ask when Lance continues speaking.

"Anyway, I don't know how long Sunny's planning to stay at home," he says. "I'm guessing until she gets bored or whatever. She doesn't have to work if she doesn't want to, but she's not much for sitting around."

"It must be hard for Miller to be away from them when you're out of town."

"Yeah. We've only had short runs so far but sometimes we're gone for more than a week at a time. I think it's making him antsy. I guess it's good he cares, right? Even if it might affect his game."

"Kids change priorities."

"If you're a good parent, I guess," Lance says, then changes the topic again.

Once we've finished our meal, Lance decides he still has room for dessert, even if I don't. He asks for an extra spoon, but it goes unused since he feeds me small bites of panna cotta instead. His eyes on are my mouth the entire time. I keep waiting for him to find an excuse to kiss me, but he doesn't. Not on the lips, anyway. But his mouth finds my shoulder on more than one occasion, as well as the back of my hand, my knuckles, and my fingertips.

He keeps a hand on my back as we wait for the car at the valet and rests his free one on my thigh on the ride back to my place. When he pulls up to my house, miraculously finding a parking spot, he looks as nervous as I suddenly feel again.

"I had a really good time tonight," I tell him.

He shifts the car into park and extends his arm along the back of my seat. "Me, too." He doesn't take his eyes off my mouth as he leans in and brushes his lips over mine.

"Do you want to come in?" I ask before he comes back for another kiss, possibly with tongue this time.

"I don't know if that's a good idea."

My heart sinks a little, and I drop my gaze to my lap, where my purse sits. "Oh."

"But I want to anyway." His fingers glide across my shoulder. "Even if I shouldn't."

"Why shouldn't you?"

"Because I'll want to do a lot more than just kiss you this time."

"That's okay."

"Is it?"

I bite my lip and nod. "I'll let you do a lot more than kiss me this time."

He fingers a lock of my hair. "You'll let me, or you want me to?"

"Both," I whisper.

Lance cuts the engine. "I like that answer a lot."

17

WHAT I WANT

LANCE

My palms are sweaty as I get out of the car and rush around the hood so I can open Poppy's door before she does. I want to be exactly like my parents expected me to be: refined and with manners.

But I'm not really like that. All of that fell away after my mum moved to Connecticut. I drifted even further when I was drafted to the farm team and got my own place. I shed all the pretension, the façade of civility, and fell down, down, down into a dark hole of excess.

I spent years burying all the hurt and hate and fear. I found ways to deal with the ingrained expectation of violence. I did things I'm not proud of, and right now I feel like I need to atone for every single sin so I can have this gorgeous woman and deserve her.

I'm not sure how to do that. I'm still going to take her, though. As far as she's willing to go.

I follow her up the steps to her door. A tremor in her hand makes me aware that she's nervous. She turns the key in the lock and opens the door. Her smile is full of trepidation as she steps aside to let me in.

I help her out of her sweater and sweep her hair over her shoulder. Leaning down, I kiss her pale skin, and she shivers.

"Don't be afraid. I won't take anything you don't want to give me."

She turns around, her eyes wide and innocent. "I know." She pushes my jacket over my shoulders, and I shrug out of it, letting her hang it up in the closet I kissed her in last time.

I don't want to hide in the dark with her any more. I want to see exactly what she looks like when I take off that pretty green dress.

She laces our fingers together and tugs, so I follow her down the hall. Instead of heading for the living room, she goes for the stairs.

"You don't want to have a drink or something?" I ask.

"I don't think that's necessary, do you?"

Well, this is unexpected. "Not if you don't."

The calves in her muscles work as she climbs the stairs. She doesn't swing her hips, or hike up her skirt to give me a glimpse at what's under there like a bunny would. She doesn't act coy or demure. She just links our pinkies together and leads me to the second floor.

She opens the door, but doesn't flick on the light. It's unnecessary since a small lamp illuminates the room from a nightstand beside her bed, which I don't think is even a queen.

The room is small. The walls are pale, almost white, and the comforter is minty green.

"This is my bedroom," she announces, then blushes.

I take her face in my hands and lean down to kiss her. "What do you want to do now?"

"I want to touch you," she says against my lips. "And I want you to touch me."

Poppy is nothing like the women I usually end up in bed with. She's not brazen. She's not looking to break conventions. She's the opposite, and I want to be exactly what she needs, except I'm not sure how.

I keep my hands where they are, holding her face so I don't take things too fast. Beyond wanting to be what she needs, I also want this to last in case she regrets it and it's the only time I get this close to her.

Poppy's hands rest on my waist, and one moves up to curve around the back of my neck. I tilt her head to the side, and she opens her mouth for me, giving me the access I want. *Need.* Her tongue meets mine, stroke for slow, hot stroke.

I'm so fucking anxious. I'm worried this isn't going to be like when I'm on her table—that when she touches me it's not going to be the same, that I'm going to hate it like I do with everyone else.

When she moves her hand from my neck down to my chest, I tense and cover it with mine.

She tries to disengage from the kiss, but I slide my tongue against hers. After another minute, during which my hard-on kicks against her stomach, I let go of her hand. She slows the kiss and pulls back until she can see me.

"You can tell me if it's not okay."

I huff out an embarrassed laugh. "I should be saying that to you, not the other way around."

Poppy links our pinkies again and tugs me toward the bed. "Come make out with me."

I feel exactly like I did when I was a teenager and it was my first time. But there are some major differences. My first time wasn't special. I didn't actually care about the girl. She was some random hook up at a hockey party—which was intentional. I knew by then that female contact wasn't welcome the way it should've been, and I didn't enjoy it the way the other guys on the team seemed to.

I just wanted to know what the big deal was. And after that I learned sex was going to be about making someone else feel good, because it didn't work that way for me.

As much as I want this, being with just Poppy means there are no distractions. I'm terrified of being the sole point of her focus. But I'm so tired of the emptiness. I'm tired of the endless ache, and I'm willing her to be the one who can fix that for me.

Poppy climbs up on the bed and moves over to make room for me. She pats the mattress, looking at me expectantly. I don't even bother to take off my shirt before I join her. I adjust the pillows and lean back against the headboard. If she were a bunny, she'd already be naked and ready to straddle me. If she were Tash, there'd be someone else involved.

Facing me, Poppy slides in close, kneeling beside me until her hip is against my knee. She doesn't unbutton my shirt. She doesn't put her hand on my thigh, or stroke my hard-on through my pants—all of which might actually be welcome at the moment.

Instead she skims the contour of my jaw with the back of her hand and traces my features with her fingertips. "How does this feel?

I close my eyes for a second. "Nice. Good."

Her fingers travel the same slow pattern on my skin until they're replaced with her lips. "And this? Does this feel nice?"

"It feels better than nice."

"Better than nice sounds good." Her lips move from my temple to the corner of my mouth. I turn my head and slide my fingers into her hair so she can't take her mouth away.

I'm the one who rearranges her body so she's straddling my lap. Her dress rides up high on her thighs. I run my hand along the bare, pale expanse of her legs, but I don't go any farther than the hem.

I just kiss her. I've never really gotten used to doing that. It's too intimate, and it invites too much in the way of hand-to-skin contact, because that's when they're liable to wander. But with Poppy, I don't mind. She makes these sweet, soft sounds and arches her back, pressing her breasts against my chest. In doing this, she also presses up against my hard-on. I groan into her mouth—it's a loud, pained sound. I've been hard since I picked her up.

Her hands, which I realize have been smoothing up and down my arms, freeze.

"That's not a bad sound," I reassure her, squeezing her thighs.

She leans back, but returns to press a kiss on my lips as she runs her fingers through my hair, her short nails dragging down the sides of my neck. Poppy traces the collar of my shirt and plays with the top button.

"How would you feel about me taking this off now?"

"I'd feel okay about that." I run a finger under the strap of her dress. "Can I take this off now, too?"

She smiles. "Would it be better if I go first?"

"Maybe, aye?" I haven't let anyone else undress me, ever. Not even Tash.

Poppy doesn't look away as she lifts one arm and pulls the hidden zipper on the side of her dress down.

I sit up straighter and kiss along her shoulder as I move the strap aside, revealing an emerald green bra, nearly the same color as her dress. I mutter a low curse and bite her shoulder when my cock kicks.

Poppy sucks in a breath.

"Sorry."

"Don't be."

I slide my hands under the hem, over her hips and stomach, and pull the dress up. Emerald green lace panties make an appearance, followed by the matching bra.

I lift the fabric over her head and groan. If I allowed myself to have a type, Poppy would be it. She's curvy, her lush breasts straining against the delicate lace cups.

"Fuckin'ell." I drag gentle fingertips over the swell of her breasts and drop my face into her cleavage. She smells like lavender and something sweet. I want to put my mouth on every inch of her. And my hands. Any part of her I can touch with any part of my body is what I want. Need. Crave.

Eventually I stop nuzzling her breasts and lift my head. "You're fucking perfect, Poppy."

Her cheeks are hot pink. "I'm not really."

"Perfect. Every inch."

"I could probably stand to go to the gym more."

"Fuck the gym. I'll be your workout. As many days of the week as you want. I'll be the best workout you've ever had."

She laughs and goes for the first button on my shirt. She's slow about the process, her fingertips grazing bare skin each time until she pulls my shirt from the waistband of my pants and parts the two sides.

She hums. "Your body is incredible, but I guess you already know that."

"It serves its purpose."

"Which is what, exactly?"

"It got me a great career and here, in your bed, with you."

"Your body didn't get you into this bed." Poppy plays with the tails of my shirt.

"No?"

She shakes her head.

"Then what did?"

Her expression is gentle. "Your sweetness."

I laugh. "I hate to break it to you, precious, but I'm pretty fucking far from sweet."

"I disagree. You've been nothing but sweet with me." She grins and then grows serious. "I want to touch you."

"Then that's what you should do."

She keeps her eyes on mine as she pushes the shirt over my

shoulders and down my arms. She removes one sleeve, then the other, and when I'm shirtless, she skims my chest with feather-light fingers.

I'm tense, but when her contact isn't followed by the sensation of ants crawling over my skin, I relax.

"Do you like that?" she asks. "Does it feel nice?"

"It feels fucking amazing."

Poppy licks her lips. "Do you think you might like it if I put my mouth on you?"

She's not offering to blow me—at least I don't think she is. She's just offering me a different kind of touch.

I've had a lot of women say a lot of dirty things to me. I've had a lot of fucked-up sex over the years, but this obliterates every single experience. For the first time ever, I'm not trying to find creative ways to keep her hands off me. I'm not looking for an escape. I'm not wasted and trying to feel something other than pain, or allow the pain to take me over.

"Where you thinkin' about putting your mouth?"

"Well." Poppy bites the end of her finger then touches it to my lips. "I'd like to start here and maybe work my way down. Does that sound acceptable?"

"That sounds way better than acceptable."

"I think so, too."

Poppy kisses me again. Her lips are tentative and warm. She moves along the side of my neck to my shoulder. She drops down so her ass is resting on my thighs, giving her access to my chest. Those pretty green eyes lock on mine as her tongue flicks out against my nipple.

"Ah, fuck." I want to shove my hands in her hair and guide her mouth lower. But I keep them on her thighs instead, because I can't rush this.

"Would you like to lie down?" Poppy asks.

"Sure. Yeah."

I hold on to her waist and ease down the bed so my head is resting on the pillows. Poppy's lace-covered pussy is now right on top of my erection. Based on the way her eyes go wide and dart to mine, she feels it when it jerks.

I don't let go of her hips; instead I rock her over me a few times. She makes this quiet, needy noise I want to hear a fuckton more of. Poppy reaches behind her and unclasps her bra. She holds the cups as the straps slide down her arms, keeping herself covered as she slips her arms through.

I'm still rocking her over me when she drops the bra on my stomach. She's still holding her breasts, though, being all modest. Or maybe a little playful, since so far it's been pretty fucking intense, and we're not even fully undressed.

"Maybe we should take your pants off," she suggests. "Since I'm more naked than you are now."

"Aye, maybe we should."

"That would make it a bit more fair, wouldn't it?"

"It would," I agree.

And that's when she drops her hands and goes for my belt. It's an orchestrated distraction. The freckles on her shoulders trickle down to the top of her breasts. Poppy's creamy white skin contrasts perfectly with the rosy pink of her nipples. Which I want to kiss and lick and suck, but she's busy right now, popping the button on my dress pants. The zipper goes down, and Poppy shifts so she's sitting beside me. I lift my hips so she can pull them down. I'm commando, so there's no hiding my erection as it springs free.

Poppy gives a low whistle. "You're really not compensating at all." She pulls my pants down the rest of the way, along with my socks.

"I have condoms in my wallet. It's in the back pocket."

"That's good, because I don't think the ones I have will be very comfortable." She sets my wallet on my chest.

"Probably not." I flip it open and pull one out, dropping it on the bed before I toss my wallet on the nightstand. She eyes the foil wrapper and tucks her thumbs into the waistband of her panties.

I sit up. "I wanna help with that."

Poppy drops her hands by her side. I don't go straight for her panties. Instead I cup her breasts and kiss each pert nipple, following with a lick and an indulgent suck.

Her hands go into my hair, and she whispers, "Oh, God." I stay there for a little while, appreciating the quiet, non-bunny sounds that come out of her. She doesn't shriek or squeal or scream. It makes me acutely aware of how much I don't want that any more and never really did. It was just another escape.

I pull her panties over her hips, but I have to stop with the nipple sucking and breast fondling in order to get them the rest of the way off. I've never wanted my hands in more places at once like I do right now.

I rise up on my knees in front of her. It forces her to tilt her head up. "Poppy." It's mostly a groan.

She runs her hands over my chest. "Lance." It comes out breathless.

I squeeze her hip and shift my hand, fingers drifting low. I slip one between her legs, hot and wet greeting me. "I wanna kiss you right here."

Her mouth drops open, brow furrowing, her grip on my shoulders tightening.

"Will you let me do that?" I find her clit and circle it. "Kiss you here?"

"Yes."

"Do you want me to kiss you here?" I ask, because letting and wanting are not the same. I let Tash do a lot of things I didn't want any part of. I don't ever want to do anything like that to Poppy.

"Yes." She skims my bottom lip with her fingertip. "I want to know what your mouth feels like."

"You know what I want?" I lay her down, fanning her hair out.

She shakes her head.

I straddle her, because if I get between her legs now, there's no way I'll be able to follow through on what I want. Or what she said she wants.

I kiss her before I answer. "I want to know what you sound like when you come." Then I swallow her moan as I take her mouth.

We kiss while I caress her breasts and down her sides. Then I start a languorous descent over her body, stopping at her nipples, at the dip in her waist, and to nibble at her hip before I edge a knee between hers.

Poppy parts her thighs, and I get comfortable, stretching out so my legs are hanging off the end of the bed. I spread her open and drop a wet kiss on that pretty little clit.

Poppy drags in a breath. I move my lips to the inside of her thigh and nip there before going back to her clit, again and again. I lick her until she comes, and my name is a hoarse cry on her lips. And then I do it again, because she tastes like she's made for me, and I'm already addicted to the sound of her when I give her exactly what she needs.

Which I want to be me.

She's glassy eyed and flush cheeked by the time I'm done. I hover over her and slide two fingers inside, pumping slow.

Her eyes roll up, and when they come back down, she raises a shaky hand and presses it to my cheek. "I want you."

"Right now?"

She bites her lip and nods, then searches the comforter for the condom. When she finds it, she puts a hand on my chest. "Can I put it on?"

At this point, she hasn't had her hand on my cock. I'm not sure how I'm going to handle that. I'm not worried about having her touch me; I'm worried about how quickly I'm going to come when she does. But I don't want to say no to her.

"Is that what you want?" I ask.

"Only if you want me to." She gives me my words back.

"I want." I sit back on my knees, and she follows. But she doesn't tear the wrapper open as her long hair sweeps over my thighs. She wraps her fingers around my cock, holding it steady. Then she looks up at me and bends forward to kiss the tip.

"Poppy." It's a guttural sound.

She follows with a lick. "Does that feel good?"

"Yeah, really good."

"I want to do that again, if you want me to."

"You really don't ha—"

"But do you want me to?" I can feel her hot breath as it breaks across the head. My cock jerks in her hand.

"Put my dick in your mouth?" I don't mean for it to sound so crass, and judging from the way her cheeks flush even pinker, she's not used to hearing it.

"Yes. Do you want my mouth on you?"

"Fuck, Poppy. Yes."

She opens her pretty, perfect mouth and covers the head. Her tongue swirls around and around before she pops off.

"How does that feel?"

I move her hair away from her face. "If you keep doing that, I'm going to come before I can get inside you."

"One more time, then?"

How the fuck can I say no to that? I close my eyes and give her a tight nod.

This time she licks around the entire head with an open mouth before she covers it, taking more of me in. Then she starts bobbing, going deeper with each pass. I'll definitely come if she keeps going, and while I'm positive I can get hard again, I don't want to miss this opportunity, or lose this moment.

"Precious…" I cup her cheek, my thumb following the curve of her bottom lip where it's wrapped around my cock. She looks up at me with wide, sweet eyes. Jesus fucking Christ, how did I manage to get into this girl's bed? "I need you to stop."

She makes a little noise, like maybe she doesn't want to, but she lets me ease her off. I pull her up and kiss her, probably harder than I should. She moans into my mouth when my tongue finds hers.

I need a minute to calm the fuck down before I get inside her, but Poppy seems to have other ideas. She tears the condom open.

"Just hold on, 'kay?" I cover her hand with mine.

"Is everything all right?" Worry makes her voice low.

"Yeah, yeah." I stroke her cheek. "I'm a little too jacked right now, and I don't want this to be over before it even gets started."

"Oh." She grins.

"Are you smirking at me?"

"Do you want me to smirk at you?" she asks, all sassy sweet.

"I'll tell you what I want." I lay her down, shifting her until her head rests on the pillows, her red hair spread across the pale green.

"What's that?" she asks, reaching up for me with the hand that isn't holding the condom.

"I wanna know what it feels like to be inside you."

"Then you should find out."

I straddle her hips so she can put the condom on, which I've never let anyone else do. Her fingers are gentle and warm as she grips me, and it feels so fucking good. Everything about her is perfect. She rolls the condom down my shaft, her eyes lifting to mine when I'm sheathed. I have to fight not to rush this; I want to be in her so badly.

I shift so I'm between her parted thighs. Lowering myself, I slide one hand under her shoulder so I can cradle the back of her head, and I use the other one to guide me.

And then it's so much more than just hot and wet. It's more than chasing down an orgasm. It's like I'm being enveloped in everything good, and I don't want it to stop. I keep my eyes on hers as I sink into her body.

Her mouth drops open, and my name comes out a whisper.

"You feeling that?" I ask.

She whispers a nearly silent yes, and her fingertips drift down my cheek and over my lips. I see her fear. I feel it echoing

222

around in my chest. But I smile. And after a moment, she smiles too.

I get it now, that this is the way it's supposed to be. This feeling is what I've been missing. I slip my finger under the back of her knee and pull her leg up, wrapping it around my waist.

If I could find a way to be any more inside her, I would.

I kiss her as I move until we can't keep the rhythm any more. I hold myself above her, our eyes locked. The only sounds are her soft pleas for me not to stop, and the whispered affirmation that I make her feel so good.

When I make her come, it's exactly how I thought it would be —like my world will end if I can't have her like this again. For the first time in my entire life, I understand what it means to be with someone who will give and not just take.

AFTERGLOW

POPPY

I half expect Lance to leave when the sex is over.

I don't know why. Beyond his intensity, which is high, he's been incredibly attentive—in bed and out of it. Maybe I'm expecting it because this kind of sex entails a lot of connection for someone who seems to have a significant aversion to it.

I'm wrapped up in him, both of my hands caught in one of his against his chest. I assume it's his way of keeping me close without giving me free rein to touch him. His other hand glides up and down my arm. We're still on top of the covers, never having made it under them for the sex part.

My bed is a double. Lance takes up a good two-thirds of the space, and his feet hang off the end. I've considered upgrading to a queen, but it hasn't been much of a priority as I've been sleeping alone for the better part of a year. It's not that I haven't dated. It's that I haven't found anyone I'm particularly interested in. Until now, of course.

But I have no idea what's going to happen with Lance beyond tonight. His wanting to "see where it goes" could've been a ploy to end up here. Although it seems an elaborate ploy, if that's the case.

"Do you have to be up early tomorrow?" he asks.

"No. I don't have appointments until the afternoon, and tomorrow is a light day."

There's a long pause before he asks uncertainly, "Can I stay?"

I lift my head so I can see if his expression matches his tone. "Here?"

His eyes shift away. "Or I can go. Whatever." He releases my hands and pushes up on one elbow.

"I don't want you to go."

He regards me skeptically. "So you want me to stay, or you'll let me stay?"

I flatten a palm on his chest. "Both." I go for light, because his mood seems to have darkened again. "I'd be a special kind of stupid to kick you out of my bed."

He snorts a laugh.

I kiss his chin. "I'm warning you, though, I'm a bed hog, so don't be surprised if you end up with six inches of mattress."

"I think I'll be able to manage." He settles back against the pillows. "So, um, are you tired now, or..." he trails off.

"Or?" I'm not sure what he's getting at. Maybe he wants to watch TV or talk some more, although my brain is practically fried from the orgasms. So many orgasms. More than I've ever had at one time—or in a twenty-four-hour period, actually.

His hand settles on my hip. "We could have sex again."

I blink a few times, trying to determine whether he's serious. He looks serious. And hungry in a not-for-food way. "Right now?"

"Or later. You know, if it's too soon." He moves his hand up a few inches to my waist, bringing his erection into view.

He's already half-hard again. "Oh wow." I drag a fingertip along the length of him.

His hand covers mine. "So an important thing you might want to know is that hockey players have pretty high stamina."

"I see that." I wrap my fingers around him and squeeze.

Lance's mouth drops open, and his eyes roll up. "You gotta tell me when you're tired, or you need a break, 'cause I can do this all night with you."

"All night?"

Lance hooks his palm behind my knee and pulls it up as he readjusts my position so I'm suddenly on top of him. He shifts around under me until I feel his erection right up against me, smooth and hard and almost entirely ready.

"All night," he confirms.

"What about sleeping?" I brace my hands on his chest. His muscles flex under my fingers, and that hot look in his eyes turns to fire when I roll my hips.

"We can take naps in between."

I ROLL over and notice there is no warm, solid body preventing me from hogging the bed. I crack a lid and run my hand over the empty space beside me. The sheets are cool to the touch. My stomach sinks and my heart jumps into my throat at the thought that Lance has disappeared in the middle of the night.

Except then I hear the sound of cupboard doors opening and closing downstairs. I shove my face into his pillow and grin. It smells like his cologne. My entire bed smells like Lance. And sex. So much sex. I stretch out and groan at the aches already starting to make themselves known. Not that I mind.

Lance is an incredible, doting lover. Even if Kristi was lying, she was right about one thing: he's certainly a giver.

I feel around on the floor for something to throw on so I can go see what he's up to. I find his dress shirt and push my arms through the sleeves, fastening a few buttons in the dark. The shirt is huge on me, the sleeves ending six inches past the tips of my fingers until I roll them up, and the bottom reaches almost to my knees.

I pad down the stairs in the semi-dark. The light over the oven is on, illuminating a bare-chested Lance, who is rooting through my cabinets, mumbling to himself.

I watch him for a little while, appreciating the defined muscles in his arms, the broad expanse of his back, the ripple of his abs and the deep V leading my eye down... Holy crap. He's naked. He turns a little, giving me an amazing view of his perfectly toned ass. God, his ass is unreal. Like every other part of him.

"Giving the neighbors a free show?" I ask.

Lance fumbles with whatever he's holding, and several items fall out of the cupboard, hitting his chest before they drop to the counter and then to the floor.

"Hey. Shit. I didn't mean to wake you up." He turns in my direction, and the bag of chips he's holding hits the floor. "Are you wearing my shirt?"

I glance down, suddenly a little self-conscious. It's buttoned cockeyed, one side hanging lower than the other. Half of my right breast is popping out.

I adjust it to cover myself. "It was the only thing I could find without turning on a light."

"You should throw out all your clothes and start wearing my shirts." He makes a C with both hands and holds them up in front of his face.

"What're you doing?"

"Making a mental picture for when I'm whacking off later."

I duck my head and laugh. God, he makes me feel sexy.

"You're going to give my neighbor a heart attack with this." I gesture to his lack of clothing.

Lance looks down and runs a palm over his chest and down his abs. He's half-hard right now and growing fast. "That old guy who flirts with you?"

"He doesn't flirt with me."

"Yeah, right. Anyway, he's probably sound asleep, dreaming of your face and wishing he could still get a hard-on." He pats his own, all proud and cocky about it. "Why you all the way over there?"

I round the breakfast bar. As soon as I'm close enough, Lance grabs the front of my shirt—his shirt—and pulls me up against him. Dipping his head he kisses my neck, then runs his nose along the exposed skin of my shoulder.

"Your hair's all fucked up," he murmurs. "It's sexy."

"So is yours. It's sexy, too."

He gives me a sleepy grin.

"What are you rooting through my cupboards for?"

"I was looking for a snack."

"What kind of snack?"

"Something sweet. Like gummy bears or something."

"Hmm... I'm more of a savory snack girl. Let me see what I can find."

I give Lance a little nudge so I can get to the cupboards. He doesn't give me much room. I feel his erection bump my hip as I reach up and do some rearranging. It's dark, though, so it's hard to see.

I rummage around until I find a few bags that feel like they could be gummies and grab them. There's a small bag of jelly beans, some Swedish Berries, and a bag of Jujubes. I hold out the Jujubes. "Here you go!"

Lance frowns. "Those aren't gummy bears."

I look at the package. "They're almost the same thing."

He pokes the bag and gives it a dirty look. "Not even remotely."

"They're both chewy and full of sugar—what more do you need."

"The texture isn't even close to the same."

I hold out the bag of Swedish Berries. "Well, what about these."

"They're okay, but still not the same."

"Are you always this picky with candy? When you get Skittles do you sort them by color?"

"They're all equal opportunity Skittles."

"I don't know if I believe you." I give him another nudge with my elbow so I can access the cupboard again. "Let me check one more time." I stretch up on my toes and feel around.

"Want some help?" Lance's hands settle on my hips.

At first I assume his version of help is going to include pressing his hard-on against my butt, but that's not what happens. He lifts me up until I can get my knees on the counter. I grab the shelf to steady myself—also, Lance's hands skim the outside of my thighs.

Now I can see inside the cupboard. There's a lot of junk food in there I didn't realize I had. I don't really eat sugary treats, but I keep them handy because my sister and April both like sweets.

"See anything good in there?" Lance asks as he tears open the bag of Swedish Berries.

"Maybe." I grab what could be a bag of gummy worms, or something similar.

All of a sudden I feel a draft. I look over my shoulder to see what's going on as Lance says, "I see something I wouldn't mind taking a bite out of."

I shriek at the sharp sting, followed by the wet stroke of Lance's tongue. "Oh my God! You bit my butt!"

"It's pretty damn biteable."

"Does it taste like gummy bears?"

Lance puts his hands on my hips before I can climb down from the counter. He turns me around so I'm sitting on the cold Formica.

He parts my knees so he can make room for himself.

I hold up the bag of gummy worms. "Tada!"

He grabs it from me, tears it open with his teeth, and dumps half the contents into his mouth. He hums as he chews. "These are kinda stale."

"The Jujubes are probably fresher."

He shakes his head and continues to chew. It takes him a long time before he finally swallows. The entire time he's running his hand up and down the outside of my thigh. His erection rests against my stomach, covered only by his shirt.

"I like this," he says.

"You like what? Eating stale gummy worms?"

"Me in your kitchen, you looking all sweet and sexy in my shirt. Us." Under the smirk lurks that vulnerability I saw earlier, the first time we had sex.

"I think you're missing the part where you're naked in my kitchen."

"If you're worried about that you can always give me my shirt back."

"But then *I'll* be naked."

"I don't see the problem with that." Lance skims along the buttons. "This is all wrong. Were you half-asleep when you put it on?"

He's got that grin going again. God, he's too sexy for his own good.

"Ha ha."

"I can fix it for you." He unfastens the first button and the second, approaching my navel. He parts the sides so my nipples appear and the fabric frames my breasts. "This is so much better."

I laugh and then moan when he cups them, thumbs teasing the tight peaks. I check the windows behind him, darkness the only thing on the other side.

Lance looks over his shoulder. "Everyone in your neighborhood but us is doing what they're supposed to at three in the morning: sleeping. It's just you and me and my stale gummy worms and your subpar candy selection." He covers my nipples with the shirt, though, and drags a single finger along the center of my chest, up my throat and under my chin. Then he touches his lips to mine. He pulls away before I can react. "I like that you're a little shy, though. I'm not used to that."

With the number of girls who throw themselves at him, I could see where my not tearing my clothes off the second he looked at me is unusual. Which is kind of sad. My stomach twists at the thought of all of the women he's been with. I wonder if any of them meant anything, or if they were all just sex. I hope again that I'm not some kind of conquest for him, something to play with and discard. My heart might not be able to take that, because it already feels too involved with this man.

He must read something in my expression, because he skims my cheek with light fingers. "I mean it when I say this is different."

"Different how?"

He picks up my hand, bringing my knuckles to his lips. "You're all the good things I didn't know I was missing." He presses my palm against his cheek. "And like I told you, I don't let anyone put their hands on me. Not ever."

I don't really understand how that works—how you can have sex with someone and not let them touch you. "Why not?"

"I don't usually like how it feels."

It's a vague answer. And though I wait for a moment, he doesn't seem inclined to elaborate.

"But I like how this feels a lot." He moves my hand down his chest, but stops there, rather than guiding me to touch him where I'm sure it would feel the best.

"That's good, because I really like the way you feel." I trail my fingertips lower, and his abs contract when I pass his navel. I skim the shaft, then wrap my hand around him, squeezing lightly before I give him a slow stroke.

"Fuck." His eyes close as his mouth drops. When he opens

them again, they're heavy. He cups my face and sucks my bottom lip between his teeth as I continue to stroke him.

"I want in you again." His tongue sweeps my mouth. He tastes like artificial strawberries and lime.

When I moan my agreement, he pulls back.

"Here is okay?"

My gaze flickers to the darkness on the other side of the window. "Yes."

"Want or let?" he asks.

It's my new favorite question. "Both." I've never been much for adventurous sex, usually sticking to beds and sometimes a couch, but I've never been wanted like this before.

Lance drops his hands to the still-fastened buttons on my/his shirt, popping them open. He pushes the sides apart again, revealing my nipples. Light fingers circle them before he bends to kiss and suck. Straightening, he follows the contour of my waist and grips my hips, pulling me closer to the edge of the counter.

He covers my hand stroking his erection with his own. The deep, almost pained groan that leaves him when he tightens his grip makes heat flare low in my belly. His eyes drop from my face to where we're holding him. He shifts his hips forward.

I suck in a gasp that comes out a moan when he rubs the head of his erection over my clit.

"Does that feel good?" he asks.

"Yes," I whisper-sigh.

He hums. "It feels fucking amazing for me."

He keeps rubbing the head over my clit in slow, easy circles, occasionally sliding down so the head probes low and then moving back up. I squirm and edge forward a little more, wanting what he keeps saying he can't wait for.

"Fuck," he rasps. "All the condoms are upstairs."

For a split second I consider going without, but it's a bad idea. I don't even know what this is between us yet. "I guess we should move this upstairs then."

Lance grunts his agreement. Peeling our hands off his erec-tion, he drapes my arms over his shoulders. "Hold on."

He lifts me off the counter. I shriek and wrap my arms and legs around him. I can feel him, hard against me. He slides one arm under my butt and nabs the gummies, then carries me out of the kitchen and back up the stairs, to my bed.

ADDICT

LANCE

Addictions run in my family. My mom is addicted to alcohol and violence, at least when she stops taking her medication. My dad is addicted to work and avoidance.

I have a variety of vices I try to keep from becoming addictions. It's not easy because I don't moderate well. I go from zero to a hundred in the blink of an eye, and bringing me back down or reeling me in is nearly impossible. It's the worst when I'm drinking.

My new obsession—possibly addiction—is the feel of Poppy. So I'm lying here with her sprawled over my chest—because I've rearranged her every time she's moved away from me and put her back where she belongs—staring at the clock, wondering how long it's going to be before she wakes up. And whether or not I can reasonably ask for more sex.

It's nine thirty. I have no idea when her alarm is supposed to go off, or what time her first appointment is. She just said afternoon. Anxiety twists my stomach when I consider the possibility that this isn't going to happen again with her, that this night is an isolated event, like most of my sexual exploits. Unlike most of my sexual exploits, this time I want it to keep happening. I want desperately to keep her in this bed. I want her hands on me. I want to be inside her. This is a familiar kind of want—but usually I associate it with things that are bad for me.

Poppy doesn't feel bad for me. She feels good. Which is why I'm almost positive I'm not going to get to hang on to any of this.

I wrap my arm around her and pull her closer. I don't know why I can handle her touching me when I've never been able to handle anyone before. It's like she connects to some part of me I didn't know was there. Her lips are parted, her breathing slow and even. Freckles dot the bridge of her nose. Her hair is damp and curling where her face is pressed against my skin. Poppy's hair is so screwed—a total tangled mess.

I'm so addicted to her, and I've only been inside her a handful of times. I close my eyes and try to go back to sleep, but my head is full of worry.

An hour later, her alarm goes off. She pushes her face into the side of my neck. Normally I'd cringe away from that kind of closeness, but I can't get enough of it with Poppy. She mumbles something, but I don't catch it.

"What was that?"

"No morning." She crawls over my chest, slapping at the buttons on her alarm.

"I could've helped you with that."

She says something else into the pillow. She's draped across my body, her perfect, round yoga ass right there, asking to be squeezed.

She wiggles like she's trying to move and groans.

"Everything okay?" I push her hair back from her face and she turns her head, one eye blinking at me.

"So sore." She struggles to climb back over my body, so I help put her back where she was. "Muscles hurt that I never knew existed.

"I guess that means no morning sex?" I'm kind of joking, but mostly not.

Her eyes go wide. "Wasn't that what happened at three in the morning?"

"That was middle of the night sex."

Poppy eyes the tent in the sheets. She lifts the covers to have a peek. "Wow. You're serious."

"I told you I could go all night."

"I thought that was a bit of an exaggeration meant to feed my ego. Clearly not."

I kiss her forehead and gather her hand in mine so she drops the covers. "Don't worry. That'll disappear eventually."

She bites her lip and looks up at me. "I have a really great place for it to disappear into."

It takes me a second to get that she's being funny. "I thought you were sore."

"Orgasms are a great analgesic."

"Is that right?"

"Mmm-hmm."

I roll over and fit myself between her legs, but she puts her hand over my mouth.

"I refuse to kiss you before you brush your teeth."

"What about a mint?"

"As long as you have one for each of us."

I roll off and root around in my pants pocket for the pack of mints. I pop one in her mouth and one into mine. While I suck on it, I kiss her neck, rolling my hips and nestling my cock in the warm and wet between her legs.

I'm out of my condoms, so we have to use the regular ones. It feels like I'm cutting off the circulation to my dick, but I'll take it if it means I get to hear and see Poppy come for me again.

Afterward we shower, washing away sex and sweat. Poppy dresses in yoga pants and a T-shirt, then makes coffee while she sets out cereal and milk. She eats one bowl, and I eat the rest of the box.

When she takes our empty bowls to the sink to rinse them, I get panicky over my time with her coming to an end. We don't have another date set up yet, and this week is going to be busy. I'll be away starting Wednesday for a couple days. I don't want to wait until I get back to see her again.

"Can I drive you to work? How many clients do you have? Maybe I can pick you up after if you're not busy tonight?"

Poppy closes the dishwasher and looks at me. "Um, I'm supposed to have dinner with April tonight."

"Right. Okay." I tap on the counter.

"We'll probably be done by seven, though."

"Yeah?" The anxious feeling that's tensing my shoulders eases a bit.

"I could text when we're done, and if you still want to see me—"

"I'll still want to see you."

She gives me a shy smile. "Okay."

I end up driving her into work because she can catch a ride with April on the way home. I kiss her in the parking lot until she tells me she's going to be late.

I'm running late for skate practice now too, but nothing seems to matter at the moment. I have a good thing going, and her name is Poppy. I get to see her again. Tonight. I speed back to my house to get my gear, and then book it to the rink.

I finally check my phone as I'm walking into the arena, having turned it off when Tash messaged during dinner last night. My good mood deflates when I see twenty new messages and two voicemails from her. I also have messages from Randy and Miller.

I don't check any of them before I hit the locker room to change because I don't want what's left of my post-Poppy high to disappear.

"What the fuck, Romance?" Randy asks when I enter.

"Huh?" I drop my bag beside him.

"Thanks for letting us know you weren't coming to get us." Miller slams his locker shut.

"Oh, shit." I totally forgot I was supposed to pick them up for practice. I scramble for a reason because neither of them knows what I was up to last night, or this morning. "I shut off my phone last night 'cause Tash wouldn't stop messaging me, and I just turned it back on. I totally forgot."

Miller scoffs and gives Randy a look. "Tash? What kind of fucking bullshit are you pulling, Romance?" He jams his helmet on and clomps off, red faced.

"Jesus. What's his problem?" Things have been less tense since Sunny had the baby, but now he's pissy with me again. I rush to put on my equipment so I'm not late hitting the ice.

"Have you checked social media today?" Randy laces up his skates.

"No. Why? What's going on?"

"What do you think? You went out with that Poppy girl and didn't think it was going to be all over the bunny sites?"

"Oh, shit." Now the onslaught of Tash messages makes sense.

I think about the middle of the night kitchen encounter: me naked, Poppy in just my shirt. Me contemplating how good it would feel to be inside without the condom, assuring her everyone was asleep in her neighborhood. "Is it bad? Like, are there bad pictures?"

"Depends on what you consider bad, I guess."

"Does any of it make Poppy look slutty?"

Randy strokes his beard and regards me curiously. "No. Not really. I mean, there's lots of you all up on her."

"Up on her how?"

"Like normal date stuff, I guess."

When I give him a blank look, he sighs and looks uncomfortable.

"Getting all touchy, kissing her, that kind of thing."

Oh, thank God. Nothing from the kitchen. "So? I don't get what the problem is." The locker room is emptying fast, and Randy and I are getting looks.

Waters pops his head in. "Let's go, guys. You needed to be on the ice two minutes ago."

"Be right there." I hurry to tie my laces.

Randy stands and grabs his helmet and stick. "When was the last time you took a girl out for dinner?"

I grab my helmet, stick, and gloves. My skates are loose, but we're out of time. I don't think taking a girl to The Olive Garden when I was a teenager counts. And that was only once.

"I don't know. Never? The last time I took anyone anywhere it was Tash, and that was Waters' engagement party and the whole team was there, so it wasn't like an actual date-date or anything. Plus things got kind of fucked up."

"Ya think? You lost your shit on her because you thought we hooked up."

"Well, she fucks everybody, so it was highly plausible."

"Pot, kettle, dude."

"You think I like being like this?" I snap.

Randy's eyes go wide as he opens the door to the ice.

"I just wanted to be with her. I kept telling her that, but all she wanted to do was screw with my head. She was the one who kept bringing me girls like they were fucking gifts."

"Wait. What?"

"It wasn't my idea; it was hers."

Randy looks floored by this information. "Seriously?"

"Unfortunately, yeah. They were her way of saying I wasn't enough, I guess."

"Why didn't you say anything before now?"

"What was I gonna say? That I hate the shit I did for her, but I didn't know how to make it any other way?"

"But the Tash situation wasn't isolated."

"Until her it wasn't common, though."

He frowns. "What do you mean it wasn't common? You're legendary."

"Things get blown out of proportion a lot. You know that."

He considers that a moment. "So what's the deal with Poppy then? Why the dinner date all of a sudden?"

We step out onto the ice together, nab a puck, and start skating, passing it back and forth.

"Because she's different—and not the way I thought Tash was different—like, really different. Good different. I want to spend time with her, real time." I sound like a fucking idiot.

Randy fumbles the puck a bit, but recovers and slides it to me. "Like an actual relationship?"

"Yeah, man. Like what you and Lily have. I think I want that. I got Poppy to agree to two dates, and I don't want to fuck this up. And not just because she can't be my massage therapist anymore. I for real want this girl. Like, I *need* to keep her. That sounds wrong, but this morning when I realized I didn't have anything set up with her, I got, like, panicky. So I made another date for tonight."

"Wow. Okay. You're seriously serious."

"Aye. So this bunny shit, I can't have it messing with things."

"But you can see why the bunnies are gossiping, right?"

"Because I took some girl out for dinner?"

"It's a big deal in the bunnysphere. You're a fucking legend, Romero, even if you don't want to be."

I overshoot the puck, but he's fast enough to catch it before it gets away from him.

Not once did I consider how the bunnydom would react to me taking a girl out for dinner. I also didn't consider the possibility that people might take pictures and post them. But I should've, because I've seen all this bullshit before. Back when

Miller was first dating Sunny, back when Randy was still pretending he and Lily were just "having fun."

"Remember all the nasty messages Lily got when she moved in with me, and we'd been together for, like, months? The bunnies are fucking crazy half the time, Lance. They're gonna be all over this."

"Is it bad like that already?" I ask.

"You gotta go check your page. That's where all the shit is going to be. It's the comments, man. You know how the bunnies are. Does Poppy know what it's going to be like? Especially with your reputation?"

"Fuck." I run a hand through my hair. Violet was right. I'm going to have to deal with this a lot sooner than I hoped. "*Fuck.* What am I gonna do?"

"Maybe there's nothing to worry about. I mean, maybe she's not big on social media stuff."

"She's got all the accounts."

He quirks a brow. "You been stalking her?"

"A little bit."

Randy barks out a laugh. But before he can razz me too much, Coach blows the whistle.

I'm distracted during practice. I still manage not to screw up too much, even though my head is anywhere but on the ice.

After practice, I get pulled aside by Smart who likes to ride my ass and check in about the fucking massages, which he still makes me get on a pretty regular basis. His talk today is about making sure I'm taking care of myself, but since I haven't punched anyone out recently, he doesn't have a reason to lecture me for long.

I rush through the shower, wrap a towel around my waist, grab my phone, and head for the sauna. I want to see what the hell is going on in the social media world so I can run interference.

I hit my page first and stop outside the door to the sauna to scroll through the new pictures circulating. Thankfully most of them are from the restaurant. I should've known better than to take her to a high-profile place like that. She looks sexy as hell, though, so that's good. And not in a slutty way. Poppy is classy and classically beautiful.

There are a bunch of pictures of me with my arm around her, and my lips close to her ear. Randy's right—I'm all over this girl. And the bunnies are not happy about it.

Then I see a picture reposted from a year ago. It's the night Miller, Randy, and I went out to the bar and took a limo home with three girls. One of them is Poppy, although she's in profile. I'm not touching her, though; my hand is on the waist of a blonde chick—the friend I never slept with.

Speculation is flying now. Bunnies are saying I've been keeping Poppy a secret all this time. It's a clusterfuck. I'll be lucky if she's still willing to go out with me again after this. If I were her, I'd say fuck it.

I decide to skip the sauna. Instead I get dressed, say a quick goodbye to the guys in the locker room, and get in my car—which I'm still driving over the Hummer. I stop at my house, since it's halfway between the gym and Poppy's work. I still have the flowers and candy I forgot to bring with me last night. I don't really have a plan. I want to make sure I'll still get to see Poppy tonight and that I haven't fucked this up.

It's after four when I get to the clinic. I put on my best smile when I see Bernadette at the receptionist desk. Her eyes light up.

"Oh! Hi!" She takes in the flowers and box of candy in my hand. "Is Poppy expecting you? I didn't think she had any more clients booked today."

I've had to cancel all my appointments with her, but maybe the receptionist lady doesn't know yet. "She doesn't. She isn't. Is she busy?"

"Her last client left a few minutes ago. I think she's still in her room."

"Great, thanks." I head down the hall. The door's ajar. I'm about to knock, but it's open a crack, so I can see inside. Low music is playing, some upbeat dance stuff. Poppy shimmies around the room, humming away. Her hair is pulled up in a ponytail. I want her to wear it like that the next time we have sex.

Which I hope might be tonight. Depending on how this goes.

I slip into the room, closing the door behind me with a quiet click. Poppy jumps and turns, gasping when she sees me.

"Lance." She brings her hand to her lips, and then it flutters around. "What are you doing here?" Her eyes move to the flowers.

"I uh—" I hold out the flowers and candy. "I wanted to give you these. I forgot them at home yesterday and—yeah, so here."

"Um. Thanks?" It comes out a question, most likely because I'm acting like a fucking weirdo. I wonder if this is the kind of thing Violet was talking about with Waters when they first started dating.

"Have you been online much today?" I blurt.

"Uh, no. I haven't had time. Why?"

Of course she hasn't had time. She's been working. I have no idea what I should say to her, other than don't look at any of my feeds for the next couple of days, which is like telling an addict not to take the hit of heroin sitting in front of him.

"Lance? Is something wrong?"

Shit. I'm just standing here, staring. "Some, uh, pictures showed up on social media today."

Her hand flutters to her throat, her delicate throat that I want to kiss and nuzzle and touch again. "What kind of pictures?"

"Of you and me."

"Oh my God." She sets the flowers on the massage table and drops down on the stool. Her fingers go to her lips. "Oh, God."

She's way more upset about this than I expected. "They're from the restaurant. It's gonna happen if you go out with me again. So, like, if it's a huge problem we could order in next time, or whatever." I just want to erase the panicked look on her face. Why didn't I plan the date better?

Her brow furrows, and she drops her hand. Her lips are turned down, but her frown looks more like a pout. "Wait. So we're not naked?"

"What?"

"The pictures? We're fully dressed?"

"Aye. Oh, fuck, you thought I meant naked ones?" I bite my bottom lip to keep from smiling at her sudden relief. It's not working, though.

Poppy points a finger. "Don't you dare laugh at me!"

"'At's a dirty mind ya got there, pretty little Poppy." It comes out heavily accented, which happens sometimes, like my roots can't stay buried.

She throws her hands up. "You come barging in here with flowers and candy looking all cagey; what the heck was I supposed to think?"

My grin breaks free as I round the table and crowd her into a corner. "Did ya think I took naked selfies with ya?"

"No. I thought some creeper was watching us when we were in the kitchen, but now I have to wonder."

"I told ya we were alone." I move in closer until she's almost backed into the wall. She's stopped moving away now. "And I would nae take pictures of ya without yer permission." I take her hands in mine when she raises them like she's warding me off. Unfurling them, I press her rigid palms against the sides of my neck.

Her touch is like crack. It's only been a few hours, and I'm already jonesing hard. "I'm sorry I freaked you out."

"Liar. You're still smiling."

"I'm not lying. I was worried you wouldn't want to go out with me again."

"Do I look like a troll or something in the pictures?"

"You look gorgeous, too beautiful to be hanging around with someone like me."

Poppy scoffs. "If you're fishing for compliments, it's not working."

"I'm not fishing. I'm being honest."

She makes another little noise of disbelief, but her eyes keep darting to my lips.

"I want to kiss you right now, even though you're kind of pissed at me. Maybe even because you're pissed at me." I lean in and wait to see whether she's going to tell me off. She's got a little fire under all that precious. It's the redhead in her.

"I might bite you."

"I might like it."

That gets a smile out of her. "Go ahead then."

"Want or let?" I whisper when my lips are almost touching hers.

"Want, of course."

I touch my lips to hers, the hint of a kiss. "So you're not upset about the pictures?"

"I'd have to be an idiot not to expect them. You're like a celebrity."

"I don't want that kind of thing interfering with me and you. I want to keep you to myself."

"Is that so?"

"Mmm. All mine." This time I take her mouth, and she parts her lips. It escalates quickly. I don't remember turning her around and lifting her onto the table. Or wrapping her legs around my waist, but that's where we end up.

The rattle of the door freezes us in place.

"Hey, Poppy? You in here? Why's the door locked?"

"That's April," Poppy whispers. Then she nips at my lip and does a little hip roll.

"Want me to tell her to fuck off?"

She shakes her head like she's throwing off a daze.

"You'll never believe what's on Insta!" More door rattling.

"I need to let her in." Poppy pushes on my chest.

I step back and shove my hand down the front of my pants to rearrange my now-hard dick so it's not so obvious. Poppy bites one of her knuckles and hums. She rushes around to open the door.

April bursts in and slams it behind her. "Check this out!" She holds her phone an inch away from Poppy's face.

It's then that she realizes I'm here. The phone suddenly disappears behind her back. "Oh. Oh, hey, Lance Romero. Number twenty-one for Chicago. Dating my friend Poppy here."

I wave. "Hey."

"I'll wait for you—" She thumbs over her shoulder, her eyes darting between us. "—out there." She bangs into the jamb.

"You don't have to leave. I'm about to head out since you girls have dinner plans, yeah?"

April looks from Poppy to me and then back again, doing some weird thing with her eyebrows.

Poppy's cheeks are pink. "We do."

"Before I go, can I check out whatever you were gonna show Poppy, massage therapist and girl I kissed in a closet when she was twelve, but said she was fourteen. And whose ponytail I love to pull." I tug on the end.

April has this glazed look on her face. She blinks a few times and looks to Poppy as if seeking permission.

"I guess it's okay?" Poppy looks uncertain, but April pulls her phone out from behind her back, punches a few buttons and holds it out for me to see.

I've seen a few variations on this picture today. Poppy's incredibly photogenic, and whoever took the pictures is good with a camera. I'm adjusting the strap of her dress and kissing her shoulder.

Her head is bowed. The freckles dotting her nose and sprinkling her cheeks make her look soft and innocent. Her lashes almost touch her cheek, and her bottom lip is caught between her teeth. It's the perfect combination of sexy and sweet.

"It's a great picture, isn't it?" I ask April.

"It is."

"I might need to make it my screensaver."

"You should totally do that." April nods vigorously.

"Am I allowed to see this, or is it just between the two of you?" Poppy asks.

"I guess you can see it." I smile at her slightly annoyed expression.

I take April's phone and move in behind Poppy, almost mirroring the pose in the picture. "See how pretty you are?" I whisper in her ear.

April makes an odd noise. When Poppy and I look at her, she turns it into a cough and looks at the ceiling.

"At least I don't look trollish."

"You're perfect."

Her smile is as addicting as her touch, but we're not alone, and we won't be for a while, so I back it up and pass April her phone, turning back to Poppy. "So I can still come over later?"

"Sure. If you want to."

"Around seven thirty is okay?"

She glances at April. "That should be good."

"Can I stay again?"

"I actually need to sleep tonight."

"Okaaayyy. So I'm going to wait out there for you." April slips out the door, but leaves it ajar this time.

"I'll *let* you sleep, even if I don't *want* to," I say.

"I'm not sure I believe you."

"I promise."

"We'll see how good you are at keeping promises."

"So that's a yes?"

"Yes. It's a yes."

I tuck a loose tendril of hair behind her ear so I can touch her. "Can I steal one more of those sweet kisses before I go?"

"Just one?"

"Maybe two." I tug on the end of her ponytail and steal three before I finally leave.

20

FALLING IN

POPPY

"I need details. Lots of them. All of them." April takes a hefty swig of her margarita.

"You're not getting all the details."

"Oh my God, he looked like he wanted to *eat* you. And you're seeing him *again* tonight? Sweet lord, I can't even…" She fans her face. "Did you sleep with him? You slept with him, right?"

"Can you keep your voice down?" I look around the pub. It's busy, and no one is paying attention, but I checked out the pictures of me and Lance on the ride over here, so now I'm paranoid.

There are a lot of them, with plenty of kissing and touching. Luckily everything is tasteful, but it's far more attention than

I've ever had, apart from the few images that circulated last year when I ended up back at his place. Those pictures didn't focus on me, though, and they weren't very clear, so I never worried about them.

These are much different. I am the central focus of every image. And I am very clearly Lance's primary focus. It's as flattering as it is unnerving.

"Sorry, sorry. So did you?" April leans in close.

I try to hide behind my Shirley Temple. "Yes."

"Oh my God! I knew it!" She slaps the table.

I grimace, along with all the other people she's scared the crap out of.

She makes one of her faces and lowers her voice. "How was he? Is he, you know, well equipped?"

"He was really sweet, and yes."

"Come on, Poppy, you have to give me more than that."

"What do you want me to say?" I'm not really one to talk about my sex life, although I've also never been with someone whose dinner date ends up being fodder for social media gossip.

"I don't know, based on that conversation back at the clinic, you didn't get a whole lot of sleep last night. Does that mean he kept you up aaaaall niiiiiggght long?" She sings it while making thrusting motions and wags her brows.

"I didn't get a lot of sleep, no."

"You're blushing so hard right now. It must've been amazing. I bet he can fuck like a god."

"Can we change the subject please?"

She purses her lips, clearly annoyed that I won't share more. "So he's coming over again tonight? What's that about?"

I fiddle with my straw. "He wants to see me again."

"I got that. So are you dating? Are you, like, his girlfriend?"

"I don't know. I guess we're seeing each other? There's no label on it. He wants to see where this goes."

"So he's not going to see other people?"

"We haven't talked about that."

249

"Doesn't he have an away series coming up? Are you going to talk about it before he goes?" April looks concerned.

"If it comes up, I guess."

I don't like this turn in the conversation. I can totally understand why April is asking, though. I've always been a relationship kind of girl. I never did the hook-up thing, even in college. When I date someone, it's only ever that one person.

Lance seems to be the exact opposite. As much as I'd like to believe he's not going to be sleeping with other women while he's away, I won't know unless I ask. And I'm not sure exactly how to do that, because if the answer isn't one I like it's going to hurt.

It's the middle of the week, and I should probably already be in bed, but Lance is currently stretched out on my couch—one leg on the floor, one propped up on the back of the seat—so I'm inclined to stay up. He's wearing boxers, and only boxers. The position highlights the outline of his somewhat-hard penis. We've already had sex once. After I gave him a massage.

Well, I made it about halfway through the massage before he decided there were particular parts of his body that required my attention.

He was pretty excited when I offered my services in exchange for orgasms. I haven't actually made it through a full-body massage since we struck that deal a few days ago, but he's also far less tense, so he won't have to see the team therapist as much, and that's a positive.

In the ten days since he took me out for dinner, Lance has become sort of a fixture in my house. He's spent nearly every night here. In my bed. He missed two nights while he was off on the away series, but when he's had games here in Chicago, he shows up afterward. I've had a lot of orgasms and not a lot of sleep.

Tomorrow he's leaving again for another away series. We still haven't had a relationship-defining talk, which made those nights he was away somewhat stressful. But he messaged every day he was gone, and no party photos showed up on social media, so that helped a little. I need to address it before he leaves tomorrow though, because I don't think I can handle that level of anxiety again, especially not for five days rather than just two.

As much as I'm not excited about the separation, my girl parts could use a few days off from all the attention. I've never been with someone who has such a high sex drive. Being wanted this much is as thrilling as it is overwhelming.

I approach the couch with my hands behind my back. "I have a surprise."

"Oh yeah?" Lance tears his eyes away from the TV. He's watching hockey, which is normal. I've also discovered he's a huge fan of Sudoku. When the commercials come on, if he's not looking to make out, he'll have me help him with them. Not that he needs the help. He's far more math minded than I am. But I secretly find it sexy. Or not so secretly.

I hold up a bag of Jelly Babies. They're a British treat my grandmother used to send me every Christmas. I recently found a store close by that sells them, and I know Lance loves them almost as much as he loves gummy bears. And sex.

He grabs for the bottom of my shirt—which is really his shirt —but I jump out of reach. "You have to share."

"What if I don't want to share?"

"Then I guess you don't get any."

He considers this for a few seconds. "Fine, I'll share. Now come here." He pats his chest, and I climb up on the couch and stretch out on top of him. His half-hard-on twitches against my stomach.

I expect him to steal the bag from me, but he doesn't. Instead he folds one arm behind his head, thick bicep flexing. He traces the contour of my face with the fingers of his free hand and tugs the end of my ponytail while I tear the bag open. I pop a jelly in my mouth before I offer one to him. He bites it out of my fingers and *mmmmmmm*s his candy enjoyment.

"I have nae had these in years." The hint of Scot creeps in.

"They were always my favorite. My nana used to send me a package every year at Christmas and my birthday. What's your favorite flavor?"

"The black currant ones."

I dig around in the bag, searching for one. If I let him have the bag, he'll snarf them all down, like he does with gummy bears.

I find one and hold it up. He takes it carefully in his teeth and watches me while he chews.

Things have been intense. We haven't gone out at all. It's just been Lance showing up at my house after work and staying the night. On the plus side, I haven't had to cook since Lance always brings takeout. He also likes to bring me flowers, and sometimes treats. There are bouquets strategically placed all over the main floor.

We talk, we have sex, we watch a lot of hockey on TV, but I haven't been invited to his games. Not that I'd expect an invitation to the away games, but maybe a home one would be nice. He hasn't asked to take me out on another date, either. Technically he owes me a coffee.

"What's your favorite flavor?" He tries to stick his hand in the bag, but I clutch it in my fist. "You know I can take that from you if I really want to."

I give him a look. "I like the orange ones."

"Of course you do."

The next time I try to feed him one, he grabs the bag.

"Hey!"

He holds it over his head, far enough away that I have to sit up. He winds an arm around my waist and flips us over so he's on top. "You'll never win, precious."

He proceeds to dump a hefty portion of the bag into his mouth, as predicted. Then he digs for an orange one. He doesn't offer it to me directly, though. Instead he finishes chewing his massive mouthful and puts the orange one between his lips.

I try to take it with my fingers, but he pulls back and shakes his head. "Take it wif yer teef."

I roll my eyes but lean up as he leans down. Before I can take it, he flips it into his mouth, then sticks his tongue out. "Geb it now," he urges.

"Ew! No. It's covered in your spit."

He removes it from his tongue. "That spit thing again? I have my tongue in your mouth all the time and you don't seem to mind at all."

"Your tongue in my mouth is different than eating candy you've slobbered all over."

"Suit yourself, but that was the last orange one." He chomps down on it, groaning his fake pleasure.

"What? Come on! I didn't even get one!" I try to get the bag back from him, but he won't let me have it.

He pulls out a black currant one and presses it against my lips. I suck the whole thing in and chew furiously, putting my hand over my mouth when he makes a move. Lance tries to pry my hand away, but I swallow before he overpowers me. Then his mouth is on mine. His tongue strokes, aggressive and searching, and when he comes up empty, he pulls back and frowns.

"You ate it."

"You put it in my mouth. Isn't that what I was supposed to do?"

"You were supposed to share."

He pops another one into his mouth and chews thoughtfully, then sits back on his heels between my legs. He's fully hard now, the head pushing against the elastic waist of his boxers. He digs through the bag and produces another orange one, eyes lit up with mischief.

"Want it?"

"Not if you expect me to share it, no."

"What if I hide it?"

"Your mouth is not a hiding spot," I shoot back.

He grins and pushes down the waistband of his boxers so the head of his erection peeks out. He places the candy on the tip.

"You know, if you want a blow job, you can just ask for one."

"I'm not asking for a blow job. Just a kiss for a candy."

Minutes later I'm naked and under Lance on the couch again.

Afterward I lie on his chest again, half asleep, and his phone starts buzzing on the table. The arm around me tightens as we look at the glowing screen. DO NOT FUCKING REPLY has messaged him once while he's been with me since our dinner date. And just like at dinner, he shuts off his phone.

Mum comes up this time, but that doesn't ease his tension at all.

"Do you want to get that?" I ask.

"Nope."

"Are you sure? I don't mind."

"I don't want to talk to her. We don't get along that well."

"Oh." He said his mother wasn't a good person before, but I never pushed. I've always gotten along well with my parents, even during my teen years when hormones made rational thought difficult. I think no matter how much attitude I copped, it didn't come close to what my sister dished out, so I was still the angel.

Lance watches the phone until it stops ringing.

"Can I ask why you don't get along?" Conversations about his family have been relatively limited, and his reaction to that phone call makes me question even more all the things he hides.

Lance regards me for a long while before he finally replies. "She has a mean streak."

I cock my head to the side. "What kind of mean streak?"

He fingers a lock of my hair. "Before we moved to the States, she and my dad used to get into it a lot. Well—" Derision darkens his features. "My mum used to get into it with my dad.

She'd get all pissed off and go at him, just fucking lose her shit. He used to laugh. I mean, she was a little thing. Not much taller than you, but she would just blow her lid. He never hit her back, though. Not once. Not that I saw, anyway."

My stomach dips, thinking about how that would look to the child version of the man in front of me.

"But she wasn't always like that. She had pills she'd take sometimes, and then she was a lot better, not so angry all the time—nicer but just kind of vacant. It was hard. I don't know why my dad put up with it, or let her go off the meds or whatever, but he did. She had a lot of issues. Bad childhood and all that shit. Anyway, eventually she turned that mean streak on me."

I put my fingers to my mouth. "She hit you?"

His eyes are sad. "It wasn't like she could really hurt me, you know? Not after I got a little older. The words are the things that stick, though."

When I put my hand on his chest, he picks it up and plays with my fingers.

"I had a younger brother. His name was Quinn."

I frown at the past tense.

"He was eight when he died."

"Oh my God. I'm so sorry."

He shakes his head, eyes still on my fingers. "I think it broke her mind. She kind of snapped and was never the same. That's when she really started to go at me, after Quinn died."

I want to ask what happened, but I don't dare interrupt him.

"We came to the States to get away from the memories for her. Or at least that's what my dad made it seem like we were doing. I think he'd had enough. He left us here, but she didn't want to go back to the UK. My playing hockey was a good enough reason for her to stay in Chicago."

He's silent for a while, maybe lost in a memory.

"I thought it might stop when we moved in with my aunt, and it did for a little while, but she'd get so pissed when I fucked

255

up at practice. After a while it was expected. It didn't matter how hard I tried, something would set her off."

My heart aches for him. "Did you tell anyone?"

"What was I gonna say? My mum beats the shit out of me? It was my fault—" He chokes on the words.

"What was your fault?"

He shakes his head taps his temple. "She messed with my head all the time, my mum did. That night I met you for the first time, I wasn't supposed to be at that party. I'd snuck out of the house through my bedroom window, like teenagers do. Or like I did, anyway. There was some big tryout the next morning for the top league in the city—on my birthday, right? My mum kept telling me she knew I was going to fail, and then we'd have to go back to Scotland. She said I better not dare do that to her.

"I figured what was the point? I was going to screw it up anyway, like I did everything else, so I went out, got drunk, and ended up in that closet with you." He smiles a little and brushes my fingertips over his lips.

"When I got home, my mum was waiting for me in the garage. She was so pissed. And she was wasted, or high—or both maybe. Like, so fucked up. That was the night my aunt found out what was going on. She walked into the garage right when my mom was in the middle of her smackdown. She had boxing gloves on so she didn't mess up her nails. Usually she'd keep to areas that weren't visible, but not that night."

He pauses, lost within himself for a moment. "Things got real messy after that for a while. And I shut out every single memory I could. All the good ones, all the bad ones. Everything. I buried it all."

"I'm so sorry."

"It is what it is. I can't change it now, so I try not to think about it too much. But stuff like that, it doesn't ever really go away. Even when you try to put it in a box, it finds a way out." He releases a long, slow breath, his expression pained as he touches my face with shaky fingertips. "I probably shouldn't have told you any of that."

I cover his hand with mine and turn my face into his palm to kiss it. "I'm glad you felt safe enough to share that with me."

"I'm fucked up, Poppy."

"We all have demons. It makes us human, not fucked up."

"I tried to have a girlfriend my sophomore year of high school. It didn't go so well."

"Why not?"

"I discovered how much I don't like being touched."

His aversion makes more sense now. "I touch you."

"It's different with you. I don't know if it's 'cause of our history or what, but this…closeness, how I am with you, this isn't how it usually is."

"And how is it usually?" My stomach knots. The things I want to hide from are too close.

Lance closes his eyes, and his jaw clenches. When he looks back at me, he seems as scared as I feel right now. "I don't really wanna answer that question."

"Why not?"

"'Cause then you'll know exactly how fucked up I am."

I reach up and touch his cheek. He gathers both of my hands in his and clasps them together, bowing his head and pressing his lips to my exposed knuckles, almost like a prayer. "I don't deserve this. You. I don't deserve this kind of goodness. I shouldn't be here, taking all these things from you when they shouldn't be mine."

"Lance."

He looks up at me through narrowed eyes, and his fear vibrates through him.

"You're not taking. I'm giving. Our pasts are part of who we are. They may shape us, but they don't govern our future paths if we don't want them to."

"What we're doing here is different than what I know."

"Do you want it to be different than it is?"

"No, I want this, but the last time I tried it backfired really bad."

We're talking in a circle, skirting the parts of this that could hurt us both. "Because of something you did?"

"Yeah. No. Sort of."

"I don't understand."

"Remember how I told you about that girl I was seeing last year and how it didn't end well?"

I nod.

"It was a complicated situation. I wanted something she didn't."

"Which was what?"

"For it just to be us. Her and me. But she wasn't interested in that."

"What did she want?"

"To mess with my head."

"I won't play head games. I'm not like that."

"You don't strike me as the type." His smile is almost shy. "I won't do that to you, either. That's definitely not what I want."

"What do you want?" There's a lot riding on this. I'm already past the point of no return where my heart is concerned, so I have to protect myself as best I can.

"Just you."

It seems to be a common phrase with him. I have to get clarity. "What does that mean exactly?"

Panic flares behind his eyes, and I can see he's struggling with words. In this moment I realize how much damage has been done to him. Prolonged, sustained physical and emotional abuse has a lasting impact.

So much finally makes sense now as I filter back to the first time he was on my table—and further back, to the night at the bar, where he was edgy and stressed over the way people kept bumping into him, and to the kiss in the closet when he wrapped my arms around his neck and told me to keep them there. That that was the real him.

I have the real him right here with me now, too. I have a broken boy who's become a broken man, and as stupid and naïve as it may be, I want to be part of what heals him.

"I want this. You and me. Us." He skims my side with his hand, then wraps an arm around my waist.

God. Of all the relationship conversations I've had, this one has to be the most difficult. "So you want be exclusive?"

He swallows hard. "I don't want there to be anyone else."

"So when you're away, you don't want me to see other people?" I won't take anything for granted.

His eyes flash with something dark. "Are you seeing anyone else right now?"

"No. And I don't plan to. That's not how I work."

He swallows thickly. "Okay. That's good."

"But what about you?" At his questioning gaze I press. "What about the girls who hang out after the games?"

"The bunnies?" Lance asks, looking almost horrified.

"Yes. The bunnies."

"They're just there for hook ups."

"And will you do that? Have you done that? Hooked up with them?"

Lance frowns. "No. Not since we've been together. Do you want me to?"

"Of course not."

"Okay. Good. 'Cause I don't want that. Not at all anymore."

His relief and mine match. "I'm glad."

"Miller, Randy, Waters, and Westinghouse all have girl-friends. Well, Violet's married to Waters, and I don't know what the fuck is going on with Westinghouse and his girl, but I hang out with them, so I can avoid the bunnies."

"That's good."

"I won't do anything to hurt you, Poppy. Okay?"

"Okay." I hope he means it. My heart is making big plans for this man, even though my head is telling me to slow down.

"Can I take you up to bed now? I'm not gonna get to have

your hands on me for almost a week, and I'm not gonna like that very much."

"Then we should definitely go to bed."

THE HOCKEY SEASON moves into full swing, and in no time it's mid-November. Lance is still a constant in my bed and on my couch. But those are really the only places I spend time with him.

In the weeks we've been seeing each other, he has yet to invite me to a game, or to his house, or out with his friends. We did go out for coffee once, at the same little dessert café we went to before. I wasn't allowed to get tea because then it technically wouldn't have counted as the second date I'd agreed to.

I try not to dwell on what all the seclusion means or doesn't mean because I like having him around, and he continues to be sweet and doting. Meals and flowers have continued to arrive on a regular basis. And one day I left work to find new snow tires on my car because there was a ten-percent possibility of snow.

This is obviously a lot of thoughtfulness, but I'm starting to wonder about the parameters of this relationship. Have I become a secret he's hiding? And if so, from who? DO NOT FUCKING REPLY hasn't messaged again, at least not while I've been with him, and past relationships haven't come up again when we talk.

Then someone else calls a few days before he's scheduled for another away series, with *unknown* as the contact.

He doesn't answer, but it makes him act sketchy. Just like when DNFR called before, he powers down his phone and distracts me with sex.

But I don't forget how anxious that incoming call made him, despite how focused on my needs he becomes, zeroed in on what makes me feel good. When I put my hands on him, his groan is almost pained, and he holds my palms against his skin, as if he could fuse me to his body.

One night he shows up at my place with the makings of a black eye after a home game. I have an early morning, but he's exceptionally needy in a way I haven't experienced before. I'm almost scared of what it might mean.

We're lying in my bed, me sprawled across his chest, because that's where he seems to like me best after sex. Really any time we're alone and prone, he prefers me to be tucked into his side or on top of him.

His breathing is even, but there's tension in his body. His phone buzzes on the nightstand beside mine. I feel his head turn, but he doesn't make a move to get it.

"Lance?"

He makes a sound, acknowledging me.

"Are you okay?"

A long pause follows before he finally says, "Aye." But his tone belies the word.

I lift my head and find him staring at the ceiling. I skim his lips with my fingertips, and he turns toward me.

I keep my eyes on his as I kiss his shoulder. "What's wrong, baby?"

The pet name is one I've used only a couple of times before, and only when it seems like something's on his mind. Like now. His hand comes up to cover mine, and his eyes fall closed as he kisses my fingertips.

"Tomorrow would've been my brother's twenty-first birthday," he whispers.

His intensity and introspection make sense now. "I'm so sorry."

"Me, too." He plays with my fingers, sweeping them back and forth across his lips.

"Lance?"

"Mmm."

"Can I ask what happened to him?"

He tenses for a moment, and his hand tightens around mine. But eventually he releases a breath, along with my fingers.

261

"I don't like to talk about it all that much."

"It must've been awful with him being so young. Was he sick?"

Lance shakes his head. "I killed him."

It's my turn to tense, but I don't take my hand away, because I'm aware his words are intended to shock and make me withdraw. "What do you mean?"

"The last time I told someone about this, she used it to manipulate me."

"You mean the complicated relationship?"

I get a small nod in reply.

"Manipulate you how?"

"She would use it against me. She made it worse."

"She made what worse?" I don't understand where he's going with this, and I have all sorts of scenarios running through my head that don't add up to the man taking up space in my bed and my heart.

"The guilt." He eyes me warily. "It's my fault he's dead."

Though I haven't been to see him play in person, I've seen Lance on the ice. The TV does a great job showcasing the aggression he works hard to contain most of the time. I've also seen the lid pop off and all the pent-up anger explode out of him. It results in things like the black eye he's currently sporting. I can spin my own ideas about what could've happened, but knowing Lance, his perception on this might be skewed.

"Can you explain that, please?" I ask.

Another long silence follows, and his breathing grows more anxious with every passing moment. I press my lips against his shoulder and shift so I can touch them to his neck, his cheek, his chin, and finally his lips.

"I just want to understand, Lance. I don't want to use the information to cause you pain."

He can't look me in the eye, and I don't push for it, knowing whatever he's about to tell me must be hard.

"When I was a kid I used to play ball hockey with some guys

after school. I always told my mum my brother and I had stayed for the after-school tutoring or math stuff or whatever, and she never checked, 'cause math was my thing.

"One afternoon I got a little caught up and ignored how tight time was getting.. My mum was going through a bad phase—not sleeping all that well, probably drinking too much, maybe not taking the pills the doctors gave her. Plus, my dad was away on another business trip, so she was on us more. On me more."

He pauses, eyes still glued to the ceiling.

"Being late meant bad things. Not for Quinn. He was a good kid. Always did what he was asked, followed the rules, didn't give anyone a hard time. We lived in a nice part of town. We had a big house and nice clothes. My parents drove expensive cars, and we had private education with uniforms. I took it for granted a lot; I still do. But there was an area close to where we lived that wasn't so nice, a lot of poverty there. That's where some of the gang kids came from. Sometimes they'd graffiti our school walls, hang out and threaten some of the mouthy kids, stuff like that."

Lance pauses again. He picks up my fingers, studying them, and I wait, because the end of this story is devastating. It marks a loss that I'm positive changed this man in a lot of ways, and will fill in so many missing pieces of the puzzle that is Lance.

When it seems like he's struggling to continue, I finally ask, "Did you get mouthy with them?"

He shakes his head.

"What happened, then?"

I get another headshake, more playing with my fingertips. His voice cracks when he finally speaks again.

"We were gonna be late 'cause I'd played hockey too long. Quinn, he'd just sit there watching, 'cause he was good like that. Real patient. He'd read a book sometimes if he was bored, but that day he told me more than once that we needed to go, and I ignored him, told him five more minutes. I just wanted to beat the other guys, and I did."

He swallows hard. "By the time we left, we only had fifteen minutes to get home. It usually took at least twenty, and that was keeping a good pace. Quinn had asthma, so he wasn't great at running, and he had puffers. I said we should take the shortcut. He didn't want to at first, 'cause my mum said never to go that way. But then I reminded him we'd be late, and I'd get in trouble. He knew what that meant when Mum was having one of her bad spells."

"So you took the shortcut?" I ask.

Lance looks out into the darkness as he nods. His glassy eyes are glued to a spot on the wall, and his throat bobs.

"There was this alley we had to go down; once we were through there, it wasn't so bad. There were stores and stuff. But that alley, it was dark. I'd gone a couple times with some friends, but never my brother. We got about halfway before we were swarmed."

He sounds so tortured. "Back home they make their own weapons."

My heart lurches.

"They'll take off their socks and fill them with rocks. Then they beat you with them. Usually you come out with bruises and shit, but it fucking hurts like hell. They tried to take Quinn's bag, and he knew if he came home without it we'd get in real shit with Mum, so he tried to hold on to it, and they went at him. Hit him right in the temple. One second he was screaming, and the next he was just…gone."

Lance's haunted gaze finally lifts to mine, fear and regret making his eyes shine. "It's my fault he's dead. I took him away from her. I broke her."

The *her* he's referring to can only be his mother. I see clearly that the blame has become a blackness inside that he can't erase.

I curve my palm around his cheek, his sadness my own. "Oh, baby, that's not your fault."

"I took him there. I was the reason we were late."

"You were a child."

"I knew better than to go that way. I should've just dealt with the beating I'd get, but I didn't want to, and then they fucking killed him, and I lost everything." A choked sound leaves him, and he closes his eyes, fists clenching as he tries to control the shudder that passes through him. When his eyes open, there's a vast emptiness that makes my heart ache. "I shouldn't have told you any of this."

I don't ask why. I already know. It's same thing he said the last time he gave me insight into his past. He thinks I'll do what it seems like everyone else in his life has. I push up so I can look at him, even though he's focused elsewhere. I touch his cheek, and he turns toward my hand.

"I'm so sorry the people who should've helped you through this weren't able to cope with the loss. I'm so sorry they made you feel like it was yours to own."

"It is mine."

"Lance, look at me."

His eyes shift, wary and afraid.

"How old were you?"

"Eleven."

If my heart wasn't breaking before, it certainly is now. To watch someone you love die, helpless to stop it, would be devastating to such a young child. To have your family fall apart and leave you believing it was your fault would be emotionally crippling. That Lance is as well adjusted as he is seems to be a miracle. I imagine his aunt is the reason for it.

"Oh, baby." I push his hair back from his forehead.

He brushes tears away from my eyes, frowning at the dampness on his fingertips. "Why're you crying?"

"Because I'm so sad that someone took your innocence from you like that, and that you believe it to be your fault when it was a horribly unfortunate situation out of your control."

"I made a mistake, and it cost me my brother."

"You made a mistake out of self-preservation. I'm sorry your mum didn't know how to love you without hurting you."

He traces the contour of my face. "I'm messed up, Poppy. I think there are parts of me that can't be fixed."

Loving this man isn't going to be easy, but I still want to try. "I don't need to fix you, Lance. I'll take you as you are. I just want you to be happy."

He kisses me, and I can almost taste his fear. He wants to believe me, but I can't blame him for being afraid. All the people in his life who were supposed to stand by him have abandoned him in some way. I don't want to be another.

THE NIGHT before Lance's next away series I wake at four in the morning to an empty bed. He was here a few hours ago when I fell asleep on his chest, so I assume he's gone in search of a snack. He seems to have the same nightly pattern, which explains why I don't ever get a full night's sleep.

I pull his T-shirt over my head and pad out into the hall, sure I'll find him scarfing down a bag of gummy bears in the kitchen. He stocks my cupboards something fierce. Lance eats a lot of candy despite it not being on his meal plan.

When I reach the landing, I can hear his voice, low and aggravated. I descend a few steps and pause again.

"No. That's not happening. I don't want to see you. There's nothing to talk about."

There's a pause, and I can see him pacing the length of living room. "I'll block this number like I did the last one... No—I will never fucking forgive you if you—why can't you let me have this? Why do you want to fuck this up for me?"

He runs a frustrated hand through his hair. "Stop fucking with my head. I told you I was done."

He drops down into a crouch, bouncing on the balls of his feet. "Goddamn it. You made it this way. Not me. You. Stop calling and stay away from me."

He hangs up the phone and drops it on the floor. It starts buzzing again almost immediately. He makes a low, deep sound in his throat and grabs his hair with both hands, pulling hard. It can't feel good.

I take another step down the stairs, hitting the one that creaks on purpose. He drops his hand and unfurls from his crouch, spinning around to face me.

"Who's calling in the middle of the night?" I look to his phone, lighting up on the floor.

"Fucking telemarketers," he lies. He snatches it up off the floor and powers it down, then tosses it roughly on the coffee table. I wonder if it was DO NOT FUCKING REPLY. I should ask, but I'm afraid to know.

"I thought maybe you went looking for gummy bears." I try to make my smile even. I'm not sure how successful I am.

"I'm not hungry for gummies any more." His hands ball into fists and then open as he stalks up the stairs.

His eyes are full of pain and fear. I feel it cracking open my heart.

"I need to be in you. I need you to let me get inside you."

"Are you okay?" I should demand the truth, make him open up and give me more, but I'm also scared of pushing him too far when he's like this.

"I want to be."

I run my hands up his bare chest, giving in to him, though I know that may not be my wisest move. "And I'll make it better?"

He cups my cheeks in his palms, kisses me tenderly and rests his forehead against mine. "Yes."

As much as I want to know more, I want this, too. His need for me is heady.

"Then you should take me back to bed so I can do that for you."

He picks me up, wrapping my legs around his waist, and

carries me up the stairs. Shortly thereafter, he makes me come three times. He tells me he needs me, this, us.

And I want to believe him—I think he's telling the truth—but I'm so scared.

Because I've fallen now, and someone else seems to have a hold on him.

HEAD GAMES

LANCE

I get it now. I've found someone who consumes my world, so I don't say anything to Miller about the excessive display of affection he's engaged in right now. Instead, I grab his bag from his front porch and toss it into the back of my Hummer while he cradles baby Logan in one arm and close-talks Sunny with the other.

I get his bad moods. I get why he's quiet and anxious these days. This thing with Poppy is new, and Miller and Sunny have been together for a long time now, but the restlessness that's settled in my chest is directly related to leaving Poppy this morning. And knowing I won't see her for five days dampens the usual excitement of the games. Miller must feel this times a million.

269

Randy tosses Miller's equipment on top of mine, and I use my shoulder to force the door shut.

"Two minutes, Butterson," I call, and then Randy and I get back in the Hummer and wait.

My phone goes off, so I check it, thinking maybe it's Poppy messaging me between appointments. It's not, it's unknown. "Fuckin'ell."

Randy looks up from his own phone. "What's up?"

"Tash."

"Why don't you just block her?"

"I did. She got a new phone. Or another one. I don't fucking know."

"Seriously?"

"Yeah. She won't let up. It's been pretty constant since all the pictures of me and Poppy showed up."

"Shit."

"Yeah. Shit is right. She wants to meet up and talk when we're in LA, which is Tash-speak for fucking with my head. I told her no, but she always does what she wants."

"You think she'll show up anyway?"

"I don't know. Probably. She'll want to see the team, right? It's like she *wants* to screw this up for me."

"I don't get it. Why is she still all over you like this?"

"That's a good question, and I don't have an answer, other than she gets a kick out of messing with me."

"That's fucked up."

"Yeah. I just need to avoid her in LA, and then hopefully she'll let up after that." I don't know how else to get rid of her.

"You think you can do that?"

"I'm gonna have to, aren't I?"

"I guess. How're things with Poppy anyway?"

I think about how I left her this morning: hair all tangled, lips swollen and cheeks pink from the see-you-soon orgasms I gave her.

"Good. She's good. Things are good." For now.

Randy strokes his beard. "Does she know about Tash?"

"That she's still calling me? No. That she exists. Yeah."

"Do you think you should tell her?"

"And say what? My ex, or whatever I'm supposed to call her, still fucks with my head? She already knows it was a complicated situation. I don't plan to see Tash, so it shouldn't be an issue anyway, right?"

"I guess not, but it's probably a good idea to be honest with her, especially since you seem to be turning into something serious."

Miller opens the rear passenger door and drops into the seat behind Randy. "Thanks for waiting, Romance."

"No problem. I know they're hard to leave behind."

He meets my gaze in the rearview mirror. "I really hope this gets easier."

I finally understand his worry.

We had it out last week about why he's been so shitty with me. Poppy was the issue. He thought I was going to treat her like she's just another bunny.

It turns out when Poppy was performing her dick removal last year, she happened to tell him I was her first kiss. He'd known the entire time and said nothing.

Obviously I was pissed about that in return, because if he'd just said something, we could've avoided all the fucking tension in the first place. But she'd asked him not to tell me, and he figured if I couldn't remember I didn't deserve to know. He had a point, even though I didn't like it.

And now that I know the how and the why and the where of our beginning, I'm glad he didn't tell me, because getting that memory back is probably one of the best things to happen to me in a long time.

I put the Hummer in gear, and we head for the airport.

WE WIN the first two games in the series. It's a good high we're riding, especially with the way last season ended. I talk to Poppy every day and avoid the bar scene after the games, having learned from Randy and Miller's past mistakes.

Before we landed in LA, I blocked Tash's number again. Not that it stops her from finding other ways to contact me. Today she used someone else's phone to leave me a message.

Poppy has clients all day, so I don't get in even a short phone conversation with her before I have to get on the ice. Tomorrow night I'll be back in Chicago, and she and I have plans. I just have to get through this game and the rest of the night, and everything will be fine.

I'm not on the ball, though. I'm distracted. And having lost the last game they played on home ice, LA is chippy. I end up in the penalty box more than once.

After the game, Randy and Miller decide they want to hit the bar for a beer before calling it a night. I don't go because I know Tash will show up like she does every time we have a game in LA, and this is the first one this season. The majority of the team still likes her because they have no idea what she's really about.

It's pretty late by the time I get to my room. I hope Rookie takes whatever bunny he's picked up tonight back to her place, or gets his own damn hotel room. I'm tired of having to sleep on Miller and Randy's couch.

I call Poppy, but I get her voicemail. I assume she's sleeping since it's even later in Chicago, and she told me she's been making up for all the hours she's missed since we started seeing each other.

I pack my bag so it's ready for tomorrow morning and in case I have to vacate when Rookie comes back with his hands full of bunny. I can understand now, in a way I never did before, why Miller and Randy used to get pissed off about all the bunny shit when I'd have parties.

At twelve thirty, Rookie still hasn't come up and I'm bagged. I haven't heard anything from Tash, which should be a relief. But for some reason it isn't. I send Poppy one last message about how I can't wait to see her tomorrow, turn off the lights, and attempt to get some sleep.

I'm woken sometime later by the click of the door. I wish I was a heavier sleeper. Quiet whispers and a few giggles follow, along with some shushing from Rookie, who is clearly not alone. I can't tell if he's only got one, or if he's brought along a pair.

"My roommate's sleeping. We gotta be quiet," Rookie whispers, but he's slurry and louder than he probably intends.

Not that it matters. The sound of a cricket can wake me from a dead sleep.

More chatter follows. "Can't we turn on a light?"

That voice makes the hairs on the back of my neck stand on end.

He laughs. "Then we'll wake him up for sure."

"So? Maybe he'll want to play, too."

The rustle of clothing follows, and a second female voice whisper-yells *ow!*

I should've known she'd find a way to fuck with me.

I feel the edge of my mattress dip.

"That's not my bed," Rookie says.

I smell Tash before I feel her. The scent of my shampoo and her lotion hits me like a puck to the face. I try to untangle myself from the sheets and get out of bed before she reaches me, but I'm not fast enough.

She straddles me and her palm comes to rest on my throat. The light beside my bed comes on, brightness blinding me. Long, dark hair tickles my chest, and the spiders are back, crawling under my skin. Goose bumps rise across my arms. Not the good kind. She pulls down the covers until they reach my waist, then stretches out on top of me. She's topless. Braless.

"Get off me." I reach out to grab her wrists, but she shifts around next to me.

"Whoa, Romance, calm down, bro!" Rookie says. "Hey don't do that."

Tash's cheek presses up against mine. "Smile." The flash blinds me again.

"Fucking Christ. What's wrong with you?" I'm faster than she is this time. I grab her waist and flip her so she's face down on the bed and I'm on top of her.

The other girl is staring at us, slack jawed.

Rookie tries to pull me off Tash, but I'm not seeing anything but red right now, so my first instinct is to punch him in the face. He goes reeling back, and the other girl screams.

"Give me the goddamn phone," I yell at Tash, who's laughing underneath me.

I stretch out over her, pushing her down into the mattress. In that moment I recognize how close I am to the edge. I wonder if this is what it was like for my mum, if she was always at this point with my dad, if he did the kinds of things to her Tash does to me.

The thought sends my head to dark places, where all the bad things I've done over the years taunt me.

I want to hurt Tash the way she's hurt me. But she's fucked up. Worse than I am, maybe. And as much as I hate her, I get that her head isn't right, just like mine.

"You'll have to fuck me for it," she laughs.

"Just give me the phone." I see movement out of the corner of my eye, and the other girl has her phone out. "Don't."

It's too late, though. I know it by the way her eyes jump from me to Tash and back again.

"Sent," she tells Tash.

Tash stops fighting and drops her phone on the comforter. I nab it and push off the bed as fast as I can, so I'm not touching her, and she's not touching me.

"Who did you send it to?" I ask the other girl.

She cradles her phone to her chest, seeming a little scared.

Rookie looks super confused. "What the hell is going on? Do you know her?"

I bark out a bitter laugh. "Unfortunately, yeah."

A flash of hurt passes over Tash's face before she gives me one of her sneers. "When did you stop being fun?"

"When you decided to keep bringing me gifts I didn't want." I turn back to the girl. "That picture you took, I wanna see it, and I want to know who you sent it to."

She passes over her phone. "I didn't post it publicly or anything."

A sick feeling washes over me as I take in the image. I'm wearing a pair of boxers, and I'm fully lying on top of Tash. Most of my face is in profile, and I look pissed. But it's her expression that makes the roll in my stomach become a knot. Tash, who is very clearly topless, is smiling directly at the camera. Like she planned this.

"Who did you send it to?"

"Me," Tash says. She's sitting on my bed, long hair cascading over her shoulders. She's still shirtless.

I pick her shirt up off the floor and toss it to her. "For Christ's sake, put this on and delete the damn picture," I bark.

She doesn't catch the shirt, letting it fall on the bed. "And Poppy, of course."

"Bullshit."

"She has all sorts of social media accounts. Posts all kinds of pictures of the flowers someone keeps sending her."

"You're stalking her? Jesus, Tash, what the fuck is wrong with you?" I ask again.

Her face falls, the anger I've witnessed before pushing to the surface. "Just interested in finding out what gossip is true and what isn't."

I laugh. She's said that to me before—when I said I wanted just her, when I tried to make it work. She would hit me with words, and then she'd take them all back with apologies and promises, only to slice me apart again when she brought me another present in the form of someone she could fuck.

"You don't even want me. Why can't you leave me alone?"

275

She gets up on her knees like she's thinking about touching me, so I take another step back. "What if I do want you?"

I have no idea how much of this is a show for our audience and how much is her manipulating as she does.

"You don't. And I don't want you. Not anymore. Not for a long time, Tash, and especially not after this." I motion between her, the random girl she's using, and Rookie.

Her smirk fades, like maybe she realizes, finally, that this game she's playing with me has real consequences. But Tash doesn't know how to be any other way.

I get that, because before Poppy, I didn't know I could be another way either.

Tash pulls the shirt over her head and jumps up off the bed. "Whatever. It's always the same thing with you." She holds out her hand for her phone.

"Tell me your passcode so I can delete whatever pictures you took first."

She purses her lips, then smiles, but there's a waver to it.

"Twenty-one twenty-one."

"Seriously? Did you change it just for tonight?"

She drops her chin, and for a second I'm sad for her. I understand exactly why I kept going back, over and over again, for the same crap. Because under the psycho bullshit is a broken person. And that was something I could relate to. But I can't fix her. I don't know that she wants to be fixed. And I can't be responsible for changing anyone but myself.

I spend the next few minutes scrolling through her phone, deleting the three blurry pictures she managed to take, and then deleting my contact information. Once I'm done, I go into every single one of her accounts until I find the picture her friend sent and delete that, too. I don't care that she's yelling at me, or telling me I'm invading her privacy. I don't even react when she starts slapping me and Rookie has to pull her off.

I check her browsing history; she's not lying about stalking

Poppy. She has every one of her social media accounts book-marked. It's almost creepy. Or rather, it's super fucking creepy.

"I need a minute," I say to Rookie. I point to the wide-eyed girl. "You need to take her somewhere."

"What?" He looks confused.

"I need to talk to Tash without an audience. Go hang out on the balcony or something."

"Can I have my phone back?" the girl asks.

"Not until I erase all the pictures."

"I only took one."

"You know we can have you sign an NDA right now, and if you post anything—any little fucking thing about me or Rookie—you'll have a lawsuit so fucking fast your head will pop off."

Her bottom lip trembles. "I-I'm s-sorry."

"Don't listen to his bullshit. He's pissed off that we came up here with his friend."

I spin to face Tash. "Don't you ever get tired of the head games?"

That shuts her up, at least for now.

I delete the image from the girl's phone before I pass it back to her. Rookie takes her by the elbow and heads for the door, which I sincerely appreciate.

"I'll message when Tash is on her way down."

He gives me a long, worried look. "If you're longer than twenty I'm bringing her back up."

As soon as the door closes, Tash takes a step toward me. I hold out my palm. "Don't fuckin' touch me."

She raises her hands in the air and backs up a step.

I grab my shirt from the end of the bed and pull it on, along with a pair of track pants, because there's no way I'm having any kind of conversation with Tash until I'm fully clothed.

"Seriously, Tash, why are you here?"

She just kind of wilts. "To see you."

"This thing you think is between us? That's done. It's been done for a long time."

"Are you still mad about last time?"

I run a palm down my face, trying to contain my frustration, but I can't. How did I ever think this was worth something?

I wish Poppy was here. She keeps me level. She makes me feel like there's something good in me that I can actually hold on to. I wish I had her to keep me from exploding like this, but Tash always knows how to push me to the edge, light a match, and set me on fire.

"Yes! Yes, I'm still mad about last time, and the time before that, and the one before that, and every single fucking time you brought me someone else after I kept telling you not to. I don't know why this is such a goddamn surprise for you."

"Then why didn't you say no?"

"I don't know. I don't fucking know. Because I thought maybe at some point you'd actually hear me and listen. Because I didn't think I deserved anything better at the time. Look, it doesn't matter, because you're not gonna do this again. I meant what I said. I'm done. And you need to be done too. Stop whatever this shit is." I hold up her phone and scroll through all of Poppy's bookmarked pages. "This isn't normal, Tash."

"I remember her. She was at your house a year ago. How long have you been screwing her? This whole time?"

"What?"

"Were you fucking her back then?" She vibrates with barely contained rage.

"Jesus Christ. Are you on something?"

"Answer the question!" she screams.

She's all over the place. I recognize the behavior. And it hits me. I don't know why I didn't see it before—the ultra highs, the deep-dark lows, the paranoia, the rage, and the grandeur. She's manic. Just like my mother is.

"No. I hadn't seen her in a year. I just met her again. Why is that even relevant?"

"Well, what are you gonna do when she wants to put her hands on you. How are you going to deal with that?"

"I like it when she touches me." The words are like a back-hand for her, so I keep going. "I don't get anxious. I don't need distractions. She's good for me."

She's silent for a while before a look of malice appears. "Maybe not any more, though. May not after she sees that picture."

There's no point in arguing with her. The conversation isn't rational. She only wants to cause pain.

I key the code back into her phone and go through the rest of her social media profiles, checking to see where the image was sent. I find it in a group message that included Poppy. She hasn't seen it yet. But she will.

I hold up the phone. "This was your plan?"

"You spend all this time with her, send her flowers like she's all yours, but what if she doesn't want you after this?"

"Why are you doing this to me?"

Confusion mars her face. I used to think she was attractive, but now I know what's inside her.

"I'm helping you," she says.

"That doesn't even make sense."

"Sure it does. Is she worth it if she can't get over this? I mean, does she even know the rumors about you are true? I bet she doesn't."

"You should go get your friend." I toss the phone to her.

"That's it?"

I give her a blank look.

"Okay, fine. Suit yourself. I'll be in Chicago in a few weeks."

"You're not getting me, Tash. This is it. There's no more. We're toxic for each other, and you need...something I can't give you. I won't do this with you any more. I don't want to."

"Because of this girl?"

"Yes. And because I can finally see what I was doing to myself, and letting you do to me. I don't want to be this way, and I don't have to."

"I could try—"

"I don't want you to. I don't want to try with you. Look what you just did to me. I can't trust you. I need you to stop. Leave Poppy alone. Whatever happens between her and me after this, I can't have you messing with her life the way you did mine."

"What are you going to do about it?"

I give her a look. "It would only take a phone call. You know that. It's not something I want to do, but I will if you force me."

Tash laughs, but it's a flat sound. "So that's it?"

"Aye. You need to go." When she takes a step toward me, I put a hand up and ward her off.

Her head drops. "Okay. I'll go."

"And I mean it when I say no contact. Especially with Poppy."

Her expression is broken as she regards me. "Fine."

As soon as the door clicks behind her, I drop to the couch. I'm shaky and on edge, as is typical after altercations with Tash. But there's a tiny little seed of relief within me too. Tash may not have gotten my message, but I think I did. I'm ready to move forward. Be different. Even if it's a hard road ahead.

I need something to replace all this unease, so I send a message to Poppy. She's been so trusting, and now Tash has to come in and try to fuck it all up. What a fantastic legacy that will be if I've managed to get rid of her, only just a little too late.

It's the middle of the night, so I don't expect a reply. All I can do is hope I'm the first person she calls when she gets up in the morning. If I'm not, things are going to be that much worse.

22

HOW MUCH REALITY IS TOO MUCH?

POPPY

My phone wakes me, not because the alarm is going off, but because it's ringing. I don't get to it before it stops. I have enough time to note a million and one alerts lighting up my screen before it rings again.

It's Lance.

My stomach flips. He's coming home today. He's sleeping over tonight. Well, he's staying over; based on the messages we've exchanged the past few days, I don't think much sleeping will be involved.

I answer the call. "Hi." My voice is sleep raspy.

"Fuck. Thank fuck. Hey. Hi. I woke you, didn't I?"

Something in his tone puts me on edge. I roll onto my back, willing my heart to stop slamming around in my chest. "I have to get up soon anyway. Is everything okay? You sound...agitated."

Lance clears his throat. "Everything's, uh, a little fucked up, to be honest."

The anxiety I've been working so hard to curb via extra yoga sessions, cookies and tea with Mr. Goldberg, and nights out with April this week suddenly wraps its fingers around my throat and squeezes the air out of my lungs.

"I need you—" Noise in the background makes it hard to hear him for a few seconds. "—Please, Poppy."

I open my mouth to speak, but nothing comes out.

"Poppy? You there?"

"Here. Sorry. I missed some of that."

He exhales in a rush, the sound whooshing into my ear. It matches the blood pumping through my veins. "How much you miss?"

"All I got was that things are fucked up and the *I need you* part."

"Look, Poppy, I'm gonna ask you to do something, and it's gonna make you want to do the opposite."

"This doesn't sound good."

"I know. Just hear me out, please?"

"Okaayyy." I sit up in bed and pull Lance's T-shirt over my knees. I've been sleeping in it the entire time he's been gone. It smells like his aftershave and him, and a little like sex.

"So, I need you to avoid all your social media accounts until I'm back in Chicago."

I can hear his fingers tapping on something. Maybe the phone. "That's a very specific, suspect request, Lance."

"I know, I know. And I can explain, but I need to be there with you to do it."

I try to keep my voice even. "What's on my social media that I shouldn't see?"

Another heavy breath, a pained sound, and repetitive thumping follow. Long seconds pass before he speaks again, this time in a whisper. "Someone sent you a picture, and I don't want you to see it—not without me there so I can explain."

"Is this a joke? Like last time when you showed up at my work all freaked out? Because if it is, it's not a very good one."

"I wish it was a joke, but it's not."

The lump in my throat makes it hard to swallow. "This sounds really bad, Lance."

"I know it does, and I know not explaining right now is probably making it way fucking worse, but I really need this from you. I'm getting on a plane soon. I'll be home in a few hours. Can you please, please just give me until I'm with you?"

"Were you with someone else?"

"No, no. Absolutely not, Poppy. I fucking promise. No."

My heart seems to dislodge from my throat a bit. "Then I don't understand what's so dire about this situation that I need to avoid all my social media."

"You remember the dick on Miller's forehead, and how nothing really happened but it looked like something happened?"

My heart is right back up in my throat again. "Yes."

"It's kinda like that."

"I see."

"So I'd really appreciate it if you could wait for me. So I can explain before you decide you never want to see me again, 'cause I don't wanna be that guy who sits outside your house waiting until you come home so I can talk to you."

"You're making it seem bad again."

"Shit. Sorry. I'm not trying to. I just need a chance to explain before you make any kind of decision."

He makes it sound so final, like whatever I'm going to see will end this. Us.

"You do realize how much more this makes me want to look, right?"

"I get that, but I'm banking on you being the good, rule-abiding girl you usually are and waiting for me. Will you do that? Wait for me?"

I think about the conversation we had before he left and how so many people in his life seem to have abandoned him when he needed them most.

"I'll wait for you."

"Promise?"

I sigh. "Promise."

"Thank you, precious. I gotta get on the plane. I'll see you soon."

And then he's gone, and I'm left staring at my phone, wondering exactly what could've happened to make him react like that. I can look right now and find out. But Lance is right about me—I'm a rule follower. I made a promise, and I won't break it.

I'm so glad I have back-to-back appointments all day. Otherwise I would crack and check all my social media feeds, like I promised I wouldn't. Lunch was a challenge.

I haven't said anything to April, partly because I haven't had more than four seconds alone with her, and also because she is not a rule follower and will persuade me to check. The anxiety is killing me. I feel like I've had a thousand cups of coffee when I've only had two.

I'm in the middle of changing the sheets when the door to my room bursts open, and Lance comes barreling in. He slams the door shut. His eyes are wide, his jaw is tight, and his hair is a burned field in a windstorm. He looks incredible, and like his anxiety rivals mine.

He crosses the room in two long strides and takes my face in his hands.

"Just in case," he mutters, then crushes his mouth to mine.

He smells like plane and faintly of aftershave. I try to protest, because seriously, what the hell is going on—but his tongue slips in and stops any words. He groans, despondent and low as his hand slides around to cup the back of my head. The other finds my waist, pulling me tight against him.

It feels so, so good. Five days of brief conversations and heated messages, five days of waiting for him to come home, and here he is. But there's weight in his return, and bad things are coming. I can feel it in his desperation.

I put my hands on his chest and push. He makes a tormented sound, and his tongue sweeps my mouth once, twice more before he pulls away. But he doesn't let me go. He searches my face and caresses my cheek with gentle fingers.

"You didn't look."

"I said I wouldn't."

"I was still worried. How much longer are you here? Can I wait? Can I take you home when you're done?"

"I have my car here, and I still have three more appointments." I push on his chest again until he finally lets me go.

"So you're here until, like, five?" He rakes a hand through his hair.

"About that, yes."

"I guess I should've asked that when I had you on the phone earlier, aye? Can I still wait?"

"I have a few minutes between clients now." I don't know that I can take three more hours of this kind of torture.

"I don't wanna do this here."

"None of this is reassuring, Lance. You showing up like this, the call this morning, the secrecy. You get that, right?"

"I do. I get it. I know I'm stressing you out. I just want enough time to explain."

His anxiety is enough to make me concede. "You can meet me at my house, if you want."

"Can I take your phone?"

I raise a brow, and he closes his eyes for a moment. "Okay.

Sorry. That was a stupid thing to ask. Should I wait outside or—"
He bites his lip.

Against my better judgment, I relent. "Let me get my keys for
you."

I grab them from my purse. When I turn back, his hands are
jammed into his pockets. I dangle the keys from my finger.

He takes my hand and the keys and brings my knuckle to his
lips. "I missed you."

I stare up at him, trying to decide if I'm an idiot for doing as
he asks. I missed him too, but telling him that now doesn't seem
like an option.

"I'll be waiting for you. Will you still wait for me?"

"Yes. I'll wait for you."

When he leans in to kiss me, I give him my cheek. His lips
linger there anyway.

I ARRIVE HOME at 5:09. Lance is sitting on the front steps. He's
showered and changed since I saw him earlier. He's wearing a
long-sleeved gray shirt that makes his pale eyes look even paler,
and a bouquet of flowers and bag of Jelly Babies sit on the stoop
beside him. He stands, running his hands down his denim-
covered thighs. He reaches down and grabs the gifts.

"Did the key not work?"

"It did. I wanted to be out here when you got home." He
holds out the flowers.

"Is this to soften the blow?" I try to make it come out light,
but it doesn't. The waver in my voice is far too telling.

Lance winces as if my words cause him physical pain. I
realize maybe they do, because his reality as a child was exactly
that.

I take the flowers and start to move past him to open the
door, but he gets there first, twisting the knob, then stepping out

of the way. He follows me through to the kitchen where I set the flowers on the counter.

"Would you like something to drink?"

"Just water, please." His fingers move to his mouth. He stops himself and jams them back in his pockets.

Neither of us speaks as I fill two glasses with ice and water, pushing one toward Lance. Leaving the flowers on the counter, I dig around in my purse until I find my phone.

"Do you want to have a seat?" I motion to the living room.

My stomach is a churning mess. I haven't eaten a thing today. My mouth is dry, and I want to get this over with so I can handle whatever is coming at me.

"Do you want to change first or anything? I know you've had a long day."

"I just want to have this conversation."

"Right. Aye. Okay." Lance sits in the middle of the couch, forcing me into close proximity.

I angle my shoulders toward him, but keep my knees far away from his. I take a sip of water, but my stomach revolts even against that, so I set it down on the table and grip my phone with both hands.

Lance takes a huge gulp of water before he sets the glass down and turns to me, his expression reflecting my fear. "So you know that woman I was involved with a while back?"

My body feels like it's going numb and hyper-activating at the same time. "The complicated one."

"Yeah. It was. It is."

"Is? As in still?" The conversation I overheard the night before he left, which has been plaguing me the entire time he's been gone, plays through my head. I hate that I didn't confront him about it then.

He nods. His palms smooth up and down his thighs again. I want to put my hand over his to stop the action, because it makes me even more nervous.

"She lives in LA."

A chill runs down my spine. "Where you played last night."

"Aye."

"And she was there?"

"I told her I didn't want to see her, but she's not so good at listening, and she used to work with the team, so she always comes by when we're in town."

"She worked with the team?" I don't understand how he could've been involved with someone he worked with.

"We trained with her."

"Isn't that not allowed?"

"Yeah." His head drops. "That's part of the reason it was so complicated. Anyway, I went right up to my room after the game. I didn't stop at the bar, 'cause I worried she'd be there."

I try not to fidget with my phone. "But you ended up seeing her anyway?"

"She plays head games, Poppy. She pulls this shit all the time. She's got issues. Worse than me."

I want to tell him he doesn't have issues, but that's not true.

"So what happened?"

"By the time Rookie came up, I was already asleep. I tried to call you before I went to bed, but it was late here." He reaches out like he wants to touch me, but when I jerk away; he retracts his hand, nodding like he understands my reluctance. "Anyway, he wasn't alone when he came up."

"He brought a girl with him?" I don't ask any of the questions that spring to mind, like what was he planning to do, have sex in the bed next to Lance's?

"He brought two."

"Was he planning to share?" I bite out.

Lance shrugs. "I dunno. Maybe? Every time he brings a girl up, I take the couch in Miller and Randy's room. And I'm gonna ask Coach if we can switch it up with the roommate situation before the next trip."

"He brings girls up to the room while you're there?"

He licks his lips and looks at his lap. It makes my heart ache like it's being squeezed. "Sometimes the bunnies have their own rooms in the hotel, in case of hook ups."

"Sometimes but not always." It's a statement, not a question. And I know the answer is going to hurt.

"Aye."

"So your roommate brought up two girls."

"Aye."

"And what happened?"

"One of them was Tash, the woman I was involved with. He didn't know who she was. He hasn't met her before."

"I see."

"Nothing happened with her. Not with me. Not with Rookie. But there's a picture that makes it look like something did. She wanted it that way."

"When was the last time you were with her?"

"I saw her the night before I first came to see you at the clinic. But whatever we had was over a long time before that."

I close my eyes and try not to react to that information. I try not to envision him with her the way he's been with me, in my bed. "And you slept with her then?"

He shakes his head. "No. She wanted me to, but I wouldn't. She tricked me."

"Tricked you?"

"She brought someone with her."

"Another woman."

"Aye."

His fingers go to his mouth and then drop to his thighs. His eyes dart around and shame makes it impossible for him to look at me.

I don't want him to feel shame for his actions, for the things he's done in the past. I don't want him to feel like he's worth less because of his choices. But I do want to understand why he felt compelled to make those choices.

"And this is something she did often? Even though you'd told her you wanted to be exclusive?"

289

He chews on his fingernails. It makes him look more boy than man. "Bring other girls?"

"Yes."

"Aye."

"And what happened then?"

I get more fidgeting, more avoiding eye contact.

"Lance?"

"I used to give her what she wanted."

"Which was?"

"To take care of the situation."

He's not going to come out and say it, and I can't blame him. I need to find a way to say what I want to without him shutting down.

"Did you want it to happen or did you let it?"

"Let."

"Why?"

"What?" He glances up.

"Why would you let that happen if you didn't want it to?"

"Because she expected it. Because I thought maybe eventually I'd be enough. Because I didn't think I deserved to have what I wanted."

My heart breaks for him. "What if I wanted that? Would you let it happen?"

His face crumples. "You would never want that."

"How do you know?" I'm not asking to hurt him, but because I want to understand his thought process.

"You're not like that. You're too precious for that." His voice is hard, like stone.

I place a palm against his cheek, hoping to calm the sudden surge of energy that seems to course through him. "You're right. I would *never* ask that of you. I value you more than that."

His fingers cover mine.

"Why don't you deserve what you want?"

"I've done a lot of bad things. I'm trying to rearrange the way I think about it." He sighs. "I want to be with you. I want to be what you need. That's all I want. I tried to avoid her. I really tried, but she can't seem to let this go."

I key in the passcode to my phone, because I need to see whatever it is that's causing him such distress. I check the most obvious accounts first, and then I finally come across an unfamiliar name.

"Natasha is Tash?" I ask.

Lance closes his eyes and bows his head.

I open the message. My throat tightens.

I try not to react to it immediately or look at it with judging eyes. It's difficult, though. Everything about this picture screams lies and deceit. But then I force myself to look without emotions, ignoring my aching heart, so I can see it for what it is.

I know this woman—the one smiling at the camera. The one lying on a bed of white sheets with Lance's big body. She's naked, or topless at least, based on the bare expanse of her back. She was the one who came to the house the morning after I stayed the night at Lance's a year ago.

She's gorgeous and in amazing shape, much better than what my twice-a-week yoga routine yields. We look absolutely nothing alike.

Lance is stretched out on top of her. But while she smiles for the camera, he looks like he wants to rip someone's head off. He's wearing boxers. It's better than him being naked, but not by much. A million unwanted scenarios rush through my mind, despite what Lance has told me, and despite my trying to keep perspective.

I push the phone toward him. "This is what you wanted to explain?"

"As soon as they came in the room, she climbed into bed with me and tried to take pictures. I was trying to get the camera from her so she couldn't post them, and her friend snapped that one. I know how it looks, though, which is why I wanted to be here when you saw it." He covers the image with his palm.

I'm grateful. It's like a train wreck. I can't look away, even though I want to. His hand is the shield I need.

"Is this going to end up all over social media?" I have to consider what that will be like, how difficult it will be to defend my relationship with him. How humiliating it will be.

"No. This is the only copy of that picture left."

"How do you know?"

"Because I deleted all of them."

"All of them? There were more?"

"Tash tried to take a few, but they were blurry."

Of all the conversations I've had over the years concerning exes, this is definitely the most unorthodox. "Is she going to keep contacting me?"

"I don't know. She's vindictive, but I told her not to. It wouldn't take much for me to cause her a lot of problems if she does. It won't look good for her that she's still been in contact with me after everything that happened."

"Do you think she'll send me other things? Pictures? Messages? Videos?"

"There aren't any videos, but we were together for a while. She'll have old pictures of her and me."

I consider what may lie ahead. Dating someone like Lance puts a spotlight on me. I'm not sure how I'm going to manage that. Or if I can. What if things like this keep happening?

"Did she call the night before you went away?"

"Aye."

"And you talked to her?" My chest feels tight. If I'd asked this question before he'd gone, would we still be dealing with this mess?

"I did."

"Why?"

"Because she won't leave me alone if I don't answer. It had been weeks of her bullshit before I did."

"Why not block her?"

"I have. I did. She messaged from someone else's phone."

That makes sense, but it still doesn't answer the most important question. "Why didn't you tell me about her before you went away? Why lie?"

Lance takes a sip of his water and clears his throat. "I didn't want to mess things up and make you worry while I was gone. I guess that kind of backfired, huh?"

"I don't understand the point of keeping it from me. Why not be honest that your ex was going to be there in the first place? This makes it look like you were hiding it."

"That's not what I meant to do." He's so forlorn.

"If we're going to have any chance of working, we have to be transparent with each other. Especially about this kind of thing. It's not avoidable, but I don't want to be blindsided by it. Today was horrible for me. I've spent the entire day on edge, feeling awful and wondering what was so damaging that you needed to be here before I could see it."

"I know. I'm sorry. But you get why I asked for that, right?"

"How often is this kind of thing going to happen? Are you going to avoid going out with your teammates every time you're in LA? I mean, really, even that isn't enough, is it?"

"Maybe you could come with me next time."

"To LA?"

"Aye."

"Why would I come to LA when you don't even have me come to home games? What are you hiding from me? Her?"

"I'm not hiding anything. I'm protecting you."

"From what? Or who?"

"The bunnies, the media crap. People will take pictures of you just like when we went out for dinner. But if you come to LA, you'll know exactly where I am and what I'm doing."

"It's not the media I'm worried about. I don't want to police your actions, Lance. I want to be part of your life, more than just this little slice you've carved out for us."

"I just don't want you dragged into all the shitty stuff that comes with being with someone like me."

"You mean like Tash? You said she comes to your games when you're in LA. And if she's there, then what? Will she confront me? Will she do things to hurt me? You?"

He drops his head again. "I don't know. I don't think so. I told her it was done for good this time, that I wasn't doing this with her any more. And I meant it. I don't want to be that person."

"I don't understand why you still talk to her when she does these kinds of things to you. Why answer her calls at all? Why is she still messaging you?"

"She got vindictive if I didn't respond. I didn't feel like I had a choice."

"But you gave her that power. Why let her have it at all?"

He's fidgety, struggling with my questions. "I don't know. We have similar backgrounds. She made it hard to walk away."

"You realize these are all excuses you're making for both of you. She still seems like part of your present, like you can't let her go. If it's only me, it can't be her, too."

"But she's not part of my present any more. I told her that last night. I know she's not good for me, and I don't want that any more."

"This is a discussion we should've had before you went away. We've been seeing each other for weeks. When would you have told me about her if this hadn't happened?"

"I wanted to. I would have," he says quickly.

"But when? She's called when I've been with you. Do you call her back later? When we're not together?"

"I've been ignoring her. I only talked to her that one time, and only because she kept calling, and I wanted to be clear that I wasn't going to see her in LA. I promise I won't talk to her any more. If she calls, I won't answer. I'll get a new phone so she doesn't have my number. I'll do anything, Poppy. Just please, give me a chance to fix this."

I can hear the child in him, the beaten one, the one who's

been abandoned over and over again. But I have to protect myself too.

"This is a lot to take in, Lance. I don't want to be responsible for allowing my heart to be broken."

Panic flares in his eyes. "So what does that mean? Are you saying it's over?"

"I'm not saying this is over. It's not black and white. But I need some time to process all of this."

His agitation makes the whole couch shake. His foot is going on the floor, the vibrations making the ice tinkle in his glass on the table. His elbows balance on his shaking knees, his fists clenching and releasing. I'm not sure whether to be afraid for him right now or not. I know he won't hurt me, but he has a tendency to find ways to hurt himself.

I've seen him fight on the ice before, watched him take hits over and over until he's finally had enough. He has to be pushed hard before he breaks. It's like watching a rubber band snap, a bomb explode.

He runs a rough hand through his hair and down over his face. Balling it into a fist, he presses it against his mouth and makes a low sound. "How much?"

"How much what?"

"How much time will you need?" His voice is mangled.

"I don't know. A week? Maybe more?"

He makes a noise that sounds a lot like a sob. "And I can't see you at all?"

Oh, God. The look on his face is breaking my heart more than that picture, and that picture shredded me. "It's not a good idea."

"Fuck. *Fuck.*" He rubs hard at the space between his eyes with his knuckles. "Have I ruined this? I have, haven't I?"

"You haven't ruined it. I need time to think, Lance. This has been intense right from the start—and I mean a decade ago. Every time you come into my life again, my world is turned upside down. I need to figure out if I can handle this level of intensity all the time." I also need time to figure out how to find balance with this man. I want to save him from himself, and keep myself safe at the same time. But I can't stop myself from putting my hand over his knee.

He shudders and covers my hand with his. His palm is clammy and shaking along with the rest of him. Suddenly he's on his knees in front of me. He wraps one arm around me and buries his face in my lap. The other hand grips my wrist. He presses my palm to the back of his neck, holding it there.

"I wanna deserve you. Why can't I find a way to deserve you?"

Paralyzed by shock, I watch this huge man fall apart for an agonizing, protracted moment. Because I told him I need time. And that's not unreasonable, I remind myself. Not after what I've just seen and what he's told me.

I run my fingers through his hair, and he nuzzles in closer, another tortured sound leaving him, like he's dying for the affection. I consider that for a moment—how he's gone through life prepared for the women in it to hurt him, rather than care for him.

I don't want to be that all over again, but I have to manage all the feelings I have for and about this man. I let him stay on the floor in front of me, for as long as I can, but eventually I stroke his cheek.

He turns his head like he's chasing the touch. He catches my hand and brings my fingers to his mouth. "I'm sorry," he whispers.

"I know you are."

He lifts his head, but keeps a tight hold on my hand. "But you can't forgive me?"

"I didn't say that. Just give me some time to get this all sorted out."

"That's not a yes."

"It's not a no, either. I'm not going to lie and tell you this is okay, because for me it's not. But that doesn't mean I won't get over it. I need time to process, okay? I have to figure out if I'm ready for something like this."

That someone else wields such power over him scares me, especially since she's been such a negative force in his life. I don't think I could bear it if I let him into my heart the way I want to, only to have their pattern prove impossible for him to break. What will I do if he discards me like she seems to do to him, over and over again?

23

DEPRIVATION

POPPY

I n the past, I've always managed a breakup, or a timeout, or whatever it is I'm calling this by staying busy. So that's exactly what I'm trying to do now. On Wednesday night I bring tea and cookies over to Mr. Goldberg's. It's too cold to sit outside, so we eat at his kitchen table instead.

"I haven't seen your boyfriend lately. Everything okay there?" He dips a gingersnap into his teacup. He uses fine china because it reminds him of his wife, even though the handles are difficult for him to manage.

"They've had an away series. They'll be back in a couple of days." I don't want to get into my relationship problems with Mr. Goldberg, mostly because I think it might make me cry.

"Well, if you wouldn't mind asking him to bring by some of

those special oat biscuits when he's back, that would be lovely. I think they're my new favorite."

"I'm sorry, oat biscuits?"

"I think that's what they are. Sometimes when you're still at work, he stops by with cookies and snacks."

"You're talking about Lance?" I had no idea Lance was sweet-talking my neighbor. He hadn't mentioned it even once.

"Unless you've got another redheaded boyfriend you're hiding somewhere, Miss Poppy, that's the one. He offered to help me get out all the Christmas decorations this year. Which is nice of him. Trudy loved Christmas."

I remembered last year the decorations had been missing, when usually they went up right after Thanksgiving. "I can come help, too."

He pats my hand and gives me a watery smile. "That'd be lovely, dear."

The rest of the week passes in the same slow, achy fashion. Work, which is usually a good distraction, is dragging today. I'm half-grateful, half-worried about having tomorrow off. As much as I need a day off, the free time means my mind has endless time for wandering, and I can spend the day watching PVR hockey games, unless I make alternate plans.

Lance has been gone for the past seven days, and I've watched the games obsessively. He's averaged three penalties a night, and there's been nothing to see on the bunny sites. Tonight they're finally playing again in Chicago. Knowing he'll be in the city again seems to make the hurt worse.

I hate that I don't know more about who he is beyond the confines of my house and what the media says. It's hard to gauge how truthful he's been with me because I only know this narrow aspect of his life.

"Poppy?" April snaps her fingers in front of my face, and I jerk.

"Huh?"

"Your next client is going to be here soon. Do you need help with the sheets?" She looks pointedly at the ball of cloth in my arms. I've been staring off into space for the past few minutes, it appears.

"Sure. Yeah. Thanks."

She rounds the table, takes the used sheets out of my hands, and grabs a fresh set. "Just call him."

"I'm not ready." It's been eleven days. Lance hasn't so much as texted me. As I asked. I should be happy about this.

I'm not.

The silence is painful, even though it was requested.

I've kept myself occupied by spending time with April, going to yoga, having tea with Mr. Goldberg; I even went to see my parents last weekend. It amazes me that in such a short span of time, one person could have filled so much of my life that even the busy-ness doesn't take away the ache of his absence.

"You're not ready, or you're too scared?" April prods.

"I don't know. Both maybe."

"Do you know what you want yet?"

I absolutely do. I want him. I want him to want me as his girl-friend. I want to have more sleepovers. I want to find him naked in my kitchen, rummaging around in my cupboards for gummy bears. More than that, I want him to let me into the rest of his life. I want to be invited to games, to meet his friends, to see him as a whole, and not just a series of puzzle pieces I can't fit together because so many are missing.

But I'm terrified of how that plays out for me. I think I can deal with the media exposure; I even think I can handle a bitch ex-girlfriend. And I'm not afraid to love someone who's been broken. But that's the extent of what I can control. I worry about being separated from the rest of his life, and that he's keeping me away for a reason.

"I don't know," is the answer I give April, though.

She throws up her hands. "Why can't you admit that you're into this guy and call?"

"He hasn't contacted me in almost two weeks."

"Because you asked him not to."

Now it's my turn with the hand gestures. "Why are boys so complicated?"

"Because they have penises. Or peni. What *is* the plural of penis?" She's trying to be funny, and most of the time it would work.

"You're not helping."

"Why don't we go out tonight?" she suggests. "It's Saturday! We'll get dressed up and go dancing. You can cut loose and have one drink. I'll have six or seven. We can flirt with dumb boys."

"There's a game on."

This gets me another look. "It'll be over by ten unless they go into overtime. Neither of us works tomorrow. You need something to take your mind off your boy problems, not feed into them."

"And you think being rubbed on by random strangers is the answer to that?"

"It's far better than waiting for a phone call you asked not to receive."

She's right, even though I hate to admit it. I still have that stupid picture on my phone. I know I need to delete the evidence, but I can't bring myself to do it. And like an idiot I've checked that Natasha girl's profile.

She's been posting old pictures of her and Lance—not just the two of them, but her with the whole team, or shots of them all working out. It's another reminder that I'm only on the fringe of his world, and makes me wonder all over again how much I can trust him, whether what he shows me about himself is real.

"I'll think about it." I tuck the sheets in and throw the heating pad on. My next client gets cold.

A brief knock is followed by Bernadette's disembodied head appearing around the doorjamb. She rarely leaves the comfort of her desk, so it must be important.

"What's up?" I ask nervously.

"Um...there are two women here to see you."

"About treatment?"

"Uh, no. They said they're friends of Lance."

April and I exchange a look.

"Oh. Ah, I guess I'll be right out?" It's more question than answer.

"They're right here. They were quite insistent," she whispers.

"Oh." My stomach flips. If it's a couple of Lance's former conquests, I might throw up for real—hopefully directly on them.

"Do you want me to stay?" April asks.

"Please. Yes."

Bernadette opens the door, and two women appear. Two gorgeous women. I try not to imagine them naked. Or Lance naked with them. One has short dark hair, almost black, cut in a bob. She's tiny and lean, with stunning almond-shaped eyes. The other one is a little taller, with long, wavy auburn hair, huge boobs, and a narrow little waist. I can't tell if they're real or fake —her boobs.

They both smile and look from me to April and back again.

"You must be Poppy," Boobs says to me. Then she turns to her friend. "Oh my God! She is *so* cute! Can you even imagine how adorable their little ginger babies would be?"

April cough-chokes.

"Ohh..." Boobs makes a face. "Is that politically correct? Can a non-ginger use the word *ginger* when referencing another ginger? Is that offensive?" She looks to me for some kind of response. "I mean, my hair is auburn, so I guess it's kind of reddish, but I don't know if it's red enough to qualify me for the use of the word *ginger*."

I'm so confused right now.

"Violet, tone down your crazy a notch," says the other one. She gives me a sympathetic smile. "I'm sorry. I'd like to tell you she's not always like this, but that would be a complete lie. I'm Lily, and this is Violet. We're friends of Lance."

The name Violet is familiar. I think Lance has mentioned her before.

"What kind of friends?"

This is an incredibly odd conversation to be having with women I automatically assume have had sex with Lance, because I don't see him having a lot of female friends. This makes me want to rip their faces off—and that is a very non-me kind of reaction.

Boobs, or Violet, makes another face. It rivals one of April's. "Not *that* kind of friend. I'm married."

Violet holds out her left hand and nearly blinds me with the giant rock on her ring finger. Her nails are pretty and fancy. I can't have long nails because of my job. They also can't have polish on them. Hers are painted in Chicago's colors.

She points to the girl beside her, Lily. "And this one is living with Balls."

At my furrowed brow, Lily elaborates. "I'm Randy Ballistic's girlfriend. We live together."

"In his house," Violet says. They both snicker.

"Am I supposed to understand what's going on here?" I ask.

"Um, probably not. Sorry." Lily looks apologetic.

"We're here to stage an intervention," Violet declares.

"I still don't understand."

"Me either." April moves to stand beside me. She crosses her arms over her chest. She's not very threatening, though. She's too sweet looking, and gangly.

"To get you and Lance back together," Lily explains. She looks at Violet. "Maybe this wasn't a great idea. I think we just look like nutters right now."

"It's a fantastic idea," Violet counters. "Lance is the reason Alex and I are married. Lance is part of the reason you and Nut Sac christen every bathroom in the greater Chicago area. It is our job to give Lance his happy ending." Violet scrunches up her nose and makes a jerking-off motion. "But not that kind of happy ending. Well, maybe. Hopefully, actually."

"Violet," Lily hisses. "Sorry. We're not crazy. Well, she is, but I'm not. Look, Lance is really sad, and we know it's because he's missing you. Randy says he moped around the entire time they were on the road, and he's been moping around since he got back to Chicago last night. So we want to sort of help smooth things over."

"Look, I appreciate you trying to help, but I need time to figure this out on my own." This is so weird.

April coughs a word that sound a lot like *liar*.

"I don't think we're doing a very good job here, Lily. I knew we should've brought Sunny."

"Sunny?" April asks.

"Sunshine, my sister-in-law. My stepbrother, Miller, knocked her up, so now she's like my stepsister-in-law and my sister-in-law. It's all very incesty soap opera. Except there's no actual incest," Violet explains.

"Is Sunshine a yoga instructor?" April asks.

"You know her?" Violet's eyes light up.

"We took her class until she went on maternity leave. We miss her so much, don't we, Poppy?" April nudges me.

"We do." This is the most bizarre conversation ever. Talk about six degrees of separation.

"I'll tell her that when I see her later. She'll probably cry. She cries over almost everything right now. Yesterday Logan made spit bubbles, and she cried over the cuteness," Violet says.

I've stopped speaking, because my brain can't fit all these puzzle pieces together.

"Oh my God. What a small world! Did you know this?" April gives me an accusing glare.

"Yeah, I guess I did," I say. There's a little nugget of his outside life I did know about, I suppose. "Did he ask you to come here?"

"No. Oh, hell no. If he knew we were here he'd probably shit a pot of gold." Violet shakes her head vigorously.

"He's Scottish, not Irish, Vi." Lily rolls her eyes.

I think I might like her despite all of this.

"Whatever. It's the same part of the world. Just like Canada and the US are almost the same."

Lily's eyes nearly pop out of her head. She looks so horrified. "Not even fucking close."

"You say *eh* and corner the market on all the real maple treats. We say *hey* and like the fake maple-flavored garbage, and you call mac and cheese something weird."

"It's KD, and that has nothing to do with you always mistaking Lance for Irish. That's not the same as Scottish. Anyway, we have a purpose here." Lily shoves her hand in Violet's purse, rummages around, and produces an envelope. It's bent at the corners. She flattens it and pulls out the contents. "We have two tickets to tonight's game."

"Really great seats right on center ice behind the bench," Violet chimes in.

I take them from her. "Why are you giving these to me?"

"We want you to come," Lily says.

"I don't know if that's a good idea." I finger the tickets. The seats are incredible. They must cost a small fortune. "I haven't spoken to Lance in a while." *And he's never wanted me to come...*

"Look, we know Lance's reputation isn't great, and it's not all rumors making it that way, but he's a good guy, and he's, like, totally into you. He's moping, and Lance doesn't do the moping thing, like, ever." Lily gives me an imploring look. "Violet and I both know how hard it can be to date one of these guys."

"When I started dating Alex I heard the hat trick rumor," Violet offers. "Later I found out it wasn't actually true, but when I thought it was... Well, I puked all over his shoes. It was epic. But now we're married."

"And Randy had a huge player reputation. I mean, most of it was actually legitimate because he *was* a player, but well, that's changed."

"We've known Lance for a while now, and neither of us has ever seen him this hung up on anyone."

"Not even Tash?" I arch an eyebrow.

They exchange a look. "That situation is comp—"

I cross my arms over my chest. "Complicated. So I've been told."

Violet grimaces. "He would probably kill me for saying this, but she really messed with his head, and Lance, he's not the way the media likes to portray him. I mean, yeah, he's done the bunny business, but I think it's blown way out of proportion. He hasn't had it easy. Anyway, you should come to the game. See him play. We'll all be sitting in the same section, so you can see what it's like. And Sunny will be there with the baby, too."

"Really?" April gets all excited and checks out the tickets. "Holy shit! These seats are killer! We have to go."

"So Lance doesn't know you're doing this?"

"Hell no. He's been adamant about making sure you have your space. I tried to get him to call you, but he refused. He said he doesn't want to do to you what Tash did to him."

If Lance wants this to work, and it certainly seems like he does, he has to let me into this part of his life. Which is why I decide to take the tickets.

"Okay. We'll come."

"Yes!" April begins to bounce.

"But you can't tell Lance. It has to be a surprise," Violet says.

"I don't know..."

"I bet he'll be so happy when he sees you sitting in the stands; he'll forget to be mad at me for doing this. When Alex was a stupid dick and told the world we were just friends on national TV, I stopped talking to him for a month. Then he was so excited when I showed up at the final game of the Cup championships. Chicago won, and he stole his own thunder by grabbing a microphone from a reporter and asking me to be his girlfriend." Violet sighs.

"She rambles a lot," Lily says.

Violet blinks a few times, like she's coming out of a daze. She waves the hand with the ring on it around. "Anyway, we have a car picking us up at six at my place. We can swing by your house on the way if you'd like, so you don't have to worry about getting there."

"Yes. That's perfect! Thank you so much," April answers for me. "Come on, Poppy, you've been sulking for almost two weeks."

She's right. I have. And this scenario is exactly what I need to put into action what I've already decided in my head. I'll get to see firsthand what this world is going to be like outside the confines of my bedroom and my house. And how Lance handles me being there.

We exchange numbers, which is strange all over again, and Violet and Lily high five each other, hug me, and leave.

"That was surreal," I say once they're gone.

"And awesome!" April adds. "Oh my God. We're going to a hockey game! And our seats are amazing."

I share her excitement and fear what it means that my heart is beating so hard right now. My decision is made. And my heart is terrified.

I've CHANGED my outfit three times. I've redone my makeup twice. And I'm not really a makeup girl.

I'm wearing a pair of dark jeans and a green top, because Lance has mentioned that he likes the way I look in green. I'm also wearing my pale yellow and green flowered bra and panty set. It's very feminine. I don't expect he's going to see it.

Okay. Who am I kidding? Now that I've made the decision to go to the game—and start hashing this mess out—a significant part of me wants tonight to end with him at least getting a glimpse of it. But I'm so nervous. Because this whole situation is entirely unprecedented. The wife of the captain of the team and the girlfriend of the legendary Randy Ballistic are picking up me and April so we can go to the game together. Something Lance never asked me to do. And he doesn't know.

I consider texting him.

I want to text him.

But it's just hours until the game, and by this point it's unlikely he has his phone with him. If he does, I don't want to be a distraction—the way right now he's totally mine.

The car that comes to get us is a black extended SUV limo with tinted windows. I follow April out of the house to find Mr. Goldberg, who I've had a lot more tea with over the past week or so, chatting up Violet.

"Ladies night out, Miss Poppy?" he asks.

"We're going to a hockey game, Mr. Goldberg. This is Violet; she's married to Alex Waters, Chicago's team captain."

"Is that so? Violet Waters, that's a lovely name."

I'm positive he's checking out her rack. She's wearing a form-fitting sweater with the Chicago logo on it.

"It makes me sound like a Disney princess, right?" Violet says with a big grin.

"That it does. Have a nice night, ladies. Be safe, Miss Poppy, and if you see that boyfriend of yours, make sure you remind him I'm out of those biscuits."

"I'll be sure to let him know."

"What's that about?" April asks.

I shake my head. "Nothing important. I'll tell you later."

I wave and get in the car where the rest of the girls are waiting. Lily's sitting to the left with a baby seat between her and Sunshine—or Sunny, I guess her friends call her—and

there's another woman I've never met seated behind her. She looks vaguely familiar.

Sunshine's face lights up when she sees us. "Hi, girls! How are you? It's so nice to see you!" We give each other awkward side hugs since I'm hunched over and she's sitting.

"Is this Logan?" I peek in at the tiny sleeping bundle in the car seat, covered with blankets. "Is this his first game?"

"It's his fourth." Sunshine smiles proudly. "I hope he's awake for at least a few minutes this time."

I move to the bench seat on the right where there's room to sit, and April goes in for hugs, then joins me.

The woman on the other side of Logan extends her hand. "I'm Charlene."

"She's dating Darren Westinghouse," Violet calls from the front seat. "Or whatever she's decided to call it."

I don't know what that means, but I introduce myself and April, and then we're on our way to the game. Charlene, Violet, Lily, and April drink champagne while Sunshine and I drink sparkling juice. She's breastfeeding, and I don't want to be tipsy before I'm even at the rink.

It doesn't take long to get to the arena. We're dropped off at a private entrance, and we have some kind of special pass that allows us to avoid all the line-ups and security checks along the way to the ice.

"Okay, so things to prepare for before we get to our seats." Violet laces her arm through mine. "There will be bunnies wearing jerseys like they're dresses with Lance's number on them. They'll have signs and things that say they love him. That's normal. Sometimes a few of them will be sitting close by, and you can hear their conversations. It can be funny, and sometimes disturbing."

"You mean like that time you called out one of Randy's bunny conquests before the game even started?" Lily asks snidely.

"She was asking for it."

"The humiliation was mine," Lily says.

"They're making it out to be worse than it is." Sunshine adjusts Logan, who's now strapped to the front of her body in a carrier that looks more complicated than a straight jacket.

He's resting his cheek on her boob, eyes closed and lips parted. He looks like a sleeping angel with his pale blond ringlets curling out of the tiny red hat he's wearing.

"Miller had a horrible reputation when I started dating him. Probably almost as bad as Lance's."

I don't think she's saying this to be mean. I don't think Sunshine has a mean bone in her body, to be quite honest.

"I let it interfere for way too long before I finally decided it didn't matter what the media or the bunnies said and did. Who Miller was with before me isn't important—not that it didn't bother me at the time."

Being with Lance when it's just him and me isn't a problem. It's being allowed to engage with the rest of his life that's the issue.

"How did you deal with it?"

"At first? Not all that well. I should've been prepared since Alex had a terrible rep, even if most of it wasn't true. But it's a lot different with a brother than a boyfriend."

"But you got over it obviously." I motion to sleeping Logan.

"I did. It took a while for me to figure out what I wanted. But when it comes down to it, it's about how Miller is with me. Everyone said the same thing when we started dating: that they'd never seen him like this with anyone else. It was the same way with Randy and Lily, and with my brother and Violet. And that's how Lance is about you. I know some of the rumors are true, and with Miller, *a lot* of the rumors were true. But he was worth getting over it for." She pats Logan's bottom when he makes a snuffling sound and kisses the top of his head.

She looks so in love, and happy.

"Thanks for sharing that." I mean it. That I'm being taken in by these women who obviously care about Lance—and have not slept with him—gives me new perspective. The man they're describing seems like the person I know, and that's reassuring.

Our seats are amazing. We're right behind Chicago's bench, which is currently empty. I'll be able to see the back of Lance's head the entire game.

Violet and the other girls all get drinks. Sunshine asks for hot water and produces a tea bag.

"They don't have herbal here," she explains.

I want hot chocolate, but I don't know if it will cause Lance to have an allergic reaction. I definitely want to leave open the option for kissing. Maybe more, depending.

When they announce the teams, butterflies flit around in my stomach and try to flutter their way up my throat. Chicago skates onto the ice, and I immediately search for jersey number twenty-one.

"There he is!" April elbows me in the side a little too hard.

"Ow!"

"Sorry." She's bouncy. She's almost finished her drink, which is either her second or third, depending on how much champagne she had in the limo.

I scan the ice and spot him. He's halfway around the rink and moving quickly, following right behind number sixty-nine. That's Randy, Lily's boyfriend.

As they take the bench, they knock on the glass, waving to the girls. Lance waves absently and takes a seat, his mouth set in a thin line. He's serious on the ice, from what I've witnessed in all my game watching. Randy taps the Plexiglas with his glove, winking at Lily. He scans the rest of the row and does a double take when he sees me. His eyes dart back to Lily with questions in them. She gives him a big grin, which he returns with a shake of his head. But it's not a bad look.

He knocks Lance on the shoulder and motions to where I'm sitting. Lance cocks his head to the side, looking confused, then does his own double take.

I give him a shy, uncertain wave, because I can't read his expression. Will he want me here? The smile that spreads across his face makes my heart sprint.

After that I'm high on adrenaline, and it's an amazing game. The bunnies Violet warned me about are definitely here, but they don't matter. At least not right now. My focus is exclusively on Lance. He stays out of trouble on the ice, for the most part. He gets one penalty for sticking, but keeps out of the box other than that. Chicago pulls out the win, and the crowd buzzes with positive energy, taking my nerves to the next level along with them.

When the team leaves the ice at the end of the game, heading for the locker room, Lance stops at our row. Violet is at the end, and I'm a few seats in. He says something to Violet, and there's a bit of back and forth before he motions to me.

April tugs on my arm. "He wants to talk to you."

I get up unsteadily, feeling his gaze as I make my way down the aisle. His eyes dart over my face and down my body. I feel like I'm being consumed from the look alone.

"You'll come out with the girls after the game?"

"I can."

His arms are full of gear. His hair is soaked with sweat. His face is red from exertion. He's gorgeous.

"And we can talk? If you're ready."

"I'm ready. We can talk."

"Okay. I'll see you soon." He hesitates, his eyes darting to my lips like he wants to kiss me. I wouldn't mind if he did, although the location is highly public. Public is what I've been saying I wanted, but I'd like to keep any affection fairly PG considering the number of bunnies in the arena. No need to invite drama if I don't have to.

Lance must sense my nervousness, because he graces me with another one of his grins, takes my hand in his, and brings my knuckles to his lips. Very PG. The sound he makes is inaudible over the noise, but I feel the hum on my skin. Flashes go off around us.

"Come on, Romance. You're holding up the team." A player knocks his shoulder.

His head snaps up, and he gives the guy a dirty look before turning back to me. "I'll be as quick as I can getting to you." He clomps off and disappears down the hall toward the locker room.

Most of the girls are buzzed and silly as we make our way out of the arena and back to the limo. Logan is asleep again.

"Does he ever make noise?" I ask Sunshine.

"Only at three in the morning when we're all supposed to be sleeping peacefully." She's smiling, though, and patting his bottom. "Mostly he can sleep through anything; otherwise I wouldn't have him out. And Miller's parents are taking him for the afternoon tomorrow, so I'll be able to make up whatever sleep I miss tonight." She gives me a wink. "Nap time with Miller is my favorite."

Lily falls into step beside me. "I thought cookie time was your favorite."

Sunny blushes and twirls a lock of hair around her finger. "That too."

At my confused expression, Lily's smile grows wider. "That's what Miller calls oral. Randy calls it beard conditioning."

I clap a hand over my mouth and laugh. I'd ask if they're always so open, but I assume the amount of sex Lance and I had is normal for this crowd, so these conversations must be fairly regular.

I'm all nerves by the time we get to the bar. And when we enter, it seems the bunnies have multiplied. I didn't think *that* was why they called them bunnies. So many girls in short skirts wearing jerseys hang around the bar, watching as we make our way to the closed area. Their jealousy is almost palpable.

We get comfortable and order drinks—I get a Shirley Temple. I settle in with Sunshine on one side of me and April on the other. Logan's decided now is a good time to wake up.

"Are you comfortable with babies?" Sunshine asks.

"Sure." I have cousins with little ones, and when I was younger I used to babysit all the time.

"Do you mind?" She holds him out to me. "I can't find his binky, and there's a hat I want to put on him before his daddy gets here."

"Of course!" I slip my arm under his head, and she carefully transfers him into my arms.

He's small, but he's got some heft to him. I coo as I turn him

313

around so he can see his mother. He startles at a sudden burst of noise, his wide eyes staring up at me as if I'm the reason behind it.

The team is here. I tear my eyes from the precious little bundle I've been entrusted with and look up, searching for the man I'm here for. I spot him across the bar, and his arrival sends a shot of lust from my brain to my girl parts. He's wearing a navy suit with the jacket unbuttoned, a gray shirt, and a black tie with the team logo on it. He searches the area until his eyes fall on me, his worried expression transforming into a tentative smile.

April makes excited noises beside me.

"Girl, I hope your beaver is ready," Violet says from across the table. "That look he's giving you may incinerate the clothes right off your body!"

I'd sacrifice this outfit for that end result.

24

THE PAST
IS THE FUTURE

LANCE

Some spans of time seem endless. The time between me fucking things up with Poppy and seeing her tonight, sitting on the other side of the Plexiglas barrier, felt more like years than days.

The span of time between hitting the locker room and arriving at the bar seems like it took more than an eon. Based on the messages between Randy and Lily, Poppy is here. I hope this is a want, not let situation. Between Lily's sweetness and Violet's pushiness, I'm not sure Poppy stood a chance against them.

At first I wasn't sure what to think about her being at the game. Part of me was annoyed that they'd pulled her into the whole scene. But then I realized they did it to help me. And that if this is going to work out at all, Poppy *has* to meet all my

315

friends, and their girlfriends and wives. More than that, I want her to, because they're my surrogate family, the ones I chose to have in my life.

I can see Poppy as soon as I enter the bar. She's sitting in the middle of my friends' girlfriends. Sunny's beside her. That's good. Sunny is exactly as her name implies, and she'll make Poppy feel comfortable.

"You need to chill out, man," Randy says over his shoulder. "You're more hyped up than me."

I realize I'm pushing him. I clap him on the shoulder. "Sorry. I just don't want her to disappear."

"She's not going anywhere." He strokes his beard as he scans the crowd for Lily.

It takes an entire millennium to get across the room, and when I finally make it to the table, there's absolutely nowhere for me to sit. I close in on Poppy and see that she's holding something. No, wait. Not something, *someone*. Logan. Miller's son.

I'm glad Miller and I are finally back to normal these days. After seeing me act like a mopey bitch for the past two weeks, it's clear that what's going on with me and Poppy is serious, and I really am done with Tash.

A warm feeling that overrides everything else settles in my chest as Poppy smiles up at me. She's holding one of my best friend's kids. This is the thing I've been missing—her, not the kid! There's no way in the world I'm anywhere close to ready for that kind of lifelong commitment. But I'm so grateful for this family I have, and Poppy being part of it—at least in this moment.

Big picture, I need to find out what she wants, and if she's willing to handle all the challenges that come with my life: the media circus, the long spans of time we'll have to go without seeing each other. There's more beyond that, but for now that's as far as I'm willing to let the future unfold. The next five minutes are already uncertain. I can't start planning in months until I know what she's feeling.

She's here, though. That has to mean something.

Logan's little fist is wrapped around her pinkie, and he seems entranced by her swinging ponytail. He flails, and his chubby fingers get tangled in the thick locks.

Poppy makes a surprised sound, and she looks away from me to him as he tries to shove her hair into his mouth.

"Someone's learning early how to get a girl's attention," I say.

"You've been coaching him, then?" Poppy asks.

"Oh! Logan! Ta-ta! Don't eat Poppy's pretty hair!" Sunny says, but I doubt he hears her over the noise.

I lean over Poppy as she tries to free Logan's fingers. He's got a solid grip, and he's working hard to get his fist in his mouth. I take the end of her ponytail in one hand so he's not yanking so hard on it, then wiggle my pinkie in until he's gripping that instead of Poppy's hair.

"Thanks," she says.

It's a million words all rolled into one. The weight of silence and time apart eases with that one softly uttered word.

I can feel myself smiling. "That's my thing. Can't have someone smoother taking my move."

She turns and looks up at me, our faces only inches apart. It wouldn't take much to erase the distance, but I don't. We're not alone, and I'm not yet invited into her space like that.

"He's a little too aggressive about it to be smooth," she tells me.

"So it's still my thing?"

She nods solemnly. "Still your thing."

"I'm glad you came to the game."

She raises a brow. "I'm glad you were in the penalty box for less than three minutes."

"I had a reason to behave." I finger the end of her ponytail. It's damp where Logan had it in his mouth, which should be sort of gross, but I don't care.

"Hey! There's my boy! Gimme my baby, Poppy from the

317

garden!" Miller leans down and kisses Sunny, then holds out his arms with a big, silly grin on his face.

I step back and let them make the transfer.

"Should we go? To talk?" Poppy asks as soon as Miller moves away to show Logan to the guys. Waters is all over that freaking baby. I won't be the least bit surprised when Violet's in the same state as Sunny was not so long ago.

I crouch down so we're eye to eye. "If you want. I mean, we can stay for a while, too. I like this." I motion to the table and the chatter. "You here, with all the people who are important to me."

Her smile is the balm I need.

"I'm glad you feel that way," she says. "It's been really nice to meet them. They all care so much about you. Violet and Lily were very persuasive."

"I'm sure they were."

"You're right about Violet being crazy."

"Right?"

"Let me find April. Then we can go talk without yelling at each other."

I pull her chair out and help her put on her coat, mostly so I can touch her. She spots April, and I follow her finger as she points. Shit. Her friend is currently chatting with Rookie.

"You need to warn your girl off this guy," I tell her.

"What? Why?"

"Unless she's down for the hook up, Rookie's a no-go."

Poppy frowns. "She's not like that."

"I didn't think so."

I follow Poppy, who pulls April aside to tell her whatever she plans to tell her. At the same time I make a point of telling Rookie April's not a bunny, and fucking her is off the table.

"Seriously, man, do not put your dick inside that girl. Not anywhere," I warn.

He smirks. "Tongue and fingers still work, yeah?"

I grab his shoulder and squeeze a little. "Any part you put inside her, I'll make you eat. How's that sound?"

"Okay, okay, Romance. I hear you. What's her deal?"

"You see the little redhead?"

He glances over my shoulder and checks Poppy out. "I sure do."

I snap a finger beside his ear to get his attention back. "She's mine."

He blinks a couple of times. "Right. Sorry. Yeah."

"And the girl you're talking to is her friend, so either keep your dick in your pants tonight or find someone else to be interested in."

"Right. Got it. Don't touch the friend."

"Or what?"

"You'll feed me my—" He doesn't bother to finish. His face says more than enough.

"Good man. Have fun tonight." I clap him on the shoulder and turn to find Poppy and April engaged in an intense discussion. It ends with a hug, and then Poppy laces her fingers with mine.

It takes a half hour to get out of the bar because I must introduce her to at least twenty of my teammates. When we step outside, Miller and Sunny are there, too. Miller's holding Logan, who seems to be drooling on his shoulder, while Sunny puts the car seat back in the limo.

Miller eyes Poppy, then me. "You guys want to catch a lift?"

There doesn't seem to be any cabs around.

"There's a concert at House of Blues tonight. Someone said it would take twenty minutes to get a cab, so we're using the limo. It's gonna circle back here after dropping us home," Miller explains.

I can't wait any more than I already have, so I motion for Poppy to get in first. A flash of memory hits me as I give her my hand and she steps inside: Miller drunk off his ass, me ushering girls into a limo, a red ponytail.

"Lance?" Poppy hesitates. "Do you want to wait?" She wiggles her hand in mine. I'm squeezing it. Tightly.

I loosen my grip. "No. It's okay. It's cold. We should go."

I follow after her, more memories trickling in—ones I don't want. I'm sure Poppy's familiar with all of them. She settles beside me in the limo and takes my hand, her curious gaze questioning. I give her a tight smile, but say nothing.

Miller and Sunny work together to buckle in the car seat. It takes a few minutes, and all the while Poppy keeps stroking the back of my knuckles with her thumb.

"Are you okay?" she asks on a whisper.

"Yeah. Just some memories."

"Of?"

"You before I remembered you."

Her eyes are full of sad understanding as she leans in and presses a kiss against my shoulder. I can't feel it through the layers of coat and shirt, but I appreciate the gesture.

Once the baby is secure, Miller gives the driver my address, checking with me to make sure he has the house number correct.

"We can drop you guys off first," I tell Miller.

He frowns. "Your place is on the way."

"I was thinking we'd go to Poppy's."

"Your place is fine," she says, settling the debate before it can get started.

I don't know how I feel about having this conversation at my house. The last time she was there, things didn't exactly go well. But I don't know how to argue with her, so I leave it alone.

Poppy and Sunny chat a little on the way, but it's clear Sunny is tired. She keeps yawning, and her blinks get longer and slower. I'm too preoccupied with the conversation that needs to be had to really participate. My place isn't all that far from the bar, and at this late hour, it doesn't take long to get there.

We say a quick good-bye, and I get out first, helping Poppy as the driver holds the door open. She doesn't let go of my hand as we walk up the steps to my front door. I try to see my house from her perspective, but all I have are flashes of Miller falling into my foyer and a red ponytail I didn't get to touch that night.

I key in the passcode and step aside. Poppy releases my hand and crosses the threshold. Her fingers drift up to her lips as she scans the foyer. It's open, with a view of the staircase leading to the second floor where the bedrooms are.

Poppy slips off her shoes and pads across the floor on bare feet with pale pink-painted toenails. I don't bother taking my shoes off, too intent on following her around.

Her fingertips skim the edge of the side table where I keep my keys and mail as she passes through to the kitchen.

I come up behind her, unsure whether I have the right to touch her at all. "What are you thinking about?"

"How different I felt the last time I was here."

"In a good way, or a bad way?"

"Good, I think." She rests a hand on the granite countertop. "This is nice. Do you cook?"

"Not really."

"I like to cook sometimes, but I don't think I'm very good."

"Better than me, I'm sure."

A small laugh bubbles up. "Maybe. It's not much fun when it's just for one person, and then I have to eat the same thing for lunch and dinner for four days."

She continues on to the living room, her gaze falling on the sliding glass doors. Her smile drops, and she crosses to them. Turning the lock, she slides it open. The cold makes her shiver, and she wraps her arms around herself as she steps outside.

I have no memories of her in the hot tub, and that bothers me. That whole night bothers me. I wish I could delete the entire night from her head like I'd mostly done in mine.

"I never made it outside, out here." She gestures to the hot tub. "Kristi and Felicity came out with you and Randy, and I snuck away to the bathroom."

"Maybe we should've gone to your place. I haven't had anything to drink. We can go now." I reach for her hand, but she shakes her head.

"No. I want to be here."

"But the memories are bad ones."

"We can replace them with good ones eventually, can't we?"

I squeeze the back of my neck. She's talking like there's a future, which is good. I don't want to jeopardize it with bad memories before we can even deal with the fallout of Tash.

Poppy circles the hot tub; on her way back around, she hooks her pinkie finger with mine. "Come on."

I wish I knew what's happening inside her head.

"I was so embarrassed." Her voice is a whisper of sound.

"I'm sorry."

She turns and presses a palm against my cheek. The contact is fleeting, but welcome.

"I know you are, and I know it's for the right reasons." She heads back to the kitchen and opens the cabinet next to the sink, where the glasses are. I don't ask how she knows where to find them. She must have gone searching when she was here before.

"I must've stayed in the bathroom forever. I didn't know what to do. My phone and wallet and keys were in Kristi's purse, and she had it outside—but the hot tub... I couldn't go out there. I knew Kristi wanted to hook up with you, and I just couldn't—" She shakes her head. "I felt so dumb. I never thought I'd meet you again, and I'd certainly never dreamed it would go like *that*."

I hate that she looks like she's on the verge of tears. I wonder if she's shed any in the days since I've last seen her. If she has, it's my fault. "We don't have to talk about this—"

"I want to. I need to." She turns on the faucet and pours herself a glass of water, filling one for me, too. She takes a deep breath. "Eventually Miller's pizza came. I thought maybe you'd all come back inside, but you didn't. I snuck out and went upstairs, thinking I could wait it out and grab my things from Kristi's purse." She takes a sip of her water.

"But she brought it to my room," I supply. Jesus. My stomach feels like someone's kicking a lead balloon around inside it.

Poppy nods. "I didn't know that, though. I fell asleep, and

when I woke up it was late—or early, depending on how you look at it. I went downstairs, hoping I'd find it out by the hot tub, but of course it wasn't there. So I had to stay."

I consider what that must have been like, being stuck in someone else's house with no way out. And God only knows what she imagined we were doing.

"And then in the morning I ignored you. Christ. Why do you even want to know me?"

"That one night doesn't define who you are. I should've insisted Kristi give me my things. But I didn't. I didn't have to come back here, but I made the choice to. Those consequences are my own to deal with. I should've been honest with you right from the start, just like you should've been honest with me about Tash, but we weren't."

"I didn't want to mess things up."

She gives me a small, sad smile. "Neither did I. I liked that you wanted me to treat you. I convinced myself it would be okay if I could just keep the professional boundaries. And then I didn't need to any more when you asked me out. I should've pushed for information about Tash, but I didn't."

When I give her a probing look, her gaze drops.

"I could've and should've asked you about the DO NOT FUCKING REPLY contact that kept popping up on your phone. I knew it couldn't be good with the way you reacted.

"And the night before you left for the away series, I knew you were lying about talking to a telemarketer, but I didn't say anything then, either."

"I didn't want you to worry while I was away."

"But I did."

She's still looking at the floor, where her toes are curled under against the pale ceramic.

"I'm sorry I did that to you." All I want is to touch her. "Why don't we sit down?" I gesture to the white couch. If we're finally going to hash out the Tash business, I think I need to be sitting down.

She expels a breath. "Okay."

"Can I get you something else to drink?"

"A glass of wine might be nice."

"Should I be worried that you need alcohol for this conversation?" I ask, hoping to alleviate some of the tension.

She smiles a little. "You should only be worried if I ask for shots."

I retrieve two wine glasses—they're relatively unused because I'm generally a scotch or beer drinker, or straight from the bottle if I can't manage my shit. But I've been a lot better about that lately. Miller and Randy have been keeping me in line so I don't go off the edge like I sometimes do.

Poppy sits tucked up in the corner of the white couch when I return with our drinks. One of the throw pillows the interior designer said I needed as an accent is clutched in her lap. She's so fucking beautiful. I want to keep her in my life, and I get that in order to do that I need to let her in, even if it means she sees all the broken parts of me.

I pass her the glass, and she cups the bowl to take a sip. She doesn't put it down after that, just twirls the stem between her fingers.

I sit down in the middle of the couch. I want to get closer, but we're not there yet. "Where do you want me to start?"

Poppy looks down at the glass and sighs. "I just want the truth, Lance. So why don't you start with that?"

"The truth about Tash?"

"Tash. The rumors. Any of it. All of it."

Fuck. This is the stuff I don't want to deal with. But I have to, one way or another. I hope that what I tell her makes things better, not worse.

"You mean the rumors about how I fuck?"

She cringes, probably because I've chosen to word that in the worst way possible.

My knees are bouncing so hard her wine swishes in her glass. I set mine on the table.

"I wasn't lying when I said I really don't like to be touched. Like at all. Especially by women. After my brother died, I could only ever associate hands on me with my mum's anger. So dealing with girls was really fucked up. I knew there was something wrong with my head, 'cause I didn't enjoy sex the way all the other guys on my team seemed to."

"But you must have found a way to get over that?" There's a hardness to Poppy's voice, tension that makes her words sharp and heavy.

"I thought maybe I could, but it didn't really work. I had this party once...and there were these two girls." I study my hands, unable to look at her. "They wanted me to—uh...anyway, that wasn't any better. It was worse. There were so many fucking hands to manage. The fucking panic—I hated it."

"Did Tash know this?"

"Aye."

"But she brought other girls anyway? Even though she knew how you felt about it?"

"Aye." The memories make my skin crawl. "And it just made the rumors worse, because then there was some actual truth to them."

"She's a horrible person."

"She has a lot of issues. Anyway, that's done now. And I have a new roommate when we travel. One of the guys with a girlfriend, so I don't have to deal with the, uh...bunnies and that awkwardness."

"That's good." Poppy raises the glass to her lips.

"And I've been staying away from the bar after games."

"I don't expect you to become a recluse."

"I know. I just want to stay away from any problems."

Poppy sets down her glass. "You have to give me a chance to trust you, and hiding in your room, not interacting with your teammates isn't going to do that. All it's going to do is make you resentful eventually."

"Resentful of what?"

"Of me, for taking you away from your friends. I don't want to confine you. If we're going to try to make this work, it can't be about you hiding from Tash, or the bunnies. And it can't be you keeping me separate from the rest of your life."

"I meant it when I said I'm not going to talk to her anymore. I'm done."

"Has she contacted you since you saw her in LA?" Poppy bites her bottom lip.

"I got one call from an unknown number, but whoever it was didn't leave a voicemail."

"And if she comes to your next LA game? How will you handle that?"

"How do you want me to handle it?" My knee is bouncing. Even if we're not involved, erasing Tash from my life isn't exactly easy.

"I want you to be honest with me if you think you're going to see her. I want to be able to trust that you're not going to fall back into old patterns every time you cross paths."

"I mean it when I say I'm done with her, Poppy. I didn't really understand how bad she made me feel until you came along. I get how toxic she is for me, and I told her that. I want what we have to work. I know you can't come to every LA game, but maybe you can come to some of them? The ones on the weekend maybe?"

Poppy glances at her wine and then back at me. "It doesn't have to be LA games."

"Whatever games you want to come to, I'll get you tickets, if that's what you want. But the bunnies are always there. I don't have control over that."

"I know. But who cares about them?" Her eyes flash. "And I only want to be at games if you want me there."

"I only got one penalty tonight because I was trying to be good for you."

A tender smile turns up the corner of her mouth. "I don't want to be hidden away. Tonight was good for me. Meeting some of the other girls, your teammates, it was nice to feel included in your life." Her eyes drop to the pillow she's holding. "Unless that's not what you want out of this."

I hadn't considered that keeping her all to myself could be a negative thing. "I just wanted to protect you from all the bad stuff."

"I can handle the bad stuff, Lance, if you let me. We can handle it together."

"The bunnies can be nasty."

"I know. I heard a few of them tonight."

"I'm sorry."

"It's not your fault. Don't take the blame for other people's words and choices."

"That's not always easy."

"Nothing good is easy; otherwise we wouldn't appreciate the effort it takes to make it work."

"So what now? Where do we go from here?"

She sets down her glass and leans closer. "Forward. If that's what you want."

"And you really want to do that?" I want to touch her. I want her to touch me. To ground me in this moment.

She laces her fingers with mine. "The past is in the past. We can leave it there if we're done with it, can't we?"

"What if I don't want to?"

She cocks her head to the side, uncertain.

"I've buried a lot of my past because it wasn't good, Poppy. But I don't want to bury anything about you. Now that I have it back, you're probably my best childhood memory. And to have you here as part of my present gives me hope that you'll be in my future, too."

25

WHERE
WE BEGIN

POPPY

L ance brings my fingers to his lips. This won't be easy or simple. Loving him isn't going to be a fairytale story where we ride off into the sunset and everything is perfect.

I know this.

We're both full of fire, and his past is full of pain he carries with him. But I'm willing to try, because I want him. And more than that, this man is the kind of beautiful I need in my life.

"Let's only keep the good ones then," I suggest.

"Okay. I like that idea." His lips brush my knuckle as he speaks. "I want to kiss you."

"You already are."

His smile grows and his lashes lower as he dips in close. "I mean your pretty lips."

"Then you should do that." I wait for the gentle, warm press.

"Want or let?" he asks.

"Need."

And then he's wrapped around me, lips on mine, tongue stroking slow inside my mouth, his low moan vibrating through my entire body.

It's a new first kiss. His brief absence from my life is washed away.

He pulls back to ask, "Can I take you upstairs?"

At my nod, he links our hands. It takes forever to get up the stairs because we can't stop kissing. When he pushes the door to his room open he mutters a curse. "I didn't think…"

His room is a mess. Clothes are strewn on the floor by the dresser. His bed is unmade. The light in the bathroom is on, and discarded towels are hanging on the edge of the tub. It's a big tub. A nice soaker.

"Wow. You're a real neat freak, huh?"

"Let me tidy up a bit, aye?"

He starts to move away, but I clutch his hand tighter. "Why bother when we're going to mess it all up anyway?"

"You make a good point."

And then we're back to kissing, and undressing. Clothing hits the floor, teeth clash and nip. He pauses when I'm in my bra and panties. "Look at you. So beautiful." His hands roam my body, reacquainting.

"We'll go slow later, aye?" He walks me backward to the bed.

"Aye," I mock breathlessly, tilting my head so he can kiss his way along my throat.

He bites my chin and makes a little growling noise that hardens my nipples and heats me from the inside out. Lance lays me out on the bed, pushing the rumpled sheets out of the way. He digs around in the nightstand drawer while we kiss and I touch him.

"You know, if you stop trying to multitask, it would probably be easier."

He grumbles something into my neck.

"What was that?"

"I don't wanna stop kissing you."

"Not even for a second?" His lips are on my jaw now.

"Not even for a second."

A huge crash shocks a gasp out of me as he pulls the drawer free from the nightstand, and it lands on the floor. Lance holds up a condom with a satisfied smile. Actually, it's a strip of condoms. "Got what I needed."

"Do we really need that?" I ask.

He blinks a couple of times. "I dunno, do we not?"

"I'm on the pill."

"And you think that's safe enough?"

"Do you?" I run my fingers through his hair, asking the question without putting it into words.

He regards me for a few long seconds. "You trust me?"

"Aye."

He huffs a little laugh and shakes his head. "Is that yer new favorite word, then?" It comes out with an accent.

"Maybe." I pause before adding, "Aye."

He drops his face into the crook of my neck. "Precious, you have no idea what you're doing to me right now." He kisses along my neck, and I feel him, hot and hard against me. "If I go in bare, I'm not gonna last long," he says when he gets to my mouth.

"That's okay. We have all night for you to be sweet with me."

He drops the strip of condoms on the covers and takes my face in his hands. With his eyes on mine he sinks in to me. For a moment I'm lost, and then I'm found in him.

This is nothing like the last time I was with him. This is connection in its purest form. Sensation blends with emotions that have yet to be uttered. But they will, because they're too big for either of us to contain anymore.

I come just before he does, and the world is devoid of color. There is only this man and this moment.

"Poppy?" Lance's arm is wrapped around me, anchoring me to his chest, even though I still feel like I'm floating.

"Mmm?"

"I have to tell you something."

I lift my head at his nervous tone.

He runs a finger from the bridge of my nose to the tip and touches it to my lips. "I'm in love with you."

"That's good to know." I pause, his panicked expression almost comical, except that it's genuine, so I continue. "Because I'm in love with you, too."

My words turn his fear into tenderness.

And then he spends the rest of the night, with his touch and his words, explaining exactly how precious I am.

EPILOGUE

FOREVER ISN'T JUST A WORD

LANCE

ONE YEAR LATER

I'm not sure I believe that time heals all wounds. I don't think it's as simple as that. Sure, time is a factor in washing away old pain, but it's what, or who, those losses and wounds are replaced by that makes the real difference.

I won't put my happiness on Poppy. That's a burden, not a compliment. But she's the light I needed to find my way out of the dark spaces in my head. I still go there sometimes, but I have a reason not to stay.

She's also the reason I finally heeded Coach's advice to talk to someone about my aggression. Because I never want to turn that on her. I never want to put on the person I love the most what someone else forced on me. So I'm dealing with the ghosts from my past so I can have a better future. One that includes Poppy.

This past summer I took her to Scotland to meet my extended family. And we took a side trip to see my father. I hadn't seen him in a couple years, but Poppy made it manageable. I have some perspective now. We're all products of our upbringing, but we get to choose who we bring into our lives. I choose Poppy. And I'm really fucking hopeful I'll be her choice, too.

I'm waiting at the front door, checking the time. According to my messages, Poppy left the Buttersons' place fifteen minutes ago. The girls got together to look at Miller and Sunny's wedding pictures. Poppy was there that day, of course, as my plus one. I officiated, as seems to be the trend.

I wipe my palm on my pants and adjust the collar of my shirt, checking my reflection in the mirror one more time. I look fine. Nervous, because I am, but fine.

She should be here any minute. I check the time again.

Just as I mutter *where the hell is she?* Poppy's car pulls up beside my Hummer. She's right, her Mini does look like something my car shat out. I check my pocket and rush to the closet, leaving the door slightly ajar.

My palms are seriously sweaty. I wipe them on my pants, retrieve the small box from my pocket, and wait. And wait some more. I'm more nervous than I was the first time Poppy agreed to go out with me. The stakes are infinitely higher right now.

Finally I hear the beep of the code being punched in. This is it. I've been waiting months for this. I suck in a deep breath, prepping for the inevitable.

"Lance? I'm home!" Poppy calls.

I bite my tongue so I don't answer.

After a few seconds of silence, she calls again. "Baby? You here?"

I'm a big fan of pet names. More than I thought I'd be.

She says something to herself about leaving lights on, and the door to the closet swings open. As soon as she sees me, she screams.

Which is not quite the response I was going for.

"Ahhh! What the heck?" She stumbles back, her hands pressed to her heart. Poppy isn't much for swearing. It's precious, just like her.

I grab her arm before she can get too far. "I didn't mean to scare you." I'm trying not to laugh at her horror.

"Then why are you hiding in the closet?" She buries her head against my chest. I love the way it feels when she's close like this. I love it most when she's near me and naked, which she will be soon enough, but first I have something important to do.

There's a light in here. I had it installed last week. I hit the switch and pull her inside.

"What are you—"

Her words catch as I push the coats out of the way and drop to one knee.

She covers her mouth with a palm, eyes wide. "Lance?"

I take her hand in mine and bring it to my lips. "Hi, precious." I pull out the tiny velvet box.

"Oh my God." She's shaking.

"Poppy Leigh O'Connor, you're the most precious, perfect person in my world. Yer my sunrise and my sunset. Marry me so I can spend every day loving you for the rest of my life."

I flip open the box, hoping she can see the ring in the semi-darkness. The coats are obstructing the light.

Because she is who she is, Poppy drops to her knees with me and takes my face in her hands. "You didn't even phrase it as a question."

"What?" All I know is it's not a yes.

She giggles. The sound is pure and sweet. "You didn't make it a yes or no question."

"You're really gonna gimme a hard time about this? Now?"

"Of course, I'll marry you."

"You're sure? Is that your yes?"

She kisses me, once, twice, a third time. "Yes. Of course. There's no one else I'd rather be loved by than you. Give me the ring."

I laugh, and so does she while she kisses me. Our tongues twine and tangle. I keep going until she's breathless; then I take her shaking hand in mine and slip the ring on her finger.

"It's so beautiful."

"I want you forever," I whisper.

"I'm yours," she whispers back. "I've been yours since you stole my first kiss."

"I'm still not sorry."

"Neither am I."

The End

BONUS SCENE

BIRTHDAY BASH GUMMY BEAR STYLE

POPPY

"Lance is going to jizz a bucketload."

"You should write Hallmark cards," Charlene deadpans while looking at her phone.

Violet makes a face at Charlene. "Eat Darren's dick."

Charlene gives her a saucy grin. "With pleasure."

I cringe at their completely unfiltered banter, thankful we're in my bedroom—the one I share with Lance—and not a public place. I smooth my hands over the soft fabric and check out my reflection in the full-length mirror. "You don't think it's too juvenile?"

"No way. It's freaking adorable," Violet replies.

"I don't want to look adorable. I want to look sexy. Maybe I should change into something else." When I first stumbled on the pinup style, form-fitting dress covered in a gummy bear print pattern, I thought it was hilarious. The mint green fabric is covered in tiny, three-dimensional gummy bears, the sweetheart neckline embellished with forest green lace accents, which also line the hem, and deep green satin ribbon cinches at the waist.

Charlene slips her phone into her purse and crosses her arms over her chest. "You look adorably sexy. You're not changing."

"I think the bra and panties might be overkill." They match the dress. I wish Lily was here, but she's at work and won't arrive until later, and Sunny can't come over until Logan is up from his afternoon nap.

It's not that I don't trust Violet and Charlene's advice. It's just that they're a little forceful about things, especially when they're together. I have a lot of new lingerie and bathing suits thanks to lunch/shopping expeditions with them. I try to say no, but then Violet messages Lance and then he messages me and tells me to put in the credit card he gave me when I moved into his house last year. It's all very kept woman-ish. Except I work full-time as a massage therapist, so I'm not kept at all.

"The bra and panties aren't overkill. Look, you've got this sweet-sexy thing going on." Charlene waves her hand around my face and then gestures to the rest of me. "This dress shows off your curves and it's covered in Lance's favorite gelatin-inspired sugary treat. It's not juvenile and he's going to love it."

"So much that he might jizz in his pants."

"Stop saying *jizz*, Violet. We're not making it the word of the day." Charlene rolls her eyes.

"It's a good word." Violet turns her attention back to me. "All you need is jewelry, something understated and simple, I think."

"What about pearls?" Charlene fingers hers. It's the only necklace I ever see her wear.

Violet and I share a look. "Yeah, pretty sure Poppy here isn't about to let Lance collar her as a birthday present."

337

I choke back a laugh. I have no idea what the significance of the pearls are, or what the dynamics of Charlene and Darren's relationship is, but I suspect it's a little unconventional and not in a gummy bear print lingerie/dress kind of way. Apparently, butt plugs were Violet's bachelorette party favor, courtesy of Charlene, which says something.

Charlene throws her hands in the air. "Would you stop?"

"I'm on a wicked roll today, eh?" Violet directs the comment at me.

"You sure are."

Charlene claps her hands together. "Oh! I have a great idea! What about a gummy bear necklace!"

"As cute as that would be, people are going to start arriving in less than an hour. Whatever jewelry I'm wearing needs to come from that box over there." I point to my dresser. I'm throwing Lance a birthday party. A surprise birthday party.

"I mean a real gummy bear necklace," Charlene replies.

"We don't have time for one of your art projects, Char," Violet says.

"Everything we need is right here. It'll only take a few minutes and then you'll be perfect." Charlene gestures to the bed. Instead of rose petals, it's sprinkled with gummy bear confetti, and there are bowls of gummy bears on the nightstand. I make a mental note not to let these two help me plan Lance's next birthday party. But he's turning twenty-five, and I don't think he's ever really celebrated it properly, so here I am, gummy beared out the wazoo.

Charlene roots around in her purse and pulls out a small tube. "What's his favorite flavor?"

"He likes the green ones best. What is this?" I pick up the tube she's tossed on the bed.

"It's an edible adhesive." She starts sifting through the bowl of gummies, piling up all the green ones.

"I'm sorry, it's what?"

"It's like body glue. So you can stick things to your skin. Except it's non-toxic and edible," Charlene explains.

"And you just happen to be carrying that around in your purse?" Violet asks.

"It's handy. It keeps bra straps and other strappy things in place."

Violet grabs the tube from me and inspects it. "It's a little weird that this exists and that it's like, one of your essential items, Char."

"Says the woman who dresses her husband's dick up in costumes."

"That's because Alex's peen is a super hero."

Dear lord, how are these women my friends?

"Okay. Sit here." Charlene pats the comforter.

I sit on the edge of the bed while she and Violet stick gummy bears to my chest in the form of a necklace. I have to admit, when they're done it looks pretty awesome, Also, Charlene has done a good job of drawing attention to my ample cleavage, thanks to the bust line of this dress.

Guests begin to arrive and text messages from Randy inform me of Lance's impending arrival. The boys took him out golfing this afternoon. I've been warned they've already consumed a few beers, so they're all feeling pretty good.

Lance believes we're having a barbeque with a few close friends. He doesn't realize I've invited his entire team to celebrate. It's just after seven when they come rolling in. The house quiets as deep raucous voices fill the foyer.

"Precious! Where ya at?" Lance calls out, his usually light Scottish accent heavier on account of the beers and the sun.

"Just in the kitchen!" I call back, biting my lip as he and the boys round the corner.

The chorus of "surprise" has him stopping in his tracks. His wide-eyed shock turns into a slow grin and he surveys the crowd, scanning until his eyes finally find me. They roam over me in a slow sweep I feel all over my body. He doesn't acknowledge the rest of the room, as if everyone else has ceased to exist.

"I told you he'd ji—" Charlene elbows Violet on the boob before she can finish her sentence.

Lance traces the gummy bear necklace with a fingertip. "These are real, aye." He takes my face in his hands, heedless of the sixty witnesses, and presses his lips to mine. "Ah fuck, ya taste like candy," he mutters, tongue sweeping inside my mouth, tasting the remnants of the gummy bear martini I've been sipping to calm my nerves.

I wrap my hand around his wrists and attempt to disconnect our mouths. I'm sure my face is as red as my name. "We have guests."

He blinks a couple of times, like he doesn't understand, then he looks around, a sheepish grin turning up the corner of his mouth as he raises a hand in greeting. "Everyone make yourselves at home, aye? I just need to speak to my precious Poppy alone for like, twenty minutes, maybe more, depending."

"Lance!" I shriek when he makes like he's going to pick me up and haul me off.

Thankfully, he's just playing. He sets me down and pats my bottom. "This dress is something else," he murmurs in my ear. "I'm going to enjoy taking it off you later."

Later doesn't arrive until two in the morning when the last guest has left. "You threw me a birthday party," Lance says after he closes the door for the final time and sets the security alarm. His accent is still more prominent than usual, although there were an unprecedented number of shots. "No one's ever done anything like that for me."

"I wanted it to be special. Did you have fun?"

"Aye." He cups my face in his hands, dipping down to press a soft kiss to my lips. "But it's been right painful looking at ya all night in this dress and not being able to get you outta it. I'd like to do that now, if that's all right with you."

I smile against his lips. "Aye, that's more than all right."

"Come on then. Let me take ya to bed and show you how grateful I am." He links our pinkies and leads me upstairs.

Lance moves my hair out of the way and kisses my shoulder as he unzips the dress. Coming to stand in front of me, he hooks his fingers in the straps and drags them down my arms, releasing a heavy breath as he takes in the lace-edged bra and panties that match the dress now pooled at my feet.

"Bloody hell, precious. Where the fuck did you find this?" He bites the end of his thumb and shakes his head. "You're a vision." Stepping in close, he runs his fingertips along the edge of the bra, causing a hot shiver to run down my spine. The gummy bear necklace disappeared over the course of the evening, Lance swooping in every once in a while to suck another candy off my chest before whispering into my ear about other things he'd rather be eating.

"I want to worship you for a while." Picking me up, he carries me over to the bed, stripping out of his shirt and pants as he climbs up after me.

His touch is slow and reverent. His kisses are soft and lingering. My bra stays on at first, the cups pulled down, my nipples traced first with light fingertips and then followed by the warmth of his tongue. Lance moves down my body, unhurried, despite the hours spent whispering about how much he couldn't wait to get me up here and naked.

When he reaches my navel, he sits back on his knees, hooks his thumbs into my panties, and drags them down my thighs. "Does this come as a bikini?" he asks, dropping them on the comforter.

"I don't know. I can check."

"Please do." He smooths his hand along the inside of my thighs before shouldering his way between my legs, and then his mouth is on me, laving, slow strokes that push me higher and higher until I unravel.

He prowls back up my body, hips settling between mine,

thick erection pressing against me, and then he's easing in, filling me.

His eyes drift shut, and when they open again, his expression is undiluted rapture. He pushes up on one arm, his other palm coming to rest over my heart. "This. You. What you give me. You're the best gift, precious Poppy."

ABOUT THE AUTHOR

NYT and USA Today bestselling author, Helena Hunting lives on the outskirts of Toronto with her amazing family and her two awesome cats, who think the best place to sleep is her keyboard. Helena writes everything from emotional contemporary romance to romantic comedies that will have you laughing until you cry. If you're looking for a tearjerker, you can find her angsty side under H. Hunting.

Scan this code to stay connected with Helena

OTHER TITLES BY HELENA HUNTING

Pucked Series

Pucked (Pucked #1)

Pucked Up (Pucked #2)

Pucked Over (Pucked #3)

Forever Pucked (Pucked #4)

Pucked Under (Pucked #5)

Pucked Off (Pucked #6)

Pucked Love (Pucked #7)

AREA 51: Deleted Scenes & Outtakes

Get Inked

Pucks & Penalties

All In Series

A Lie for a Lie

A Favor for a Favor

A Secret for a Secret

A Kiss for a Kiss

Lies, Hearts & Truths Series

Little Lies

Bitter Sweet Heart

Shattered Truths

Shacking Up Series

Shacking Up

Getting Down (Novella)

Hooking Up

I Flipping Love You

Making Up

Handle with Care

Spark Sisters Series

When Sparks Fly

Starry-Eyed Love

Make A Wish

Lakeside Series

Love Next Door

Love on the Lake

The Clipped Wings Series

Cupcakes and Ink

Clipped Wings

Between the Cracks

Inked Armor

Cracks in the Armor

Fractures in Ink

Standalone Novels

The Librarian Principle

Felony Ever After

Before You Ghost (with Debra Anastasia)

Forever Romance Standalones

The Good Luck Charm

Meet Cute

Kiss my Cupcake